THE MUSKETS OF GASCONY
The Revolt of Bernard d'Audijos

Armand Daudeyos

Translated by
J H M Salmon

MINERVA PRESS
LONDON
MIAMI DELHI SYDNEY

THE MUSKETS OF GASCONY:
The Revolt of Bernard d'Audijos
Copyright © J H M Salmon 2000

All Rights Reserved

No part of this book may be reproduced in any form
by photocopying or by electronic or mechanical means,
including information storage or retrieval systems,
without permission in writing from both the copyright
owner and the publisher of this book.

ISBN 0 75411 211 X

First Published 2000 by
MINERVA PRESS
315–317 Regent Street
London W1R 7YB

Printed in Great Britain for Minerva Press

THE MUSKETS OF GASCONY
The Revolt of Bernard d'Audijos

Cover illustration from a painting of a cavalry ambush in a mountain pass by Philip Wouverman, c.1640. All rights reserved. © Prado Museum, Madrid.

Preface

It happened many years ago, when I had nearly completed my research on a revolt in Gascony against the *gabelle*, or salt tax, in the 1660s, led by a former officer of light horse named Bernard d'Audijos. In those days, before theoretical debates about postmodernism blighted the writing of history, it was fashionable for historians of early modern France to study popular revolts, and if one was lucky enough to find an unstudied rebellion in a province with good local archives and even better cuisine, one's profession became a pleasurable pursuit.

I was staying in Pau at the Hôtel Gramont. After spending most of the day in the Archives Départementales, I used often to walk up the hill towards the celebrated château where Henry of Navarre was born, and stop for my evening meal at a small restaurant run by my friend Monsieur Dupaty, who cooked a miraculous steak Béarnais and kept a reserve of the best Jurançon wine to accompany it. He took a lively interest in my researches, although he deplored my focus on the way Audijos's rebellion had exacerbated institutional rivalries under the regime of Louis XIV. He was much more intrigued by the perilous trips I took in my battered second-hand car to explore the terrain where Audijos had fought his battles and found safe places of refuge, especially in the foothills of the Pyrenees. To him this was the *pays* where Dumas' musketeers had originated, and he wanted to invest Audijos and his supporters with the same aura of seventeenth-century romance.

On this particular evening my host was so excited that, before I could even scan the menu, he burst out with the news that he had made a discovery to put my humdrum investigations to shame.

'Voilà!' he said, thrusting a thick bound manuscript into my hands. 'Here is a book that tells you what Bernard d'Audijos really accomplished. It was given to me this morning by a friend to whom I had mentioned your work. He wants you to keep it.'

Instead of my usual after dinner stroll in the park beside the château, I returned to my hotel, braving the velos which at this hour the youth of Pau raced noisily round the square where the Gramont was situated (it used to be a set rule that one should never take a room in a provincial hotel fronting the town square, but in this instance I had had no choice). As I began to read the yellow pages, I forgot the din of the velos outside, and became immersed in the story it told. It was a novel, written in the mid-nineteenth century by someone named Armand Daudeyos, who claimed to be of the same family as the rebel leader (the name was often spelled in that Gascon fashion in the lifetime of Bernard d'Audijos). The author was more a disciple of Prosper Mérimée than of Alexandre Dumas, to whom the plot was more important than historical accuracy. Like Mérimée's *Chronicle of the Reign of Charles IX*, his book followed the facts of what had really happened, while bringing the actual characters to life, adding some extras from his own imagination, and filling in gaps where the record was missing. Not only had he read the memoirs of the time, but he had also studied carefully the relevant archives, later to be gathered together in a volume of the *Archives historiques de la Gascogne* (1893). I had come to know the same sources well, and noted the way he had integrated them into his narrative.

Apparently, Armand Daudeyos never bothered to find a publisher, but his historical novel deserves to be remembered. Here it is in an English version prepared for modern readers.

J H M Salmon.

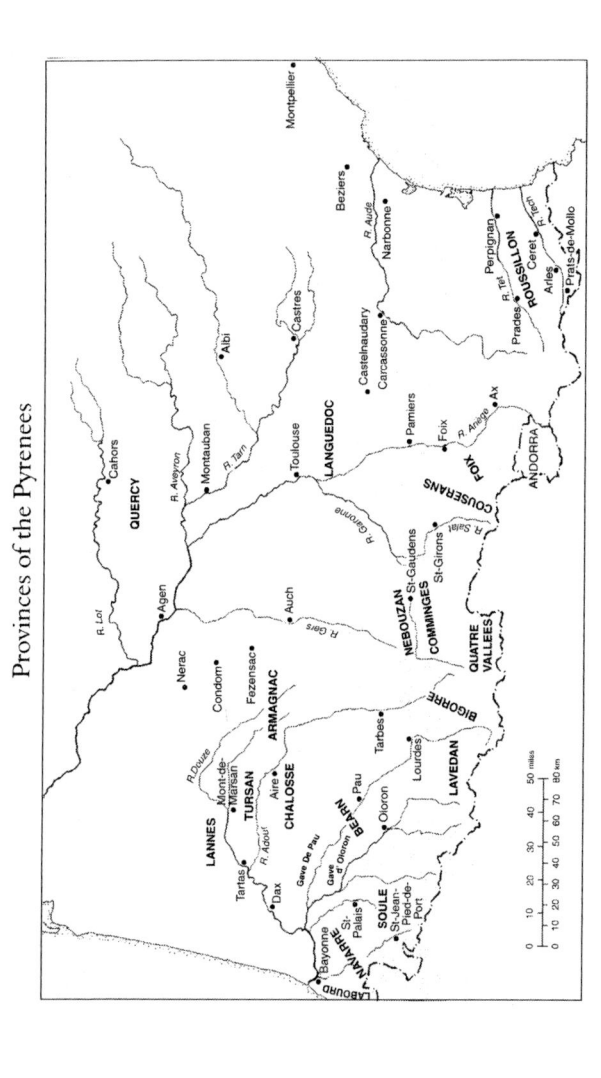

Provinces of the Pyrenees

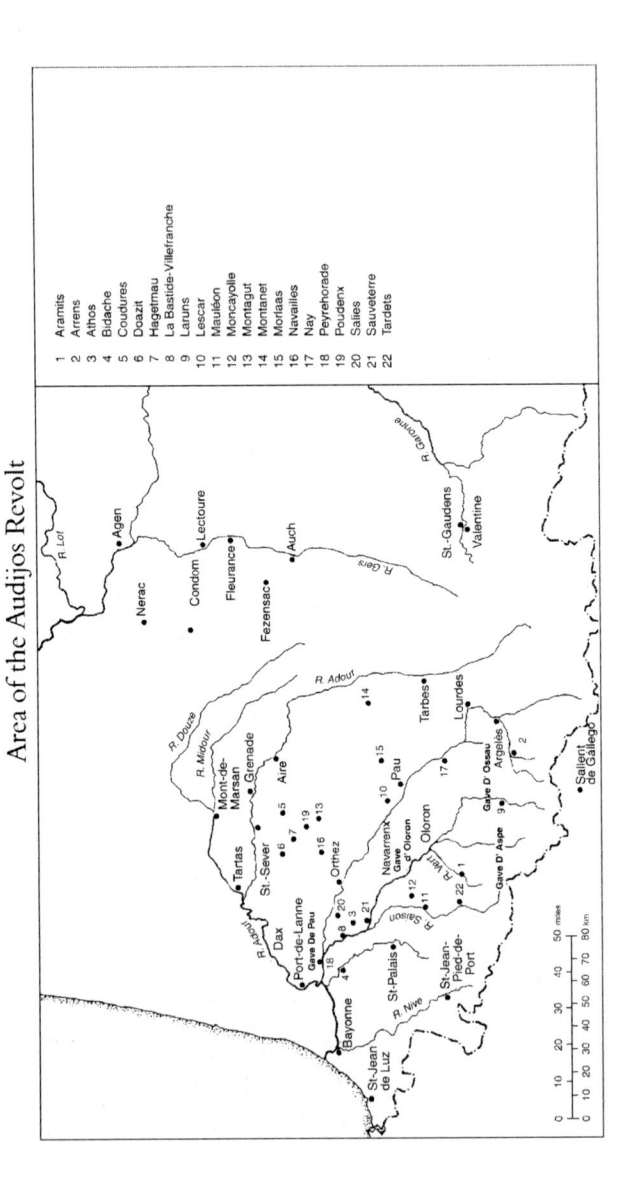

Area of the Audijos Revolt

1 Aramits
2 Arrens
3 Athos
4 Bidache
5 Coudures
6 Doazit
7 Hagetmau
8 La Bastide-Villefranche
9 Laruns
10 Lescar
11 Mauléon
12 Moncayolle
13 Montagut
14 Montanet
15 Morlaas
16 Navailles
17 Nay
18 Peyrehorade
19 Poudenx
20 Salies
21 Sauveterre
22 Tardets

Contents

1. The Créquy Cavalerie — 11
2. The Duc de Navailles — 16
3. Madame de Motteville — 20
4. The Châtelaine — 26
5. The Gabeleurs — 30
6. Saint-Sever — 34
7. Coudures — 40
8. The Cabaret — 46
9. Journey to Bigorre — 51
10. Roger Dubourdieu — 58
11. Lavedan — 65
12. Arrens — 72
13. The Caves of Bétharram — 77
14. Reunions in Bayonne — 80
15. The Witch of Bidart — 86
16. The Royal Marriage — 94
17. The Intendant — 100
18. Return to Chalosse — 109
19. Prelude to Revolt — 116
20. Three Meetings — 125
21. Jeanne-Marie Escapes — 132

22. The Battle of Hagetmau	137
23. Revenge	143
24. Repression and Response	149
25. Mission to Béarn	156
26. Execution at Hagetmau	162
27. Death of A Gallant Man	171
28. The Revolt of the Mountain Men	177
29. Negotiations at Lourdes	183
30. The Double Agent	191
31. Riot in Bayonne	197
32. Lake Trasimene	205
33. The Bishop and the Charter	211
34. The Net Tightens	221
35. Across the Pyrenees	231
36. Sallent de Gallego	242
37. Conspiracy and Betrayal	250
38. Bordeaux	259
39. A Perilous Rescue	267
40. Deception and Disaster	274
41. The Châtelaine's Date with Destiny	284
42. The Pardon	297

1. The Créquy Cavalerie

On a cold, wet evening in February 1660, a company of light horse clattered into the fortress town of Saint-Jean-d'Angély. They were the advance guard of the regiment of Créquy Cavalerie, moving northwards, like so many other units, after the peace between France and Spain had been definitively established. They looked a tired and despondent lot on their mud-spattered horses. Their commander, it is true, provided a splash of colour, with his red cloak flying in the wind and the white plumes of his hat still standing erect. Captain Boisset had always provided an example to the fifty bedraggled riders who followed him. Immediately behind him rode two less inspiring figures: one square, dark and heavy on his raw-boned gelding, the other a tall, ungainly man, slouched forward on his dainty black mare with his carbine carefully wrapped against the damp and slung over his shoulder.

The two were cousins, despite their contrasting appearance. They were Gascons, born in the town of Coudures, not far from the point where the River Gabas joined the Adour on its way to the sea at Bayonne. The region of Chalosse, in which lay Coudures and its sister town, Saint-Sever to the north, contained the ancestral lands of the marshal-duke, Antoine de Gramont, one of the greatest soldiers and courtiers of the age. Roger Dubourdieu and Bernard d'Audijos, the two ill-matched junior officers in Boisset's company, had been brought up in the circle of local officials who administered the Gramont estates. Both had been reared to speak the cultivated French of the north as well as their native Gascon, and both had some knowledge of the Béarnais that was spoken further south. Dubourdieu's father was a minor magistrate in Coudures and in Hagetmau to the west, where Gramont had been born. Audijos was the grandson of a merchant, who had married the sister of Dubourdieu's grandfather. His father, who called himself the sieur de Renung, had risen in the world by his marriage to the noblewoman Diane de Talazac-Bahus, the daughter of Philibert de Talazac, baron de Bahus, and Isabeau de Foix-Candale.

Seven years earlier, when Dubourdieu and Audijos had enlisted in the Créquy Cavalerie at the respective ages of sixteen and fifteen, the boys had seen action in the final months of the civil war of the Fronde. They had served under the command of the marquis de Poyanne in a desultory campaign against the forces of the German Balthasar, the general of the rebel prince de Condé in Gascony. Like their opponents, their regiment had lived off the countryside, and the local population had reacted with fear and resentment to both royalists and frondeurs, who had pillaged their towns and commandeered their livestock. Both cousins, however, had acquired a sympathy for the plight of the unprivileged from Antoine Legrange, their preceptor at the school of Saint-Sever, whose knowledge of local law and peasant rights had brought him into frequent conflict with authority. The two young cavaliers had deplored the treatment of the common people, although their older comrades had paid scant regard to murmurs of protest from such raw recruits. Their reputation with their commander, himself a man of sentiment, had not suffered from reports of so unusual a compassion. Despite their youth, they had been promoted a few years later for their courage and élan. During the regiment's subsequent service in the war against Spain in Catalonia, their friendship was sealed by the fact that they owed their lives to each other. Dubourdieu had saved Audijos when he had been wounded in an ambush, and the latter had returned the compliment when, a few weeks later, his cousin had nearly been captured by irregulars. Such episodes seemed now to belong to an irrecoverable past. It was not just the weather that lowered the spirits of the two friends as they entered Saint-Jean-d'Angély. The rumour was widespread that peace would result in the regiment's disbandment.

Captain Boisset halted the company before the derelict building that was to be its quarters for the night. Leaving his two lieutenants to attend to the comfort of the men and their horses, he rode off to convey his compliments to the governor of the town. The cavaliers dismounted and began to lead their tired horses towards the stables, where, they suspected, many of them would themselves have to bed down beside their mounts. Dubourdieu moved towards the main door of the house, but he had taken but a step when it was flung open in his face, and a tall figure wearing a black sash over his doublet confronted him, sword in hand. Behind him the sound of voices raised in revelry burst out into the night air.

'You cannot lodge here, monsieur,' the officer declared. 'These are the quarters of the regiment of Navailles, and I, Sébastien de Nogent, have occupied this house with my men on the express command of the duke whose name we are proud to bear. Take your ragtag fellows and sleep elsewhere.'

'A horse's turd for your Navailles!' responded the choleric Dubourdieu, drawing his own sword. 'Morbleu! We are the Créquy Cavalerie, and our captain has a warrant from the maréchal de logis assigning us these lodgings. Our duke and his ancestors proved their worth in battle, while yours was carrying the chamber pot for his so-called eminence the cardinal de Richelieu.'

It so happened that this altercation reflected a rivalry during the Catalan campaign, when the two regiments fought side by side under command of the general-duke, Charles III de Blanchefort-Créquy. The Créquy Cavalerie was certainly the senior formation, for it had been raised by the general-duke's grandfather to serve against Savoy in 1598. Moreover, the cavaliers had been issued with shortened versions of the new experimental flintlock fusils, which they used to good effect. The regiment of Navailles, on the other hand, still relied on cold steel, although some of them were equipped with standard wheel-matchlocks modified for cavalry. They had been formed in 1641 by the duke, Philippe de Montac de Bénac, who had indeed served as a page to Richelieu before seeing action in Flanders and rising to the same rank of lieutenant-general as his rival, the present duc de Créquy. The latter was with the court in Provence at this time, but Navailles, having returned from a diplomatic mission in Italy, happened to be visiting the castle of Saint-Jean-d'Angély on the very evening when his regiment seemed about to have an affray with the

Créquy Cavalerie. The coincidence was to have a profound effect upon the career of Bernard d'Audijos.

Nogent was inflamed by the words of Dubourdieu, and lunged wildly with his sword. Stepping back, his opponent parried the thrust effortlessly. As Dubourdieu gave ground he noted that two more men had emerged from the house, and sought to take him from either side. Nogent sneered triumphantly and prepared to dispatch his enemy, who turned this way and that to challenge his new adversaries. At that moment the sound of a musket shot resounded and Nogent clutched his wrist as his broken sword flew from his hand. Audijos, still in the saddle but now erect and watchful, lowered his smoking carbine. If his cousin was renowned for his swordplay, he was the undisputed marksman of the regiment. At the sound of the shot the other two assailants fell back, and their comrades put down their wine, began to open the shutters of the house and to move cautiously into the street, clutching whatever weapons had come to hand. Meanwhile most of the Créquy cavaliers had turned to support their lieutenants, while others took the bridles of several horses at a time, and moved them to cover. Some began to reload their carbines, and some held their weapons at the ready, hoping the rain had not dampened the powder. Two opposing lines of soldiers formed in silent confrontation.

Then Audijos, having drawn his flintlock pistol from his belt and levelled it at the officer of the Navailles company, called in stentorian tones: 'Tell your men to lay down their arms, fellow, or my next shot will take you to hell, where you belong.' A wolfish smile spread across Nogent's face.

'Men of Navailles,' he shouted, 'aim your weapons at this cut-throat dog.' The click of cocking pieces or wheel-locks ran like a rippling wind down the two opposing lines of light horsemen. Just as a bloody exchange seemed unavoidable, rapid hoofbeats sounded and three cavaliers swept round the corner of the lodgings from the castle road. They were none other than Navailles himself, accompanied by a squire, and Boisset, who on his way to the castle had met the duke as he set forth down the hill to inspect the quarters of the newly arrived contingent from his regiment, and had learned of the double assignment of the lodging house. Boisset had joined the duke to help solve the confusion. At the noise of the musket shot the three men had spurred forward into a gallop.

The three horses reared as their riders reined them in firmly at the scene before them. Navailles, who was wearing the black sash of his regiment, was immediately recognisable, but it was Boisset, not the duke, who was the first to react.

'Hold your fire!' he shouted. 'Créquy Cavalerie, mount up, form line ahead, and follow me.' An audible sigh ran down the two opposing lines as the tension was released, and the cavaliers turned to seek their horses.

For his part, the duke rode forward to his captain, and asked for an explanation of events. He listened calmly to Nogent's expostulations, and instructed him to order his men back to their quarters. He then rejoined Boisset, whose company was still forming column.

'There is room for you all in the castle stables,' he said. 'I shall accompany you, and I expect you and your two hot-brained ensigns to join me for supper. But first, I would have you tell your marksman to replace my lieutenant's sword with his own.' It was a gesture of reconciliation, but Boisset, knowing the symbolic meaning of a sword to a Créquy cavalier, seemed loath to comply. However, Audijos had overheard the words of the duke. He dismounted, stepped up to Nogent, and proffered the hilt of his weapon to his former opponent. The officer removed his hat, bowed with a flourish, and took the sword. His gallantry masked his true feelings.

'On the next occasion we meet, monsieur,' he whispered, 'I trust it will find your heart.' Impervious to the insult, Audijos fixed Nogent with an unblinking stare from his light blue eyes. Then, remounting his mare, he gave an ironic salute, and took his place in the column. With Navailles and Boisset at their head, the Créquy Cavalerie moved up the hill towards the castle.

2. The Duc de Navailles

Like the rest of the fortifications of Saint-Jean-d'Angély, the old castle was in a dilapidated condition. Less than a century before it had been the heart of resistance to the royal army during an epic siege in the Huguenot wars. Subsequently the town had generally remained under French Protestant control until Louis XIII had taken it in 1621. Since then the walls had crumbled into ruin, and now that the Huguenots were no longer a military presence, no one had bothered to repair them. The governor's rooms in the castle had, however, been restored to a state of comfort, if not provincial splendour. The governor and his family happened to be absent on a visit to their estates, leaving their quarters to their patron, the duc de Navailles.

The duke was sitting before a fire in the great hall that had once been the guardroom of the garrison. From the tips of his curled moustache to his elegant boots he epitomised that section of the high aristocracy that had distinguished itself in the king's service. His reputation was scarcely less than that of Gramont or of Créquy. He had led the advance guard of the royal army at Saint-Antoine in 1652, when Condé's frondeurs had been pinned against the eastern walls of Paris and obliged to retreat into the city. Two years later he had been in the vanguard of the assault on Arras in the Spanish war. As a roving ambassador in Italy he had been appointed to command the French forces opposing the enemy in the peninsula. Most of his estates lay in Bigorre, adjoining Béarn, and his château of Bénac looked southwards to the central Pyrenees. He was, of course, well informed in diplomacy and high politics, but it was his practice to sound out the opinions of his social inferiors in such matters – hence his invitation to the junior officers of the Créquy Cavalerie. Their conduct in the affair of the lodging house had impressed him, and he also had in mind a personal mission, which he hoped to entrust to one of them.

Boisset was the first to enter the room, his lieutenants being occupied with settling men and horses into the capacious but half ruined stables of the castle. The duke questioned him closely about the service and background of Audijos and Dubourdieu. He seemed pleased that they were of the new gentry with close affiliations to the bourgeois notables of Chalosse. The fact that Audijos was related to the house of Foix-Candale also delighted him.

'We need such men,' he remarked. 'Now that we have peace with Spain we must settle our own problems, and nowhere more than in Gascony, where tumults and seditions against the king's taxes have long been rife.'

'Yes, monseigneur,' Boisset replied, 'but if the regiments are to be disbanded, the taxes His Majesty exacts should no longer be needed.'

'God grant it may be so! Yet I fear the financiers will not easily withdraw their claws. You should realise that our cardinal Mazarin, who governs both His Majesty and the queen mother, spends all his time in negotiating with the powers of Europe, and leaves financial matters to the controller-general, Nicolas Fouquet – a man hand in glove with those vultures, the tax-farmers, to whom the kingdom is mortgaged.'

'I know little of such high affairs,' said the captain. 'It saddens me to think our fine regiments and their traditions will disappear, and I know not how so many brave men will find a livelihood.'

'I share both your regrets and your apprehensions. Some may join the guards that intercept the salt smugglers who evade the tax of the gabelle. These men are bandits who stir up troubles in the land with their armed convoys and their assaults upon the bureaux of the gabeleurs. It is true that the latter are the agents of the tax-farmers, but the king's law must be observed.'

'That I know well, monseigneur. The poor need cheap salt to preserve their meat, and perhaps it is unjust that the peasants bear the burden when their superiors enjoy the privilege of exemption from the direct taxes.'

Navailles seemed surprised at such sentiments, but he took the point.

The Duc de Navailles

'At least,' he resumed, 'the officers in our regiments, and some of the rank and file as well, are seigneurs, however small their estates. It will be their duty to protect their peasants, to reconcile them with the system, and to work to improve their lot through the institutions in which nobles, clerics and bourgeois have a voice in the Pyrenean provinces.'

'My two young lieutenants happen to hold such views,' said Boisset. 'I have heard that when they were first enlisted they tried to protect the countryside against the rapine our troops committed in the Fronde. It was reported that on occasion they sent prior warning of our approach to the villages. I did not discipline them, for their motives were good, even if at times we lacked provisions in consequence.'

At this moment a discreet knock on the door signalled the arrival of Audijos and Dubourdieu. At the duke's bidding they entered and bowed to their host. Dubourdieu was awkward in such surroundings, while Audijos, who had visited the châteaux of some of his mother's relatives, seemed more at ease.

'You are welcome, gentlemen,' said Navailles. 'I trust your men are more comfortable in these stables than they would be brawling in the street with my own ruffians.'

'They have ridden far,' Audijos replied, 'and would rather sleep than fight. They thank your lordship for your hospitality, and for the food and wine you have sent them. Yet I believe our claim to the lodgings in the town was the better one.

The duke glanced at him sharply.

'That's as may be, but remember, young man, that we are all in the king's service. Captain Boisset tells me you have a passion to see justice done, even to the point where you claim that the peasants in the fields have their rights.'

'That they do, my lord, for they, like us, have immortal souls, and the king's writ should protect all, regardless of rank and privilege.'

'And where did you come by such notions? From your father, the first of his line, I believe, to be ennobled? Surely not from your widowed mother of the house of Foix-Candale.'

'No, monseigneur. My father, God rest his soul, was like most men with a newly acquired title – anxious to demonstrate his superiority and to have me find a noble career at arms. My mother, who is of the true nobility that cares for underlings, knew a teacher at the school of Saint-Sever and sent me there with my cousin Dubourdieu. My teacher had once studied the law and had then sought to be a priest. He had been in the company of Father Vincent de Paul, the shepherd boy whom the pope should make a saint for his labours on behalf of the oppressed. I am as proud to have had such a master as he was to have learnt from Father Vincent.'

Dubourdieu had turned red with embarrassment at this exchange, and Boisset seemed about to intercede when Navailles held up his hand.

'No, captain, I like the spirit of this man, and I have decided that he should fulfil a mission I have in my mind. With your permission, I shall have him seconded from your company to escort madame the duchess and her party to Bigorre. I have been recalled to my post, and she wishes to travel by dangerous ways, and even to visit the valleys of Lavedan in the mountains. She will be accompanied by her friend, madame de Motteville, lady of honour to the queen mother. I need someone of strength and resourcefulness, and these are qualities I discern in your Audijos. Besides, it is no bad thing that these ladies, who move in the highest society in the land, should learn something of the lowest. Audijos does not appear to hide his support for the latter. But we shall have to teach him something about court society if he is to hear their conversation.'

'You have my permission, my lord,' said Boisset. 'We are deeply honoured.' He looked towards his lieutenant, who clearly hesitated to accept his new role.

'Here,' said the duke, reaching for the weapon he had placed upon a nearby table. 'Take this sword of Navailles in place of the one you surrendered, and with it defend the honour of my lady.'

'I accept, my lord,' Audijos replied.

3. Madame de Motteville

The duke led his guests through the old armoury of the castle to the salon where they were to dine. While they were eating he made good his promise to trace the course of recent diplomacy and to provide some background to affairs at court. He explained how after the preliminary signing of the peace in the previous summer cardinal Mazarin had spent months negotiating with his Spanish counterpart, Don Luis de Haro, on the Isle of Pheasants in the middle of the Bidassoa River that formed the boundary between France and Spain in the south-west. The main sticking point had been the terms on which France could accept the restoration of the prince de Condé, who since the Fronde had been commanding Spanish armies against his king. Navailles told his audience that a messenger had recently brought the news that Condé had made his submission to Louis XIV at Aix-en-Provence and received the royal pardon. Another issue had been the proposed marriage alliance between the young king and the Spanish Infanta, Maria Teresa. The gallant Gramont had been sent to Spain to ask for the hand of the princess on behalf of the king. Here the duke was particularly well informed, for the brother of madame de Motteville, his wife's closest friend, had actually been in Gramont's retinue. Moreover, a notorious scandal had cast a blight upon this aspect of the negotiations.

The king's love affair with Marie de Mancini, the cardinal's niece, was common gossip at court. At the onset of the negotiations she had been sent into exile at La Rochelle, and both Mazarin and the queen mother had instructed His Majesty that he must put the good of his country before his passion. Nevertheless, Anne of Austria had ceded to her son's ardent wish to see Marie when in the autumn the court had passed close to La Rochelle, and halted at Saint-Jean.

'It was in this very place,' said Navailles, looking at Audijos, 'that they bade each other their last adieux. The court moved on to Bordeaux before spending the winter in Provence. You will find the duchess and madame de Motteville incessantly discussing the details, which have all the ingredients of a tragedy by Corneille. The queen mother gave her lady of honour permission to stay on at Niort with my wife, and the two of them subsequently went to call upon the Mancini girl at La Rochelle. They told me that she was utterly distraught, and the only advice her uncle could give was to write to tell her to read Seneca for consolation. But now she will be finding solace of a different kind. Last month our good cardinal allowed her to return to Paris.'

Audijos had been taught to read Seneca at Saint-Sever, but he had never heard of Corneille. He did not wish to display his ignorance, and in any case Boisset had a point of his own.

'Some might suggest, monseigneur,' he remarked, 'that his eminence had much to gain by letting the affair with his niece proceed.'

'Whatever you may think of our first minister, and you will remember how greatly he was vilified in the Fronde, he is too much the realist to conceive of his own family allied to the crown of France. Besides, the royal marriage, which is likely to take place in a few weeks somewhere near the frontier, is an essential part of the peace for which the cardinal has striven harder than any.'

The duke went on to discuss madame de Motteville. 'You will find,' he said to Audijos, 'that she is a lady of great learning. In the Paris salons they called her 'Socratine.' She is also a person of great discretion, as indeed she must be as one privy to the highest secrets of the kingdom. Her devotion to the queen mother is absolute, and my lady duchess says she keeps a diary, which is a kind of biography of Her Majesty. She belongs to no court cabal, nor has she family ties to distract her. She was born Françoise de Bertaut, the daughter of a gentleman valet in the king's chamber. When she was still but a girl she was married to old Langlois de Motteville, the presiding judge in the Rouen chamber of accounts. He was eighty at the time, and at his death left her a substantial fortune.'

'I fear, my lord, that a country gentleman such as myself is no fit company for such high ladies,' said Audijos.

'I do not expect you to display the wit and learning of the Paris salons – nor to exchange gossip about the great,' Navailles returned. 'Yet it will be well if you know something about great affairs. You are to serve as escort and to protect the party from the dangers of their route. Moreover, it may be, as I have suggested, that the ladies will learn something of the ways of the common people. There will be occasions when your charges may turn to you to ask about the customs of the lands through which they are to travel.'

Audijos felt distinctly uncomfortable at the prospect before him, but he had agreed to the mission, and he was not the kind of man to go back on his word. When he and Dubourdieu retired to their makeshift quarters, the latter congratulated him upon his good fortune.

'If you play the right cards,' Dubourdieu remarked, 'you will find yourself some position at the court.'

'That is not in my destiny,' said Audijos. 'I could never play the courtier, as you well know, my friend. Would that it were you who had been chosen. It will be a brief service, and I shall soon rejoin you and the rest of the company.'

Dubourdieu reflected for a moment.

'We both must wonder,' he said, 'if as soldiers of the king we can fulfil the charge our master laid upon us to restore to the people the liberties they were given under the ancient *fors*.'

'Those charters of freedom that maître Legrange knew so well are kept hidden by the powers that be. Some day they will be proclaimed once more,' said Audijos, 'and you will remember how he spoke of those old parchments, which have lain hidden for centuries and which must be found and restored to light. But in any case it does not seem that our service will last much longer, and perhaps when the Créquy Cavalerie is disbanded we can commence our quest.'

'Better that than to join the enforcers of the evil gabelle. By the wounds of Christ, I should rather aid the salt smugglers with my sword than associate with those who attack them. But here you are, a poor gentleman of Chalosse, about to rub shoulders with the high and mighty!'

Audijos did not respond, and the two friends wrapped themselves in their blankets and fell asleep. Early next morning they awoke to the swish of a sword whipped from side to side. Captain Boisset stood above them, brandishing the sword of Navailles.

'It is a fine Toledo blade the duke has bestowed upon you, Bernard d'Audijos,' he said. 'He is up betimes and awaits you to ride to Niort to join his ladies. He will leave you there to start your journey while he takes ship at La Rochelle.'

After embracing his cousin and bidding farewell to Boisset and his men, Audijos joined Navailles and his squire. The forty-mile ride was uneventful, passing through the flat lands of Aunis and interrupted by a halt for a meal at Dampierre. For the second part of the journey Audijos rode beside the squire, since the duke wished to commune with his own thoughts. The squire, a younger son of the vicomte de Parthenay, was a surly young man who owed his position to his birth. Clearly he resented the bestowal of such responsibilities upon a petty gentleman from Chalosse, and his few remarks belittled the boastful ways and quarrelsome habits attributed to Gascons. The Gascon reputation fitted Dubourdieu well enough, but it was far from apt for his introspective cousin. Audijos did not rise to the bait, and felt relieved when the church spire of Niort appeared on the horizon.

Upon the arrival of the cavaliers at the duke's substantial mansion on the outskirts of the town, Audijos noted that preparations for the journey to the Pyrenees were already in train. A cumbersome baggage wagon stood in the courtyard beside a more elegant vehicle evidently intended for the ladies. As he followed Navailles inside Audijos perceived a tall and elegant woman, a few years older than himself, pushing her way through a crowd of servants who stood ready to attend the duke's needs.

'Madame,' said the duke, 'allow me to present the sieur Bernard d'Audijos, who is to escort your mistress's party on your journey. Audijos, this is the lady Bernadette de Méru of the house of Montmorency, widow of the châtelain de Sèvres.'

Audijos swept off his plumed hat and bowed, a little awkwardly, for he saw the lady appraising him shrewdly with her strikingly green eyes. With her white complexion, her auburn hair falling in soft curls, and her sensuous figure, he thought her the most beautiful woman he had ever encountered. She led the men into the salon, where the duchess and madame de Motteville were awaiting them.

The duchesse de Navailles was a tall, rather prim woman, who had the habit of pursing her lips as if she strongly disapproved of most people's opinions. Madame de Motteville looked older than her forty years. She gave the impression of someone with a mission who felt the world had failed to recognise the importance of her role. As Audijos was to discover, that mission was to elevate her mistress, Anne of Austria, to the part of the all-seeing controller of the destinies of France – a woman whose political sagacity had survived persecution at the hands of cardinal Richelieu and was now displayed in her manipulation of his successor, cardinal Mazarin, in preparation for the day when her son, the king, should assume the reins of power. With her layered wig of artificial curls and her abundance of lace, madame de Motteville was very much the grand lady of the court who contrived to give the impression of knowing all its secrets while guarding them jealously. Her discretion, however, was less rigorous than it seemed. She disliked Mazarin and resented his intimacy with her adored mistress. The queen mother had always treated her as a confidante, relishing the opportunity to converse with her in Spanish, which Françoise de Bertaut had learnt at her mother's knee. They had endured much together – from cardinal Richelieu, who had once dismissed madame de Motteville from her mistress's retinue as one who encouraged Anne of Austria to take an independent stance against her husband, the king, to his successor's tribulations in the Fronde, which had occasioned scabrous pamphlets about Mazarin's relationship to Anne. Malicious tongues still wagged about the two, for their apartments in the Louvre adjoined each other, and they seemed to adopt a familial attitude to the upbringing of young Louis XIV. However, no one could deny the cardinal's obsequious observance of public proprieties.

The duc de Navailles presented Audijos, and explained that he had selected him to escort the party to Bénac and beyond. The ladies accepted this with some reservation, for they had not expected a strange officer to command their guard. At the same time they contrived to greet Audijos graciously, and he, for his part, was too overawed by the company to do more than mumble an expression of the honour done to him. His eyes remained fixed on the châtelaine de Sèvres, who stood behind the duchess's chair. Navailles told him to be ready for departure next morning, and promised to inform him later of the composition of the party and the route that they should take. Sensing that his presence was no longer required, Audijos bowed, and turned to Parthenay to conduct him to his quarters.

4. The Châtelaine

Audijos supped with Parthenay and some other gentlemen of the household. He was too conscious of his provincial ways to enter a conversation, which became progressively freer as the evening wore on and the duke's wine flowed plentifully. Someone had mentioned the charms of the châtelaine de Sèvres, who was dining with Navailles and the other ladies. Parthenay turned to his silent companion.

'What do you think of the fair châtelaine?' he asked. 'I note she held your eye, and perhaps you should be warned that she has a lust for strangers such as you."

Audijos blushed and stammered. 'I – I hardly think she would look to me. Besides, you are too ready to besmirch the lady's honour, monsieur.'

'So! You would be a champion to a woman who has bedded more men than you have in your company.'

Audijos struggled to contain the anger that welled up within him.

'I do not know the lady,' he replied, 'but I am prepared to defend her against the slanders of a foul-mouthed ninny whose manners do not befit his birth.'

Matters might have gone further, but at that moment a servant brought Audijos a message that the duke required his attendance to brief him on his duties. He was ushered into a book-lined room where Navailles, having left the ladies after their repast, was consulting a number of maps laid out on a table. He outlined the roads to be followed and listed the châteaux of his friends and clients who would provide hospitality.

'My secretary will provide you with an itinerary before your departure tomorrow,' he said. 'I am more concerned with the danger points along the route. You will follow the roads where you will be unlikely to meet bandits or smugglers, but there are places that could be perilous. Ten armed and mounted servants

The Châtelaine

will accompany you, although I cannot vouch for their skill in combat.'

As Audijos walked along the corridor that led to his quarters a door opened and a voice called to him softly. It was the châtelaine, clad in revealing night attire.

'I have heard, monsieur,' she said, 'that you defended my honour against one who would traduce it.' She looked at him seductively, and shook her barely concealed bosom alluringly beneath her robe. Audijos felt a wave of desire that almost overcame him.

'I am your ladyship's servant, madame,' he replied with a bow.

'Perhaps,' she said, 'we shall see each other often on our journey.' She stepped backwards, closing the door behind her.

Audijos trembled, recovered himself, and resumed his path along the passageway. He had had little amorous experience. He remembered Dubourdieu's twelve-year old sister Jeanne-Marie, who had worshipped him as he was growing into manhood, and had promised him when he enlisted that she would wait for his return and hope that one day their families would negotiate their union. He thought of her elfin face and innocent ways, and of the times he and Roger had teased her when she followed them on their boyhood games. He called to mind his sexual initiation, when his elder sister, born of his father's first marriage, had persuaded a worldly female friend to seduce him in a barn at the time of the harvest festival. Then there had been encounters with Catalan women during the Spanish campaign. Unlike most of his comrades, Audijos had treated them with respect, and made sure that they were willing partners. But the châtelaine was someone beyond all his secret imaginings. He reflected that Parthenay's remark might not have been far from the truth, but, cautious though he was of the dangers of such a liaison on his present mission, his senses had been enthralled.

The duke and his personal entourage departed early the next morning, and Audijos, after receiving his instructions, marshalled the servants and carriages while he waited impatiently for the ladies to appear. They came at last, and nodded to him condescendingly as he swept off his hat and helped them ascend the steps of their conveyance. Then, after various anxieties about the proper stowage of their baggage, the duchesse de Navailles told him to mount and give the signal for departure. Audijos had carefully organised the order of march. The two most reliable of the duke's armed retainers rode several hundred yards ahead to provide early warning. He himself led three mounted men in front of the carriage containing the duchess, madame de Motteville and the châtelaine. Behind them came another carriage with the ladies' female servants followed by two more men with spare horses and the lumbering baggage wagon. The remaining three armed retainers brought up the rear.

Day after day the convoy moved slowly southwards, stopping by night in the main towns or at the country seats of local magnates. Audijos had expected to meet Boisset and his company, as well as Nogent and his men, on the road, but at Saint-Jean-d'Angély he learned that the itinerary of the regiments had been countermanded, and that they were returning to Gascony.

As the convoy approached Bordeaux the châtelaine left the main carriage for part of each day and rode beside Audijos on the most spirited of the spare horses. She pretended that the incessant chatter of the two great ladies wearied her and that they, for their part, welcomed the opportunity to be alone together. The truth was that the châtelaine was regarded with some distrust by the duchess and her friend, for the aura of scandal that surrounded her was not to their taste. In fact her presence on the journey was due to the specific orders of the duke, who had promised her Montmorency relatives to accept her temporarily into the duchess's household. Despite her high connections, her marriage had been to one of the lesser nobility. She had received various proposals of marriage in the years following the death of her husband, but had preferred to remain single. It was of course, not uncommon among the nobility for one spouse to ignore the infidelity of the other, for marriage among the great was an arranged matter of property and dynastic alliance. The châtelaine de Sèvres preferred, however, to pursue her predatory course unfettered even by nominal ties, and for the most part she was sufficiently discreet to avoid offending her more strait-laced travelling companions. She had ambitions of her own to secure a place at court, and she knew that madame de Navailles coveted the post of lady of honour to the Spanish Infanta, soon to be queen of France. Madame de Motteville's possession of the ear of Anne of Austria was important to the success of the plan.

After their first meeting at Niort, Audijos looked constantly to the châtelaine for some sort of encouragement, but for many days she remained aloof and scarcely glanced in his direction. Her manner changed when she began to ride at his side. She overcame his shyness with questions about the campaigns in which he had fought, and as they approached his native province she showed an interest in the countryside through which they passed. Then at Langon, where the party crossed the Garonne, she began to speak of her own life, playing the role of a woman who had suffered much from deception and betrayal. Audijos responded with sympathy, even though a doubt hovered in the back of his mind. The châtelaine placed a hand on his bridle arm as they rode together, and Audijos felt his reserve melt away. Two nights later, while the party was enjoying the hospitality of the château de Roquefort on the Douze River, the châtelaine came by night into his room and fell into his arms.

5. The Gabeleurs

The châtelaine came secretly to Audijos on two subsequent occasions, but their lovemaking proceeded in purely physical terms without any exchange of intimate confidences. This troubled Bernard, who sought some expression of sentiment from the châtelaine.

'You must take me as you find me,' she responded. 'Can we not take pleasure in each other without indulging in foolish talk of love?' One morning he observed her flirting with the son of their host for the previous night. When they were next alone he reproached her for her inconstancy.

'You are under some misapprehension, sir,' she said. 'This is my life, and I owe you nothing.'

'I understand, madame,' returned Audijos, thinking that Parthenay had not been so wide of the mark after all. 'Perhaps you should find some other man to cater to your pleasures.'

The châtelaine glared at him in fury. 'I am not accustomed to being rejected, monsieur. You will live to regret this.'

Meanwhile the slow moving cavalcade proceeded steadily southwards, passing through the regions of Landes and Tursan and approaching Audijos's home county of Chalosse. The duchess intended to visit the small town of Navailles, whence her husband drew his title, but she was willing, at the request of Audijos, to make a slight change in the duke's itinerary and to travel by way of Saint-Sever and Coudures. This detour led to an incident that shattered their peaceful progress.

As the party ascended the forested hill, beyond which lay the valley of the Adour and the ford a few miles west of Saint-Sever, a burst of musketry sounded, followed by shouts and screams from the direction of the river. Audijos halted the cavalcade and rode forward to meet one of his scouts, who came galloping back from the crest.

'It is the gabeleurs from the salt bureau,' he burst out. 'They have ambushed a convoy of salt smugglers, and they are shooting down man and beast.'

Audijos rode forward to the top of the hill to join the second scout. Below him was a scene of pandemonium. Two barges were grounded by the bank. Beside them on the shore men and horses lay dead or dying. From the taller trees that lined the further slope came puffs of smoke, followed by the noise of musket shots. The surviving smugglers had boarded the barges, which they tried desperately to push into deeper water. Some of them were returning fire to cover their comrades, but clearly their targets among the trees were largely invisible. A short, burly man standing waist-deep in the river caught Audijos's attention. It was Roger Dubourdieu, straining his mighty muscles and oblivious of the musket balls that cut the water around him.

'Ride back to the duchess,' Audijos ordered the second scout, 'and tell her that it is necessary to leave the road and take shelter behind that rocky outcrop we noticed half a mile to the rear. I have some business with those ahead.'

With the remaining scout by his side Audijos cantered into the valley and made for the ford five hundred yards downstream. They crossed it unobserved, and rode up the hill into the trees, turning eastwards to outflank the gabeleurs. When they were above the ambush they dismounted and moved cautiously towards the guards of the bureau. By this time resistance from the barges had almost ceased. Through a gap in the vegetation Audijos glimpsed Dubourdieu standing on board the nearest barge with sword in hand. At that moment the guards broke cover and advanced towards the shore with their firearms at the ready. Dubourdieu gave a cry of defiance, but it seemed that he and his surviving friends had no more ammunition. Audijos crouched beside a rock and unslung his musket. His first shot took the leading guard in the back and he pitched forward and lay still. His second, fired from the musket handed him by the scout, hit the officer commanding the gabeleurs in the leg. The six remaining guards fled back towards the trees, dragging their wounded leader with them. Audijos reloaded, but did not fire again. The guards mounted the horses they had tethered behind their place of ambush, and took the road towards Saint-Sever.

When Audijos broke cover and strode towards the river, his friend gave a cry of astonished recognition.

'By the white plume of Navarre,' Dubourdieu shouted, 'I might have known that only you could have hit two targets at two hundred paces. How come you here to save my carcass a second time?'

'I heard the first shots of your ambush as I brought my ladies to the far side of the northern hill,' Audijos responded. 'But what misfortune led you to be among the salt smugglers when our company marches forty leagues from here?'

'I was granted leave to visit Coudures, and there I heard that some of our boyhood friends were riding along the banks of the Adour in escort to the two salt barges. The cause was good, for these base fellows of the bureau threaten our liberties and impose the gabelle without due warrant. Now they have murdered horse and man alike without challenge or warning.'

As the two friends embraced, Dubourdieu winced, and Audijos perceived that his left arm had been wounded by a musket ball, and was bleeding copiously. He tried to staunch the flow, but Dubourdieu pushed him away.

'Morbleu! It is only a graze. Let us look to the wounded who lie beside us.

There were indeed three men who lay groaning on the shore, and several wounded horses still thrashing helplessly. Audijos put the horses out of their agony while Dubourdieu tended the injured. In the midst of their ministrations they heard a female voice call to them. Looking up, they saw the châtelaine and four retainers riding towards them from the ford. 'What, sir, have you done?' she exclaimed. 'The duchess and madame de Motteville are in a terrible state of alarm. It is no part of your duties to fight battles with the gabeleurs. And who is this who stands beside you, bleeding like a pig?'

Audijos introduced Dubourdieu, who was visibly impressed by the châtelaine's charms, and became quite speechless as she dismounted, tore off a segment of her dress, and bandaged his wounded arm. Audijos stammered out some explanation of the circumstances, but the châtelaine reacted to him coldly.

'We are supposed to continue to Saint-Sever,' she said. 'If, as you say, the guards of the bureau have withdrawn there, they will surely recognise you upon our arrival, and the duchess will be more than embarrassed if the commander of her escort is arrested as a rebel against the king and a murderer of his officials.'

'You exaggerate, madame,' he responded with rising anger. 'The king would not sanction the killing of innocent men from ambush – men who are acting in accordance with the privileges of the region against false laws enforced by ruffians. In any case none of these fellows saw my face in this encounter.'

Four unwounded men had also disembarked, and proceeded to round up the surviving horses that were browsing on the edge of the woods. The dead were buried, and the wounded placed on a cart acquired from a local farmlet and harnessed to one of the horses. It was decided that Dubourdieu should mount another horse and lead the injured men to Coudures by back roads, while the salt convoy should continue as best it could. The barges were pushed offshore and set off downstream with the current. They were now without escort, although one man led the remaining horses along the bank. Well before the completion of these preparations Audijos and the châtelaine were obliged to leave the scene to rejoin the party sheltering over the hill to the north. They rode back together in silence.

6. Saint-Sever

The duchess and madame de Motteville were already in their carriage when Audijos and the châtelaine approached the rocky crag behind which the main party had been sheltering. Madame de Navailles looked disapprovingly at Audijos, and appeared alarmed at the evident disarray of the countess's dress.

'Fear not, madame,' said the châtelaine. 'My robe was torn to make a bandage for a brave and wounded man.'

'In truth,' Audijos added, 'I felt it was my duty to help a friend and his comrades when they had been unjustly set upon by the guards of the bureau. These fellows have retreated to Saint-Sever, while my friend and others hurt in the affray have gone to Coudures. The guards had no opportunity to see who I was, so we may proceed on our journey without danger of reproach.'

'It is you, sir, who deserve reproach,' replied the duchess. 'Your mission to command our escort should have taken precedence over your wish to embroil yourself in wayside brawls. My husband will not think well of you when he hears of this.'

At this moment Audijos received support from an unexpected quarter.

'I think, my dear, we may pardon our hot-headed lieutenant,' said madame de Motteville to the duchess. 'It appears that we are not compromised in this affair, and no one in Saint-Sever is likely to connect him with it.' The châtelaine endorsed this viewpoint, and after some further discussion of the incident madame de Navailles relented. She ordered Audijos to set the cavalcade once more in line of march. 'But make sure,' she told him, 'that none of our people mention the matter when we reach the town.'

Instead of crossing the river and passing the scene of the ambuscade, Audijos kept to the north bank, and followed a road that intersected the route from Mont-de-Marsan. There he turned south to pass the Adour by a bridge leading directly to Saint-Sever. As he rode into the town he looked carefully to left and right for signs of his recent enemies, but neither the guards nor their horses were visible. Passing the school, he vowed to return to revive his boyhood memories by a visit to maître Legrange, if indeed his former teacher still lived in the adjoining house. It took an hour or two to settle the ladies and their entourage into the mansion of the sénéchal, whose officers had been apprised of their coming by a messenger, sent on in advance. As he was making his way to seek leave from the duchess to absent himself, Audijos encountered the châtelaine de Sèvres, but she turned her head away from him when he tried to greet her.

Bernard d'Audijos tethered his mare beside the tree in the middle of the school courtyard, and looked round at the familiar scene he had known eight years earlier. The school was one of those founded in the previous century by the good bourgeois who sought to prepare their sons for advancement in a more effective way than the church establishments for the young had done. As his mind retraced memories of the games he had played and the Latin tags he had learnt from maître Legrange, he was startled by the snorting of horses in the storehouse to his right. He moved to the door of the main building and found it open. No one responded to the sound of the iron bell when he rang. He stepped into the vestibule, and then into the principal classroom. There, seated upon a bench with his wounded leg upon a desk, was the officer of the guards of the bureau. Beside him some of his men were finishing a makeshift meal. The schoolhouse had been commandeered by the gabeleurs.

Audijos was wearing the sword presented to him by the duc de Navailles, but he had left both pistol and carbine at the sénéchaussée, and there was nothing to associate him with the recent affray. 'Forgive my intrusion, sir,' he said to the officer. 'I was seeking the schoolmaster.'

'You will not find him here,' came the reply. 'He does not approve of those, such as myself, who enforce the king's gabelle. When he received the order for our being quartered here, he cursed us soundly and went to consult the curé in the vicarage at the end of the street.'

Audijos had no intention of arousing the man's suspicions, so he mumbled a word of thanks and went outside to his horse. He found his old teacher talking animatedly to the curé outside the vicarage. Maître Legrange had changed little through the years. He was perhaps a little balder and a little more rotund, but he still displayed he same irrepressible energy that Audijos remembered so well. His eyes sparkled and he gesticulated wildly as he expatiated on the misdeeds of the gabeleurs and the inconvenience they had caused by occupying the schoolhouse. He looked up as he heard the sound of Audijos's horse, and cried out in pleasure as he recognised the rider.

'Bernard, by the Odes of Horace. How you have changed – you are quite the soldier now! What brings you back to Saint-Sever?'

'And you, maître, are the same as ever, and even more like the prince of satirists, whose Latin lines you made us learn with the help of your cane. I am detached from my regiment, escorting the duchesse de Navailles and her party on the road to Bigorre.'

Audijos dismounted, greeted the curé, and was ushered inside the house. A fine Jurançon wine was produced, and before long Legrange had reverted to his diatribe against the evils of the gabelle. It was a familiar discourse – one that Audijos had heard many times as a schoolboy, when the teacher had digressed from his Latin tags to indoctrinate his pupils with the story of the liberties of the region and their infringement by the agents of the king.

'It is not the king who is to blame,' he said. 'Those who speak in his name never inform him of the tyrannies they perpetrate. They contravene the old laws, and there is no one to tell His Majesty of the suffering of his people.'

Audijos knew he could trust Legrange with the details of the ambush, although he was modest about his own part in the encounter. The schoolmaster listened attentively.

'It is not the first of such incidents,' he said. 'New storm clouds are gathering, and before long we may expect the people to take arms as they did in Bayonne nearly twenty years ago. Your recent battle is, I fear, the prelude to many that are to come. In the last phase there was a similar killing near Mont-de-Marsan in 1649, when the guards attacked a convoy of over one hundred carts of salt.'

Legrange knew the history of the long struggle against the gabelle, going back a century to the great revolt in Guienne. He had taken a law degree at the University of Toulouse, but had been disbarred from practice for his outspoken opinions. He was aware how bitterly the salt tax was resented among all the social orders, and he knew, even better than the legal fraternity, how the old constitutional restraints in the provinces bordering the Pyrenees had been subtly undermined. The regions of the Landais, including Chalosse and Tursan, paid a special sum to obtain exemption from the gabelle, and thus acquired the status of 'redeemed districts.' However, this could be revoked by royal authority and they were less secure than provinces in the extreme south such as Labourd, Navarre, Soule, Béarn and Bigorre, where the tax-farmers who ran the gabelle had no jurisdiction. From time to time the towns along the Adour and its tributaries (Bayonne, Dax, Tartas, Mont-de-Marsan, Saint-Sever and Aire) were the subject of edicts establishing the bureaux of the gabelle with their guards and salt depots, but local resistance and the promise of further lump sum payments had secured suspension of the edicts in the past. Meanwhile cheap salt from the salt fountains in Béarn was carried northwards by the smugglers, resulting in a covert war with the guards. Understanding these complexities had been Legrange's avocation in the years following his association with Vincent de Paul, and he brought to it all Father Vincent's concern for the unprivileged.

'There is another incident I must relate,' said Legrange. 'Three years ago, when you were serving in Catalonia, a brigade of guards were terrorising the people of Aire, the very seat of our good bishop who strives to protect the people from the misdeeds of those who pretend to execute the king's warrant. His grace had in his possession an old manuscript of the ancient charter of Chalosse, granted four centuries ago by Gaston de Monçade, who ruled not only Béarn but all these lands to the north. This *for* was lost in the subsequent wars with the English, but the liberties it established were fully as wide as those in Béarn and the mountain valleys in the south. The document passed out of memory until a friend of mine, an antiquary of Aire, discovered a copy and passed it to the bishop. He in turn gave it to the town councillors so that they might confront the officer in charge of the gabeleurs and tell him that the actions of his men contravened our sacred rights. This officer laughed in their faces and confiscated the piece of vellum. That very night the daughter of one of the councillors was raped by three of the guards. The gentry of the town and the surrounding countryside gathered in the château of Viella, and launched an attack upon the bureau, killing the rapists, holding the officer to ransom and driving the rest of his men from the district. In due course the officer was released, but the *for* was recovered and given secretly to me for safe custody.

When royal troops arrived in Aire some months later to re-establish the salt bureau, they were accompanied by agents who began an inquiry about the fate of the document. At this time I was being visited by the curé of Arrens in the Lavedan, who had trained with me in the seminary. As the search came closer I gave the *for* to him to take back to the mountains and hide in a secure place. The time is coming when we shall need the charter to give us judicial protection, and somehow it must be brought back from Lavedan.'

Audijos listened carefully to the schoolmaster's story, his light blue eyes hardening as he heard about the *for*. Seeking to elicit more detail from Legrange, he assumed at first an air of scepticism.

'I remember how you taught us to revere such ancient laws, maître,' he replied, 'but can you truly believe that the ruffians who enforce the gabelle will respect a piece of vellum centuries old? And why do you think the tax-farmers are planning some new campaign against the people of Chalosse?'

'The magistrates of the *parlements* in both Bordeaux and Pau respect our ancient customs as they do the edicts of the king,' Legrange answered, 'and they can issue an order to restrict the ravages of the gabeleurs until they have examined the matter. Further, the governor may intercede with the royal council, for he knows well that the good King Henri and his successors have sworn to uphold our chartered liberties. As to your second question, I can tell you in greatest confidence that I have a secret source in Bordeaux who has tapped the correspondence of the financiers with the minister, Fouquet. They are planning a new series of bureaux for the gabelle, and they intend to recruit many new guards. What is more, they are setting up a network of spies and informers to report on those who aid the salt smugglers. I have even heard that they have in their pay a woman of noble birth whose task it is to inform upon the gentry who support our cause.'

Audijos was startled by these words.

'You are more deeply embroiled in these affairs than I had imagined, maître,' he replied. 'Perhaps I may be able to serve you in retrieving the *for* of Chalosse from the curé of Arrens. I am to escort my ladies into the mountains of Lavedan. But now I must return to them, for they await my presence to take them to Coudures.'

7. Coudures

Audijos took his leave of the schoolmaster, promising to send word about his search for the precious document. For his part, maître Legrange undertook to keep his former pupil informed of events concerning the enforcement of the gabelle in the district. As he passed the school on his way back to the house of the sénéchal, Audijos saw the officer he had shot standing at the gate with the aid of a cane. The officer stared at him intently, but did not return Audijos's salute.

The duchesse de Navailles was in some distress when Audijos found her, for it seemed that the châtelaine had disappeared and no one knew her whereabouts. An hour later she returned on horseback, just as Audijos was about to organise a search. Coudures lay only six miles to the south-east, so there was still time to reach the village before nightfall. The cortège proceeded in its customary formation by the road that followed the course of the Gabas River. Soon after crossing a tributary stream, the Bas, they passed through a dark wood of black oak and saw ahead of them open fields and the outskirts of the village.

Coudures contained less than a hundred dwellings, most of them lining the long central road that ascended gradually to the church with its square, flat-topped bell tower constructed at the beginning of the century. There were some substantial houses, notably those of the Dubourdieu family and that of Audijos's parents. Clearly, the cortège was expected, for the people flocked into the street and waved to Audijos as he rode at the head of the duchess's carriage. They halted at the gate of the Dubourdieu home, which was large enough to accommodate most of the party. Standing in the portal of the house was someone whom Audijos recognised, after a moment's hesitation. It was Roger's sister, Jeanne-Marie – no longer the elfin figure who had joined in their boyhood escapades so many years ago, but a woman of striking beauty with long brown tresses tied at the nape of her neck and falling almost to her waist. She was no taller than Audijos remembered, but her figure had filled out and combined a hint of sensuality with an impression of strength and determination. She blushed as Audijos swept off his plumed hat, and ran inside to summon her father.

Arnaud Dubourdieu appeared within seconds. His portly frame moved with a dignity appropriate to his many local offices as judge of Coudures and Hagetmau and attorney to the countship of Louvigny within the lands of the duc de Gramont. The common folk respected him no less for his fairness in arbitrating litigious matters between peasant communities and their overlord than for his firmness in dealing with malefactors under his master's right to dispense high justice. The local nobility knew him as one who, however obsequious in his demeanour to his betters, administered seigneurial laws with an impartial regard for the rights of both high and low. He felt honoured at the visit of such great ladies as the duchess and madame de Motteville despite considerable embarrassment at his son's involvement in the battle with the gabeleurs. Roger had informed him of the rescue by Audijos, but since the latter remained in charge of the safety of the cortège it was unlikely, he reflected, that his own family would be implicated. Nonetheless, caution had persuaded him to have his wounded son transferred to the house of Audijos's mother, Diane de Talazac-Bahus.

'Your ladyships are most welcome to my humble abode,' said the elder Dubourdieu as he assisted the ladies to descend from their cumbersome carriage. 'We have prepared lodgings for your entourage, and my stables and courtyard stand ready for your horses and conveyances.'

The duchess and her companions swept past the judge and his daughter as they entered the house, the châtelaine observing Jeanne-Marie with a scornful and penetrating glance. She had not failed to notice Jeanne-Marie's reaction to the arrival of Audijos, and the hostility she now felt towards Bernard inclined her to seek revenge.

As soon as Audijos had settled his party into their quarters he sought out Jeanne-Marie alone, and asked for news of her brother.

'He is with your mother,' she replied, 'and his wound is likely to heal within days. But have you nothing else to say to me after these years of waiting and watching for your return?'

Audijos looked down into the brown eyes staring intently into his. He felt an urge to kiss her half-open lips, but restrained himself.

'I have never forgotten you,' he said, 'but you must remember that we were very young, and doubtless we have each learnt much from life since we parted.'

'By that you mean you have loved others, I suppose – or perhaps you think I have not been loyal to the pledge I gave you. It is true that my father wishes me to respond to the rich and opinionated sieur de Prugues, who has been pursuing me. But you have always been in my heart and I have thought of no other man since you rode off as a boy of fifteen to join the Créquy Cavalerie.'

'And you were a girl of scarce twelve years, Jeanne, and more given to climbing trees and playing the hoyden than thinking of love. This is no more than a fancy conjured from the stories of dragons, knights and fairies in that old romance we read of the '*Amadis de Gaule*'

Jeanne-Marie turned her face away, her eyes clouded with the tears she could not repress.

'I do not care what you say,' she burst out. 'I shall make you love me.'

The sun had set and they were standing in the half-light behind a spinney at the rear of the house. Jeanne-Marie seized Bernard's hand and placed it upon her breast. At the same time she put her left arm round his neck and dragged his mouth onto hers. Audijos did not try to resist and kissed her passionately. At that same moment there was a movement on the other side of the spinney, and the châtelaine stepped through the bushes and confronted them.

The couple stepped apart in consternation. It was the châtelaine who broke the silence.

'I did not mean to interrupt so tender a tryst,' she said with a scornful note in her voice. 'I have just learned that the man whose wound I tended is a son of this house, and is lodged nearby. They told me that you, monsieur could take me to him.'

Conflicting emotions raced through the mind of Audijos. On one hand the meeting of the woman to whom he had made love and someone for whom he had just acknowledged a deep affection left him speechless; on the other, his suspicion at the interest the châtelaine expressed in Roger, coupled with his surprise at her discovery of his friend's identity and whereabouts, inspired a profound disquiet. Had the châtelaine wormed the information out of one of Roger's parents by talking about the ambush? Could she be the spy of whom Legrange had spoken? He glanced at Jeanne-Marie, who had gathered up her skirts and was clearly about to retreat into the house.

'Stay, my dear,' he said. 'Madame shall see your brother. We shall take her to my own home, where he is recovering.'

'You may do so, Bernard,' she returned. 'As for me, I should help my mother see to the comfort of our guests.' She tossed her head, turned her back upon the châtelaine and left the scene.

Audijos and the châtelaine walked side by side down the main street of Coudures, each wondering who would be first to break the silence. Finally it was the châtelaine who spoke: 'I note, sir, that you are as quick with your kisses as you are with your musket.'

'That is unworthy of you, châtelaine. We were childhood friends. In any case, why have you chosen to ignore me, and why do you now pursue my friend, Roger Dubourdieu?'

'He interests me and you have chosen to insult me.'

No other word was uttered until they reached the portal of Audijos's home. Bernard asked his companion to wait for an instant while he informed the household of their unexpected visitor. He found his mother seated with Dubourdieu before a fire. Their effusive greeting was checked by a warning gesture from Audijos.

'The châtelaine de Sèvres waits without, Roger,' he said. 'She is the lady who tied up your wound after the ambush. I am told that your graze is on the mend, but be careful what you say to her, for I know not her motives in coming here. I regret, mother that I must withhold my joy at seeing you again until our guest has taken her leave. There are secrets in the air that force us to be on guard.'

Madame de Talazuc was taken aback by her son's manner, but she welcomed the châtelaine gracefully when Bernard presented her. The châtelaine, for her part, clearly knew madame's distinguished ancestry and treated her with great respect. After some brief enquiries about the house of Talazuc and the fortunes of the Foix-Candale, she turned to Dubourdieu.

'I came to ask about the health of my brave patient,' she said with her most charming smile. 'I can see that you are fit enough to support some new band of smugglers.'

Dubourdieu, whose left arm was supported by a sling, bowed and curled the tips of his long moustache with his right hand. 'I am honoured by your interest, madame,' he responded, 'but I have to rejoin my regiment and have no intention of further escapades against those scoundrels of the bureau.'

'Perhaps,' said the châtelaine, 'you will escort me back to the house of your parents. The duchess will be asking for me, and I know that monsieur d'Audijos wishes to spend some time with his mother.'

Audijos felt some alarm at this manœuvre, and was on the point of suggesting that a servant should fulfil the châtelaine's request when Dubourdieu expressed his willingness to perform the service. Seizing his plumed hat and strapping on his sword with some difficulty, he ushered the châtelaine to the door. She chattered flirtatiously to the muscular, swaggering figure at her side as they walked along the street. By the time they reached their destination she had not only extracted from her ingenuous escort the names of the more considerable gentry of the area sympathetic to the salt traffic but she had also secured a new and fervent admirer.

When Audijos returned to the Dubourdieu mansion an hour later he took Roger aside and told him his suspicions about the châtelaine. It was soon clear to him however, that nothing he could say to his friend in this vein would make much of an impression. He suppressed his own lingering passion for the lady, newly excited by a pang of jealousy, and it became easier for him to do so when he examined his own reaction to Jeanne-Marie's embrace. He sought her out before they retired, and as they discussed old memories of life in Coudures he was increasingly attracted by her direct and simple ways.

'You must think I had taken your pledge too lightly,' said Bernard, 'and to tell you the truth, I did not think of you as often as I should through these long years. We were but children then, but now I realise how much you mean to me.'

'My dearest love, those are the sweetest words I have ever heard. I cannot tell you how much I have thought about you, and worried you might be lying dead on some distant battlefield. But now you have come back to me alive and well.'

'I love you, Jeanne, and though my duties force our continued separation, I shall return.'

The lovers embraced. They could hear voices raised in altercation in the salon, and made their way there, entering by different doors.

8. The Cabaret

Audijos took in the scene before him at a glance. His friend, Roger, stood red-faced in the middle of the room, his parents pale and worried, behind him. Madame de Motteville and the châtelaine de Sèvres still reclined in their chairs, but the duchess had risen to her full height and her tightly pursed lips betrayed an evident anger.

'Let me repeat myself,' she said loudly to the elder Dubourdieu. 'Is it not enough that my journey should be interrupted by bandits that I should now be insulted by finding that one of them is the son of my host and dares to come into my very presence?'

'I crave your grace's pardon,' replied Roger's father. 'I am a man of the law, and I can assure you that no insult was intended. It can be said that the officers of the gabelle are the ones who must take the blame for this unfortunate affray.'

To the surprise of all present, the châtelaine now assumed the role of conciliator.

'I regret, madame,' she said, 'that I should have answered your question so rashly when I presented this brave man, and you asked how he had come by his wound. Would it not be best if you allowed him to withdraw and we could forget this whole incident?'

'He may leave,' said the duchess, in no way mollified, 'but I shall certainly not forget this matter. The duke shall hear of it. Moreover, the gentleman supposedly responsible for our safety himself participated in this murderous business.' She looked severely at Audijos.

Bernard bowed and ventured to reply. 'Your grace's welfare will always be my first consideration while I continue to command your escort. I could not leave my friend to die, and I repeat my request that you accept my deep regret for causing you distress.'

The duchess chose to ignore these words, and Roger, still scarlet with embarrassment, bowed somewhat clumsily and left the room. It was time for madame de Motteville to intervene.

'Come, my dear,' she said to her friend. 'Do you not remember how you admired the magnanimity of the emperor in Corneille's play *Cinna* when he pardoned all those who had offended him? Our host and his family are worthy people, and it is not for us to indict two hot-headed young lieutenants whose loyalty to the king is not in doubt.'

'I can hardly claim to play the part of the mighty Augustus,' replied the duchesse de Navailles, whose pursed lips, nonetheless, seemed to relax a little. 'This affair is more like a scene from *Horace,* where the champions of Rome and Alba are at each other's throats. But I shall not pursue matters further. You, monsieur d'Audijos, had best make preparations for our departure in the morning.'

Bernard hurried after Roger, narrowly anticipating the châtelaine, who had risen with similar intent. He found his friend outside in the street, muttering a stream of Gascon oaths.

'Let us visit the cabaret on the corner,' he said. 'We may find some of our old companions there, and at the least we may drown our sorrows.'

Audijos turned and noticed the châtelaine standing outside the Dubourdieu house, but she did not attempt to follow them when they entered the doorway on their left. Roger's gloom disappeared as soon as they were inside. Familiar faces surrounded them. Among the score or so of men present in the tavern were Duplantier, the proprietor, whose broad face, surmounting a massive frame, was perpetually wreathed in smiles; the sly, diminutive Bernard de Labat, the sole notary in Coudures; Jean Lacourt, the curé, who preferred the career of a poacher to his duties in the pulpit, which he abandoned to his vicar; his brother Simon, a surly fellow who had been a man-at-arms; and, nearer the age of Bernard and Roger, two share-croppers from the neighbouring village of Ancos, Arnaud Corade and Géronce Baillet. Corade was a muscular fellow with a twisted lip that gave him a sardonic expression, Baillet a slim man with a smiling, open face that made him look younger than his thirty years.

The Cabaret

The two latter men were the first to greet the cavaliers, but others in the cabaret were quick to follow suit. From the general enthusiasm it was evident that they had been discussing the ambush, and that they knew all about the parts played by Audijos and Dubourdieu. A few, however, were rather less approving.

'My welcome to you both,' said Duplantier, producing a flagon of dark red wine. 'We have been wondering how badly you were wounded, monsieur Dubourdieu, for the news of your exploit and your return to Coudures has been on everyone's lips. And welcome to you, monsieur d'Audijos. The holy saints of Chalosse will bless your taking time off from the fine ladies who grace our village to rescue our friends and their salt from the accursed gabeleurs. The wine is on the house, and we drink it to the health and good fortune of you both.'

The curé did not seem to share the company's fervent response to Duplantier's words.

'That's as may be,' he grumbled, 'but the saints are not likely to endorse such flagrant abuse of the law as that which stained the waters of the Adour with blood.'

'Look who is talking!' said the tavern keeper. 'Despite the cut of your cloth, you are not priest enough to tell us what the saints may think of these brave gentlemen, and as for the law, we all know where you found the rabbits on your table.'

'Come!' said the notary in his silken voice. 'Père Lacourt has no more respect for the gabelle than any of us. We must band together in defence of our rights. He speaks only in regret for the violence that has occurred, and for my part I condemn the guards for their cruelty.'

Corade and Baillet, who had been regaling themselves without restraint, felt it was time for the younger generation to be heard.

'Bravo!' cried the latter. 'Death to the gabeleurs! If they shoot at us, we should return fire.'

'Vive monsieur d'Audijos! Vive monsieur Dubourdieu!' shouted Corade.

At these words Simon Lacourt rose with a scowl, and stepping over to the table where the two young farmers were seated, threw the contents of his goblet in Corade's face.

The Cabaret

'That's what I think of trouble makers,' he snarled, 'and there will be worse for anyone else who does not respect my brother's words.'

'Hold!' said Audijos, fixing the man with his piercing blue eyes. In a flash Lacourt drew a knife from his shirt and threw it at the cavalier's stomach. Any other man would have been transfixed, but Bernard's reflexes were as quick as a cat's. The knife hummed past him as he jumped sideways, and stuck quivering in the wall. A second later Dubourdieu struck the man-at-arms a mighty blow with his right fist, and sent him sprawling on the floor, whence the tavern keeper picked him up like a dead hog, carried him to the door and threw him into the street. Trembling with fear, the curé backed towards the exit and followed his brother. The notary also took the path of prudence and left the scene.

'A pox on those scurvy rogues,' said Roger. 'May the devil take his own. Let us return to the business at hand. We thank the rest of you for your welcome, and we drink damnation to the gabeleurs.'

The company lifted tankards and goblets and roared with approval. Duplantier threw more wood on the fire, and as the flames flared up Audijos noticed that there was someone sitting alone in the shadows, quietly sipping a glass of armagnac without sharing in the festivities. Taking the tavern keeper aside, he asked the identity of the stranger.

'I do not know, sir,' Duplantier replied. 'He came in here an hour ago and has kept to himself entirely.'

The man saw that he was observed, and rose from his chair. As he left the room, walking with a pronounced limp, Bernard gave a start of recognition. It was the officer who had commanded the ambush. Audijos moved towards his cousin, who had been too engrossed with his carousing to notice his former adversary.

'Roger, my friend,' said Audijos, 'I think we had best leave before we are beset by those gabeleurs. Their leader has been spying on us, and we must not compromise our friends.'

With the excuse that they had preparations to make for the morrow, the two cavaliers took their leave of the company, and made their way back to Dubourdieu's home. As they approached

The Cabaret

they distinguished three figures taking leave of each other near the gate some fifty yards ahead. It was impossible to see them clearly in the darkness, but there was just enough light to see that one was a tall woman, the second a slight, stooping man who seemed to resemble the notary, while the third, who was holding the reins of a horse, was surely the commander of the gabeleurs. The woman entered the house, while one of her companions made off down the street and the other mounted clumsily and rode past him. The two cousins speculated what business the châtelaine, if indeed it was she, could have to do with Bernard de Labat and the officer. Audijos recalled her disappearance at Saint-Sever, and things began to fall into place in his mind. But it grew late and there was much to attend to. Roger turned back towards his friend's house, embracing him and bidding him adieu with the hope that they would soon be reunited. He, too, had to ride in the morning, for his leave would expire within three days.

9. Journey to Bigorre

Audijos spent some time instructing the escort on the duties they were to perform as soon as it was dawn. Before retiring he knocked softly on Jeanne-Marie's door. She opened it so swiftly that Bernard knew that she had been awaiting him. He entered and they embraced each other passionately. She broke away and stepped back, and it was clear that she had something to tell him nearly as important as their profession of mutual love.

'Bernard,' she said. 'Strange events have occurred in your absence. A messenger arrived for that woman who calls herself a châtelaine, and when she had read the missive he carried she went straight into the salon, where my parents were entertaining mesdames. I followed her and heard her say that she must leave their company to go to Bordeaux. The duchess was more than a little surprised, but I sensed that both she and madame de Motteville were by no means upset to be rid of her. She gave the sudden illness of a near relative as the reason for her departure, but I felt that this was some subterfuge. I believe the great ladies thought so too, but they did not press her. When they asked how she would travel and what was to be done about her baggage, my father, bless his heart, offered to provide a conveyance and two servants as escort.'

'I think, my love, that she really is a châtelaine,' Bernard replied, 'but there is not much else about her that is genuine. She has been behaving oddly, to say the least. Your brother and I saw her in the street talking to that notary fellow whom I do not trust, and – what is even more sinister – to the officer who directed the ambush on the Adour. He had come from Duplantier's tavern, where there was heated discussion of the gabelle.'

'Well, I hope that you are as glad as the ladies about her leaving your party,' said Jeanne, looking quizzically at her lover. Bernard had the grace to blush, but he made no comment. They would have wished to spend more time in each other's company, but, with her parents nearby, discretion prevailed, and they merely kissed again before parting.

Audijos spent the rest of the night at his mother's house, where Dubourdieu was already asleep. He rose at first light to superintend preparations for the cortège, and heard Roger still venting stentorian snores as he said farewell to his mother. It was more than an hour after Audijos had informed the ladies that all was ready before they took their places in the coach. He was about to give the signal for departure when the châtelaine emerged and climbed into her own conveyance. She waved sardonically as her vehicle with its two attendants moved off on the road to Saint-Sever. The cortège set off in the opposite direction, meeting Dubourdieu on his heavy roan, trotting gently along. His wound was sufficiently improved to hold the reins in his left hand, and he gallantly doffed his hat to the ladies with the other. He turned his horse and rode for a few moments beside Audijos.

'If you ride a little faster, my friend,' said Bernard, 'you will likely catch up with that mysterious châtelaine, who, for some reason known only to herself, has decided to return to Bordeaux.'

'Morbleu, how the plot thickens! Perhaps if I ride with her a while I may discover what devilry she has in mind.'

'Watch your step, for she has all the subtleties of an enchantress and all the instincts of a viper. I wish you bonne chance. We shall meet again when my accursed mission is over and we are both back with our regiment.'

Thus the two friends parted. Some time was to pass before they saw each other again.

The cortège took the road to the village of Doazit, where the party lunched at the château of Candale – well known to Audijos since it belonged to his mother's family. Thence they proceeded south-east to the Gramont town of Hagetmau and spent the night there. The mood of the ladies seemed to have lightened since the departure of the châtelaine. They talked of Henri IV's mistress, Diane d'Andoins, who had married Antoine de Gramont's grandfather in Hagetmau.

'I have heard,' said madame de Motteville, 'that Henri de Navarre rode all the way from Coutras, where he had defeated the royal army and killed its commander, the duc de Joyeuse, to lay the standards he had captured in the battle at the feet of his lady in Hagetmau.'

This romantic legend of good king Henri was familiar to all Gascons, but Audijos took a wider view of the matter.

'Some say,' he remarked, 'that the fair Corisande, as we call the comtesse de Gramont in these parts, would have been better served if her lover had taken his victorious army to join his German allies, and thus put a speedy end to those wars of religion. Yet I believe he was a strategist in war as well as in love, for he became the ally of the king, Henri III, whom he was to succeed.' Bernard spoke with more freedom than he had previously employed in the presence of his august charges, but they did not seem offended. He went on to discourse on the wealth of the Gramont lands administered by his family, and reminded the duchess that their host in Coudures was the leading magistrate in the place.

On the next day they stopped briefly at the imposing château of Momuy, where they were met by the vicomte de Poudenx, a man of considerable influence through his role as the syndic of the standing committee of the representative estates of Béarn. He held lands in Chalosse as well as Béarn, and Momuy itself was situated just north of the Béarnais border. Moreover, he was a member of the house of Foix-Candale, and recognised Audijos as a distant cousin. He did not hesitate to voice his opposition to the gabelle, which persuaded the duchess to take a more favourable view of the involvement of Bernard and Roger in the affair on the Adour. Yet, as madame de Motteville observed, the vicomte did not wish to appear disloyal to the king, and took the customary line that His Majesty was ill informed of the nefarious doings of the gabeleurs.

Poudenx rode south with the cortège to the ducal village of Navailles beside the river Luy de Béarn. They rested there for the following day while the duchess made some perfunctory inquiries about the administration of her husband's estate, and received the respectful homage of the local notables. The vicomte viewed these ceremonies with approval before returning to Momuy.

It was now late in March, and as the party made their way by the road skirting the Luy they found the river swollen by the melting snows of the Pyrenees. The route suggested by the duc de Navailles avoided the fortress town of Orthez, and proceeded more directly to the Béarnais capital of Pau. Audijos felt uneasy about this decision, for the road was bad and the countryside far wilder than that which they had traversed. High hills, forested with black oaks, lay on either side of the valley, and there were few villages along the way. Beside the river were elms, willows and poplars, interspersed with thick scrub alive with small game such as hares and partridges. From time to time the advance scouts caught glimpses of wolves, which vanished into the underbrush on their approach. The cortège might have been able to cover the thirty miles to Lescar, on the outskirts of Pau, in a day's march, had not the road become mired by heavy rain. The valley had opened out into wide, flat marshes in imminent danger of flooding when Audijos decided they should seek some shelter for the night. The village of Mazerolles lay close at hand, and the scouts reported a large manor house in the vicinity.

Audijos halted the cavalcade and rode through the gates with two retainers. Clearly, he had been observed for the door of the house opened, and a gigantic figure with a musket under his arm appeared.

'Who are you that dares enter unbidden the domains of the sieur de Mazerolles?' came the stentorian challenge in the Béarnais language.

'I, sir, am Bernard d'Audijos, lieutenant of the Créquy Cavalerie, escorting her grace, the duchesse de Navailles and her party, on the road to Lescar. We crave your hospitality for the night.'

'I know your regiment, sir,' came the reply in distinctly less aggressive tones, 'but I am but a poor gentleman and my house is scarcely fit for such fine company. How many are there in your party?'

It turned out that Mazerolles had commanded a battery of cannon in the Catalan campaign, but, despite his preparedness to allow the travellers to shelter under his roof, he seemed ungracious and unwilling to look Bernard in the eye. Further, he claimed to have inadequate provisions for so large a number of guests, and it became clear that he expected to be paid for the privilege of entertaining them. Audijos rode back to ask the duchess her wishes. The rain was still falling and, short of attempting to bivouac in the village, there was little alternative to their staying in the manor. They found the interior to be rustic in the extreme, but, surprisingly, it seemed to be a veritable armoury, with weapons stacked in profusion in the central hall. They dined with great simplicity from a table before a blazing fire, while their host remained surly and taciturn, refusing to engage Audijos in conversation about military matters, and answering the inquiries of the ladies with the utmost brevity. Mazerolles did, however, surrender the main bedroom to the duchess and madame de Motteville, who accepted their none-too-clean accommodation with polite reserve. He watched attentively as their heavy boxes were carried upstairs. Audijos was to bed down in an outhouse with the servants.

Bernard had sent two of his men to the village to procure extra food, and had instructed them before departure to pick up what gossip they could about their host's reputation. The skies had cleared, and late that night, as he listened to wolves howling to the moon, they came to him to report their findings. Their news was alarming. Mazerolles, it seemed, was the leader of a band of brigands who had been terrorising the neighbourhood and intercepting travellers for ransom. Audijos woke the duchess's servants and, collecting his weapons, made his way silently back to the main house. As he skirted the courtyard in the shadows, he saw a group of armed men gathering near the stables. Some of them were moving towards the outhouse, others towards the manor. Bernard slipped swiftly up the stairs ahead of them, and knocked softly at the bedroom door.

'Mesdames,' he said, 'it is d'Audijos. Open quickly. You are in mortal danger.'

A dishevelled madame de Motteville opened the door within seconds, and Bernard entered and closed it behind him.

'We have entered a nest of bandits,' he said. 'Go back to bed and pretend to be asleep. They have come to rob you, at the least, and are now at the door below.'

The two ladies knew Bernard well enough by now to obey without question. They climbed back into their primitive bed, while Audijos took up his station behind the door. Within seconds muffled footsteps could be heard ascending the stairs. The door burst open, and three men, led by a bearded ruffian with a sword in one hand and a lantern in the other, came into the room. He placed the lantern upon a bench.

'Awake ladies!' he said hoarsely. 'You are the prisoners of the sieur de Mazerolles.'

Then Audijos struck. He ran the nearest man through with his sword, and brought the butt of his pistol down on the head of the next. The bearded man turned and lunged wildly at his adversary. Audijos had not withdrawn his sword from the side of his first victim. He stepped inside the thrust, and used his pistol butt again to strike his opponent in the face. The man staggered back, but he was still on his feet and came at Audijos again, his nose and mouth spurting blood. Audijos calmly cocked his weapon and shot his enemy through the heart.

'A thousand pardons, mesdames,' he said. 'I had no other way to defend you. I fear I must leave you at once. Mazerolles is leading others to attack our servants in the outhouse, where he expected to find me.'

The duchesse de Navailles was having hysterics. Madame de Motteville, on the other hand, remained as calm as Bernard himself. She helped her rescuer tie up the two wounded men, one still unconscious, the other groaning with the pain in his side. Audijos reloaded his pistol and passed it to her. He then picked up his musket and bounded down the stairs.

As he approached the outhouse he heard shots and cries. Stepping through the entrance, he shouted: 'Bernard d'Audijos, at your service, gentlemen!' In the smoke filled room, lit by torches, he saw two of the servants lying dead, and the others trying to defend themselves as best they could against Mazerolles and six followers, three of whom had been wounded. Before leaving, Audijos had warned his men to be on guard, and they had been ready for the assault. One of them now seized the opportunity occasioned by the unexpected arrival of Audijos to snatch up a loaded carbine and shoot down another attacker. Others disarmed two more of them, leaving the leader of the band to face Bernard. The latter, seeing that Mazerolles was armed only with a sword, put aside his musket, and drew his own weapon. The two circled each other for a few seconds. There was a clash of steel, with thrust, parry and counter-thrust before the sword of Navailles pierced Mazerolles in the chest and he fell to the floor with a mighty crash.

'A good night's work, mes braves,' said Audijos.

The surviving bandits, wounded and unwounded, were placed under guard, and Audijos returned to the main house, where he found the duchess in a calmer state and madame de Motteville still levelling the pistol at the two men tied up on the floor. Both ladies expressed their gratitude to Bernard, who thenceforth enjoyed their trust and admiration in a way he had not done before. Indeed, madame de Motteville gave him the title of 'El Cid.'

No one had much sleep for the rest of the night. In the morning the dead were buried, and the cortège set off with the prisoners tied by ropes to the horses of the escort or, in the case of the severely wounded, stowed in the baggage wagon. As they passed through Mazerolles the cavalcade was loudly acclaimed by the villagers, now freed from their tormentor and his band. At Lescar Audijos made a full report of the affair to the lieutenant-criminel, and handed over the surviving bandits, many of them in urgent need of medical attention. Wounded or not, their fate on the gallows or in the king's galleys was assured.

At Pau the party rested for two days. The ladies were made welcome in the château, the birthplace of Henri de Navarre, by the lieutenant general of Béarn, the marquis de Poyanne, who had commanded the royal forces in which Audijos had served in the last months of the Fronde. He did not remember Bernard from those times, but on hearing of his exploits at Mazerolles he bestowed upon him a special commendation.

A further day's journey brought the cortège to Tarbes, the capital of Bigorre. There their host was Gramont's brother, the comte de Toulongeon, who bore the title of sénéchal of the province. Bénac lay only six miles to the south-west, and there was a general feeling of relief when the tall towers of the château appeared in sight.

10. Roger Dubourdieu

After leaving Audijos and the cortège Roger pressed the roan into a canter in order to catch up with the châtelaine. Unfortunately his horse cast a shoe, and he stopped at the forge in the village of Eyres-Moncube. By the time the blacksmith had done his work the châtelaine and her escort were far ahead of him, and he failed to come up with them before reaching Saint-Sever. There he repaired to the schoolhouse, and informed maître Legrange of the events at Coudures. Legrange reinforced the warning Audijos had given his friend about the châtelaine, whom he had had followed for some miles on her journey. She had already passed through the town an hour earlier, and had joined forces with the officer of the gabelle and his men, dismissing the two servants of Arnaud Dubourdieu. The party had taken the road westwards towards Mugron.

Roger considered the risk of a new meeting with the gabeleurs, but he had promised Bernard to keep an eye on the châtelaine, and he was not the man to let danger deflect him from his path. Moreover, he was not insensible to the châtelaine's charms, to which her now open association with the gabeleurs gave an added piquancy. He had, of course, no inkling of Bernard's affair with the châtelaine, for the latter, having confided in him his love for Jeanne-Marie, had been careful not to mention his experience with a woman who was in every respect the antithesis of Roger's sister. He said farewell to the schoolmaster, promising to send back a message if he discovered anything of interest. Legrange, for his part, did not hide from Dubourdieu that he had his own network of informers seeking news about the agents of the gabelle.

Dubourdieu rode hard, stopping only to inquire from wayfarers when it was that his quarry had passed them. At the village of Montaut he calculated that the châtelaine and her party were less than half an hour in advance. The day was bright and cold, but the road twisted its way through patches of forest and he had no clear view of what lay ahead. Finally, as he began to ascend the hill on which Mugron was perched, the path straightened and he saw the cavalcade about to enter the town about half a mile away. He slackened his pace, and, when he reached the summit, took a side road that brought him into the back of the place. Leaving his horse at an inn to be watered and rested, he walked cautiously towards the main road. There, as he had suspected, he saw the châtelaine's conveyance and the horses of the gabeleurs outside a rather large establishment, where the party had stopped to dine.

Roger was more used to armed confrontation than to playing the spy. He moved to the back of the building, and asked a servant to summon the landlord.

'Are you aware, fellow,' he asked when the man appeared, 'that you are harbouring the agents of the accursed gabelle?'

'I know it well, my lord,' came the reply, 'but who am I to turn them away? Though they may be the oppressors of our fair land of Chalosse, they pay good money.'

Dubourdieu had no gift for subtlety.

'I shall be frank with you,' he went on. 'I speak for those who defend our privileges, and I need to know the burden of the conversation between the lady and the officer who commands the gabeleurs.'

'I can tell you this, sir. It is the lady who commands. I heard enough to know that the guards are making for Dax, where a salt bureau is being established. They plan to spend the night in the inn at Montfort, about an hour's ride from here.'

This was all that Roger needed to know. Swearing the landlord to secrecy, he collected his horse and made his way to Montfort, where he installed himself at the inn well in advance of the gabeleurs. As at Mugron, he thought he had gained the confidence of the proprietor, but on this occasion he proved to be mistaken. The man professed his hatred for the gabelle, but in reality he sought to profit from the occasion. For the moment, however, he chose to bide his time and see what opportunity offered. He showed Dubourdieu into a small room adjoining the main hall, where, with the aid of a spyhole through a thin partition, he himself customarily kept watch on troublesome guests. Roger placed sword and pistol on the table, ordered food and wine, and waited for the arrival of his enemies.

Soon after dark the châtelaine and her party entered the inn. The guards took some time to settle into their quarters, while the châtelaine, after refreshing herself in the best bedroom in the establishment, was shown by the landlord to a table set some distance apart from the rest. It happened to be very close to Roger's observation post, and he noted that the officer soon limped over to her and sat down at her side. All his instincts rebelled against eavesdropping on someone else's conversation, but he appeased his conscience by reflecting that on this occasion the stakes justified his playing the spy.

'Well, lieutenant de Labaume,' said the châtelaine, 'you have been curious about my role in these affairs since the start of our association, and now, perhaps, I have seen enough of you to confide in you.'

'I confess, madame, that after seeing your warrant from the intendant at Bordeaux I have wondered how a high born lady such as yourself would stoop to meddle in the secrets of the gabelle. You ride like a man, you command like an officer of the king, and you deign to sit in a common tap room.'

'These things amuse me, lieutenant,' said the châtelaine, arching her delicate eyebrows and smiling at her companion. 'I have chosen the path of adventure because, if truth be known, it is part of my nature. I have no liking for salons and elegant badinage. My warrant to test the strength of sentiment against the gabelle, and to identify those who are likely to use violent means to oppose its extension, has given me the kind of excitement I crave. The journey with the duchesse de Navailles provided an excellent cover. At first I thought to probe the sentiments of the young commander of her escort, and later, for similar reasons, I took an interest in his friend, the man whom you wounded on the Adour. That is why I summoned you to Coudures after our meeting at Saint-Sever.'

Roger was so startled by these revelations that he placed his hand on his sword, and in so doing knocked over the bottle beside him. The noise could be heard on the other side of the partition, and immediately the châtelaine and Labaume were alerted. The officer rose and limped over to the place where the landlord was superintending his staff.

'Mine host,' he asked, 'do the walls have ears in your tavern? Who is it that hides in the room behind the châtelaine's table?'

The innkeeper's shifty expression intensified.

'These are difficult times, monsieur,' he said. 'There are dangerous men about, and I am a poor man with no means of defence against desperadoes who threaten my house.'

'So it is money you want, fellow,' Labaume replied, producing his purse.

'If your lordship could spare a mite for my aged mother, I can tell you all I know. But you must assure me protection, for it was only under dire threat that I did what I did.'

A gold coin produced the facts that the man behind the partition had arrived some time before the guards of the gabelle with the intention of spying on the party, that he appeared to have a wound in his left arm, and that he had the bearing of a cavalry officer. The landlord indicated the spyhole in the wall to Labaume, and suggested that if he wished to surprise the man he should make his arrangements outside his line of vision.

Dubourdieu could not, of course, hear what was being said on the other side of the room. Nor did he see the officer passing money to the innkeeper. When the officer moved out of his line of sight, he began to feel uneasy, but his sang froid returned in a minute or two when he saw Labaume limp back to the châtelaine's table and report that there was no cause for alarm. He picked up the bottle from the floor and noted with approval that not all its contents had spilt. He had scarcely turned his attention back to the châtelaine's conversation when a pistol shot shattered the lock in the door behind him and the gabeleurs burst into the room.

The struggle was brief, for Roger was completely taken by surprise. A musket ball whistled past his head. He managed to fell one of his assailants, but the others were upon him like hounds on a wounded deer. By the time Labaume entered the room, he had been securely trussed to his chair.

'This time, monsieur,' said the officer, 'there is no one to rescue you. You will be taken to the cellars and kept under guard until we are ready to interrogate you. There are, I believe, a few scores to settle.'

Dubourdieu sat on a cask in the darkness below stairs with his hands tied tightly behind his back and the wound in his arm aching. Hours passed. He tried to loosen his bonds without success. He could hear the rats squeaking among the detritus that littered the cellar floor, and, for a time, the sound of footsteps passing overhead. At intervals the trapdoor at the top of the cellar stairs would open and the man on guard would descend a few steps to inspect the prisoner. Then a longer lapse occurred, and Roger began to wonder whether the sentry had left his post and he could try to escape. While he was considering such a move the trapdoor suddenly opened, and a figure bearing a dim lantern descended. It was the châtelaine.

'So, we meet again, monsieur,' she whispered.

'Madame, the sentry...'

'He will not trouble us. I placed a sleeping potion in the flask he carried before he went on duty. But others may be astir, so we must be silent.'

She moved close to him and he smelt the warm fragrance that enveloped her. She drew a knife that was concealed beneath her dress, and Roger started back, fearing she had come to assassinate him.

'No, monsieur,' she said with a smile. 'I have need of you alive. My knife is to cut your bonds. Turn round.'

She put down the lantern, cut the rope and massaged his aching wrists. Then, as he turned back to face her, she put her arms about his neck and kissed him lingeringly upon the lips before stepping back.

'Your wound has reopened,' she said, 'but we have little time to tend it now. First, tell me how much you heard when you were spying on me above.'

'Madame,' replied Roger, torn between desire inspired by her sensuous kiss and caution born of the dangers he knew she represented, 'I can only think of your lips upon mine. I—'

She took a step back and held up her hand.

'Tell me!' she commanded.

'I could not hear clearly. It was something to do with the gabelle, but I could not catch the gist of what you were telling that fellow.'

The châtelaine chose to believe this lie, or, at least, to pretend that she did. 'I think you know how much I like you, monsieur Dubourdieu,' she went on. 'I shall confide in you. You are surprised, I am sure, by my association with the agents of the gabelle, but that is only because the intendant in Bordeaux knows a secret about my past, and has threatened to reveal it to my family unless I co-operate with him. I have been deceived and ill treated, and many malign me. Yet my heart is with you. I can provide you and your friends with information about the plans of the gabeleurs, and perhaps there are other favours you would want of me?'

'Yes,' whispered Roger hoarsely, forgetting the pain in his wrists and arm.

The châtelaine smiled seductively in the half-light of the lamp, and moistened her lips with her tongue.

'But not now,' she said. 'You have only a few minutes to escape before the guard is relieved. There will be another occasion. We must find a second exit from this place, and place a broken bottle beside the rope, smearing it with a little blood from your arm so that it will seem you freed yourself.'

For a moment Dubourdieu thought of seizing the woman in his arms, but he reconsidered and made the arrangements she suggested, muffling a bottle in his jacket so that the noise of its breaking would not awake the partially drugged guard. With the aid of the lantern he found a second trapdoor, and placed a cask below it to climb up to the floor above.

'Au revoir, madame,' he said. 'I trust it will not be long before we meet again.'

'You will find your regiment at Bayonne,' she replied. 'I must travel north to Bordeaux, but it is likely I shall soon go south, for they say the king is to marry the infanta of Spain somewhere near the border – a ceremony I would not miss for worlds. Take care as you emerge. There is a sentry posted at the door of the inn.'

'Madame, I thank you from the bottom of my heart. Will you grant me a last embrace before I leave?'

'No, monsieur,' said the châtelaine. 'You must remember the kiss I gave you.'

Dubourdieu hoisted himself through the trapdoor, leaving splotches of blood from his wound as he went. He made his way cautiously to the front door of the inn, where he took the guard unawares and stunned him with a blow to the back of the head. Taking the man's sash, Roger bound his own wound tightly and then equipped himself with the unconscious sentinel's weapons. He found his horse in the stables, saddled up, and within minutes was on the road for Dax.

'Morbleu!' he muttered to himself. 'I shall attend to that innkeeper's reckoning some other day, and I shall pay it with the flat of my sword.'

11. Lavedan

The duc de Navailles was the titular seigneur of Lavedan, where foaming torrents cascaded from the mountains and ran through narrow valleys in the foothills of the Pyrenees. Seigneur he might have been, but the vicomté he ruled in name gave him neither economic advantage nor any real authority. Few nobles resided in the district. The people of the valleys were a rude and independent lot, whose village syndics expressed their views forcefully in the estates of Bigorre, and whose priests paid little attention to the demands of their bishop in Tarbes. It was partly because of their strange manner of life, and the tales of their uncouth doings reaching the ducal entourage, that the duchess and her friend had resolved to visit the district. Audijos felt more trepidation than curiosity about the venture. He had once visited the valleys, and he knew the propensity for violence possessed by their inhabitants.

The party rested for several days at Bénac. The weather was clear, and from the battlements of the château the snow covered peaks to the south could be seen stretching for range upon range in tumbled confusion. When the duchess instructed him that they should leave on the morrow, he took particular care to see that the baggage wagon was well stocked with provisions and the weapons of the escort made ready for possible action. Their route lay south-west from Bénac to Lourdes, whence they would commence the ascent into the valleys of Lavedan. Lourdes had been heavily fortified in case of a Spanish incursion across the Pyrenees. Its governor, Germain d'Antin, had drawn up the garrison of the castle to receive the duchess and her party with all due ceremony. When he heard that they intended first to visit the Navailles fief of Juncalas to the south-east, and then to move west through the mountains to Argelès and follow the valley of the Gave d'Azun towards Aucun and Arrens, he insisted on providing local guides.

As the party ascended the winding road beside the swift flowing Néez, they passed through small villages whose inhabitants came out into the street to watch them. Madame de Motteville later recorded in her diary:

The churches are well attended, and there are a number of priests. The people are no less ill natured on that account, for the rigours of the climate make them cruel. At the same time they are pious in their own fashion, and on every road one comes across wayside chapels and images of Our Lady. Their language sounds like a corrupt kind of Spanish, which is difficult to understand. The peasants are all tall. They dress and carry themselves well. In former times they went armed with pistols and daggers, but the bishop of Tarbes forbade them to carry arms because they so often killed each other in the murderous small affrays in which they engaged.

Such were the impressions of a great lady of the court, based upon the explanations of one of the guides, who was more concerned with what he thought the duchess and madame de Motteville wanted to hear than with the actual state of affairs. The guide himself had all the lowlander's suspicion for the mountain men, and as he had once served as a servant to the secretary of the bishop of Tarbes he represented things through episcopal eyes. The peasantry of the central Pyrenees were certainly capable of violence, but their communal bonds were strong and the raids that one village might practice against another had long been ignored by the rulers of Béarn and Bigorre, as they had been by the monarchy itself. The valleys of Lavedan would unite against such common dangers as royal tax collectors and troops sent to interdict the trade in contraband. Despite the anarchic ways of the mountain men, the authorities were well aware that they had their uses in this all but uninhabitable terrain. It was they who guarded the passes against military invasion more effectively than any royal garrisons, and they did so because they had traditions in common with their counterparts on the southern slopes of the mountains that set them apart from the people of the lowlands on both sides of the Pyrenees. Moreover, despite the commands of the bishop of Tarbes, they still carried arms, and were often joined in their enterprises by the priests who served and led them. Of this Audijos was soon to encounter unexpected proof.

The bailiff of the duc de Navailles at Juncalas had arranged a meal for the party in the largest of the white stone houses of the bourg. Audijos was the last to enter the building, and as he did so someone caught him by the arm. He was about to draw his poniard when the man placed a finger to his lips and beckoned him aside.

'The archpriest wishes to see you,' he whispered. Audijos knew the reputation of the formidable figure whose ecclesiastical authority in the valleys exceeded that of the bishop. He sent his excuses to the ladies, and followed the messenger up the slope away from the Néez and over a crest to a wooded area on the reverse side. Standing on a grassy knoll that dominated the clumps of trees dispersed in irregular fashion over the plateau before him was a tall man clad in a soutane with a cuirass across his chest and a plumed hat on his head. With heavy eyebrows, hooked nose, deep-set eyes and a full beard, the face created a sense of ferocity, and yet there was something in its expression that also conveyed a hint of gentleness. He turned as Audijos approached and greeted him with courtesy.

'The Lord's blessing upon you, Bernard d'Audijos,' he said. 'I am Jean de Cauterets, archpriest of Juncalas, and I was told of your coming in a missive from my friend, maître Legrange. He has asked me to aid you in your quest for the charter of Chalosse.'

'I am indeed blessed, father,' Bernard replied. 'Here in the valleys your ancient rights are recognised by all, but in Chalosse the agents of the gabelle ride roughshod over our privileges.'

'Maître Legrange has informed me of your problems,' the archpriest continued, 'and he also wrote of your affray on the Adour. You have found me at a time when I am exercising my brothers of Lavedan in similar pursuits. Our time of troubles is soon to come, and, under the protection of Our Lady, we shall be ready to defend ourselves.'

'I have heard something of your politics in schooling the deputies of the valleys at the estates of Bigorre,' Audijos responded with a laugh, 'but, truth to tell, I had not expected a warrior priest to advise me in the tricks of my own profession.'

'Then stand still and watch,' said the archpriest. 'When I have done, I shall tell you what I know of the *for* of Chalosse.'

The archpriest drew a whistle from the satchel at his side, and blew a single blast. There emerged from a stand of trees a group of armed peasants, who marched forward purposefully in military formation.

'Those are the sheep or, rather, a mock company of troops,' said Cauterets. 'Now you will see the wolves.' He whistled twice, and suddenly a hillside covered with low bushes began to move in pursuit of the supposed soldiers. More whistles sounded and groups of camouflaged men could be seen on either side of the column, training their muskets on the marchers. Finally, a fourth group appeared among the taller trees on the crest of the slope the column was ascending. The sound of musketry was heard, and the dummy soldiers fell to the ground or dived this way and that, only to find fire directed at them from all sides.

'That,' said the archpriest, 'is the way to conduct an ambush. Note that the men on either side are at different elevations, so that they will not shoot each other if they miss their targets. The Lord knows, they need practice with their weaponry. For this exercise, of course, their muskets and pistols are loaded only with powder and wadding.'

Audijos could not conceal his admiration.

'We in the light horse,' he said, 'know something about ambushes and the use of cover, but this surpasses any manoeuvre I have known. I could, perhaps, teach them a thing or two about the use of their arms.'

They walked over to the nearest group of peasants, where the archpriest ordered one of them to surrender his musket to Audijos. The man was a surly looking fellow who seemed loath to hand over his weapon. Audijos inspected it carefully and noted that it was of Spanish make.

'Yes,' said the archpriest. 'We rely upon one of my friends, Miguel Joan from Sallent de Gallego, to supply us. He is a well known merchant in these parts, and few goods are smuggled across the frontier without his having a hand in the transaction. At present he is staying in my house, and you may wish to make his acquaintance.'

Audijos nodded hesitantly, for he feared to compromise his escort duties again. Clearly, Jean de Cauterets was a law unto himself in the Lavedan, but his co-operation was needed if the *for* of Chalosse were to be secured for maître Legrange. At the moment, however, it was the musket in his hand that engrossed his attention. Unconsciously he reverted to his professional role.

'This musket,' he said in Béarnais, 'is in a disgraceful condition. The bore is fouled and should be scoured with boiling water, and the lock is corroded and needs to be cleaned and oiled.' The man angrily seized his firearm and shook it threateningly at Audijos.

'Enough, Orso!' said the archpriest. 'Go clean your musket, and bring it to me at the church for inspection.'

Audijos had no time to reflect upon the curiously mixed roles of priest and warrior, for the archpriest took him by the arm and led him towards his residence, explaining that he would not keep him long from his duty to the ladies. As they walked through the village Jean de Cauterets began to talk about the *for* of Chalosse.

'My friend, the curé of Arrens,' he said, 'took charge of it for maître Legrange. As he took the road from Pau to Lourdes he was followed by agents of the gabelle, and he turned aside near the caves of Bétharram to hide the charter somewhere in that labyrinth. It was as well he did so, for his pursuers caught up with him and searched him. They took no account of his cloth and tortured him to reveal his secret, but God was with him and he held firm. When the mountain men of his parish heard of the outrage, they tracked down and murdered the gabeleurs. As far as I know, the *for* still lies hidden in the caves, and no one is likely to find it without the map the curé drew later to record its location.'

Audijos had planned to call on the curé when his party passed through Arrens, and now the visit was doubly necessary. In the meantime he entered the archpriest's dwelling and waited while his host divested himself of his military accoutrements. Cauterets returned accompanied by a short, broad-shouldered, dark-complexioned man whose face seemed set in a saturnine kind of smile. Behind them padded an enormous dog whose thick white coat was marked with patches of brown.

'Señor Joan - Le sieur d'Audijos,' said the archpriest, adding, to complete the introductions, 'and his mountain dog, Pastoure.'

'A fine animal, señor,' remarked Audijos, as the two men bowed to each other.

'Yes, monsieur,' returned the Spaniard. 'If you like the breed, there is one left in the litter she bore six months ago, and you can have him for a price. He has been trained as far as is possible at such an age, and has all the instincts that will protect his master from danger.'

In response to a whistle a Pyrenean dog even larger than his mother shambled, puppylike, into the room, and made his way straight to Audijos with all the assurance of one who can detect a human with a fondness for his kind. Audijos hardly needed to bend to fondle him, while the dog responded by licking his hand.

'I call him Patou,' said Joan. 'He is cheap at fifty reals, and if you buy him I ask only that you give him some of the respect and affection he will offer you.'

The archpriest showed evident amusement at this.

'My friend Miguel,' he said with a smile, 'never lets slip a chance to sell his wares with a moral, but you will find he gives good value. The dog will serve you as well as a wagonload of Spanish muskets in times of trouble.'

Audijos reflected briefly. He had enough on his hands without having to complete the training of a Pyrenean mountain dog. Yet he felt drawn to Patou, and certainly the animal would have its uses. Besides, he remembered that Jeanne-Marie had once doted on a family dog of the same breed. If he had to go on campaign again, it would be a good companion for her in his absence.

'I shall take your Patou,' he said, 'and I shall tell my ladies that he is good protection against bears and wolves on the rest of our journey.' He handed over the money, and stayed another half-hour to drink some wine with the archpriest and his guest. In the course of the conversation he came to realise that Miguel Joan was himself a force to be reckoned with in those parts. The Spaniard clearly saw the mountain people on either side of the border as having a common culture that made loyalties between them more important than their ties to far-off kings and governors. Moreover, he had friends and agents in the lowlands as well as in the mountains. If the archpriest of Juncalas commanded a peasant militia as effectively as he controlled the clergy of Lavedan, Joan was at the centre of an intelligence network as necessary to local politics as it was to trade and contraband.

Calling Patou to follow him, Audijos set off for the house of the bailiff. The dog looked back for a moment at his mother, and trotted off at the heels of his new master. The duchesse de Navailles and madame de Motteville were entranced by the new acquisition to their party. It was their intention to reach the Navailles castle of Bossein on the slopes of a nearby mountain before nightfall, and the cortège was soon on the march. Patou was accustomed to such journeys and took position beside Bernard's mare, his head reaching as high as the stirrup leather.

12. Arrens

The carriages swayed and bumped perilously as the cortège climbed upwards along a rough mountain track. To the south, snow covered peaks soared over nine thousand feet towards the heavens. As they rounded a steep bluff the walls of the fortress of Bossein appeared before them. It seemed a fairytale place with its half-ruined towers, and madame de Motteville, torn between apprehension at the wildness of the scene and admiration for its grandeur, remarked to the duchess that she expected it to be inhabited by sprites and spirits, like the fabulous castles depicted by Honoré d'Urfé in his popular romance, *L'Astrée*. The duchess, however, was too frightened by the precipice at their left, and the water cascading over the rocks ahead, to pay much attention to literary allusions. In any case reality soon replaced fantasy as the party entered the castle gates. Guarded by five soldiers of the duc de Navailles, the place was cold and inhospitable. The group passed an uncomfortable night and was glad to retrace their path to Juncalas on the following day.

The cortège descended the valley of the Néez to the point where it joined the Gave de Cauterets. Melting snow in the mountains had rendered the ford difficult to cross, but Patou disported himself joyfully in the icy water and stood barking on the further bank while his master and the retainers struggled with the conveyances. Thence they climbed westwards to Argelès and along a high ridge overlooking the wide and fertile valley of the Gave d'Azun to the south. Audijos took note of the hostile looks of the villagers in the small places through which they passed – Arras, Arcizans, Gaillagos and Aucun. There were a few stone houses, but most of the dwellings were constructed of sod, and in some instances were largely underground, with green smoke issuing through vents from the fires that warmed them. The most elaborate buildings, as madame de Motteville noted in her diary, were the churches. At Aucun, where they stopped for the night, the local curé greeted them in front of the renaissance portal that graced his church. He had already received notice of their coming from the archpriest, and did his best to make them comfortable in the rectory and in a large barn. He explained apologetically that the surliness of his parishioners, and of the other villagers along the way, was due to their isolation and their natural suspicion towards lowland folk. Audijos, however, knew the reputation of the mountaineers, and took no chances, posting a strong guard throughout the night.

At every opportunity Audijos attended to the training of Patou. The dog was quick to learn, and his master had to teach him to distinguish between the signals he used for his mare and those which applied to him. The horse, for example, knew how to wait unmoving when Audijos left her unattended, and then to come to him when he called. Now Patou had to learn the same drill, but with a different kind of whistle. A close bond developed between the two animals, and each in its own way idolised its master who, for his part, never forgot to attend to their needs. When the party arrived at Arrens on the following morning, Patou was to show his worth.

Arrens was a picturesque hamlet, nestled among tree covered hills, with bare rocky outcrops denuded of snow to the north, where the gave descended from the mountains to a precipitous cliff below the village before veering eastwards. The ladies wished to lunch at an inn that was unexpectedly substantial for such a place, but none of the local notables were there to receive them. It turned out that a child had been taken by wolves on the previous day, and a party, headed by the curé, had set off down the gorge in search of the killers. Audijos talked to the innkeeper about the likely route the hunting party had taken, made his excuses to the ladies, and, leaving his horse in the stables, set off to climb down into the gorge, Patou at his heels. It was a steep descent, man and dog leaping from rock to rock. When they reached the stream, they made their way by a rough trail along the bank, crossing the gave from time to time as the water ran close to cliffs. Audijos pointed to footprints in patches of mud, and Patou, after sniffing them, took up the scent at his master's bidding.

With the dog in the lead, they came to a bend where Patou stopped and growled, his fur bristling along his back. Audijos urged him forward, but the dog seemed to want to diverge from the track the hunting party had followed. Then, a few paces from the trail, Audijos discerned barely perceptible wolf prints in the rocky soil, and Patou bounded forward, disappearing round an outcrop. His master hesitated, wondering whether to recall the animal, and then scrambled in pursuit, his musket banging against his back as he forced his way through the vegetation. Patou was not to be seen, but within a minute or so a deep-throated bark and savage snarling sounds were to be heard. When Audijos came upon the scene of the battle, he saw the dog towering above four wolves, while a fifth lay dead and bloodied on the ground. Patou had his back against a boulder, while his assailants were darting and snapping but not daring to take hold. Audijos unslung his musket and primed it quickly. He was panting from his exertions and fearful of missing his aim. Holding his breath, he fired and saw the wolf furthest from Patou leap in the air and fall dead. At the sound of the shot the remaining beasts turned and fled, but not before the dog had sprung upon the hindmost and broken its neck with his mighty jaws. He would have pursued the two survivors, but Audijos commanded the dog to be still. He came forward and embraced Patou, careless of the blood on his clothing from the superficial bites the dog had sustained.

They had rested beside each other for several minutes when they heard a shout from the direction of the stream. Audijos answered, and before long the hunting party came up with them. A tall, ferocious looking fellow was the first on the scene, clad partly in rags, with a bearskin over his shoulders and a long knife at his side. Behind him was a swarthy, diminutive figure carrying a musket. Four peasants followed him, each armed with knives and a miscellany of outdated firearms. They stared amazed at the scene in front of them before the small man stepped forward and introduced himself.

'Greetings, my lord Audijos, for I assume that it is you,' said the man, 'I am Jean de Lanusse, priest of Arrens, and I have long awaited your coming. We heard your musket shot, and retraced our path.'

The figure with the bearskin drew his knife, and Patou uttered a low growl. There was no need for alarm, for the man stepped up to the dead wolves and cut off their tails.

'This will serve in memory of my daughter, carrion,' said the fellow in his mountain dialect, addressing the dead animals. The curé intervened.

'Let us return to Arrens,' said the priest to Audijos in impeccable French. 'We shall tend your dog's wounds, and there is much to tell.'

As they made their way back down the gorge, the curé and Audijos exchanged details of the wolf hunt. Within an hour they were back in the village, where Bernard accompanied the priest to the rectory and stood by while he put salve on Patou's wolf bites.

'He has suffered no serious harm,' he remarked, 'and should heal within a day or two. The peasants hereabouts believe the pack are werewolves from the Col du Souler and think their bite fatal. But that is the kind of superstition these primitive folk credit.'

'I marvel that you, an educated man and a friend of my teacher, maître Legrange, should live in this wild place and cater to these people,' Audijos observed.

'It is my mission,' said the priest, 'and I am well content to preach the gospel to them. Yet we have important matters to discuss. We clerics have our own network, and I have already had news of you from the archpriest of Juncalas, who sent me word of your search for the *for* of Chalosse.'

'Yes, father,' Audijos replied. 'I bear a letter from maître Legrange, who entrusted you with the charter.'

'I hid it safely in the caves of Bétharram,' said the priest, glancing at the paper Audijos produced, 'and surely no one can find it without the map I have made of its hiding place.' He raised a flagstone in the floor, and drew out a dust covered scroll. Audijos scanned it carefully, and questioned Lanusse on how to find the entrance to the labyrinth for which the curé had sketched the details.

With the map safely stowed inside his doublet, Bernard made his way to the inn. News of the wolf hunt had already preceded him, for the whole village was aware of the exploit. Madame de Motteville insisted on a full account of the matter.

'I had not known,' she said 'that El Cid could deal with wolves as well as Moors.'

'The Campeador had no Pyrenean mountain dog at his side,' replied Bernard. 'The victory was Patou's, not mine.'

13. The Caves of Bétharram

The entire village of Arrens turned out to farewell the party. Gone were the surly looks and suspicious glances they had come to expect from the mountain folk. As he rode in front of the duchess's carriage Audijos and his dog received shouts of approval for ridding the area of the wolf pack. A little stiff from his wounds, Patou held himself proudly, as if he knew to whom the plaudits were directed. The cortège continued along the ridge to the Col du Souler, where the ladies were entranced to see the shepherds driving their flocks up the slopes to spring pastures. Each man was accompanied by a Pyrenean, while the sheep were worked by collies that seemed miniatures in contrast with the gigantic guard dogs. Patou glanced longingly at the scene, but a word from his master kept him at his station.

The party turned sharply southwards at the col, and began the steep, winding descent to Arbéost and Ferrières. There was a danger that the primitive brakes with which the conveyances were equipped would not hold the wheels, and from time to time Audijos ordered some of the escort to dismount and restrain the carriages with ropes. Progress was slow in such circumstances, and they did not reach the town of Nay on the Gave de Pau until nightfall. The Grottes de Bétharram lay only ten miles upriver from Nay.

Audijos could think of no excuse to divert the party from the route to Pau, nor would it be easy to explain a long absence on the following day. He therefore decided to entrust the duchess with the secret of his mission and hope for her approval for a pause in the journey. Luck was on his side, for one of the ladies' maids had come down with a fever, and needed rest from the jolting motion of the second wagon. The duchess readily gave permission. Although she had no sympathy for charters of liberty, she felt that not only the maid, but herself and madame de Motteville also, would welcome a day's respite from travel, and the quarters they occupied at Nay seemed reasonably comfortable. Besides, since the adventure of Mazerolles Bernard could do no wrong. As he left the room in the inn, Audijos was alarmed to see one of the guides moving furtively down the hallway ahead of him. He wondered if the man had been listening at the door. Now that they were back in the lowlands the guides would be returning to Bénac, but a spy who might have acquired his secret would likely cause new problems in the future.

At daybreak Audijos saddled the mare and set off with Patou for Bétharram. When they reached the place it took some time to find the entrance to the caves, which lay in a forested and hilly area some distance from the road. Bernard dismounted and cut himself some brush to bind into torches. He ordered Patou to stay beside the mare, and climbed into the mouth of a limestone cavern that branched inside into several low tunnels. Lighting the first of his torches, he consulted the curé's map, and took the fork immediately to the left. After twenty yards the tunnel ended, and he emerged into a vast space where light from the torch could not reach the roof. Before him were strange columns and fantastic limestone shapes formed by slowly dripping water. Père Lanusse had described it as a kind of underground cathedral, showing it clearly on his chart, and Audijos marvelled at the place.

He was about to light another torch when he perceived a strange glow emanating from an exit on the far side of the chamber. This too had been mentioned by the curé, and Audijos stepped through the gap to find himself in another cavern whose vault was lit by a myriad of tiny lights. He was not superstitious but, in his ignorance of glow-worms, he began to think of the fairies madame de Motteville read about in her favourite romances. He could hear the gurgling of running water on the far side, and he guessed there was another entrance to the labyrinth by a subterranean stream. At the same time he smelt a fetid odour coming from a narrow tunnel to his left. Thrusting a newly lit torch into this place he noticed the stinking remains of the carcasses of small animals. However, the chart suggested another tunnel, and this he took, emerging in a smaller chamber filled with a limestone formation in the form of an altar. Audijos felt his pulse begin to race. He moved behind the altar to see a small wooden pointer. The floor in which it was placed was not of rock but of loose earth. He dug with his hands and discovered a bottle with a scroll within. He had found the *for* of Chalosse!

At that same instant a menacing growl came from the entrance to the chamber. There, in the torchlight, stood erect an enormous brown bear, with saliva dripping from its fangs and the long claws on its front legs extended towards him. Bernard believed his last moment had come. He had brought neither sword nor musket into the cave, his pistol was loaded but unprimed, and his only effective weapon was his poniard. The bear had for long lived in the caves. It had grown more savage and carnivorous with age, and had killed several men in its time when they wandered into its domain. The torch disconcerted it, and the limestone block lay between it and its intended prey. As Audijos tried to keep the so-called altar between himself and the beast, he remembered that he had an ally. He uttered two piercing whistles, hoping that the sound would carry to the exterior. Lighting another torch so that he held fire in each hand, he circled the stone while the perplexed animal followed him menacingly. Audijos knew that the bear could move more quickly than he could and dreaded the moment when the beast, now on all fours, came at him with a rush. The stalemate lasted for perhaps two minutes. Then suddenly there was a growling roar, and Patou appeared at the entrance and launched himself on the animal's hindquarters. He was only half the size of his enemy and no match for those terrible claws. The bear turned on his attacker. Before it could rake the dog or seize him in a death-dealing embrace, Audijos dropped one torch, thrust the other into the beast's jaws, and drove his dagger into its side. The bear squealed in pain, beating the air with its forepaws. Bernard slipped past it and called Patou to release his hold. Man and dog raced through tunnel and cavern, but the bear did not follow. They emerged breathless into the open air. For a moment Audijos considered re-entering the caves with his pistol at the ready, but he preferred to place his arms round Patou's neck and to thank providence and the bravery of his dog for their escape.

The mare came at his call. Audijos mounted and rode slowly back to Nay, Patou at his side and the precious bottle in his saddlebag.

14. Reunions in Bayonne

Audijos had no wish to boast about his new adventure, but the ladies insisted he tell them of the recovery of the charter and of the marvels of the caves of Bétharram. Moreover, Patou's wounds had been reopened by his encounter with the bear, and this could not pass without explanation. The dog was fussed over as much as Audijos, but the latter cut short these demonstrations by calling for the reassembly of the convoy. They made their way in leisurely fashion along the bank of the Gave de Pau, eventually reaching Orthez. They had missed the walled city and ancient capital of Béarn on the journey out, but now the duchesse de Navailles wished to stay there a day or two, partly to enjoy the hospitality of the local nobility and partly to attend to her sick maid, whose fever had worsened.

It was only a few hours ride northwards from Orthez to Hagetmau and Coudures, and Audijos asked leave to deliver the *for* of Chalosse to maître Legrange. He had also decided to leave Patou with Jeanne-Marie. The wolf bites now seemed to be infected, and, even if the dog could make the journey to Bayonne, it might not be possible to keep him when his master resumed service with his regiment. The reception they received in Bernard's native town varied from the raptures of Jeanne-Marie through the reserved affection of madame de Talazuc to the warm praise of maître Legrange, who happened to be visiting Coudures. Bernard told them all that he hoped soon to return if the Créquy Cavalerie were indeed to be disbanded. He would have wished to spend more time with Jeanne-Marie and his friends, but this was not possible. He heard news of further activities by the gabeleurs from the schoolmaster, who took delivery of the charter with renewed cautions about the need for secrecy. Both expressed concern about the apparent link between the châtelaine and Labaume. When Audijos visited the inn, Duplantier asked if he might accompany the duchess's party to Bayonne, for he had been invited there by his sister. Bernard readily agreed, since his presence would strengthen the escort on the final stages of the journey.

He said goodbye to his mother, and rode on to the Dubourdieu residence. He was close to tears when he parted from Jeanne-Marie. Despite his normal reserve, he found it difficult to command his emotions with someone he loved so much.

'I cannot tell what the future will hold,' said Bernard, 'but you will always be in my thoughts.'

'Come back to me when you can,' she replied between her sobs. 'I shall wait for you for ever.' She looked down at the massive head of Patou, and cradled it in her arms. 'You have left me a part of yourself, and I shall care for him well until you return to us.'

The dog licked her face, and then looked at his master as if he understood. Audijos kissed her gently, and caressed Patou. He swung himself into the saddle, and rode back to the inn, where Duplantier was waiting. When they reached the end of the street, he turned and waved his plumed hat in farewell. Dubourdieu and his wife had joined their daughter, and waved in return. But Jeanne-Marie was hiding her head in Patou's fur.

Next day the cortège followed the road to Bayonne beside the Gave de Pau. When they reached the bourg of Peyrehorade, where the Gave d'Oloron tumbled between massive boulders into the larger river, they heard news of troubles with agents of the gabelle in the area. The party was settling down for the night in a local manor house, and Duplantier went off to visit the hostelry in the place. He returned, burning with indignation, to relate the arbitrary arrests of several men accused of illicit trade in salt. Despite sharing his sentiments, Audijos knew it would be imprudent to intervene at this stage of the journey, and he told Duplantier to content himself with reporting the details to maître Legrange on his return to Chalosse.

In the morning they reached another river junction, the confluence of the Gave de Pau and the Adour. Late on the afternoon of 5 May, they attained Bayonne itself. The city was a prosperous port with several ships at anchor near the further bank of the river, and others docked on the southern shore. The Adour was far too broad to be bridged and its level rose and fell alarmingly with the tide from the sea four miles to the west. This proved a constant problem for shipping, which was frequently stranded on mudbanks. There was some settlement on the northern fringe, but Bayonne sheltered behind its defensive walls to the south. It was not an easy town to protect, for it was bisected by the River Nive, which joined the Adour near the town centre. Behind the western walls rose the battlements of the so-called Château Vieux, while the Château Neuf, whose foundations were actually older than its rival, reinforced the eastern defences. Of course, the church was just as important as sea borne trade or military fortification in the external appearance of Bayonne. The Basque city was dominated by the twin spires of the cathedral of Sainte-Marie.

The cortège of the duchesse de Navailles had arrived from the north, and had to be ferried across the river. The boatmen had been busy with many such crossings since the royal court had entered Bayonne a few days earlier. Before the marriage of Louis XIV and the Spanish infanta, Maria Teresa, could be formalised there remained a number of diplomatic problems that were under discussion between the two chief ministers, cardinal Mazarin and Luis de Haro. In the meantime the king was busy issuing proclamations to guarantee the liberties of Bayonne and the adjacent lands – liberties that affirmed local structures of government, freedom from the gabelle, and protection from royal imposts on shipping. For her part, the queen mother was preparing for the court's move to Saint-Jean-de-Luz, close to the frontier, and for a personal meeting with her brother, Felipe IV of Spain.

Anne of Austria welcomed madame de Motteville effusively, but she was reserved in her greeting to the duchesse de Navailles, whom she knew to be seeking the post of lady of honour in the household of the future queen of France. Shortly after this interview Audijos had asked the duchess if he might now be released from his escort duties so that he might rejoin his regiment, cantonned outside the eastern city walls so as not to offend the susceptibilities of the notables of Bayonne. At first he was disappointed. Madame de Motteville had taken such a fancy to him that she wished to find him a place in the queen mother's household. To her astonishment Bernard had begged her not to make the request. Despite the honour such an appointment would entail for a petty Gascon gentleman, he could not forget his promise to Jeanne-Marie, and in any case he had had his fill of dancing attendance on highborn ladies. However, he could not entirely escape madame de Motteville's demands. The queen mother had told her of the impending journey to Saint-Jean-de-Luz, and had mentioned that a troop of cavalry would be detailed to escort them in addition to the gentlemen who normally formed part of her retinue. Madame de Motteville had immediately informed her mistress of the prowess of Audijos, and an order had been sent to the commander of the Créquy Cavalerie. So even if Bernard had turned down the chance to enter the fringes of court society, he was committed in the immediate future to serving the great.

Audijos was greeted by his fellow junior officers with a certain raillery when he rejoined his regiment.

'Welcome to the lackey of Navailles! Make way for the ladies' man!' came the shouts when he entered the mess room. Captain Boisset had already received the orders sent from court, and congratulated Audijos upon his success. Roger Dubourdieu greeted his old friend with his usual warmth and a profusion of Gascon oaths. As soon as they were alone together Roger recounted his adventures with the châtelaine and Audijos told of his fight with Mazerolles, his travels in Lavedan, his recovery of the *for* of Chalosse, and of Legrange's forebodings about the gabeleurs when the charter was returned to him in Coudures. He repeated to his friend his feelings for Jeanne-Marie, and Roger, who warmly welcomed this confirmation, was delighted to learn that Bernard had left Patou in her care. When Dubourdieu heard that Duplantier was staying in Bayonne at an inn where the patron was husband to Duplantier's sister, the two friends resolved to visit the place.

Soon after dark they found the inn tucked away in a side street behind the cathedral. At first they could make little of the conversation within, for the majority of the drinkers were Basques and their language was unintelligible to the Gascons. Duplantier soon came forward with his brother-in-law to make them welcome. They talked of the royal proclamation, and it soon became clear that the Bayonnais, whether French or Basque, were sceptical about the intentions of the king's advisers. The innkeeper, Cambo Jatxou, was half Basque himself, and, like most of his clients, was bilingual. It was obvious to the Gascons that there were both racial and social divisions within Bayonne. The notables in the city, whether magistrates or wealthy merchants, were French, but there was a minority of Frenchmen among artisans, shopkeepers and sailors. When it came to conflict between the city fathers and the populace, racial differences ceased to be important. It was also apparent that when the independence of Bayonne was threatened all classes and races came together and accepted the leadership of the notables against the external officers and soldiers of the central government. At the same time there was an underlying loyalty for the crown, and a readiness to suppose that the king was not aware of instances of oppression. The high nobility, especially Gramont and his brother Toulongeon, who was the non-resident governor of Bayonne, were also respected. While the royal court was present in the city and the peace with Spain was about to be confirmed by the Spanish match, there was a groundswell of enthusiasm, tempered only by doubts about future taxes and rivalry between royal troops and the city militia.

Some of these political subtleties were lost upon Audijos and Dubourdieu, despite their support of the unprivileged in the countryside. Duplantier understood them better. He and his brother-in-law sympathised with the plight of the poor within the city. Jatxou was also a defender of Basque culture, and a critic of the French prejudice that thought his people cruel and superstitious. He spoke eloquently against the witch-hunts that had occurred in the Basque lands at the start of the century, and of the writings of Pierre de Lancre, their instigator and recorder.

'Even in these more enlightened times,' said Jatxou, 'there are reports of a new witch trial at Bidart to the south.'

The Gascons drank little and learnt much from the conversation. Boisset had designated Dubourdieu as second in command of the troop that Audijos was to lead into the Basque country, and the two friends speculated about their role in the protection of the queen mother and her retinue. On the following day they received their orders from Boisset. They were to lead a troop of fifteen light horsemen, and would be under the command of the marquis de Gontier, the administrator of the queen mother's household. To avoid the reproach of favouritism, a similar troop had been commissioned from the regiment of Navailles. Boisset made a point of telling the two ensigns that there was to be no repetition of the confrontation of Saint-Jean-d'Angély.

Bernard and Roger inspected their cavaliers carefully to ensure they looked their best. With polished equipment and well groomed horses, they made a brave show as they rode into the courtyard of the Château Neuf, but there an unpleasant surprise awaited them. Standing beside his horse in front of the line of his own dismounted troop was lieutenant Sébastien de Nogent. Audijos saluted his former foe with courtesy, and Nogent responded in peremptory manner, a scowl upon his face. An orderly rode up with orders from the marquis to prepare for departure, the men of Navailles to take the van and the Créquy Cavalerie to bring up the rear.

'An appropriate order of march,' Nogent remarked loudly, 'true cavaliers in the advance guard, and the ragtag behind.'

Remembering Boisset's injunction, Audijos contented himself with a stony glare. Nogent's men climbed into their saddles and waited at the main gate of the castle. A number of gentlemen, whose splendid apparel suggested their courtier status, then rode up behind them, followed by the carriages and wagons of the rest of the queen mother's household. Audijos and his men fell into double line abreast in the rear, and the column took the road for Saint-Jean-de-Luz. It was an impressive sight, but a small thing when compared with the two regiments, two hundred gentlemen, and thirty carriages which made up the king's retinue departing from the Château Vieux two hours earlier.

15. The Witch of Bidart

The queen mother's convoy took the coast road south, and reached the outskirts of the village of Bidart within a few miles. There were reports that the way ahead had been blocked by a landslide, and the marquis de Gontier ordered the column to halt. He sent Nogent forward to see if the route was truly impassable, while Audijos was sent into the village to inquire about an alternative road. When Bernard entered the place with five of his men, he found an angry crowd assembled outside the largest building in the square. They were shouting in Basque at a man wearing a red robe, and denying him access to the house. Perceiving the man to be an official of some kind, Audijos fired his pistol in the air. The shouting ceased immediately, and the crowd divided to allow the cavaliers to ride forward.

'Bernard d'Audijos of the Créquy Cavalerie, at your service, sir,' said the ensign, doffing his hat.

'Joseph de Lespès de Hureaux, lieutenant-criminel of Bayonne,' the man replied. 'I need your protection, for I am on the king's business. I came to suspend proceedings here against some poor woman accused of witchcraft. This unruly canaille must have got wind of my mission. They threaten violence and bar the doors against me.'

Audijos was faced with a dilemma. He recognised that Hureaux was a royal municipal judge with power to command his assistance, but at the same time his orders required him to find a route for the convoy, and one did not lightly cause delay to the king's mother. When he explained this to the judge, Hureaux offered to sign a warrant authorising his intervention.

'Without your help,' he said, 'my sergeant, my clerk, and I may be torn apart by this mob. They are terrified of witchcraft and seem to think us emissaries of the devil.'

The crowd had remained silent during this interchange, but at that moment a woman's scream was heard from inside the building and voices in the square called: 'Death to the witch! Put her to the question.'

'They are torturing her,' said the judge. 'The *parlement* of Bordeaux has banned such procedure except in the last resort.'

Audijos determined to act. He and his men dismounted. Those blocking the door stepped aside at the sight of his drawn sword, and Hureaux and his party were ushered inside. Three of the cavaliers were detailed to tether the horses and hold their carbines at the ready in front of the entrance, while Audijos and the two remaining soldiers followed the judge into the hall where the trial was being held.

It was a long, low room crammed with people, most of them female. At the far end an almost naked woman was bound to a table, her long black tresses hanging to the floor. Beside her stood a masked man holding a pair of pincers he had been heating in a glowing brazier, and a second man, the interrogator, wearing the garb of a Dominican friar. A third, sitting at a desk, was copying down the victim's words. The friar turned to challenge the intruders.

'You may wear the robe of a magistrate, sir,' he said to the judge, but this is God's tribunal and we shall not hand over this limb of Satan to execution by the secular power until we have extracted her full confession. Witnesses have already attested to her spells, and we have examined her body and found the devil's mark upon it. Now we have begun to put her to the question so that she may implicate her confederates at the devil's sabbat she has confessed to attending.'

As a man of the law Hureaux did nothing unless by due process.

'I have a warrant here of supersedeas,' he declared. 'This case is hereby removed from your jurisdiction, and the prisoner is to be delivered into my custody.'

The friar seemed unwilling even to scan the writ the judge held out to him.

'You cannot take her until we are finished,' he said. 'The good father, Pierre de Lancre, knew how to deal with vermin such as this, and I shall fulfil the role with which the holy church has entrusted me, and continue the work he began in these parts.'

Hureaux was well read in the literature of witchcraft, and shared the reservations of the new generation of jurists.

'You may cite Lancre until you are blue in the face,' he went on, 'but we in the law prefer to follow the learned Father Alonso de Salazar, the Spanish inquisitor who tested confessions obtained across the border by such methods as yours, and found them false. The sovereign *parlement* of Bordeaux refer to his reports in their condemnation of proceedings such as this. Again, I call upon you to cease.'

The friar turned defiantly to his assistant and signalled him to continue the torture. A murmur of approval came from the audience as they saw the masked man stoop to reheat the pincers in the glowing embers. The supposed witch had fainted. Audijos had stood by impatiently while the debate had been going on. He could wait no longer. Since he had had no opportunity to reload his own weapon, he seized the pistol of one of the soldiers who stood beside him and fired at the brazier. The burning coals scattered from their container and the instrument of torture flew against the legs of the torturer, who yelled in pain. There were screams from all parts of the room as flames caught the wooden planks of the walls and the desk of the recorder.

Audijos sprang forward, followed by his men. Pushing the friar to one side, he cut the bonds of the unconscious witch and picked her up in his arms. By this time the exit was blocked by the crowd surging to escape from the fire.

'Seize him!' he said, pointing to the inquisitor. The two soldiers pinioned the friar's arms. 'Now, brother, there must be a back entrance to this place,' Audijos said threateningly. 'Tell me where it is or you will suffer the fate you intended for this unfortunate woman.'

'Sacrilege! Sacrilege!' called the friar. The two cavalrymen pushed him towards the flaming desk, and he screeched as he felt the fire. 'Behind the arras, may the Lord have mercy,' he quavered. One of the soldiers tore some hangings aside, and opened a low door. They crossed a second room and burst out into the open air, the friar following. As they rounded the building they came upon a scene of panic. Those watching the interrogation had managed to join the crowd outside, and the entire mob was fleeing the scene. The judge and his two supporters had been the last to exit by the main doorway. They stood calmly beside the three cavaliers left on guard, who had untied the frantic horses, and were about to try to re-enter the burning structure in search of their leader.

The alleged witch had regained her senses, and Audijos had covered her with his cape before placing her gently on the ground. Her seared and bloody legs bore testimony to the torture she had endured. She was in great pain and as yet unable to stand, but she clearly understood the circumstances of her rescue and looked at Bernard gratefully. He had little time to attend to her needs, for he could feel the heat of the fire behind them as the flames began to burst through the roof of the building, while at the far edge of the square the crowd was already reforming. Audijos ordered his men to mount, with the judge and his two assistants, as well as the witch, riding pillion behind them. They rode across the square to a hostelry where Hureaux and his party had left their horses. As they were reclaiming their mounts from the stables the mob surrounded them, waving pitchforks, staves and other weapons and calling in their own tongue, 'Death to the witch and the foreign devils.'

Audijos realised that they were trapped. Some of their assailants had firearms, and to try to break through the ring of nearly a hundred peasants would entail disaster. The only course of action seemed to be to abandon their horses and retire into the inn to withstand siege as best they might. Before Audijos could order such a move help arrived from an unexpected quarter. A trumpet sounded, and Nogent rode into the square with the five men he had taken to reconnoitre the road ahead. The shouts of the peasants died away. Nogent turned in his saddle and called loudly to the rearmost cavalier: 'Ride back and summon the rest of the company.' The soldier grasped his officer's stratagem and galloped out of the square. Even if there were few in the angry crowd who knew enough French to understand the order, the departure of the soldier had an immediate effect. Within a minute or two the mob had melted away, and Audijos rode forward to thank his deliverer. His expression of gratitude was rudely acknowledged. 'You are supposed to be serving Her Majesty's needs, sir,' said the lieutenant. 'If all you can do is to provoke this canaille into attacking you, you would be better off tending pigs in Chalosse.'

Once again Bernard chose not to respond. He had no desire to tell Nogent of his involvement in the witch trial, but he needed to know whether the officer had found the road ahead passable.

'I have no time to bandy words with you,' he said, 'but I am supposed to find an alternate route, and would appreciate knowing whether the convoy can pass through the landslide.'

'Yes,' Nogent replied. 'The blockage is not as severe as we were informed, so you may return to your post at the fag end of the column, taking, no doubt, these odd recruits you seem to have acquired.' He looked quizzically at the witch and the judge's entourage, but made no further inquiry.

As the Navailles contingent rode off, Audijos turned to Hureaux.

'I cannot guard you and your prisoner on your way back to Bayonne,' he said. 'I have to escort Her Majesty's party to Saint-Jean-de-Luz.'

'This I know well,' said the judge, who had been amused by the exchange between Audijos and Nogent. 'You acted impetuously, but I should have given you my approval had you asked me. Now I fear the whole countryside has been aroused against the woman, and we shall be attacked again if we take her. In any event she is likely to be acquitted of sorcery by my tribunal. May I discharge her into your protection?'

The alleged witch had heard these words with increasing agitation.

'Please, my lords,' she said, 'do not let these people burn me. I have done no wrong. Take me to Saint-Jean-de-Luz, and I shall invoke the spirits to reward you.' She looked appealingly at Audijos.

'I doubt if my superiors would authorise such a thing,' said Bernard. 'But you have suffered enough, and I cannot abandon you.'

'Then that is settled,' said Hureaux. 'I shall ride back with you to your station, and relate the details to your commander if you deem it necessary.'

Bernard thought it best not to explain his diversion from his mission officially, so he declined the offer. On returning to the column he said farewell to the judge, and sought out madame de Motteville. He was fortunate to find her dining alfresco with some other ladies beneath a tree. The queen mother was lunching with a group of nobles some distance away. Audijos signalled to the lady of honour, who rose and walked over to him.

'Once again I have been rash, madame,' he said. 'With the sanction of the lieutenant-criminel of Bayonne, who had come to remove a poor woman from the jurisdiction of a friar torturing her as a witch, I have taken the victim under my protection. The Basque peasants in the area are so incensed against the woman that it is impossible for the judge to conduct her to Bayonne. May we allow her to ride in one of the wagons, and have one of your servants tend her wounds?'

Madame de Motteville smiled.

'You are incurable, El Cid,' she said. 'Her Majesty would not be pleased if we attract the hostile attention of some superstitious mob. Yet I have never met anyone accused of witchcraft, and I should be interested in her story. You may take her to my servant Louise, and when she is rested I should like to talk with her.'

The convoy, it seemed, was in no hurry to continue the journey. Anne of Austria wished to see the coast of her native country, which was clearly visible from the cliffs along the shore at Bidart. While the queen mother and a group of gentlemen departed on this expedition, Audijos visited his new protégé, who was being cared for by Louise. He thought it would be prudent to find out more about her before madame de Motteville spoke with her. He found her lying comfortably among the stores in a baggage wagon. At first he could hardly believe she was the same woman he had rescued from the torments of the inquisitor. Her long hair had been combed and adorned with ribbons, and she was dressed quite fashionably in the spare clothes of one of the ladies in waiting. Audijos estimated that she was about forty years of age. She would have been a striking beauty had her face not been lined and careworn. Even so, her eyes had a strange hypnotic quality, and when she smiled they projected a singular warmth and vivacity. Her face lit up with just such a smile when she saw Bernard approaching.

There was something about her that made Bernard treat her as though she were a gentlewoman. He swept off his hat, bowed and introduced himself.

'You are my rescuer,' she said, speaking French with a thick accent. 'I am the widow Carla Baroja. My husband was lost at sea twelve years ago.'

'I wish to find out more about you,' said Bernard. 'A great lady of the court, madame de Motteville, has allowed you to travel with us to Saint-Jean-de-Luz. She wants to converse with you about your supposed craft, and since there is need for prudence, I must warn you about what it would be impolitic to say. Hence you will forgive my asking about things I do not understand. Are you really a witch?'

Carla smiled.

'You may call me an *azta*, but not a *sorguin*,' she said, using the Basque words for enchantress and witch. 'I have certain powers to see into people's minds, and sometimes to make them do what I will. I have visions about things that happen in other places and at other times. I know about the herbs of healing, and I care for the sick. But I do only good and am no servant of the devil.'

'Then you do not attend the sabbat?' asked Bernard, who shared popular beliefs in magic and spiritual phenomena without crediting the wilder excesses that characterised the witch-hunts of an earlier generation.

'If you mean those supposed ceremonies in which Christian rituals are reversed and women indulge in abominable practices with the devil in the form of a man-goat,' Carla responded, 'then the answer is 'No'. Nor do I believe that the real devil participates in orgies, which some misguided persons use to indulge their own perversions. Then there are some deluded women who, believing they possess black powers, live in an imaginary world of the mind, and cast malevolent spells that are for the most part ineffective.'

The relief of Audijos at these explanations was patent. There was no need to warn Carla Baroja against possible indiscretions with madame de Motteville. Despite himself, Bernard could not help but be drawn to the Basque woman, who continued to fix her eyes on his.

'What was it,' he asked, 'that led you to be interrogated by the witch-finder?'

'I have had a reputation for healing both animals and humans,' she replied, 'but sometimes my herbs have not sufficed, and then someone will say I am the agent of death. Recently the syndic of Bidart fell ill with a fever. I had foreseen his death in a dream, and refused his wife's request that I treat him because I thought that I would be blamed for his passing. As it turned out, I was blamed in any case when he died. A chorus of denunciations followed, and then the friar came from Bayonne to arrest me.'

'And what about the devil's mark?' Bernard asked.

'It is but a natural birthmark. I shall show you.' She pulled her dress up over her bandaged legs to reveal a strawberry blemish on her thigh. Bernard bent forward, and felt an unexpected surge of desire.

'I see you are getting to know our witch better, monsieur,' came a voice. There stood madame de Motteville, escorted by Roger Dubourdieu.

16. The Royal Marriage

An embarrassed Audijos presented Carla Baroja to madame de Motteville, who expressed such interest in the witch's story that the incident of the birthmark was soon forgotten. While the two women were talking Bernard took Roger aside and explained the events that had occurred at Bidart.

'By the horns of the devil,' exclaimed Dubourdieu, 'you are treading a dangerous path. Who knows if she will not turn her enchantments in your direction, and what defence can one have against someone who can read one's mind?'

'That's as may be,' returned Audijos. 'We must hope that madame will take her under her protection, for captain Boisset is likely to recall us once we reach Saint-Jean-de-Luz.'

'There has already been news of that,' said his friend. 'I hear the whole regiment is to join the king's guards at the Bidassoa when His Majesty goes to claim his bride. Let us hope Nogent and his men do not receive a similar assignment.'

When the cavaliers rejoined the conversation between madame de Motteville and Carla Baroja, they found the two women to be on the best of terms. Madame de Motteville remained sceptical of the powers claimed by the enchantress, but she was fascinated by her strange personality and entirely convinced that she sought to heal rather than to harm. Audijos wondered whether the Basque woman had exerted the kind of subliminal influence that he had himself experienced. In any case, Carla Baroja had been assured transport to Saint-Jean-de-Luz, where she could seek refuge with a cousin. Bernard felt relieved that he would no longer be responsible for her safety and at the same time regretful that their ways might part. As things turned out their association was not to be so easily terminated.

Several hours later, as the queen mother's cortège threaded its way through the narrow streets of Saint-Jean-de-Luz towards the house reserved for Anne of Austria on the banks of the River

Nivelle, Audijos had occasion to ride past the wagon in which Baroja was travelling. He felt an inexplicable urge to speak with her.

'So you have answered my summons,' said the witch. 'The cousin who will shelter me lives on the next corner, but there is something else I wish to say apart from asking you to set me down in safety. You have saved my life, and, whether you wish it or not, our destinies will not diverge as swiftly as you seem to think. I have a presentiment to tell you. You have an enemy awaiting you at the end of this journey. And now stop the wagon and help me to my cousin's house.'

Bernard halted the conveyance and, having dismounted, helped Carla to alight. She held his arm and insisted on walking on her bandaged legs as they approached the house.

'You see,' she said, 'I can manage better than you imagine. I know you would like to carry me as you did in Bidart, but I have need to grow strong, for there will come a time when you will want my help.'

Audijos did not know whether to resent the way she read his thoughts or to take her predictions seriously. He knew only that he felt the same longing he had known when they had first spoken.

'It is true,' he said. 'I do not want to part, and I shall hope to see you again.'

'You shall,' she replied, 'but remember to be on guard against the dangers you will encounter.'

Someone inside the house had clearly observed their approach. The door opened suddenly, and Audijos caught a glimpse of a squat, dark man who ushered Carla inside and shut it abruptly in his face. He remounted his mare, and told the driver of the wagon to resume his place in the convoy. A few moments later they entered the courtyard of the mansion allotted to the queen mother and her retinue. There, standing on the steps that led up to the main entrance was the châtelaine de Sèvres, welcoming Anne of Austria. Audijos recalled Carla's presentiment. Was this the enemy against whom she had warned him, he wondered?

The châtelaine had arrived from Bordeaux by ship several days before, and had been given the task of preparing the queen mother's residence. A detachment of the royal guards was already on duty there. The officers of the escort from Bayonne - Nogent, Audijos and Dubourdieu - were summoned to receive Anne of Austria's thanks. Bernard noticed both madame de Navailles and madame de Motteville smiling at him from the terrace where the queen mother stood. Behind them was the châtelaine, an expression of disdain upon her face. Audijos and his companions bowed in acknowledgement of the honour it had been to serve Her Majesty. They returned to their men and rode off to the barracks assigned their respective regiments. Nogent, who had been perplexed by the favour Audijos received from the duchesse de Navailles, the patroness of his regiment, was polite enough in his farewells when they parted, but it was clear from his manner that his hostility towards Bernard had not abated.

When the two friends entered their quarters after reporting to captain Boisset, they were surprised to find Duplantier awaiting them. He had arrived by sea from Bayonne, bearing letters that maître Legrange had sent him for delivery to the two cavaliers. Legrange had complete trust in the innkeeper, and had thought it better to use him as an intermediary than to have his messenger track down the officers. As it happened, the package arrived in Bayonne after the departure of Bernard and Roger, and Duplantier, knowing the importance of its contents from a missive he had himself received from the schoolmaster, had set out immediately for Saint-Jean-de-Luz.

'You will find letters from Coudures as well as from Saint-Sever,' said Duplantier. 'Maître Legrange wrote to me too, and said he was enclosing mail from the Dubourdieu household for you both.' He looked meaningfully at Bernard.

Audijos did not want to admit his eagerness to read what - Jeanne-Marie had sent him, so he asked: 'What else did maître Legrange have to say?'

'He had heard of the king's declaration in Bayonne about protecting our liberties, and told me to tell our contacts in the town not to let down their guard, for the gabeleurs are likely to ignore the royal promise as soon as His Majesty has left the region.'

Audijos quickly scanned the letter Legrange had sent him.

'Yes,' he said, 'the good master has said the same thing here. He also gives news of plans for new bureaux of the gabelle to be established in Chalosse. He reports on his own measures for creating a network of informants against the gabeleurs, and I note that you, mine host, are expected to establish such a ring in Bayonne through your brother-in-law. He wants monsieur Dubourdieu and me to sound out cavaliers from our area who are thought to be reliable so that we have fighting men available if the regiment is disbanded.'

Duplantier turned the conversation in a new direction.

'My brother-in-law, Cambo Jatxou, has asked me to inquire if you heard anything of the witch trial when you passed by Bidart. He fears a new panic among the Basque people and a new surge of persecution. They say that the friar who conducts the inquiries deliberately holds them in public to inflame the people and thus provide him with more victims.'

'I can give you more details than you would expect,' replied Audijos. He proceeded to retell the story of Carla Baroja, asking in turn whether Jatxou knew of her and believed in her magical powers.

'Yes, I believe he has had some contact with her,' said Duplantier. 'He thinks she is a wise woman who commands many secrets unknown to ordinary mortals but would have no truck with Satan. Perhaps she may aid us in the conflict with the gabeleurs.'

'Morbleu!' said Dubourdieu, swearing and crossing himself simultaneously. 'Let us not meddle with witches. We have troubles enough without enlisting spells and enchantments.'

When Duplantier had left, Roger opened the letter he had received from his parents while Bernard retired to a corner of the room to read what Jeanne-Marie had written:

My dearest love, the days pass slowly without you, and I tell Patou you will come back to us one day. May God guard you from perils – and also from all those fine court ladies whom you have to serve. Send me word when you can and tell me that you love me as I love you. A thousand kisses from your Jeanne-Marie.

When Audijos retired to his pallet he dreamed uneasily of the châtelaine, the witch, and Jeanne-Marie circling round him.

On the following day the regiment received its marching orders to proceed to Hendaye, a fortress town on the north bank of the Bidassoa confronting its Spanish counterpart, Fuentarrabia, on the other shore. They remained there for several days while important personages from the two royal courts moved through their lines to cross and recross the river. The king of Spain left San Sebastian for Fuentarrabia, and on 2 June, according to Spanish protocol for a royal princess leaving the country, had his daughter married by proxy to the French king, using his minister, Luis de Haro, as the substitute for Louis XIV. A group of French ladies, including madame de Motteville, witnessed this ceremony, and were received by Maria Teresa. Madame confided to her diary that most of the Spanish women were dark and thin, and dressed in lace. The infanta, she wrote, was like a little round machine with far too much material in her skirts and too much false hair on her head.

Two days later Anne of Austria met her brother, Felipe IV, while the duc de Créquy, having first inspected his regiment on the riverbank, carried gifts across the Bidassoa to the king of Spain from the king of France. On 6 June, the two kings met on the Isle of Pheasants to swear eternal peace, while their troops lined the opposing shores, and wondered when they would next be joined in battle. Then Felipe IV surrendered his daughter into the care of his sister, and Anne of Austria established the household of her future daughter-in-law in accordance with the instructions she and Mazarin had suggested to the king. The duchesse de Navailles received the appointment of dame d'atour, a step towards the position she coveted as lady of honour. Then the French court retired to Saint-Jean-de-Luz, where the royal wedding was to take place on 9 June. Audijos and his fellow officers heard something of these high affairs, but for the most part were too busy with the guard duties required of them to observe the doings of the great. However, on the eve of the wedding they received orders to secure the streets through which the royal cortège was to proceed.

Early next morning captain Boisset and his company took up their station on the south side of the square facing the church of

Saint-Jean-Baptiste. They had to position themselves between massive temporary structures festooned with flowers, which had been erected for the occasion. The jurats of Saint-Jean-de-Luz had spared no expense to celebrate the honour bestowed upon the town by the royal nuptials. Additional funds had been voted by the Bilcar, an assembly of the syndics of the Basque communities of the province of Labourd. The sound of trumpets heralded the arrival of the procession that wended its way from the lodgings of the court on the banks of the Nivelle. A company of Swiss guards was followed by several hundred noblemen, with cardinal Mazarin behind them. Then came the young king, dressed in black and ornamented with cascades of lace. The infanta walked a few steps in his rear, wearing a silver robe, a cloak of purple velvet, and a crown upon her head. Then came the king's brother and Anne of Austria, supported by their respective entourages.

For three hours the men of the Créquy Cavalerie waited outside while the bishop of Bayonne conducted the ceremony. When all was completed the king led the new queen out of the church, and the procession reformed to march back to the houses beside the river. There Mazarin and the king dispensed commemorative coins to the watching crowd. Audijos and Dubourdieu were on duty with their men below the balcony from which the coins were thrown, watching for trouble. The two officers had been carefully observing the reactions of the spectators to the royal procession, and had noted that while there had been a few cries of 'Vive le Roi!' many in the crowd had remained curious but unimpressed by so much grandeur and display. This reserve vanished when the coins rained down upon them. A violent scramble took place as men and women clawed their way forward to share in the largesse. None of this provided any threat to the royal party, but then, without warning, a group of armed men emerged from the house opposite the king's lodgings.

17. The Intendant

The armed men who had swaggered into the square did not seem to belong to any military unit. They bore a miscellany of weapons, some with old-style muskets, others with pistols, daggers and long swords. Their dress was as varied as their arms, but the green scarves they wore suggested they belonged to some kind of irregular formation. They were led by a pale, emaciated man whose large head, beetling brows, and cavernous eye-sockets gave the impression of a corpse freshly risen from the grave. His diminutive frame was clad in black, and he carried no sword at his side. Audijos started in recognition. Once, when he had carried a message to his regimental headquarters during the Catalan campaign, he had seen this man in company with the commander, the marquis de Poyanne. It was the king's intendant to the army of Catalonia, Claude Pellot, whose sinister reputation had been widespread within the officer corps. He had been known for his puritanical morality, his insistence upon strict discipline, and his remorseless pursuit of economy in military administration. He was feared and disliked as a civilian trained in the law whose brevet required him to report directly to the royal council with respect to supposed irregularities on the part of field commanders.

Although Bernard's apprehension about a possible threat to the king's safety from this ragtag group was allayed by the anomalous presence of Pellot, he felt it necessary to confront them and discover their business. As they approached the crowd below the balcony where the king's largesse was being distributed, the alms-seekers began to turn and vilify the intruders with shouts of 'La brigade! A curse on the gabeleurs!' At the same time that Bernard realised that he faced the guards of the bureau, he perceived a manacled prisoner in their midst whom he recognised as his friend, Duplantier.

Followed by some of his men. Audijos strode forward and addressed the intendant: 'We are the Créquy Cavalerie, responsible for the protection of His Majesty in this place. By what warrant do you bring your prisoner here to disturb the royal almsgiving?'

Pellot looked contemptuously at his interlocutor and then glanced upwards at the balcony, noting that the young king and his first minister had retired into the upper level of the house.

'I need no warrant, monsieur.' he responded. 'I am the king's intendant, and His Majesty has no wish to waste more gold on this riffraff. He would take it ill if you try to impede my path with this traitor who plots against the gabelle.'

'I can vouch for this man,' said Audijos. I know him well as a loyal subject of the king. If you have information against him, deliver him to my custody, and I shall see he has a hearing before the lieutenant-criminel.'

Pellot's jaw stiffened with anger at this defiance, but his voice retained its icy calm.

'If you know this man so well, you are perhaps yourself associated with the rebels who seek to overturn the salt laws. We are sending the prisoner to Bayonne, where he will be put to the question and forced to reveal his confederates. Take care, young man, or the same fate will befall you.'

Audijos knew this was no idle threat. Neither his rank nor his connections could save him if he crossed the intendant's will. Discretion seemed the only way.

'I did but question your business because of my duty to safeguard His Majesty,' he answered, sweeping off his hat and bowing low.

'Then order your soldiers to stand aside,' said Pellot, signalling his men to move forward.

At that moment Duplantier shouted:

'Seigneur d'Audijos, save me! Tell my brother-in-law that—' His words were cut off, as one of the guards struck him savagely with the butt of a musket.

This proved too much for Roger Dubourdieu, who let out an oath and began to draw his sword. Bernard placed a restraining hand on the sword arm of his impetuous friend, and instructed his troop to open a path for the intendant. As Pellot and his men dragged Duplantier into a side street, Bernard called to a sergeant he trusted. 'Follow them at a distance, and find where they lodge the prisoner.'

The Créquy Cavalerie remained on duty in the square for another hour, when Boisset arrived with orders to stand down. As they returned to their quarters, they passed a contingent of the household guards escorting the new queen of France, her mother-in-law and their ladies to the king's dwelling. Audijos and his men stood aside and saluted respectfully, but Dubourdieu, less awed by the occasion than his companions, whispered hoarsely: 'I wager a golden crown that a dauphin will be engendered this night.'

Boisset smiled. 'His Majesty is of an age with yourself,' he said.

Bernard looked closely at the ladies in the royal retinue, but did not find the châtelaine among them. He was soon to receive news of her that made him apprehensive. Later that night the sergeant reported that he had followed Pellot's party without arousing their suspicions. They had stopped at a door near the northern ramparts of the town, and a woman of evident rank had answered the intendant's knock. She had stepped into the street and closely examined the prisoner. The sergeant had been near enough to hear her words.

'He is indeed the man,' she had said. Then Pellot had instructed the guards to lodge Duplantier in the basement of a fortified house nearby, and to keep him under constant watch. As the rest of the group departed, Pellot had entered the house with the lady. The sergeant had continued to follow the guards, and noted that after the prisoner had been placed under lock and key several of them entered an adjoining tavern. He had divested himself of those items of clothing that might identify him as a member of Audijos's troop, and managed to find a table close to the gabeleurs.

'They say,' he heard one of them remark, 'that she is named madame de Sèvres, and that our good intendant uses her as his agent in his inquiries about those who conduct the salt trains from Béarn.'

The sergeant had heard nothing more of interest, and Bernard thanked him for his pains and then dismissed him, cautioning him to keep the information to himself. Not long afterwards, as he was discussing Duplantier's arrest with Roger and expressing his alarm at the continued involvement of the châtelaine, captain Boisset summoned them to his office.

'Messieurs, I have received a complaint from monsieur Pellot,' he said. 'He claims that you tried to impede his progress across the town square when he was escorting a notorious salt smuggler.'

'We knew not at first that it was the intendant,' Audijos replied. 'We were concerned for the king's safety, and the rascally gabeleurs in his band seemed a threat to His Majesty.'

'There is more,' added Dubourdieu. 'They were maltreating a man we know well from our village of Coudures, and we did but ask why they had him in manacles.'

'You do not realise what kind of man you have affronted,' said Boisset sternly. 'True, his commission as intendant to the army of Catalonia has expired with the peace, but they say he has been told to gather information about resistance to the gabelle before he receives some new assignment. He has the ear of the king's council, and after your brush with him he will have no high regard for our regiment when it comes to decisions about disbandment.'

'But, captain,' said Audijos, 'you would not want us to stand by while some injustice is committed. These guards of the gabelle are little better than bandits.'

'Listen to me carefully,' Boisset returned, his voice growing in intensity. 'It is not for us to judge these affairs. The gabelle exists by the king's command, and I forbid either of you to take any action in defence of your friend from Coudures. We are here to obey orders and to defend the honour of the regiment. I shall not bandy words with you. Return to your quarters.'

The two friends knew better than to protest further, but they did not want to abandon Duplantier. Before they retired for the night Audijos had a strange feeling that someone was trying to communicate with him. Then an idea drifted unbidden into his mind. Duplantier had Basque connections. If the witch was still in Saint-Jean-de-Luz, perhaps she might find a way to save the innkeeper. The house where Bernard had left her was not far away. Despite Roger's misgivings, the two friends set off to find her.

They went fully armed, Bernard with his loaded musket at the ready. He had a premonition of danger. The moonlight cast heavy shadows from the houses across the narrow and deserted streets. Twice they stopped, thinking that they had heard furtive footsteps following them, and on the second occasion they turned to glimpse a form flitting from shadow to shadow. Dubourdieu muttered an imprecation and was about to go back to confront their stalker, but Audijos knew better.

'Whoever it is,' he whispered, 'he could elude us in the maze of side streets in this quarter. Besides, the house where Carla Baroja is lodged is at the next corner if I am not mistaken.'

They crossed the road through a patch of moonlight. As they reached the further side a woman's voice suddenly rang out from an upper window: 'Run! He is about to fire.' Roger leapt sideways and Bernard threw himself on the ground as a musket shot sounded, and a ball slammed over his head into the house behind him. He had broken his fall with his right hand, holding his own musket in his left. Steadying himself for a second, he returned fire at the shadow from whence the shot had come. His bullet hit home, for there was a screech as his assailant staggered into the road flailing his arms, fell, and lay still. A door opened and Carla called to them: 'Enter, my lords. You will be safe here.'

As they entered the house, two burly men brushed past them.

'Have no fear,' said the witch. 'They will hide the man's body. There may be other assassins, and we do not want this house to be known to their masters.'

'You saved my life,' Audijos replied. 'How did you know we were coming and that we were being followed?'

'I did but return a favour,' said the witch. 'I knew you were coming because I summoned you, and I watched from above and saw the man in the shadow. My associates in this place have their own means of finding out what your enemies are planning. I know you want me to help rescue your friend who is held by the gabeleurs, and this is something we may be able to arrange for you.'

'But how?' blurted out Bernard in his astonishment.

'You do not understand my powers,' Carla responded with a smile. 'I can send my thoughts, and sometimes, when he at whom they are aimed is sympathetic, they will be received. You and I have a secret bond, and I should warn you that at times I can read thoughts too. But come, there is wine to drink and we have plans to make.'

These events occurred several hours after the meeting between the intendant and the châtelaine. Saint-Jean-de-Luz and the Basque province of Labourd in which it was situated were not subject to the gabelle, but rumours that it was soon to be introduced were widespread. The irregular party of guards that had come from the north to support Pellot in his investigations had already been identified by the underground network of the Basque resistance to which Carla Baroja's cousins belonged. Since the Basques were as much involved in the salt trade as any of the local peoples, it was in their interest to publicise the presence of the gabeleurs as much as possible, and to excite protests against them. All this intensely irritated the intendant, who found his own network of spies to be constantly outwitted by his opponents. When he had been in Bordeaux the châtelaine had already briefed him on the results of her mission to Chalosse under cover of the entourage of the duchesse de Navailles. She had told him the information about the ancient charter that the spy at Nay had eventually passed on to her. The intendant attached little importance to such documents. Had he known of the identity of its custodian, and maître Legrange's role in opposing the gabelle, he would certainly have been more interested, but the spy had not heard this part of Audijos's conversation with the duchess. It was the châtelaine who had recognised Duplantier in Saint-Jean-de-Luz, and her information had enabled Pellot to arrest him. She had also told the intendant of the political sympathies of the two junior officers of the Créquy Cavalerie, and when Pellot had discovered that it was they whom he had encountered in the square he had considered ordering their immediate indictment. However, at the suggestion of the châtelaine, he had decided to hold his hand, and merely sent a note of reproof to Boisset. She had confirmed their part in the incident on the Adour, but she gave Pellot to understand that her romantic intrigues with them might enable her to make later use of them if further resistance to the gabelle developed.

The Intendant

Madame de Sèvres was not entirely frank with the intendant in these matters, for she had her own games to play. In particular, she was determined to revenge herself on Audijos for slighting her. She had used her charms upon Dubourdieu as much in the hope of dividing the two friends as of worming information from him. She had been courting the favour of madame de Navailles, now in the retinue of the new queen, in the hope of securing her own advancement. The duchess treated her coldly and did not reveal the confidences with which Audijos had entrusted her. At the same time her admiration for Bernard was so strong that she could not forbear to report his latest exploits and his presence in Saint-Jean-de-Luz. Such praise excited in the châtelaine a wave of vindictive hatred for the man who had first accepted her advances and then spurned her. Soon after this interview she commissioned the assassin to shoot him down. Pellot, of course, knew nothing of this.

The intendant had had long experience in the king's service. His father had entered the ranks of office-holders in the royal administration as a provincial treasurer. The son acquired an office in the judicial *parlement* of Rouen soon after the ruthless suppression of a peasant rising in Normandy in 1639, where he had learnt that mercy would win him no credit in the eyes of his superiors. He placed his foot firmly on the ladder of ascension through a marriage into the judicial nobility. His mother-in-law was the aunt of an even more ambitious civil servant, Jean-Baptiste Colbert, the personal assistant to Mazarin. Pellot became an intendant in Dauphiné, where he earned notoriety through insisting upon the execution of a woman accused of infanticide when the evidence was not conclusive. From Grenoble he was transferred to the intendancy of Poitou, and thence to Catalonia. The châtelaine knew something of his career and reputation, and he, for his part, knew her to be an unscrupulous adventuress well suited to his present purpose.

On the day after their conversation about possible resistance to the introduction of the gabelle in the area, the intendant and the châtelaine received a rude surprise. Duplantier had escaped. In the early hours of the morning he had been taken by some kind of fit, and his guards had then summoned a physician from the neighbourhood. It seemed that when this man and his female assistant had entered the house the guards had fallen into a trance and could recollect nothing of what subsequently transpired. When they came to their senses Duplantier had disappeared, and the body of a man shot through the chest had been left in his cell. Nor could any trace be found of the physician and his aid. On interrogation neighbours said they had never heard of them, and the man standing outside the house, who had recommended the doctor when Duplantier had begun to froth at the mouth, had also vanished. The corpse substituted for the prisoner was subsequently identified as a former soldier known as a hired assassin. Pellot bit his lips in fury at this news. Madame de Sèvres suspected that the witch, whom Audijos, as she had heard from the duchesse de Navailles, had rescued at Bidart, might have had something to do with these supernatural occurrences. But she was too fearful that Pellot might learn of her own connection with the assassin to take matters further.

Audijos, who had adopted a disguise to play the part of the physician, was delighted by the success of their stratagem, and even Dubourdieu, whose superstitious fears had been heightened by his friend's account of the manner in which Carla had hypnotised the guards, gave due credit to the witch. Duplantier, whose feigned illness had been directed by her telepathic powers, at first found it difficult to accept his miraculous deliverance. Yet the danger of discovery was pressing and the mingled joy and awe experienced by the Gascons soon took second place to the need for evasion. The witch and her cousins arranged immediate passage to Bayonne on a fishing sloop, taking Duplantier with them. Bernard and Roger prepared to return to their lodgings, hoping their absence had not come to the ears of Boisset.

'You have more than repaid any debt you owed me,' Audijos said to Carla Baroja before her departure. 'I shall never forget you.'

'That is true,' the witch replied. 'Perhaps we shall meet again. I know what you feel for me, and because I also know that you love another I have not done more to excite your passion.'

The two officers rejoined their company, which had received orders to ride northwards with other formations in advance of the royal court. Soon afterwards Pellot received instructions to proceed to Foix to investigate the credentials of false nobles in the area. He sensed, however, that his duties in the western provinces of the Pyrenees were by no means finished. Whatever the king's assurances to respect local liberties, he expected a new mission from his patron, Colbert, to extend and enforce the gabelle.

18. Return to Chalosse

The two squadrons that composed the Créquy Cavalerie rode back to Bayonne several days before the court left Saint-Jean-de-Luz on its slow progress back to the royal residences on the Loire. Captain Boisset's company jingled into the courtyard of the Château Neuf, dismounted, and led their horses to the stables. Audijos and Dubourdieu had suffered no repercussions from their brush with Pellot, and it seemed that the authorities had taken pains to conceal the affair of Duplantier's rescue. The regiment was to stay in Bayonne for some time, so that the two officers were able to contact Cambo Jatxou at their leisure and to learn that his brother-in-law was in hiding.

When they found Duplantier holed up in the corner of a warehouse in the wharf area, he was still mystified by the circumstances of his escape. He was even more concerned that Pellot's men had known of his mission against the gabelle, and had been able to track him down in Saint-Jean-de-Luz. Could there be a spy in the network Legrange was trying to establish? Further, there had been new reports of trouble with the guards of the bureau in Peyrehorade, at the confluence of the Gave de Pau and the Gave d'Oloron. It was rumoured that troops were to be sent to the town, and this caused concern for the city council of Bayonne, for, like the towns on the Adour, Peyrehorade was a vital link for the city's trade with the interior. However, one of their own members, a prominent barrister named David de Cheverry, had gone to Paris and become a client of the finance minister, Nicolas Fouquet. He could be relied upon to defend the liberties of Bayonne and local privileges in the hinterland, even when these served as obstacles to the tax-gathering plans of his master. De Cheverry, it was hoped, would work on Fouquet to have the order for the quartering of the troops countermanded.

The mills of the central government ground slowly. After performing garrison duty in Bayonne for several months, the

Créquy Cavalerie was chosen to occupy Peyrehorade and suppress resistance to the gabelle. This was a bitter pill for Bernard and Roger, who could not help but suspect that it was the influence of Pellot that had forced their unit to support the hated gabeleurs. However, in February 1661, soon after their arrival in the town, De Cheverry sent news to Bayonne that he had succeeded in obtaining an order for the withdrawal of the troops. His argument that the presence of soldiers in Peyrehorade adversely affected trade in the area had persuaded Fouquet to intercede. Audijos knew about this before the actual order had reached the regiment in Peyrehorade. Legrange's secret network included De Cheverry's secretary, and the schoolmaster was delighted to be able to pass the information to his former pupil. In any case, the salt trains had given Peyrehorade a wide berth during the occupation of the town by the Créquy Cavalerie.

There followed in rapid succession two events of major significance. A decision was made for reasons of economy to disband nearly all formations of light horse, including the regiments of Créquy and Navailles. Further, officers such as Boisset who had bought their commands were not to be compensated. Hard on the heels of this decision came the news that Mazarin had died, and Fouquet was expected to take over his role as first minister. Yet the young king made no move, and it was known that other factions at court sought to overthrow the superintendent of the finances. In the meantime Fouquet did nothing to restrain the activities of the gabeleurs in Gascony, who launched another ambush of a salt train, this time in the vicinity of Aire. Then in September, when the regiments were finally disbanded, news arrived that Fouquet had been arrested at the instigation of Colbert, and that Pellot had played an important part in the coup by seizing the papers of Fouquet's secretary.

Details of these high affairs filtered down into the provinces piecemeal and in distorted fashion. Audijos knew more about them than most of his fellow officers because of the secret missives hand-delivered by the agents of maître Legrange, which contained political news as well as reports about the gabeleurs. The disbanding of the Créquy Cavalerie was, of course, an immediate reality. The colonel of the regiment undertook to use his influence to find employment for the officers, but it was clear that most of them would have to return to their lands. Few captains had the means to buy other commands, and in any case, short of another war, no new formations were likely to be raised. To the distress of Bernard and Roger, the impecunious Boisset began to talk of seeking a post with the bureau of the gabelle. Their thoughts, however, turned more to the prospect of returning home than to the possible defection of their captain.

The course of true love had not run smooth for Bernard and Jeanne-Marie. Many months had passed since their last meeting. His requests to take leave to visit Coudures had been refused by Boisset, evidently on instruction from higher authority, and Bernard suspected that this was because he was thought to be plotting against the gabelle in the area. He had been too proud to challenge Boisset on the matter, and his letters to Jeanne-Marie had gone unanswered. Dubourdieu had also been denied permission to visit his home, but he slipped away nonetheless, under cover of a patrolling assignment. He returned with disquieting news. His sister had not received the letters Audijos had sent and it seemed the despairing pleas she had addressed to him had also gone astray or been intercepted. Since each of the lovers was unaware of this circumstance, they had feared that the silence of their partner had been intentional. At the same time Jeanne-Marie had been besieged by the advances of the sieur de Prugues, a match that her parents favoured. On one occasion, she had told Roger, Prugues had come upon her swimming naked in the river. He had lain in wait and attempted to take her by force when she emerged. Her screams had summoned Patou on the further bank. The dog had crossed the river in a fury of flailing paws and bounded up the bank with his teeth bared. Jeanne-Marie had called off her protector, and Prugues had retired in confusion.

Audijos found it difficult to control his emotions.

'God knows,' he said, 'she must feel I have abandoned her, but there will be a day of reckoning for that scoundrel.'

'Yes,' responded Dubourdieu. 'My sister's honour will be avenged. Morbleu! You know how headstrong she can be. Who but she would bathe alone in the woods?'

'Not quite alone,' said Audijos. 'Thanks be to the saints that the dog was with her. Did you tell her about me?'

'Of course. I told her how much she means to you, but she tossed her head in that way she has, and refused to believe you had written. I would she had given me some note to pass to you. I think she still loves you, but I cannot tell. She has told no one but me about this incident.'

A few weeks after Roger's return from Coudures the regiment assembled for the last parade of the Créquy Cavalerie. After the formalities of the occasion he and Bernard made their farewells to their companions and took the road for Chalosse. As officers they were able to keep their arms and accoutrements, although their men had had to surrender their muskets and horses. They rode by way of Orthez and spent the night at Hagetmau. They set off again early next morning and, soon after crossing the Bas, saw the outskirts of Coudures before them. Dubourdieu urged his horse forward into a canter, but Audijos hung back, apprehensive as to the welcome that awaited him.

'Ride on,' he shouted to his friend. 'I shall go straight to my mother's house, and you can send me word there about Jeanne-Marie.'

Diane de Talazuc-Bahus greeted her son warmly, yet with a certain air of reserve. The reason for this was soon disclosed. The Dubourdieu family had broken off relations after Jeanne-Marie had told her parents of her love for Bernard.

'As if we were not good enough for these jumped-up officials of the law,' said madame de Talazuc. 'We have the blood of Foix-Candale in our veins, even though we have not the lands and money that mean so much to people like the Dubourdieu. It seems they have in mind some suitor of greater wealth for their daughter. I wish you had confided in me, and then, perhaps, I could have served you in this matter.'

'There must be more to it than that, madame,' Audijos responded. 'I was well enough received in their house. I did not ask them for Jeanne-Marie's hand because I had to rejoin my regiment and knew not what the future held. Now much time has passed, and neither of us have received any letters of late. I no longer know what her heart may tell her.'

Soon after this conversation Roger Dubourdieu brought news that gave even greater cause for alarm.

'My parents have been threatened by some agent of the gabelle,' he said. 'They have been told that you and I are at the centre of a plot against the gabeleurs, and if they do not co-operate, my father's offices will be taken from him, and he will be placed under restraint as an accomplice. They have allowed the correspondence between you and my sister to be intercepted, and they have told Jeanne-Marie that she must marry that snivelling rogue who calls himself the sieur de Prugues. She, of course, refused, and now they have sent her to Saint-Sever to be locked up in the convent of the Sisters of Mercy.'

Audijos tensed as though an icy hand had gripped his heart.

'Small mercy there,' he said bitterly. 'How could they have done such a thing? And what has become of my dog?'

'My mother broke down in tears when I reproached her,' replied Dubourdieu. 'She told me that Jeanne-Marie tried to flee into the woods, Patou with her. They caught her, and one of the servants stunned the dog with a club. He must have recovered from the blow, for at night he is heard howling in the forest. He mourns for his lost mistress, but there is no trail for him to follow. No one has dared to recapture him. By the wounds of Christ, shame upon my kin!'

Bernard's jaw tightened.

'This is no time for blasphemy,' he said. 'We shall find this skulking agent of the gabelle. I shall ride to Saint-Sever and consult maître Legrange about these spies. Then we shall free Jeanne-Marie, whether she cares for me or not. But first I must find the one being I know she loves.'

It was late in the afternoon when Audijos entered the woods fringing the banks of the stream that was named the Bas. He decided not to call the dog until he was well out of earshot of the village. He had penetrated about a hundred yards into the tangled black oaks when he trod upon a fallen branch that broke with a snap. Immediately a low growl sounded behind the bushes to his left.

'Patou!' he shouted, and a large furry body bounded out of the undergrowth into his arms. It took some time before the dog's exuberant greeting calmed down. His fur was matted and caked with mud, and Bernard noted the dried blood from a wound behind one of his ears. Man and dog walked back together through Coudures, Patou whining softly as they passed the house of the Dubourdieu.

Before leaving for Saint-Sever on the following day Bernard asked Roger to see if he could discover the identity of the gabeleur who had threatened his father.

'I think he will tell me,' Dubourdieu replied. 'Like most folk in Chalosse, he views the gabelle as a thing contrary to our liberties, and I believe he secretly approved of our part in the affray on the Adour. But he fears for his rank and status, and he sees us as hotheads who will compromise the family. Above all, he has set his heart against having you as his son-in-law.'

'I intend to see Jeanne-Marie in Saint-Sever,' said Audijos. 'I bring the dog with me so that he may soften the heart of the abbess.'

'You are a strange one, my friend. No one else, save my headstrong sister, would bestow affection on an animal as though it were human.'

'You are mistaken. Patou has emotions just as we do, and loyalties superior to the calculations and deceits of men. I have discussed the matter with madame de Motteville, and she told me that she disagreed with a philosopher called Descartes who claims that beasts are mere machines and have no soul.'

'A pox on philosophers!' Dubourdieu responded. 'But whether your Descartes is right or wrong, that dog has his uses. May he lead you to my sister.'

Audijos rode slowly on the road to Saint-Sever and Patou had no trouble in keeping pace with his master's horse. Maître Legrange greeted him warmly, and bestowed an admiring glance on the dog, who on Bernard's command lay down in the stable beside the mare.

'You have a new recruit for our cause,' said the schoolmaster. 'At least our enemies will worm no secrets out of him.'

Legrange was as much disturbed by the news of the pressure brought on Arnaud Dubourdieu as he had earlier been at the arrest of Duplantier in Saint-Jean-de-Luz.

'At least they have not suborned our own messengers,' he remarked. 'They must have expected to find information that would serve them in the letters you sent to your lady.'

'The châtelaine must have left spies in this area,' returned Bernard. 'Let us hope maître, that they do not find the chain leads back to you. Is the *for* of Chalosse well hid?'

'For the moment, yes,' said Legrange. 'I am thinking of lodging it with a much respected judge in the *parlement* of Pau, président de Gassion, who is the part-owner of the salt fountain of Salies in Béarn and has a personal interest in the matter. He has acquired the château of Saint-Martin du Salies from the family of Gontaut-Biron, and has been elevated to the high dignity of marquis. But apart from that, we must ask ourselves why no action has been taken against you and young Dubourdieu if your actions on the Adour are known to the gabeleurs.'

'It may be that they are biding their time - or that they do not yet want to provoke a response among the nobility of the land, who may be willing to defend us. Yet I do not think of myself so much as of Jeanne-Marie, who lies imprisoned in the convent here by her father's order.'

'I shall see what I can do,' said Legrange. 'This is not one of those libertine places where the sisters enjoy a more free and easy social life than they would in the manors of their parents. I know and respect the abbess, but she is a stern woman and allows no departures from the discipline of her order. Fortunately, the woman you love has taken no vows and is not even in the position of a postulant. I may be able to arrange a meeting between you, but I cannot promise more. Under the law no one can challenge a father's order.'

Legrange and his former pupil spent several hours discussing the likely extension of the gabelle, the intrigues of its agents, and the ways in which they could oppose its machinations. But throughout the conversation Bernard's thoughts constantly reverted to the prospect of seeing Jeanne-Marie.

19. Prelude to Revolt

While Audijos was in Saint-Sever, Roger sat down for a serious talk with his father.

'Sir,' he said, ' you have insulted the nobly born mother of my best friend and sent my sister to a convent to prevent her seeing him. All this, so my mother tells me, is because some scoundrel of a gabeleur has threatened you.'

Arnaud Dubourdieu reddened and puffed out his cheeks.

'Who are you, sir, to question your father? We have a certain dignity to maintain, and your consorting with young Audijos - not to mention your fighting with the guards of the bureau - is likely to place us all beyond the very law that I, a judge, have a duty to enforce.'

'Sir, with respect, the gabelle is no true law. Do you not serve the maréchal-duc de Gramont, one of the greatest powers in the land? What would he - or the marquis de Poyanne, under whom Bernard and I have served - think of your conduct? How will it sit with the duc de Navailles, who entrusted Bernard with command of his wife's escort, or the Créquy family that raised our late regiment, or the vicomte de Poudenx, syndic of the estates of Béarn, governor of Dax, and a member of the family of Bernard's mother?'

This list of the high and mighty had a considerable effect upon the elder Dubourdieu.

'Perhaps I have been hasty,' he said. 'But I shall not revoke my order concerning Jeanne-Marie. Your friend is an adventurer and I want no truck with him. Let her stay in the convent until she cools down and considers the suit of the sieur de Prugues.'

'Bernard is a natural leader of men, sir,' replied Roger. 'Though I am older than he, I would follow him into the cannon's mouth. He is a man of true honour, and your Prugues, from what I hear, has nothing but money to recommend him.' He said nothing of the incident in the woods.

Arnaud Dubourdieu had never met such defiance in his usually respectful son.

'Leave me,' he said. 'You are an unnatural son. I want no more of your insolence."

Roger, his temper rising slammed the door behind him. He realised that his anger had prevented him from asking his father the identity of the blackmailer. Yet all was not lost. His mother, who was waiting in the antechamber, and had evidently overheard the exchanges, signalled to him to follow her.

'You must not excite your father,' she said. 'I shall do my best to persuade him to change his mind, although he is stubborn and it will take time. I certainly prefer Bernard to that Prugues fellow. Do you know that it was to him that Arnaud passed the letters intended for Jeanne-Marie? I saw them both in the garden when it was done, but I could not hear all their words.'

'Thank you, mother,' said Roger. 'Things begin to fall in place and now I have a mission to perform.' He slung on his sword belt, curled his ferocious mustachios, and called a servant to fetch his horse. Within a few hours he reached the Prugues estate near Urgons to the south-east of Coudures, and was ushered into the presence of its owner, a sharp featured, elegantly dressed man some forty years of age.

'You are welcome to my humble house, monsieur,' said Prugues, bowing and rubbing his hands. 'How may I be of service to you?'

Roger had not given much thought to what he should say to the would-be ravisher of his sister, whom he had had previously met casually on two or three occasions and despised as an effete popinjay. Now he knew better.

'Morbleu!' he spluttered. 'It is my sister's service that I have in mind.'

'Ah, such a lovely lady!' Prugues simpered. 'Perhaps you bring a message on her behalf?'

'I believe you have some of her letters which you tricked my father into giving you."

'Come, sir, that is not the way to address a gentleman.'

Dubourdieu exploded, throwing discretion to the winds.

'Gentleman! You are a scoundrel, sir! Not content with assaulting my sister, you are hand in glove with the filth of the gabelle. And you dare to menace my house with exposure. By the hounds of hell, you deserve a beating with the flat of my sword.'

Prugues became preternaturally calm.

'How very charming! You deserve your reputation as a braggart and a bully. Have a care, monsieur, or I shall teach you a lesson you may not live to learn.' As he spoke he opened a drawer of the desk at which he had sat down and drew out a loaded pistol, which he cocked. 'Now, sir, leave my house this instant or you will be carried out feet foremost.'

Roger turned on his heel as if he were about to withdraw, and then hurled himself downwards at the desk. The ball from the pistol passed over his head. The heavy piece of furniture shattered at the impact of the cavalier's charge and collapsed on top of Prugues. Roger rose to his feet, clutching a bruised shoulder, and saw that his foe lay motionless. As he stooped to make sure the man was indeed unconscious, he saw a sheaf of papers tied with a ribbon lying beside Prugues. He picked them up and read a note inscribed on an enfolding leaf: 'For the eyes of Jean de Labat.' Extracting one of the sheets, he recognised the handwriting of Audijos.

'So I have the letters,' he murmured, 'and also the identity of another traitor.'

Dubourdieu could hear the sound of hurrying footsteps, as the servants responded to the sound of the pistol shot. Drawing his sword he flung open the door, to be confronted with three white faced men.

'Stand aside, you limbs of Satan,' he bellowed. 'Your master has need of you.' He strode out of the house, sprang into the saddle, and galloped off on the road to Saint-Sever.

While these events were passing at Urgons, Audijos, who had spent the night at Legrange's house, was awaiting word as to whether the abbess would allow him to see Jeanne-Marie. Eventually the schoolmaster returned, his brow creased with a frown.

'Good news and bad,' he said in answer to Bernard's anxious expression. 'The abbess refuses your request without a written order from Arnaud Dubourdieu. However, I have risked my good name by playing on the feelings of one of the nuns whose father attended my school. She will arrange for Jeanne-Marie to be at the western portal of the convent in half an hour. She knows that she is disobeying her superior, and I have promised her that the visit will not be repeated without proper authorisation. It is all I can do. When you have seen her you must return at once to Coudures, where I shall visit you in a week's time.'

'My thanks, maître,' said Audijos. He saddled his horse, and set off immediately with Patou at his side. Leaving dog and horse in an alley behind the convent, he cautiously approached the western gate in the surrounding wall. A low voice sounded at the grating in the portal: 'Bernard, you have come at last.'

'Jeanne-Marie, is it really you?'

'After all these months, Bernard. Why, why, did you not send me word?'

'I wrote you several times. They would not give me leave to visit you.'

'But Roger came. He said you had written. Why did I not receive your letters?'

'It is a complex story, my love. You must believe me when I say someone took the letters, as they also took those I think you consigned to me. It is the agents of the gabelle who thought they would find evidence of my plotting against them.'

'How can I believe you? Why, the sieur de Prugues - that is, in the days when I was still speaking to that man - told me you had made love to that horrible châtelaine. He had it from his friend Parthenay, squire to the duc de Navailles.'

'I was deceived. I am deeply sorry. It was before we re-met. Can you not forgive me? I do not hold your romance with Prugues against you.'

'Romance, indeed! That man attacked me in the woods, and had it not been for Patou... Does Patou still live? The servants wounded him when I fled my father's house.'

Bernard had forgotten the dog in the anxiety of the moment:

'He is well, and he is here. Perhaps you will believe him.' He gave a low whistle, and within a few seconds Patou was at his side. As soon as he heard Jeanne-Marie's voice behind the grating he whined and scratched at the doorway. But another voice was heard behind the wall: 'Jeanne-Marie, you must come at once. The abbess has entered the garden.'

'I must go, Bernard.'

'I love you, Jeanne-Marie. Tell me that you love me too.'

'I cannot tell. I must think. Somehow we must meet again. Make my father release me from this place.'

She was gone, and Bernard felt a lump in his throat. Patou answered his summons unwillingly, and they returned to the place he had left the mare. They had hardly set out on the road to Coudures when Roger arrived in a cloud of dust.

'I have your letters to Jeanne-Marie. I have the letters,' he repeated.

'It is too late,' said Bernard glumly. All the way back to Coudures he would do nothing but grunt acknowledgement of Roger's breathless explanations.

In the week that followed Audijos's thoughts were divided between Jeanne-Marie and the oppression of the gabelle. On the one hand the rational part of his mind told him that he must wait and somehow persuade Arnaud Dubourdieu to relent, while rallying opinion to secure the abolition of the salt tax; on the other, his instinctive urge for action led him to consider the possibilities of carrying off Jeanne-Marie from the convent by force and leading an armed revolt against the gabeleurs. Yet violence would make him an outlaw. He would be hunted through hill and dale, and in any case he could not be sure that either Jeanne-Marie or Legrange would accept such a course of action. For all he knew the woman he loved might no longer return his affection, and the schoolmaster's carefully laid plans would be totally disrupted. In the meantime he moved out of Coudures to a cottage on his small estate, and Roger also left his parents' house to manage his lands nearby.

When Legrange arrived from Saint-Sever, he brought disturbing news on both counts. The sister who had arranged the interview had been severely disciplined by the abbess, and Jeanne-Marie was now under constant watch. In the wider world Colbert, who now managed the king's finances, had granted a new tax lease for the gabelle to the financier Gervaisot in Bordeaux. A levy on shipping was to be imposed upon Bayonne, new bureaux for the gabelle were to be established in the towns along the Adour and its tributaries, and a much stronger force of guards was to be recruited. Boisset was their new controller, and lieutenant Nogent was to lead a force of dragoons to assist the guards. Legrange had received some of this news from an agent in Bordeaux, and some from the secretary of De Cheverry, who had survived the fall of Fouquet and was still working at court in the interests of Bayonne.

The meeting with Legrange took place in a back room of Duplantier's tavern. Duplantier himself had returned secretly from hiding in Bayonne, and reported upon the dismay of the merchants and city fathers of the town at the shipping tax, which had already been put into effect there. There was a rising groundswell of popular discontent among the artisans and sailors. The cabaret owner's jovial disposition seemed to have changed under the stress of the secret life he had been obliged to live, and his face was sombre as he gave details of the network he had established of those popular leaders loyal to the cause.

'There may come a time,' said Legrange, 'when we shall have to mobilise those discontents, but for the present we must try to influence those in high places who respect our liberties and detest the gabelle as much as we. Above all, we must be sure that we confide only in those we trust. There are spies close to us. The notary is clearly among them, and also the sieur de Prugues.'

He glanced at the two share-croppers from Ancos, Arnaud Corade and Géronce Baillet, whom Bernard and Roger had asked to attend the meeting.

'Yes,' said Corade, 'there have been comings and goings at the Prugues manor house, and that lily-livered lordling was absent for several days. I found out from one of his servants that he had gone to Bordeaux."

'He is a more dangerous man than you might think,' added Dubourdieu, who had earlier given Legrange details of his adventure at Prugues. The schoolmaster had shown great concern to find that the sieur de Prugues had prepared the bundle of Audijos's letters for transmission to Bernard de Labat. The notary was evidently playing a double game. He had visited the Dubourdieu household in Roger's absence, and his contact with Prugues made him a major suspect.

Legrange had also spent some time alone with Audijos, and while he clearly sympathised with Bernard's despair at Jeanne-Marie's continued imprisonment, he made it clear that he thought the campaign against the gabelle should receive first priority. Bernard had mentioned the possible need for general armed resistance.

'That depends,' Legrange had replied, 'upon how far the new guards of the bureau are prepared to go. They have recruited many disbanded soldiers, but some of them are from this area and might defect to us if it comes to fighting. Moreover, there are others whom we can directly recruit and train in our cause. That, Bernard, should be your task.' Before the meeting in the cabaret broke up, Audijos arranged for a rendezvous of a core of trusted men to receive instruction in the techniques of guerrilla warfare he had seen practised by the archpriest of Juncalas.

Legrange kept in touch with his lieutenants in the months following this meeting. For long it seemed that the influence of Gramont and other members of the high Gascon nobility was restraining the attempts of Colbert to augment the revenues of the state in the south-west. Early in the year 1663, the guards of the convoy, as the farm of the salt tax and its bureaux were called, attacked a salt train near Doazit, some six miles to the west of Saint-Sever. A few weeks later riots in Bayonne forced Gervaisot and his agents, who were visiting the port, to take refuge in the Château Vieux. The city fathers called an assembly to condemn the violence, and calm was eventually restored. Back in Bayonne, Duplantier reported to Legrange that popular passions had boiled over without any instigation from the members of his own network, although many of them had perforce to join the agitation. Colbert then tried a new tactic, with an edict declaring the king to be the rightful owner of the Béarnais salt fountain at Salies. The edict had to be revoked in face of the constitutional rulings of the *parlement* of Pau, where président de Gassion was the far-from-disinterested leader of the opposition. The *parlement* went on to authorise the use of armed guards to defend the salt convoys against the attacks of the gabeleurs. One such attack had again occurred near Doazit, where the men of the brigade had slaughtered the animals pulling the salt carts.

As the guards of the gabelle went over to the offensive, Colbert renewed his plan to install bureaux in the main towns on the river system. Saint-Sever was itself chosen for this purpose, and at Legrange's suggestion the town consuls sent a delegation to Bayonne, asking for the city's support. The city government then petitioned for the convocation of the representative estates of Landes to discuss all imposts contrary to the privileges of the region. This was a body incorporating all the subprovinces in the area, and it had not been assembled for several generations. Not unexpectedly, the request was denied. Eventually the gabeleurs appeared before the gates of Saint-Sever, where they were turned back by a force of masked men led by Audijos. This action afforded merely a temporary respite. Troops were sent to the town accompanied by magistrates instructed to inquire into the affair. The inquiry proved abortive, and the town was required to pay thirty thousand livres in return for the privilege of avoiding the installation of the bureau. The same fate befell other towns such as Dax, Tartas, and Mont-de-Marsan, also under pressure from the gabelle.

During this interval Audijos thought constantly of Jeanne-Marie. The elder Dubourdieu was as adamant as ever, and it seemed he had lost all sympathy for his headstrong daughter. Madame Dubourdieu was more understanding. She had visited Jeanne-Marie from time to time, and while she refused to disobey her husband by passing messages between the lovers, she gave each of them covertly to understand that a bond remained between them. This was some comfort to Audijos, although he could not know precisely what Jeanne-Marie was thinking. Meanwhile he busied himself on his estate, went hunting in the woods for wild boar with Patou, and attended to the training of his irregulars. Their confidence grew after repulsing the gabeleurs outside Saint-Sever without having to fire a shot.

Always it was Legrange who kept a hand on the pulse of the changing situation, and disseminated news and counsel through his agents. However, a new factor appeared at the beginning of 1664. Pellot was installed as the intendant of Guienne. He came with the firm intention of reducing all the south-west to obedience, and this at a time when sentiment against the gabelle was reaching a crescendo.

20. Three Meetings

One of Claude Pellot's first actions on assuming his duties was to meet with the tax-farmer Gervaisot in Bordeaux.

'Until now,' he said to the financier, 'the profits from your lease have been restricted by the opponents of the gabelle. It is my intention to enforce His Majesty's orders with an iron hand. I shall crush resistance wherever it may occur, and my connection with monsieur Colbert will enable me to discipline the nobility as well as the common people.'

The financier, a large man who towered over the diminutive intendant, became visibly nervous at these words.

'I – I would wish to avoid violence,' he stammered. 'As you know, my accountants and I were manhandled by an angry mob in Bayonne when I went there to supervise the collection of the shipping tax. I do not understand why the king's taxes should excite such animosity from those who call themselves loyal subjects.'

'They are stirred up by disloyal agitators who pretend their ancient rights are being denied,' replied Pellot. 'They do not realise that the king's will is the true law, and we, his agents, must enforce it with the executioner's rope and block if there be need.'

'But we might gain more by yielding a little. I have heard from my colleague monsieur Pierre-Paul Riquet, the farmer of the gabelle in Languedoc, that last year, when his men used force to collect the tax in our new province of Roussillon, a revolt began in the mountains.'

'Monsieur Macqueron, the intendant in those parts, has already informed me of these circumstances. They call the rebels 'Angelets', but it is not force so much as foolish attempts to conciliate these Catalan angels of death that has led to war in the eastern Pyrenees. It will be the same here with Gascons, Béarnais and Basques if we allow talk of special privileges. Yet we are better placed than the government of Roussillon to anticipate revolt. There is someone whom I should like you to meet.'

A fire seemed to glow in the sunken eyes of the intendant. Gervaisot quailed and stepped back. Then Pellot called to a servant: 'Summon the châtelaine de Sèvres.'

The châtelaine swept into the room as if she were a duchess presiding at a salon filled with inferiors. She seated herself in the largest armchair without invitation, and the two men sat down beside her.

'I have met monsieur Gervaisot in the house of madame de Saint-Luc,' she said. 'What can I do for you, monsieur Pellot?'

'My guest is concerned at the rising tide of opinion against the gabelle,' said the intendant. 'He is not aware of the information you have gathered, particularly about the disaffected gentry in Chalosse and Tursan. Show him your list, so that he may know we are ready to anticipate any move these vermin may make.'

Madame de Sèvres smiled enigmatically.

'Vermin?' she asked. 'You are disrespectful of my noble friends.' She produced a scroll and handed it to the financier. It contained some forty names, each of them annotated with remarks such as 'took part in an affray with the guards of the bureau at Doazit', 'allowed the escort of a salt convoy to shelter in his château near Dumes', 'expressed support for the delegation protesting the gabelle.' There were further comments on the characters of the seigneurs on the list such as 'incorruptible,' 'timorous and easily swayed', 'venal', 'can be blackmailed through his family scandal', 'susceptible to feminine wiles.'

'You see,' said Pellot, who had already looked through the list and had asked the châtelaine if the last of these characteristics was the result of her own charms, 'we are ready to act when the time comes, and that time is now upon us. Further, we have reports about their network of spies, including town notables, former soldiers, and even peasants. Madame de Sèvres has traced those links that the disaffected have with the great, and she has personal links with some of the most dangerous of the petty seigneurs, such as Audijos and Dubourdieu, whom I have mentioned to you. Most important of all, she has identified the mastermind that unites the disaffection - a schoolmaster at Saint-Sever. He will be eliminated. For the time being we have withdrawn the men we sent to Saint-Sever, and now I intend to occupy the mighty duc de Gramont's personal estate at Hagetmau. We shall see who really has the king's ear – his true servants on the royal council or these courtier dukes who attend to his pleasures.'

'I can see how useful madame's information can be,' said Gervaisot, who was clearly astonished to discover such a role in one who by repute was engrossed in the amours and gossip of high society. 'But is it wise to challenge the greatest names in the land? If it comes to military action, will you not have to depend upon lords such as the lieutenant general of our province, monsieur de Saint-Luc, or the marquis de Poyanne, or the vicomte de Poudenx?'

'We shall see,' Pellot responded grimly.

Early in April 1664, twenty well armed men of Gervaisot's bureau were despatched to Hagetmau. Legrange had had word of their coming, and had called an emergency meeting at Saint-Sever of the innermost circle of the resistance. Audijos, Dubourdieu, Duplantier, Corade and Baillet were among those present.

'Not long ago,' he said, 'we decided to challenge the guards who were sent here to our own town, and we were able to turn them back without any killing. We cannot hope for such an outcome at Hagetmau. I have learnt that the new intendant has resolved to crush our opposition. The outposts he is establishing along the main routes of the salt trains from Béarn to Guienne will have orders not just to interdict the convoys, but also to arrest any who support them in the towns and villages. Pellot is a ruthless man. The fact that he has chosen to challenge our worthy duke by setting up a bureau in his very birthplace at Hagetmau means that he is prepared to defy the noble lords upon whom we have hitherto depended. Our campaign can no longer be a matter of persuasion and local defence. We must sound the tocsin and call our people to war against the gabeleurs in just defence of our rights.'

'We are ready,' said Audijos. 'We have a band of some sixty men who have been trained in battle tactics in town and countryside, and many more in reserve. We have contacted all the local seigneurs upon whom we can rely, and who will provide us with places of refuge. I have instituted the system of communication you suggested, and my men can be summoned to rally within a few hours at any designated assembly point. They are well mounted and can fight with sword and fusil as well as any company of light cavalry.'

'It is well,' said Legrange, 'and now that we are faced with general combat, it is you, Bernard d'Audijos, who must take command. Henceforth I shall play a subsidiary role. In any case my days may well be numbered, for there are spies who shadow my movements. Even tonight I had to elude them before coming to this place.'

'We shall guard you as well as we can, maître,' responded Audijos, 'but if we fail someone must know your contacts and codes and, above all, where the *for* of Chalosse lies hidden.'

'I have prepared a dossier to pass to you,' said Legrange, handing Audijos a scroll tied with a ribbon. 'I fear, however, that our network will become largely ineffective when the outside world brands us as rebels against the king, whose true interests we serve. There are many who have helped us in the past, but who will not risk their office and status once we are at war. My agent in the bureau in Bordeaux can no longer be relied upon, and the secretary of De Cheverry will be unlikely to send information, despite his own and his master's continuing sympathy for our cause. As to the *for,* I rode to Pau last week to deliver it into the hands of the new président de Gassion, who recently succeeded to his father's marquisate and to his office in the *parlement*. I think he can be trusted. There is a rough copy in the papers I have given you, although it is only the ancient document that will carry weight. I expected to be waylaid, for there was a rider who followed me at a distance throughout the journey.'

'That was rash, maître,' said Audijos.

'True, but the matter was urgent, and I knew you and your men were training in the woods near Serres-Gaston. It may come to pass that your muskets will serve better than the law, but remember that we must always maintain the legality of the privileges His Majesty has promised to support.'

'I doubt whether there is much legality in the command you have bestowed on me. There will be suffering and bloodshed. All I can say is that those who follow me will face death with honour.'

'Our cause is just, and you are the one we look to to defend it.' Legrange turned to the others assembled in the room. 'Will you draw your swords for Audijos and justice?'

Swords leapt from their scabbards.

'Vive le roi sans la gabelle! Vive d'Audijos!' came the answering shout that was to become the battle cry of the movement.

A week later a very different kind of meeting took place at Coudures. The local notables who attended it had been convoked by the notary Jean de Labat in his house. Arnaud Dubourdieu was there, as were Bernard Dumartin, syndic of Coudures and seigneur d'Ancos, and Christophe de Labat, bailiff of various large estates and cousin of the notary. Others present were also local judges and officials administering feudal law and supervising the accounts of the lands held by Gramont and other lords. They all lived nobly, avoiding any kind of manual labour, and gave themselves an air of importance associated with some small property from which each derived his petty title. The ostensible purpose of the meeting was to deal with Jean Lacourt, the curé who preferred poaching to his ecclesiastical duties, and his brother Simon, the former soldier who had arbitrarily encroached upon the common lands. The real purpose, as everyone knew, was to explore communal reaction to the new initiatives of the gabeleurs.

'It seems to me,' said the notary in his silken voice, 'that while we all resent the salt tax, we need to make some statement to show we condemn those who take matters into their own hands. What could be better than to have our recalcitrant curé resume his pulpit and preach against those who resist the gabeleurs?'

'Why not leave church discipline to the archpriest in Urgons?' said Dumartin. 'We shall merely antagonise our people if we take a stand that appears to favour the gabelle. Besides, some of us are more closely concerned with the resistance than is good for Coudures.' He looked meaningfully at Arnaud Dubourdieu.

The judge reddened but remained silent. Jean de Labat took up the thread.

'I need not name the two young gallants who have been foolish enough to use their swords against those who have the king's warrant. There are rumours that they are training other desperadoes in the forests. I have seen a copy of a proclamation from the intendant in Bordeaux placing one of them beyond the law and offering a reward for his arrest. It is soon to be issued, and when it is we should compel our godless curé to read it to the congregation.'

This was too much for the elder Dubourdieu.

'You will bring dishonour on my house. Where is the evidence for what you dare to allege? The noble duc de Gramont will intercede if this outrage is perpetrated.'

'We can no longer count upon the protection of the marshal-duke,' returned Labat. 'Have you not heard that the guards of the bureau are about to invade his estates at Hagetmau? We must make some gesture to protect our community from similar measures.'

At this point Christophe de Labat, who was totally unaware of the double game his cousin was playing, interceded.

'This is all very well, but you invited us here to deal with the Lacourt brothers. The curé is not likely to agree to such a demand. Do you not recall that when we asked him to desist from pouring lime into the Gabas and ruining the fish runs, he treated us with contempt? And his brother is a dangerous man who may assault any sergeant we send to evict him from the common land.'

Arnaud Dubourdieu rose to his feet.

'I shall take no further part in these proceedings,' he said. 'We are not here to play politics. The law should take its course against malefactors, and I believe the true wrongdoers are the gabeleurs.'

'Do not be too hasty, messieurs,' said the notary. 'These are dangerous times and we must make what provision we can in the interests of Coudures.'

These words were lost upon the audience, who followed the example of Dubourdieu, and abruptly left the house. Jean de Labat accompanied his guests to the door, pretending to observe customary civilities. As soon as they were gone he entered another room, where the Lacourt brothers were waiting.

'You heard what transpired,' he said. 'They have reacted exactly as we planned. Next Sunday at mass you must return to your pulpit and read the proclamation, monsieur le curé. And you, Simon, get you to Saint-Sever and plant your dagger in the schoolmaster's heart. When you have done so, find any documents about the gabelle he may have, and bring them to me.'

21. Jeanne-Marie Escapes

The days seemed interminable to Jeanne-Marie. Her mother told her on one of her visits to the convent that her father showed signs of a change in attitude, and was talking of the infamies committed by the gabeleurs. Yet he would not authorise her release until she promised never to see Audijos again. This she would not do and she began to weigh the possibilities of escape. She had gained permission to tend one of the kitchen gardens within the convent walls. She watched the lizards climbing the masonry, and wondered if she could find a ladder to scale the wall. She observed a squirrel digging holes in a vain attempt to find the nuts it had buried, and thought of tunnelling her way beneath. Neither of these ideas was feasible, for there were always sisters who came regularly to check her activities on the instructions of the abbess. One day she was talking to the gardener who supplied her with seedlings, and discovered that he made a daily journey in a horse-drawn wagon to fetch provisions for the convent. After matins on the following day she hid herself under some sacking in the back of the wagon.

As the wagon jolted over the cobbles through the convent gates Jeanne-Marie expected every instant that someone would find she was not in her room and raise a hue and cry. They reached the outskirts of Saint-Sever, and the wagon came to a stop in the busy street. Jeanne-Marie slipped to the ground and plunged into the crowd. Such was her desperation that she had made no plans as to what she would do once she had evaded the sisters who held her captive. She could not return to her home, nor did she know how she might find Audijos. Then she remembered Bernard's stories about maître Legrange and she determined to throw herself on the schoolmaster's mercy. A passer-by directed her to the house.

Somehow the place seemed grim and foreboding. She did not dare approach the front door, but made her way cautiously round the side of the house, glancing from side to side to see that she was unobserved. The door at the back was open and she entered with palpitating heart. All was quiet. She was about to call out, when suddenly she heard a commotion above stairs, followed by a terrible cry. Prudence suggested flight, but that was not her way. She climbed half way up the stairs noiselessly, and saw on the landing a figure standing over a man, who was bleeding copiously.

She could not repress a gasp, and the figure turned towards her, a bloody knife in his hand.

'Who the devil are you?' said Simon Lacourt through his clenched teeth. Then he recognised her. 'You are the Dubourdieu bitch, and you will die for your meddling.' He bounded down the stairs towards her, his weapon poised to strike.

Jeanne-Marie threw herself at his oncoming feet. As the assassin tripped, his momentum carried him all the way to the foot of the stairway. There was a crash and a screech. Lacourt had fallen on his dagger and transfixed himself. He lay there unmoving.

Jeanne-Marie rose unsteadily, and heard a harsh gurgling noise from the man on the landing. She re-climbed the stairs and bent over the dying Legrange.

'May God preserve you,' she said. 'I am Jeanne-Marie Dubourdieu, the friend of Bernard d'Audijos, and I came here to seek your help. Let me find something to staunch your wound.'

'It is no use,' Legrange whispered weakly between each laboured breath. 'Tell Bernard that this... this is the work of the gabeleurs. Tell – tell him that I die for the cause of which he is now the... leader. Have the *parlement* proclaim the *for*. Find the papers at the back of the armoire, and give – give them to Bernard. God have mercy upon...' He shuddered, tried to rise, and fell back lifeless.

When she was sure that the schoolmaster breathed no more, Jeanne-Marie rummaged in the back of the wardrobe in the bedroom, and found a valise stuffed with documents. Then she descended the stairs, gripping the bag tightly as she went. She stepped over the dead assassin and made her way to the door. Who now could help her? She must find Bernard and tell him of the murder. Strangely, she felt more concern for the murdered Legrange than she did for her own predicament. As if fortified by the scene of terror she had experienced, her mind began to race in search of some solution. Then she thought of the parish priest who had come to the convent to hear confession. He had been kind to her, and when she had asked for absolution for loving Bernard and defying her father, he had said there was no sin to forgive. And the church stood close to Legrange's house.

Jeanne-Marie found père Anselme in the sacristy.

'Father,' she said, trying to control the tremor in her voice,' I have fled from the convent and entered the house of maître Legrange to beg his assistance. I arrived just before the death of the worthy schoolmaster by the hand of that evil brother of the curé of Coudures, who then killed himself by accident in attempting to assault me. I have to find the sieur d'Audijos. Help me, I beg you, for the love of God.'

Astonishment and grief were reflected in the face of père Anselme.

'My daughter,' he said, 'this is a most dreadful thing. You have more courage than most of us. Maître Legrange and I have been old friends. He confided in me about the abominations of the gabelle. It was at this very place that your Audijos came to seek him after the affray on the Adour. Audijos has gone to Hagetmau to defend us against the gabeleurs. There will be more killing, and you cannot go there at this time.'

'I must go, father. I care not for my own life. I must give Bernard the message maître Legrange asked me to transmit with his dying words.'

This information persuaded the priest to revise his opinion.

'So be it, my daughter,' he said. 'You must not repeat this outside the circle you trust, but I am one of many in the church who aid those who resist the gabeleurs. It so happens that Géronce Baillet arrives here in an hour with ten men on his way to join Audijos at Hagetmau. I shall find you a horse and you can ride under their protection. As to the convent and the lady abbess, you can rely on my discretion.'

Père Anselme was indeed discreet. He did not wish to examine the valise Jeanne-Marie was still clutching, nor did he question her about Legrange's message, or ask how exactly Simon Lacourt came by his own death, although he wondered what the words 'by accident' entailed. He sent a servant to the local constable to report an intruder in the schoolmaster's house, and persuaded his guest to rest while she awaited the arrival of her escort. Meanwhile he arranged for a horse to be saddled and brought to the vicarage stable. It was a fresh and fiery animal, but the priest was aware of Jeanne-Marie's unusual skills as a rider.

Ballet and his men, all heavily armed, arrived soon afterwards. They had ridden hard, and dismounted at Legrange's school to water their horses and refresh themselves. Their leader was at first dismayed to learn that he was expected to include the demoiselle Dubourdieu in his party, but he changed his attitude when he heard père Anselme's explanations and the news of the murder of maître Legrange.

'I shall try to keep her safe at the rear of the column,' he said, 'but who knows, with a woman such as she, what madcap action she will undertake?' When Jeanne-Marie emerged he welcomed her, and presented her with a loaded pistol to place in her saddle holster.

'I hope you can shoot as well as ride,' he said. 'It may be you will need a weapon.' Jeanne-Marie thanked him. She was so elated at the prospect of seeing Bernard that she gave no thought to the dangers ahead.

'You had best set forth at once,' said père Anselme. 'I do not want you here when the constable arrives to discover the bodies in the house across the street. God be with you.'

Daylight began to fade as the cavalcade reached the château near Dumes on the road south to Hagetmau. Baillet, his slight frame tense in the saddle in expectation of immediate action, had sent two scouts ahead in case of ambush. By the time they reached the woods north of Hagetmau it had become completely dark. The hooting of an owl sounded from the trees beside the road. It was answered with a similar call from the leading scout, while the other turned back to warn the rest of the party that they were approaching the rendezvous. A man stepped out of the forest, and led them along a path for about a hundred yards. There, sitting by a small fire in front of a woodsman's hut, were Bernard, Roger and three other men.

'Well met, and not before time,' said Audijos. 'Corade has just returned from the town to report that the gabeleurs, after being harassed by the populace, have established themselves in a fortified house near the church of Saint-Girons. We shall move before dawn.'

'There is news for you, brought by someone you do not expect,' said Baillet. The last of the riders dismounted as she entered the clearing, and ran into Bernard's arms.

'Jeanne-Marie, how on earth did you find your way here? Wait – let me summon one who stands guard in the woods.' He gave a low whistle, and within seconds Patou bounded into the circle, and greeted Jeanne-Marie with a rapture his more inhibited master could not display in public. Forgetting the need for silence, the rest of the party burst into applause, led by Roger, who was overjoyed to find his sister in such unexpected circumstances.

Bernard's face became sombre as he learnt of the details of the escape of Jeanne-Marie and the death of Legrange.

'Fate has dealt us a sad blow,' he said. 'At least, my love, you were there to hear his last words. When we have disposed of the vermin who have infested Hagetmau, I shall ride to Pau and ask the marquis de Gassion to proclaim the *for* of Chalosse in the *parlement*. And this murder will be avenged. Simon Lacourt may be dead, but it is someone else who directed this foul deed.'

Food and drink were provided, and most of the men tried to snatch an hour or two of sleep. Bernard and Roger examined the contents of the bag brought by Jeanne-Marie as best they could in the flickering firelight. It was full of the correspondence between Legrange and his agents. Audijos already possessed the names and addresses in the dossier the schoolmaster had given him. He threw the bag on the fire, lest by mischance it should fall into the hands of the servants of the gabelle. Then the two lovers drew apart from their companions and related to each other all that had passed in their lives during their long separation. They embraced fervently knowing their estrangement was over.

Two hours after midnight, Audijos roused the men and told them to prepare for action.

22. The Battle of Hagetmau

Jeanne-Marie was deputed to remain in the clearing with the horses and Patou. Audijos led the party silently through the woods to the western side of Hagetmau. From time to time a crescent moon shone out fitfully between the clouds, but as they entered the narrow streets of the town they moved in almost complete darkness. Audijos knew the maze of alleyways tolerably well, and Corade's reconnaissance on the previous day had provided a detailed description of the place occupied by the gabeleurs and its immediate environs. They stole stealthily along either side of a deserted street in the direction of the church of Saint-Girons, alert to the possibility of a gabeleur outpost or patrol. All seemed quiet at first, but when they paused they heard footsteps ahead, and glimpsed in a ray of moonlight shadowy figures flitting silently from door to door some fifty yards in advance. Audijos was about to pass a whispered order to fan out through the side alleys when a man stepped from a doorway, and levelled a pistol at Audijos.

'Stand, whoever you are!' he said. 'Are you friend or foe of the gabelle?'

Bernard glanced across the street, and sensed that Dubourdieu and those following him were moving to his support. By the sounds ahead he knew that those for whom the man with the pistol had been acting as rearguard had also heard the challenge, and were retracing their steps. For an instant he feared he had encountered a gabeleur patrol, and a desperate struggle was about to take place in the darkness. But the challenge had not been phrased in the terms he would have expected from the enemy.

'I am Bernard d'Audijos,' he said. 'We have come to drive out the guards of the bureau.'

'You are doubly welcome,' came the reply. 'I am Robert Lacroix, leading the militia of Hagetmau against the gabeleurs who have invaded our town. They are fully armed and have set men on watch through the night less than half a mile from here. Let us join forces and move indoors to discuss our plan of attack.'

'By all means, friend,' said Audijos. 'We must be in position before daylight, and we have little time to spare. Let us send scouts forward to keep watch on our enemies while we confer.' Lacroix sent some of his men to report on activities in the house held by the gabeleurs, while the rest of the two groups moved into an adjoining tavern opened by one of the militiamen, who happened to be the owner. Corade had already met him when he had made his reconnaissance, but having found someone he could trust to tell him the location of the gabeleurs, he had thought it prudent to say nothing of his own party.

'We expect to have to fight,' said Audijos, 'but to avoid needless bloodshed we should first give the guards the opportunity to withdraw peacefully.'

'That is not our intention,' said Lacroix. 'Already they have spilt blood. When they entered the town they shot dead an urchin who threw a stone at them. The people of Hagetmau demand vengeance.'

'Vengeance they shall have,' returned Audijos. 'I accept your wish that we should not attempt to parley, but I think that from this point you should accept my advice. We shall not succeed if we have divided counsels.'

'You must take command,' said Lacroix. 'We know your reputation, monsieur. There are ten of us here who can fire a musket and use a sword, but few have had much experience of combat. Make your dispositions, and we shall obey.'

Audijos had already improvised a plan. Before first light two or three men should take up positions in each of the four houses overlooking the place the gabeleurs had occupied. It had originally been part of the town's defences, with thick stone walls surmounted by a crenellated tower. The combined forces had a slight advantage in numbers, but not enough to take the place by frontal assault. Audijos's strategy was to blockade the guards and convey the impression the besiegers were far more numerous than in fact they were. The main force of twelve men under Audijos's immediate command would be held in reserve behind the church, and wait until opportunity offered to create a diversion in front of the strongpoint, whereupon the reserve would attack from the rear.

Things did not go exactly as planned. The local militia were assigned the task of entering the houses, since they would be known to the inhabitants. They executed their task somewhat clumsily. Dogs barked and lamps were lit, and it was apparent that the gabeleurs on watch knew something was afoot. As dawn began to break, Audijos moved silently from house to house to see that each party had taken up its post. He was checking the lines of fire from the building opposite the front of the strongpoint when he saw six of the guards, led by an officer, emerge into the street. To his surprise it was his former commander, captain Boisset.

'Hold your fire,' he called to the two militiamen beside him.

Boisset recognised the voice.

'So, monsieur d'Audijos,' he shouted, 'you have become a rebel in a wrong cause. Tell your men to throw their weapons into the street, and I shall see they are given justice.'

'Not the king's justice, captain, but the executioners employed by monsieur Pellot. You are surrounded. It is you who must surrender. If you do so you may leave the town under safe-conduct'

Boisset had no opportunity to reply. The militiamen had lost patience with this exchange, which seemed contrary to the agreement they had made with Audijos. A crackle of musketry came from the adjoining house. The shots were poorly aimed and missed their targets. Boisset and his men retired precipitantly into the strongpoint. The siege had begun.

Audijos withdrew from the house by its rear entrance and joined Dubourdieu at the back of the church. He was pleased that he had been able to make his offer known to Boisset, but angered that the militiamen had fired on impulse.

'Their discipline is as poor as their marksmanship,' he said to Roger. As the day wore on an erratic fire was sustained against the strongpoint, the militiamen as well as some of the men from the reserve moving from house to house and window to window. The gabeleurs returned fire from time to time, but no one on either side was hit.

Audijos racked his brains to think of some diversionary tactic. He could not afford to let the siege drag on for more than a day or two because the bureau would be bound to send reinforcements as soon as reports of Boisset's predicament were received. Nor would it be possible to restrain for long the impatience of the people of Hagetmau, who were already flocking into the back streets of the Saint-Girons area in anticipation of the massacre of the gabeleurs. Indeed, it was as much as Lacroix could do to control armed volunteers who joined the militia in the houses from which the inhabitants had been evacuated. While Audijos could assume that this popular agitation would be observed by Boisset and might well persuade him to seek terms, he did not want to see an uncontrolled mob suffer heavy casualties from the fire of the guards. Meanwhile he did not forget Jeanne-Marie, who had been left in the woods with Patou to guard the horses. On the first night of the siege he sent Corade and Baillet to bring them to a safe place in the town designated by Lacroix.

On the second morning an opportunity to resolve the stalemate presented itself. Corade's friend, the tavern keeper, offered to have a local farmer drive a herd of cattle down the street in front of the strongpoint, and suggested that this might create the necessary confusion for an attack to be launched. Audijos adapted this proposal to fit his original plan. He ordered a cart with bales of straw to follow the cattle, as if some peasant from the country, knowing nothing of the siege, was proceeding to the market. When the cart drew level with the main gate of the strongpoint, men hidden in the back of the cart would place the bales against the walls of the gabeleurs' refuge and set alight to them. This would provide the diversion to allow a successful assault on the rear of the building.

While these arrangements were being set in train, the gabeleurs attempted a sortie in the direction of the church to test the strength of the investing forces. They were met with a hail of musketry from the reserve under Audijos, while Dubourdieu, sword in hand, led a counter attack. The gabeleurs were driven back into the strongpoint with three of their number wounded and one dead. The second night seemed to pass without incident, apart from false alarms and stray shots fired at venture. In reality, however, the situation inside the strongpoint had changed dramatically.

Boisset had spent much of the time in the tower observing the activities of the besieging forces. After the failure of the sortie he realised that he could not break out of the strongpoint. While time appeared to be on the side of the defenders, supplies were running low. He knew that Audijos was a resourceful opponent who would think he had to make some kind of move before help was sent to the guards of the bureau, and Boisset wondered what kind of stratagem his former lieutenant would devise. As he sat cogitating in the tower on the late afternoon of the second day, one of his men came puffing and blowing up the winding stairway.

'Captain,' he said breathlessly, 'we have found a way to escape. There is a tunnel in the cellar that leads to the ruined walls on the western side.' Before it had become dark, Boisset had personally reconnoitred the escape route and found the exit from the tunnel unguarded nearly a hundred yards away. He gave orders for the evacuation of the strongpoint in the early hours of the following morning.

As dawn came, a dank mist roiled through the streets and rose above the chimney tops. The bellowing of cattle sounded as the long-horned animals were driven between the houses by the cries of the herdsman and the barking of his dogs. A covered wagon lumbered behind. Shots came from the strongpoint, one of them wounding the driver as he brought his clumsy vehicle level with the gateway. A barrage of covering fire sounded from the surrounding houses as four men jumped from the wagon, hurled the straw at the gate and beneath the lower windows, and set it alight. Thick smoke mingled with the fog to create a dense blanket through which none of the musketeers could aim with certainty.

At the rear of the building Audijos and Dubourdieu led their men forward. They carried a heavy battering ram and swung it rhythmically against the heavy doors. Someone fired from one of the upper windows, and Baillet fell as the bullet grazed his thigh. Then the door splintered and gave way. Sword in one hand, pistol in the other, the attackers stormed through the opening. But there was no one to confront them. The men spread out through the building, Audijos climbing the stairway with three others behind him. A pistol shot passed over his head. Standing at the head of the stairs holding his smoking weapon was captain Boisset. Bernard could have fired at point-blank range, but seeing the captain at a disadvantage, he came at him with his sword. The sword play did not last long. With a deft twist of his wrist, Audijos disarmed his opponent.

Roger ascended the stairs soon afterwards.

'There is no one else here,' he said. 'There are muskets beside the windows, some discharged and others still loaded.'

'Where are your men, captain?' Bernard demanded.

'I ordered them to retire. It seems you have had the best of it this time. Yet I fancy my stratagem was better than yours.'

The building was searched from top to bottom, and eventually the secret tunnel was discovered. Clearly, Boisset had chosen to remain behind to cover the escape of the guards, and had gone from window to window firing at random. Meanwhile some of the crowd had entered the strongpoint, and were clamouring for the death of the prisoner.

'Hang him – burn him – death to the gabeleur,' came the shouts. Audijos turned to Boisset.

'You would not accept my safe conduct when it was offered, but I think you could profit from it now.'

'I thank you, monsieur. One day, perhaps I may repay you.'

'Roger, escort our gallant captain through the tunnel,' said Audijos. 'Make sure he has a horse to carry him beyond the clutches of the good people of Hagetmau. Then see if it is worth pursuing the cut-throats he commands.'

So ended the first battle of Hagetmau.

23. Revenge

Reverberations from the events in Hagetmau made themselves felt at a variety of levels. In Bordeaux Pellot's anger knew no bounds, and he wrote at once to Colbert asking for a regiment of dragoons to enforce his orders. In Paris, the duc de Gramont protested vigorously against the invasion of his lands by the gabeleurs, and sent instructions to his officials in Chalosse telling them to trust in his protection. Reactions in Doazit, Saint-Sever and Coudures were exultant and, at the same time, apprehensive. Meetings of seigneurs in the châteaux and manors of the countryside expressed open support for Audijos and his band, while local notables in the towns cautiously suggested petitions to defend their privileges.

The victors of Hagetmau returned quietly to their homes. In his office of judge at Hagetmau, Arnaud Dubourdieu felt sufficiently assured by the promise he had received of the continued patronage of the duc de Gramont to express open sympathy for the movement against the gabelle. He had felt outraged at the news of Jean-Marie's flight from the convent, but he decided to yield to the pleas of his wife and to accept his errant daughter back into his home, although he made it clear to Roger that he continued to frown on her association with Bernard.

For his part, Audijos received a warm welcome from his mother, and accompanied her on a visit to the château at Doazit, where he was greeted by the aged baron, Sarran de Foix-Candale, and an assembly of local lords who had gathered to celebrate his exploit. Among them were the baron de Navailles-Banos, who was related to the duc de Navailles and held the château near Dumes, the seigneur de Serres-Louts, who had himself participated in the defence of a salt convoy against the gabeleurs, and his close friend, the seigneur de Montaut, who had also acted as an escort to a salt train. But what reassured Audijos even more than the presence of these members of the local elite was the attendance of two officials from Saint-Sever, Pierre de Borrit, the royal provost of the town, and Louis de Barry, the chief judicial officer.

It was the baron de Foix-Candale, toothless and bent with years, who spoke for the assembly in his thin, quavering voice. 'We bid double welcome to you and your son, cousin,' he said to madame de Talazuc, 'because he has taken a stand in a cause, which is dear to our family and our friends.'

'My lords,' replied Audijos on his mother's behalf, 'we marvel that the news from Hagetmau has spread so fast, and it seems the identity of those who fought the gabeleurs is already known to many."

'This is true,' said Pierre de Borrit. 'It would have been better if there were more secrecy in this matter, for I fear there will be reprisals. It is not only those who have shown their courage in resisting the gabeleurs by force who must take precautions. Those of us who hold the king's warrant, and believe the perfidies of the bureau are not known to His Majesty, will face penalties if our sympathies become known to the servants of the intendant.'

'Yes,' said Audijos, 'I know something of monsieur Pellot, and he will not let our resistance go unanswered. He has spies in many places, and your discretion is as vital to our cause as the support we hope you will afford us. From now on I and others who are known to his informants will be treated as outlaws to be hunted down. When the need arises, we shall take to the woods and strike the gabeleurs when they least expect us.'

'I am proud that a member of my house has become the leader of this cause,' interposed old Sarran de Foix-Candale. 'You may count upon our help and that of all who serve us.'

Audijos and madame de Talazuc enjoyed the hospitality of their kinsfolk until the following day, when they returned to Coudures. On their return journey they discussed other members of the family. They had seen little of the old baron's son and heir, Jean-François, who was bedridden with a wasting disease, which the physicians could not diagnose. Bernard had talked to him at his bedside, and had felt a sense of unease.

'He questioned me closely about the details of our organisation,' he said, 'but I thought it prudent to say little. Perhaps it was as well I was discreet, for he asked me if I knew that scoundrel the sieur de Prugues, who seems to be hand in glove with the gabeleurs.'

'I believe they were boyhood friends,' replied madame de Talazuc. 'I recall that the old baron was disturbed at his son's licentious behaviour before his illness, and attributed it to Prugues' evil influence. There is little sympathy between father and son, and the pattern of estrangement has repeated itself in the next generation. Henri, the baron's grandson, who is absent studying at the University of Bordeaux, is said to be divided from his own father. But you need not be concerned. There are others in our family who feel as you do about the gabelle, especially our cousin the vicomte de Poudenx, who has so much influence in Chalosse and Béarn and is widely known as a defender of our privileges.'

'This is true, mother. The cause in which I have taken up arms would certainly fail if we did not have such wide support throughout Gascony and Béarn. What worries me most is the existence of secret enemies who work to betray us. Those who serve monsieur Pellot know neither honour nor scruple. My concern is that they may act against those most dear to me. You yourself may be in danger.'

'My dear son, I cannot conceive that the nobility of this land of ours would allow me to be threatened. And as to your Jeanne-Marie, she is surely safe enough if she stays with her parents. Your friend Roger may have chosen to fight by your side, but the father sits astride every fence where there are political choices, and I cannot see him endorsing armed resistance to the gabelle.'

'I pray to God you are right, madame,' said Audijos, and lapsed into a brooding silence.

Over the next few days, events in Coudures bore out these premonitions. Père Lacourt, angered at the mysterious death of his brother and suspecting that the supporters of Audijos were responsible, summoned up the courage to resume his pulpit, and obeyed Labat's instruction to read to the congregation the intendant's decree branding Audijos an outlaw. Most of those in the audience, Arnaud Dubourdieu included, reacted by rising from their seats and leaving the church, some expostulating and shaking their fists as they left. Bernard de Labat and his family, however, remained in their pew. It was as well for the movement of resistance that they did so, for two of the followers of Audijos had taken advantage of the notary's attendance at mass to search his house.

Both Labourde and Desbordes had taken part in the attack on the gabeleurs in Hagetmau. The first had been better educated than most of his kind. He had become a clerk in Labat's service, and had suffered dismissal for ferreting through papers that were not his concern. He had suspected the notary of being an informer for the gabelle even before Labat had excited the suspicions of Audijos and Legrange. It was Corade who chose him to search the notary's house while Labat and his family were at church, but, since Labourde was a small nervous man who was more accomplished with a quill than with a musket, his friend Desbordes accompanied him to the house to keep up his spirits and to stand guard during the burglary. Desbordes was the local butcher, a massive man who was something of a street orator, known for his colourful invective against the salt tax that increased the expenses of his trade.

Labat lived within a hundred yards of the church. Desbordes stood in the roadway, pretending to occupy himself with the broken wheel of a cart, while Labourde climbed over a wall to gain entry to the back of the house. Twice he emerged fearfully at the front door to assure himself that his friend was keeping a proper watch. Finally he came out carrying a small sack, and whispered to Desbordes: 'I have found what we need, hidden in the cabinet he always kept locked. Quick, let us go before we are discovered.' The butcher suddenly found his cart to be operative, and the two unlikely thieves made their way to Duplantier's tavern. A few moments later the angry crowd who had reacted to the curé's announcement about Audijos flocked into the street.

Since the notary would not be long in finding that his house had been forcibly entered, the lock to his cabinet broken, and the compromising documents removed, immediate action was demanded. Duplantier had to attend to his customers, so Corrade and Baillet, already recovered from his wound, went to a back room and helped Labourde scan the papers he had stolen while

Desbordes stood at the door. While the full import of all that the documents revealed would take time to discover, it was soon clear that Prugues, Labat and the Lacourt brothers were the centre of the network of secret agents who worked for the gabelle in the district. More striking still, it was apparent that Labat had received instructions to murder Legrange and had passed them on to the assassin.

The four conspirators found Audijos and Roger Dubourdieu in the hideaway they were preparing in the woods beside the Gabas. It was a secure place, consisting of a large cave with a concealed entrance surrounded by massive trees, in the tallest of which a kind of watchtower had been constructed with a wide view over the surrounding countryside. Bernard sat down with his lieutenants in a council of war.

'We are all in your debt,' he said to Labourde. 'Now that we have certain knowledge that Labat was responsible for our master's death, we shall act at once to avenge him.'

'What about Prugues and the curé?' asked Dubourdieu. 'By all the devils in hell, they deserve to die as surely as he.'

'Not yet,' replied Audijos. 'Pellot will take some time to find out that we have discovered the identity of some of his other spies, and the longer we wait before we strike them, the more we may turn affairs to our advantage. We can feed them with false information about our plans.'

'Then let us kill the notary before he informs the intendant of our theft,' said Corade. 'I beg you, let me have the pleasure of cutting his throat.' He fingered his dagger and twisted his face into a malevolent snarl.

'Blood for blood,' exclaimed Audijos, 'but it is I who shall shed it to avenge maître Legrange. It shall be done in such a way that the people of Coudures know the reason for the deed, and those who are not with us may be warned of the penalty of betrayal. Saddle your horses and don your masks. Our friends will recognise some of us, but they can feign ignorance if they are interrogated.'

Late on that Sunday afternoon six masked men rode into the main street of Coudures, and dismounted before the house of the notary. Two of them moved to the rear of the place to prevent any attempt at escape, while two others covered the front windows with their muskets. Dubourdieu shattered the door with a massive blow, and Audijos strode into the vestibule.

'Come forth and meet your fate, Labat,' he called. 'I am are here in the name of maître Legrange.'

There was a shuffling noise on the landing, and the white-faced notary appeared carrying a pistol unsteadily in his hand. He pointed the wavering weapon at Audijos, but the latter ignored it and leapt up the stairs, his sword before him. Labat's shot went wide, and the sword passed through his heart. He made a gurgling sound and fell to the floor. Downstairs there was a scream from the notary's wife. She and her sixteen-year-old son ran out by the back door, where they were shot down by Desbordes and Baillet. The killers returned to their horses, mounted, and road slowly out of the town.

'May God have mercy on us for shedding the blood of innocents beside that of the guilty,' said Labourde, who alone of the party seemed to shudder and sway in his saddle.

'We are embarked on a course of blood and terror,' Audijos responded sternly. 'God knows we do not want to kill lightly, yet if these people lived they might tell our enemies that we have Labat's papers. Our good master is avenged.'

24. Repression and Response

Colonel Podewiltz, commanding the regiment of the Dragons Etrangers at Bordeaux, was a veteran officer who well knew that problems of internal disorder required as much political *savoir faire* as the military skill he had demonstrated on foreign campaigns. His men were German speaking, most of them from Alsace. They were rough, merciless fellows, experienced in pillage and rapine. Well armed and well mounted, they wore cuirasses and took pride in the blue cloaks that distinguished the regiment. Podewiltz had already received orders from Pellot to send two companies to Chalosse and Tursan, but he learnt also from his military superior, the marquis de Saint-Luc, that the matter was still being debated in the royal council and final authority had not yet been given. Hence he temporised, and merely instructed his officers to prepare for a new mission in support of the gabeleurs. Late in June, Colbert prevailed over those ministers who supported Gramont, and the preliminary orders issued to Pellot were confirmed. The first detachment of the Dragons Etrangers, with Boisset's guards in their train, was to occupy Hagetmau and punish its rebellious inhabitants.

News of the approach of the dragoons reached Hagetmau several hours ahead of the column. Most of the local officials, Arnaud Dubourdieu among them, did not live in the town itself, and chose to remain absent. Robert Lacroix sent a messenger to Audijos in Coudures, and had the militia rouse out all able bodied citizens to build barricades and reinforce the gates. Their efforts were in vain. The dragoons rode into the town like a whirlwind, brushing aside the opposition and scattering the improvised defences. About a dozen defenders were killed, Lacroix among them. As the people of Hagetmau began to stream out of the eastern gates, the soldiers rampaged through the streets, burning and looting as they went.

Audijos and his band of thirty men arrived later that night, meeting the flood of refugees on the way. They waited until the dragoons and the gabeleurs had settled down for the night in their cantonments, and launched a series of hit and run attacks on the outposts of the invaders. Three soldiers and one of the guards of the bureau were killed in these assaults, and at dawn Audijos, knowing it would be folly to engage the enemy in pitched battle, withdrew his men to the woods. The second battle of Hagetmau was a victory for the gabelle.

In the days following the seizure of Hagetmau, the dragoons and the guards sent raiding parties into the countryside, confiscating livestock from village communities and threatening the châteaux of the seigneurs. Audijos and his men ambushed one such party in the hamlet of Horsarrieu, a mile or two north of Hagetmau, and shot three more dragoons. The invaders then marched on Doazit, but refrained from sacking the place when the inhabitants bought them off with money and the promise of supplies. Another troop occupied the château of the baron de Navailles-Banos at Dumes, and yet another destroyed the hamlet of Mus and took arms, foodstuffs and equipment from the château of Candale nearby. The seigneurs de Serres-Louts and de Montaut were arrested and held for interrogation, as were many humbler folk from disaffected parishes.

The old baron de Foix-Candale sent messages to Audijos reporting these indignities, but the raids occurred so swiftly that it was not possible to intercept their perpetrators. It seemed suspicious to the baron that most of the nobles who had been in his house when he had entertained Audijos were singled out for persecution, and he suspected that a subsequent visit to his bedridden son by the sieur de Prugues had provided the channel by which information had been sent to the gabeleurs. The raid on Candale itself, he suggested, had been intended to divert suspicion from his perfidious heir. In all this the old man seemed to take a perverse pleasure in dictating his reports to Audijos, despite the troubles that had descended on his house. But Audijos himself was too occupied with counter measures to pay much attention.

The intendant played a personal part in the next phase of the repression. Early in August he arrived in Mont-de-Marsan with two judges from the *parlement* of Bordeaux, two executioners, and a strong escort. From there his party moved to Saint-Sever, and then to Hagetmau itself. It was his intention to inflict summary justice on the prisoners he had taken, to extract what information he could by torture, and to direct operations against the Invisibles, as Audijos and his band had come to be called. The tribunal sentenced some of their victims to execution, others to the galleys. Most of those arrested had little or no connection with the Invisibles, so that rack and pincers did not elicit much information of use to the intendant. A number of victims who appeared to be more compliant were taken from village to village to identify further suspects. Where names were known, but their possessors had eluded capture, a bizarre ceremony was enacted in which the suspects were condemned and hanged in effigy. At Hagetmau gibbets bearing corpses and dummies lined the streets, but there were few to observe them apart from the garrison of dragoons. Most of the inhabitants had fled to Momuy to the south. As Pellot became aware that support for Audijos was more extensive than the reports of his informers had led him to believe, he called in more soldiers to occupy Grenade, Saint-Sever and Tartas.

Pellot wrote to Colbert to inform him of the measures he had taken:

'It is impossible to imagine a more open or outrageous rebellion than this one. The inhabitants of this place are the most to blame. They have been the authors of the whole disorder and they have excited others. There is evidence that the gentry were part of it.'

When he had returned to Mont-de-Marsan, the intendant sent a more detailed account on 20 August:

'There was a plot between the neighbouring parishes, and Hagetmau was its centre. Most of the gentry and persons of note in the town, including the officials, were resolved not to tolerate the bureau of the convoy and its guards anywhere in the neighbourhood, and to hunt them down wherever they were. They stirred up the peasants and canaille, and at their head were men experienced in bearing arms whom they call the Invisibles. If we had been able to

catch more of them, we should have made more extensive punishments, as the crime assuredly merited, but they all disappeared at my approach and at that of the troops.'

Meanwhile the Invisibles appeared from nowhere, ambushed guards and dragoons, and vanished into the forests. Audijos decided that the time had come to deal with local traitors. Père Lacourt was killed by a musket shot on the threshold of his vicarage in Coudures, and an attack was planned on the manor of the sieur de Prugues at Urgons. Prugues, however, had stationed sentries on all the approaches, and was warned in time to escape Audijos and his men. He sent messages to a troop of dragoons stationed at Grenade and to Boisset in Hagetmau, while he himself rode westwards to meet the captain of the guards. Audijos was not to be trapped so easily. Dubourdieu intercepted and killed the messenger to Grenade, and Audijos himself, finding Prugues' house deserted, sent three men to the ford across the Gabas, where they saw Prugues crossing the river in company with Boisset and sixteen guards. The party was shadowed by the Invisibles to the vicinity of Aubagnan, where Bernard had posted marksmen in the woods beside the road. Two of the guards fell in the encounter and a third was gravely wounded. The rest turned and galloped back to the ford, Prugues in the lead. Boisset slowly and regretfully followed his retreating men to the accompaniment of taunts from the undergrowth. Audijos prevented his band from firing at his former commander, but he could not stop their jeers.

Members of Boisset's command who had chosen to live in their native villages began to find that the hatred expressed towards them by local society now took the form of physical assaults. After one of the guards was killed in an affray of this kind, orders were issued for all the men of the gabelle to reside in the bureaux established in the towns. In Saint-Sever, the royal provost did little to inquire into the countless instances of violence throughout the sénéchaussée in which he was responsible for law and order. Nor was the investigation performed by his colleague, Louis de Barry, into the death of the curé of Coudures more than a pure formality, although he recorded some detail about the murder of Legrange and the death of his presumed assassin. As the conflicts between the Invisibles and the guards, the depredations of the soldiery, and the activities of Pellot's tribunal began to assume all the aspects of revolt and repression, normal procedures of law enforcement were superseded. The inhabitants of many villages fled into the woods and fields on the approach of the tribunal and the prisoners it brought in tow to identify suspects. The seigneur de Serres-Louts was one of those suffering the humiliation of being dragged in chains from place to place to name persons associated with the resistance. On the other hand, his friend Montaut was released for lack of evidence on the insistence of the two judges from Bordeaux. They were less scrupulous about accusations against lesser folk.

Coudures itself was occupied by a military detachment under command of lieutenant Labaume, who rode into the town with a bravura lacking on his previous visit. Jeanne-Marie watched his coming from a window of the Dubourdieu house, and was shocked to recognise two figures riding at the rear of the column. They were the sieur de Prugues and the châtelaine de Sèvres. Arnaud Dubourdieu was nearly as indignant as his daughter, but his customary prudence restrained his tongue when Labaume addressed a meeting of the notables of the community, telling them that Coudures was a nest of traitors, and that a curfew would be imposed,

Jeanne-Marie's immediate fear was for madame de Talazuc. With Patou at her heels she made her way to the house of Bernard's mother.

'Madame,' she said, 'you are in great danger of being arrested and held as a hostage. Come with me and I can show you a safe place of refuge where they cannot find you."

Madame de Talazuc might have stood upon her dignity, but the presence of the châtelaine in the town convinced her that her son's enemies would have little respect for her rank.

'I accept your offer, my child. I might find shelter with my relatives,' she replied, 'but even that is uncertain when these devils think nothing of pillaging the château of Candale. Yet consider yourself. You must be in equal peril, for there are many here who know of Bernard's affection for you.'

'This is true, madame. I fear that dreadful woman is herself aware of our love. Yet I think I can serve Bernard best if I remain in Coudures and discover all I can about the doings of the gabeleurs. I shall be on constant watch, and at the first sign of danger I shall join you in the secret place that Bernard has prepared. There is food and drink there, and a rough lodging.'

Madame de Talazuc packed a few necessities, instructed her maid to accompany her, and set off on foot for the woods beside the Gabas with Jeanne-Marie and the dog. The three women looked back from time to time to ensure they were not being followed. Jeanne-Marie carried in her bag the loaded pistol Baillet had given her at Hagetmau. Bernard had shown her the hidden paths to the hideaway. When she had made madame de Talazuc and her servant as comfortable as possible in the cave, she took her departure, leaving Patou as guard and companion.

As she was about to emerge from the forest about half a mile away, she heard the neighing of a horse, and, peering between the trees, saw a patrol of gabeleurs riding along the edge of the trees to her right. They were some distance off, and she felt it safe to take the path across the fields in the opposite direction. She was so intent upon the patrol that she was unaware of the two figures who were watching her.

'What a delightful coincidence,' said a familiar voice. It was the sieur de Prugues, and with him was the châtelaine.

Jeanne-Marie could see no means of escape. Prugues and his companion had been concealed in a grove of oaks that formed a kind of island in the open ground to her left. They were dismounted, holding the bridles of their horses, and she had no hope of outpacing them on foot.

'So, it is the demoiselle Dubourdieu,' said the châtelaine gloatingly to Prugues. 'I think you told me, monsieur, that she was unwilling to accept your amorous advances on an earlier occasion. Since there is no one here to disturb us, I should be interested to observe your technique in taking her by force. She looks ripe for the picking, and think what a juicy memento that would provide for my friend, monsieur d'Audijos.'

Prugues cast a lascivious glance at his victim, and ran his tongue over his thin lips.

'She is a wildcat but resistance heightens pleasure,' he lisped, drawing his dagger and moving towards her. Jeanne-Marie stepped back apprehensively, but Prugues was too quick for her. He lunged forward, seizing the front of her dress and ripping it to the waist.

'A good beginning,' commented the châtelaine. But neither she nor her companion were prepared for what followed. Jeanne-Marie swung the bag containing the pistol at the face of her attacker, breaking his nose with an effusion of blood. Prugues screamed and dropped his dagger, which Jeanne-Marie picked up and plunged into his stomach. As he fell she darted past the châtelaine, grabbed the reins of one of the horses, and vaulted into the saddle.

'Adieu, madame,' Jeanne-Marie called, as she dug her heels into her mount and galloped off in a cloud of dust that slowly descended on the châtelaine and her dying escort. The vengeance of Audijos was completed.

25. Mission to Béarn

The campaign of the Invisibles had now reached such an intensity that they remained united in two bands of thirty men, and no longer rode from village to village gathering their forces as circumstances dictated. The garrisons established by the dragoons and the guards had been augmented by companies of infantry, but they preferred to conduct their raids and patrols separately since it had become clear that the Invisibles were targeting the gabeleurs rather than the other formations. Although they did not co-ordinate their attacks with any precision, Pellot's troops followed an identical pattern of living off the countryside and inflicting maximum suffering on the populace. This policy served only to unite the forces of resistance, and the Invisibles were provided with an early warning system that enabled them to intercept their enemies more effectively.

Audijos had handed over command to Roger Dubourdieu and taken the road for Pau in fulfilment of Legrange's dying injunction to have président de Gassion proclaim the charter of Chalosse. The notoriety that the decree of outlawry had brought upon his name had made Bernard a grimmer and more determined man than the young cavalry officer who had blended idealism with adventure. He had no illusions about the strength of the forces Pellot had arrayed against him, but he also knew how strong was the sentiment in his favour throughout the provinces bordering the Pyrenees. Apart from the difficulty of co-ordinating his attacks against the gabeleurs and the soldiery, he worried about the suffering that reaction to his campaign had imposed on the countryside and, more particularly, about the safety of those he loved. He had less confidence than his late mentor in the ability of the law to defend local privileges against the power of the intendant, but as he rode through Béarn he managed to convince himself that his mission to the *parlement* of Pau might somehow lead to royal acknowledgement of the injustice of the gabelle in the lands of the south.

It seemed his arrival in Pau was not unexpected, for he had no sooner settled himself into an inn when a servant of the vicomte de Poudenx brought him a message from his master.

'We all know of your deeds, monsieur,' said the man, 'but the vicomte cannot compromise himself by receiving you publicly. He asked me to tell you that he will be waiting in the stables of the château at nine this evening.'

Poudenx stepped out of the shadows as Bernard arrived at the stable gate.

'It is a sad consequence of these troubling times, cousin,' he said 'that I have to conceal any contact with you. When we last met at Momuy and Navailles, you were the proud escort of two great ladies, and now you are an outlaw, fighting against the soldiers of the king.'

'It is not against His Majesty that I have taken arms, my lord, but against the imposition of the gabelle in violation of our just rights.'

'It is a distinction that monsieur Pellot and others of his kind do not recognise,' returned Poudenx. 'As for me, I know you have a good cause, and one which I shall put before the estates of Béarn. But I am also the faithful subject of the king, and things have reached such a pitch that I would not be immune from prosecution if it were known that I have been consorting with a rebel. The intendant has little regard for rank and status when he meets opposition to what he considers the king's service.'

'I understand,' said Audijos, 'and those who follow me appreciate whatever support you can give us. It cannot be open aid – that I know, for you have lands in Chalosse as well as in Béarn. It is my mission to seek out président de Gassion and ask him to proclaim through the *parlement* the old charter that would render Chalosse as privileged as Béarn.'

'I wish you good fortune, but you must remember that the judges who wear the long robe have to tread as fine a line as those of us who live by the sword. Pellot has no jurisdiction here, but His Majesty is sovereign in Béarn through his inheritance from his grandfather, the good king Henri, and I doubt if those who advise him would accept new restrictions on the royal power. We in the estates believe our resolutions are more effective than the decrees of the law courts. Even so, there is a new spirit in the royal council since the late cardinal de Richelieu made the law equivalent to the will of the king. The best we can do in the estates is to bargain with the king's commissioners, and that counts for something, since we still have the power of the purse.

'But His Majesty swore to preserve the privileges of these lands when he was in Bayonne.'

'True, but promises are evaded for reasons of state.'

'There is one other thing I should like to ask of you, my lord,' said Audijos. 'We are being hard pressed in Chalosse, and I have thought that we may have to seek refuge in Béarn.'

'I can give you no authority to cross the frontier, but I can tell you unofficially that the people of Béarn will give you shelter. I hope it will not come to that. I fear that your presence here may lead the king to invade the province, as his father did when he reimposed the Catholic religion forty-four years ago. In those days Louis XIII also swore to protect our traditions, but many of us know such oaths to be empty formalities. Because of my office I myself may have to act against you as an outlaw. Now go, before my meeting with you is discovered.'

Audijos derived little comfort from this political discussion. At best he could hope for covert support from the pragmatic Poudenx. He felt even less confident of a favourable response from Gassion, and his forebodings were borne out by what followed. The judge at first did not answer the note Bernard had passed to him as he emerged next day from the *parlement*, and he took even more elaborate precautions than Poudenx had done to conceal their interview. He was led from the inn by a law clerk to a deserted dwelling on the outskirts of the city where the président awaited him. He was a large, bald-headed man with a pompous demeanour, who paused between his words with his head on one side, as if he expected his audience to value each one of them in gold.

'You had no – uh – right, monsieur,' he said, 'to accost me in a public – um – place. What if someone had – uh – recognised you? I have my reputation as both président and marquis de Gassion to

Mission to Béarn

consider. I have agreed to your – uh – demand to see me only because of my respect for your late – er – mentor, maître Legrange, who was my friend at the university of Toulouse.'

Bernard's heart sank as he confronted the man before him, who looked for all the world like a raven contemplating some glittering object with a greedy but uncertain eye.

'I regret to have embarrassed you, my lord,' he said,' but I could find no other way to fulfil my dear master's last request. He brought you, I believe, the only known original of the *for* of Chalosse.'

'It may be that – perhaps – I have the document.'

'Did he not say to you that it should be registered and proclaimed in the full chamber of the *parlement* when the time was ripe? That time has now come.'

'My dear young man,' said Gassion. 'We must not be – er – too hasty. Do you not realise that this is Béarn? In Chalosse the *parlement* of Bordeaux, not that of – um – Pau, has superior jurisdiction. In any case I represent the law, and you have chosen the path of bloodshed and rebellion. Do you ask me to serve the cause of an outlaw?'

'My lord,' replied Audijos. 'The cause is just, and is not the law to give justice? The judges of Bordeaux are unfavourably disposed to this matter. At this moment two of them serve the intendant in condemning innocent souls. Besides, when the charter was granted Chalosse and Béarn were under the same jurisdiction, or so, at least maître Legrange informed me.'

'Do you dare to dispute with me, the président, as if you were –um – some unruly young advocate at the bar?'

'I crave your indulgence, my lord. Surely the gabelle is of concern to us all. Did not the *parlement* of Pau authorise the guarding of the salt convoys within the province, and is not the salt of Béarn of profit to some of the greatest in this land?'

Gassion reddened at this allusion to his own interest, and Audijos realised he had made a tactical mistake.

'Here,' said the judge, casting his mannerism aside in his anger. 'Take your charter, and find someone else to back your ill-advised revolt.' He took a scroll from the pocket of his cloak and thrust it into Bernard's hands. Turning on his heel, he strode out of the room.

On the following morning Audijos rode out of Pau on the road to Orthez. His mood was grim, but he carried the *for* of Chalosse in his saddlebag and he still hoped that somewhere there must be a legal authority who would recognise the significance of the document. In any event he was determined to continue the campaign against the gabelle. At Orthez he was received in such a fashion as to lighten his spirits and strengthen his resolve. He was known almost as soon as he entered the old walled city he had last visited in company with the duchesse de Navailles and madame de Motteville. The notables of the place gathered to acclaim him and to promise their support. Some of the local gentry even asked to join the Invisibles, and others undertook to shelter his men if they were obliged to seek refuge south of the Chalosse border.

Fortified by these assurances Bernard set out on the road to Sault-de-Navailles, where he had arranged to meet Dubourdieu and the main band of Invisibles in the woods north of the village. The news that awaited him there was disquieting. Desbordes and Labourde had been captured when reconnoitring the activities of a group of gabeleurs near the hamlet of Morganx, and taken to Hagetmau, where they had been condemned to be broken on the wheel as an example to the inhabitants. There had been an action on the Adour at Toulouzette thirty miles northwards, where a salt convoy had been virtually destroyed by a force under Bernard's old antagonist, lieutenant Nogent.

Most alarming of all, the châtelaine had reported the death of Prugues as an unprovoked assassination by Jeanne-Marie, and a massive inquiry had been launched from Saint-Sever to bring her to justice. So far the elaborate hiding place near Coudures had not been discovered, and Jeanne-Marie and madame de Talazuc were safely ensconced there with Corade and three of the Invisibles watching all the approaches. But in Saint-Sever itself Borrit, the royal provost, and Barry, the lieutenant civil et criminel, had dared to question the châtelaine's account, and had promptly been suspended from their offices and arrested by the personal order of the intendant. Nearby, lieutenant Labaume had tightened his grip on Coudures, and his men, when not pillaging and burning the houses of suspected supporters of the Invisibles, were scouting the environs in search of Jeanne-Marie. Audijos began to feel that the tide was turning against him.

26. Execution at Hagetmau

Since the death of Prugues, the châtelaine had adopted Labaume as her regular escort, and, to the scandal of Arnaud Dubourdieu and other notables in Coudures, had moved into the house where the lieutenant had established his headquarters. Soon after he had ordered the arrest of Borrit and Barry, Pellot summoned madame de Sèvres, together with Labaume, Boisset and Nogent, to a council of war at Saint-Sever. He did not on this occasion include the higher commanders of the military forces, for he was aware of the friction between them and the guards of the bureau, and wished to confine the meeting to those closely in touch with the gabeleurs. Since he made it his business to know as much as possible about the personal affairs of his agents as well as those of his enemies, he was aware of the new liaison between Labaume and the châtelaine. While his puritanical soul was revolted by the promiscuous habits of the latter, he knew their value to his cause, and he did not imagine for a moment that her seduction of Labaume would inhibit her from using her charms in other directions should it prove necessary.

There were tensions within the room as soon as the meeting began. The gallant Boisset and the saturnine Nogent viewed each other with a suspicion based on the rivalry of their former regiments and the incidents at Saint-Jean-d'Angély and the road to Saint-Jean-de-Luz. Neither of them was prepared for the presence of the châtelaine, although they knew of her dubious reputation and her role as a spy for the gabelle. Boisset had met madame de Sèvres briefly at the time when Audijos was appointed to command the escort of the duchesse de Navailles, but he could place no trust in a woman who scorned the moral code he had been brought up to respect. Labaume, whose unimaginative dedication to the suppression of the movement against the gabelle had known wider horizons since his passions had been roused by the châtelaine, felt an instinctive jealousy for the two other officers. Madame de Sèvres herself felt a disinterested amusement in the presence of four men whose attitudes differed so widely.

The intendant made some brief introductions and came straight to the point.

'We are here,' he said, 'to appraise our success in imposing the gabelle and crushing the resistance. Thanks to the dragoons you are again in control of Hagetmau, captain Boisset, and you, lieutenant Nogent, have set an example in destroying a salt train at Toulouzette, but you, monsieur Labaume, have yet to bring to book the criminals who destroyed our network at Coudures. We have terrorised the countryside, and yet the gentry and common people still support these rebels who hide in the forests and ambush our men.'

'What news do we have of the outlaw Audijos and his plans, madame?' asked Nogent, looking at the châtelaine. 'I understand from monsieur Pellot that it is you who collect the news our informers provide.'

'We have a source in the château of Candale,' replied madame de Sèvres. 'Before his murder, the sieur de Prugues acquired some information from the baron's son, which has enabled us to arrest the two traitors at Saint-Sever, Barry and Borrit. They were plotting sedition with Audijos at the gathering convened by the old baron.'

'We shall make a public example of them as royal officers who consorted with a rebel and refused to bring the assassin of monsieur de Prugues to justice,' said Pellot.

'What is more,' the châtelaine continued, 'we had a spy follow the schoolmaster Legrange, who before his death was some kind of mentor to Audijos, when he went to Pau to deliver the supposed charter of liberties they hold so dear to président de Gassion of the *parlement*. We have reason to believe that Audijos himself was in Pau in an endeavour to have the charter proclaimed, but the président refused him aid, or so he has informed us. Moreover, he intimated that the outlaw was granted an interview by the vicomte de Poudenx.'

'It is unfortunate,' Pellot interjected, 'that those who wield great influence in Béarn should be so misguided as to sympathise with rebels. We must tread warily in such cases and persuade His

Majesty to bring the great lords to heel by his direct command. With the authority of the king there is nothing we cannot do. Consider what we have done in the lands of the duc de Gramont – although I hear from monsieur Colbert that the duke is moving heaven and earth to have the troops withdrawn from Hagetmau.'

'Surely that is his lordship's privilege,' said Boisset, who was feeling increasingly uneasy with the direction of the conversation. The intendant gave him a piercing glance, but said nothing.

'Is it not true,' asked Labaume, 'that we have arrested two of the followers of Audijos at Morganx? Why not execute them in the square at Hagetmau, and demonstrate to all who is in control?'

'Good!' said Pellot. 'They shall be broken on the wheel.'

'Yes,' said the châtelaine. 'If we make it widely known that they are to be publicly executed, we can set a trap for Audijos, for he may well attempt a rescue.'

'Better and better!' Pellot commented. 'But let us look to a wider strategy. Let us arrange with the dragoons and infantry to block the roads with outposts and see if we can fence in these so-called Invisibles. You, Nogent, must arrange to occupy Navailles and stop their escape by the road south to Orthez and Salies. We know that Audijos has been well received in those parts and may seek shelter across the border there.'

The discussion moved to other detailed dispositions, and the châtelaine, who began to be bored by the conversation, begged leave to withdraw. She resolved to ask the intendant on a later occasion to have the search for Jeanne-Marie intensified, for she had little confidence in the measures Labaume was taking. Nogent and Labaume were filled with surprise and admiration at the role the châtelaine performed in these matters. Boisset, on the other hand, felt more and more uncomfortable, and realised that he must conceal his disquiet if he were not to excite Pellot's suspicion of his loyalty.

Meanwhile Audijos and the inner circle of the Invisibles made their way secretly to the hideout in the woods by the Gabas. His mood was dour, although he responded in lighter vein to the greeting he received from his mother, Jeanne-Marie and Patou. There had been news from Cambo Jatxou in Bayonne, where the movement in support of Audijos was gathering strength. It was agreed that Duplantier should return to the port to see if he could gain further support in the Basque lands to the south. Bernard saw that the odds were stacked against his little band in Chalosse, and envisaged a grand union of the forces of discontent in Labourd, Béarn and Bigorre. Roger Dubourdieu, on the other hand, wanted to increase the attacks of the Invisibles on the occupying forces. They were agreed, however, that their first priority was to rescue Desbordes and Labourde.

When the news came through, a few days later, of the intended execution of the prisoners at Hagetmau, Audijos was ready with his plan. He foresaw that the town square would be heavily guarded, and that any attempt to attack the place in full strength would result in the death of most of his comrades. His best hope was to enter the town disguised with two or three men among a crowd of townspeople returning from Momuy, where most of them had taken refuge after the occupation by the dragoons and Boisset's guards. To do this imposed high risks, because he had to persuade the refugees to move, and he could not tell so many that they were acting as a cover in the rescue without the danger of some informer betraying the attempt. After long discussion it was resolved to trust the loyalty of the people. Baillet and Corade were to accompany Audijos. Dubourdieu, who resented not being included in the rescue party, was to bring a band of thirty Invisibles to the woods where they had sheltered before their first attack on Hagetmau, and provide defence in the event of pursuit. Roger was only persuaded to accept this secondary role after being convinced that no disguise, short of shaving his mustachios, would adequately conceal his identity. In any case, Bernard had reasoned, someone had to take over command if he were to fall in the course of the enterprise. As to the mechanics of the actual rescue, that would depend on the reconnaissance Audijos would undertake once he had entered the town.

It was a grey day in mid-October when a hundred or so of the inhabitants of Hagetmau and some peasants from the environs set out on the road from Momuy. There had been instant enthusiasm when the word was spread that the sieur d'Audijos had asked them to aid his plan. With some misgivings, women and children formed part of the motley throng to convince the guards that this was indeed a return to their homes on the part of the townspeople who pretended no longer to fear for their safety. With the permission of Poudenx's bailiff a market had been established in Momuy to replace the one that had been closed down in Hagetmau. It was the time of the harvest, and some of the better-off peasants from the area brought grain, hay and vegetables, as well as assorted livestock, with the intention of selling their produce to the occupying troops. One enthusiastic supporter offered Audijos a cartload of apples, and insisted that his family ride on the lumbering vehicle beside him. He knelt before Bernard, saying, 'Lord, you are the saviour of the poor, and we would place our lives in your hands to serve you.'

Bernard was more than a little embarrassed by this show of devotion and raised the man to his feet.

'This is a common cause for us all,' he said. 'We are all equal before God, yet He would not have you endanger those dearest to you.' Eventually he yielded to the man's insistence, and, disguising himself as a peasant woman, sat beside the peasant's wife and child among the barrels of apples on the back of the cart. Beneath it were strapped an array of weapons wrapped in sacking. Baillet and Corade followed the vehicle, decked out respectively as a nun and a friar.

A patrol of dragoons halted the procession a mile south of Hagetmau. Upon learning of the crowd's intention, their commander gave leave for them to proceed, and sent one of his men back to warn the garrison. As they approached the town the returning inhabitants were met by a detachment of Boisset's guards, who searched them individually for weapons and examined the produce carts.

'You have arrived just in time to witness the death of two of the bandits who follow Audijos,' said one of the gabeleurs to the driver of Bernard's cart. 'At noon tomorrow they are to be stretched till their bones crack – a pretty spectacle for you all!'

'We shall be there,' replied the driver. 'Perhaps you would care to buy some of my fine apples.'

Glancing carelessly at Audijos and the peasant's wife and child, the guard moved to the rear of the cart, and tipped one of the barrels into the dust.

'No weapons there,' he remarked. 'We shall keep this lot as the price of your entry. Pass on. You,' he said to Baillet and Corade, 'set up the barrel by the road and put the apples back in it.'

'I am a man of the cloth, ' returned Corade, hiding his face in his cowl. 'This is no fit work for a servant of God.'

'Get to it,' said the guard, 'or we will strip your doxy as well as yourself to see if you carry arms beneath your robes.'

'Holy Mother,' shrilled Baillet in a high-pitched voice, 'protect me from these ruffians.'

Happy to escape the search, the pretended friar and nun complied with the order, and then followed the applecart into the town. They made their way to the inn where they had met before the siege of the strongpoint, and found the innkeeper in occupation. Still in the guise of a peasant woman, Audijos set out to inspect the intended scene of execution and to locate the place where Desbordes and Labourde were imprisoned. Baillet and Corade shed their disguises and took the weapons into the house.

'This is no work for a friar either,' said Baillet, 'but you fit the part well.'

The muscular ex-friar looked at his slim, smooth-complexioned companion.

'And you, sister,' he said, 'display more charms in your habit than you do as a man.'

Audijos returned two hours later. 'If I have to traipse another yard in these confounded skirts,' he said, throwing off his woman's cap and peasant dress and unstrapping the padding beneath it, 'I shall put a curse on womankind. But it has served me well. I passed the good captain Boisset in the street, and he failed to recognise me.'

'It is as well you did not share the scruples of monsieur Dubourdieu about your moustache,' said Baillet. 'But what news is there?'

'The worst,' replied Bernard. 'Our friends are held in the town hall with twenty dragoons around them, and from the gossip I heard in the street they have been so badly tortured that I doubt if they can walk. There are barricades to hold back the crowd in the square where two engines of death have been erected on a platform, and I am sure the place will be guarded by a full company of soldiers on the morrow.'

Once again the innkeeper had a suggestion.

'I have a friend,' he said, 'who has rooms at the top of a house overlooking the square, and it is within range of the scaffold.'

Day was beginning to break on the following morning as Audijos, Baillet and Corade made their way towards the town square with their weapons concealed in bundles of faggots. No one challenged them, and they found the innkeeper's friend waiting at the door of his lodging house. He led the three men to the upper storey, packed his few belongings, and hurriedly left the place.

'He is a man of prudence,' remarked Bernard as he and his supporters loaded their muskets and checked their lines of sight. 'May we escape as easily after this day's work.'

By midday a sullen crowd was massed behind the barricades, while a phalanx of dragoons and guards surrounded the scaffold. A lieutenant of dragoons checked the disposal of his men, and watched the movement of the crowd from the platform. Beside him captain Boisset, whose expression suggested an extreme distaste for the proceedings, sent patrols of guards through the mass of people, who hissed and jeered as they approached but stood hastily aside to let them through lest they receive the butt of a musket in the face. Other guards and soldiers blocked the streets and alleys that fed into the square, and one of these detachments returned to the town hall escorting a cavalier whose jaded horse indicated that he had ridden hard to reach the place.

The new arrival mounted the scaffold and had a few words with Boisset. The crowd hushed and waited expectantly, hoping for a reprieve for the prisoners.

'Good people of Hagetmau,' the officer shouted, 'I bring news from your lord and master, the noble duc de Gramont. He wishes it to be known that His Majesty the king has graciously restored to him full jurisdiction over his fief of Hagetmau in the countship of Louvigny. The troops and the agents of the bureau are shortly to be withdrawn.' These words were greeted with mild applause, but the conclusion of the speech was the reverse of what the populace hoped for. 'Our noble duke has also proclaimed,' the officer continued, 'that he condemns the outlaw Audijos, and orders his pursuit and arrest, dead or alive.'

There was a sudden silence. Then someone shouted: 'Vive d'Audijos! Death to the gabeleurs!'

'It is our friend, the driver of the applecart,' said Corade to Audijos, whose keen eyes had also picked out the man from their vantage point above the square.

'Yes,' said Baillet, 'our noble duke has evidently struck a bargain with the king to recover his rights at our expense.'

A group of guards were trying to force their way through the throng to apprehend the author of the seditious cry, but now the crowd, disregarding threats and blows, closed ranks to impede their progress.

'See,' said Bernard, 'he has escaped and has circled behind them to hide in a house on the west side.'

This diversion was forgotten as two executioners, masked in black, dragged Desbordes and Labourde on to the scaffold. Both men seemed more dead than alive after their suffering. Desbordes, the rabble-rouser, had had his tongue cut out; Labourde, the clerk who had rifled Labat's papers, had had his right hand amputated, and blood still dripped from the bandaged stump. The executioners bound them to the two circular machines as the crowd groaned in unison. Gramont's emissary looked aghast at these proceedings, and retired precipitantly into the town hall. A priest stepped forward to offer the victims the last rites, but both men seemed to have lapsed into unconsciousness. The executioners laid hold of the levers on the machines that would stretch the bodies of the unfortunates to breaking point.

'Now!' said Audijos. He aimed the first of the two muskets he had prepared at Desbordes, and the bullet hit him in the temple. The second shot killed Labourde in like fashion. Corade and Baillet were less skilful, but their shots struck the bodies of the executioners and sent them writhing in pain to the floor of the scaffold. There was a moment of profound silence and then a swelling tumult rose from the crowd: 'Vive d'Audijos! Vive d'Audijos.'

Boisset drew his sword and led a dozen guards towards the house from whence the shots had come. The lieutenant of dragoons sent those of his men who were surrounding the scaffold to find their horses and block all escape routes from the town. Audijos and his two supporters had flung aside their fusils as soon as they saw their purpose had been accomplished, and had bounded down the stairs to the back entrance to the house well before their pursuers reached it. They ran through the maze of back alleys, and attained the strongpoint on the western boundary of Hagetmau without being intercepted. They lay concealed in the cellar for several hours until the hue and cry had died down. When night fell they entered the tunnel that would take them beyond the city walls. They emerged with caution, but were only a few paces from the mouth of the tunnel when they heard a familiar voice.

'I was expecting you, gentlemen,' said captain Boisset, stepping out from some broken fortifications. 'Allow me to return a favour. I have tethered two horses beyond the embankment on your left.'

'You are a brave and gallant man, my captain,' replied Bernard. 'I should have guessed that you would have anticipated our plan of escape. We thank you for your courtesy, and trust you have not compromised your future by your generous action.'

'I have no stomach for this business,' said Boisset. 'The cause I serve and the riffraff I command fill me with disgust, but I must fulfil my duty. Get you gone. Pray God we do not have to cross swords again!'

Out of the corner of his eye Audijos sensed a shadowy form moving between some bushes on the bank, but when he looked more intently he could discern nothing.

'Such is also my hope,' he said, 'but beware of Pellot's spies. I trust you have not been followed. Again, my thanks. Adieu.'

The three men mounted the horses, Baillet riding pillion behind Corade. Within an hour they were reunited with Dubourdieu and his band waiting in the woods. They encountered a patrol of dragoons on the road to Sainte-Colombe and Coudures, but the soldiers, seeing the Invisibles were in force, turned their horses and rode off in the direction of Horsarrieu.

27. Death of A Gallant Man

News of the latest exploit of the Invisibles reached the intendant while he was still in Mont-de-Marsan. His immediate reaction was to summon madame de Sèvres and Labaume. The châtelaine brought with her disturbing information about captain Boisset that increased Pellot's wrath at the events in Hagetmau and the order obtained by Gramont for the evacuation of his forces in the town.

'I fancy our good captain has betrayed us,' the châtelaine remarked. 'One of my spies reported that Boisset actually aided the escape of Audijos after he interrupted the public execution of our victims.'

'The devil looks after his own,' responded Pellot with a scowl. 'We had hoped to strike terror into the hearts of the canaille who inhabit the place, and instead we provoked a popular demonstration in favour of that vile rebel. What is more, the people will assume that the king has two minds about our mission after his order in favour of the noble duke. I doubt if the message brought by his emissary for the pursuit of Audijos will be taken seriously. As for that traitor Boisset, we shall string him up by his heels. He has been privy to our plans and has doubtless disclosed them to his former lieutenant.'

'I doubt that, monsieur. Boisset lives by a code of honour. He is unlikely to have passed our secrets to the rebels, despite his friendship for Audijos. I think it probable that he was repaying a debt. You will remember that his escape from the strongpoint at Saint-Girons was little short of miraculous.'

'Perhaps, madame, but in any case we shall make an example of him. We need to frighten the gentry of Chalosse as well as the peasants and townsfolk. Besides, the judges from Bordeaux on my tribunal are showing some hesitation in punishing the seigneurs, and this is so clear a case they cannot refuse to condemn him.'

'I have a better plan,' said the châtelaine. 'You can use the provost and the lieutenant-criminel of Saint-Sever for that purpose. What if we have Boisset assassinated in circumstances that make Audijos appear responsible? The killing can be staged as one that no gentleman would perpetrate against an officer under whom he had served. This could destroy the illusions the local gentry hold about our friend.'

A light gleamed in the sunken eyes of the intendant.

'As always, madame, you are one step ahead of me in your devisings, but whom can we trust for such a task?'

'Leave that to me, monsieur Pellot. It will give me pleasure to find a suitably grisly end for the good captain. Lieutenant Labaume and I shall ride at once to Hagetmau.'

'So be it, madame,' returned Pellot, rising from his chair and contorting his hunched body in the semblance of a bow.

After the reunion of the Invisibles in their secret rendezvous beside the Gabas, a council of war was held to determine their future action. They had sustained several casualties in their battles with the guards and the dragoons, but none had affected them as much as the death of Desbordes and Labourde.

'We failed in our attempt at rescue and had no other choice but to end their suffering,' said Bernard. 'They have died for our cause, and many of us will follow them if we do not change our strategy. Our enemies are closing in on us, and if we remain here in force our hiding places will be discovered - especially this one.' He looked beyond the circle of his lieutenants towards the mouth of the cave, where his mother and Jeanne-Marie were sitting beside a fire.

'You may be right,' said Roger Dubourdieu. 'It is clear that there is not a village in Chalosse that does not support us, but every time they give us shelter they are exposed to the retribution of Pellot and the gabeleurs. By the bones of Christ I could wish our struggle did not fill the gibbets with rotting corpses of the innocent and man the king's galleys with oarsmen whose only crime was to cry 'Vive d'Audijos.'

'There is also support for us in Bayonne,' added Audijos,' as there is in Béarn and Bigorre, where the writ of the intendant does not run. We should spread the fight and at the same time recoup our losses. The leaves are beginning to fall, and the forests of Chalosse no longer afford the concealment we need. It is time to move to the south where we can go more openly.'

'But you have said,' Corade put in,' that the vicomte de Poudenx warned you that to cross into the privileged provinces might result in their invasion by the armies of the king.'

'Why not come to Bayonne?' asked Duplantier. 'There are many there who would welcome you, and the province of Labourd is as good a base as any.'

'You must return there,' Audijos replied. 'The day may come when we shall need to mobilise the Basque people, and in Carla Baroja you have someone who commands powers that may stand us in good stead. But in the immediate future our best prospect lies in Orthez. The town lies close to the border and we can strike northward against the gabeleurs as the need arises. The sympathies of the vicomte de Poudenx are with us, and it seems that the duc de Gramont is regaining enough influence at court to defend the liberties of Béarn. Who knows, we may yet persuade the *parlement* of Pau to proclaim the ancient charter of Chalosse.'

So it was decided that the Invisibles should ride south. The only objection to this plan came from Jeanne-Marie, who feared a long separation from Bernard.

'If you must go, let me and Patou accompany you,' she begged. 'I can ride and shoot as well as any of your men.'

'I wish it could be so, my love,' said Bernard, 'but someone must attend my mother, and I shall leave three or four of our company here to guard you both and to act as couriers. We shall also lead the gabeleurs to think that you and my mother have gone to her relatives in Foix. The town farrier is one of the spies on Labat's list, and I shall see that this false news gets to him.'

'Think also of the dog, sister,' added Dubourdieu. 'If he accompanies us half the province will say that there rides Audijos. Here he is the best of sentinels: there he is a target for the musketry of our enemies.'

'The mare shall stay with you too,' said Bernard to Jeanne-Marie. 'She is Patou's companion and has seen enough danger.'

On the following day Duplantier set off for Bayonne, and Audijos, bidding farewell to those who were dearest to him, took a circuitous route to Béarn, avoiding the checkposts Nogent had established on the principal roads. With him went fifteen of the Invisibles, the rest having dispersed to various safe havens in the forests. Baillet stayed with three men in the hideaway by the Gabas and Corade was despatched to Lavedan with a message to the archpriest of Juncalas informing him of their plans.

While Audijos rode south Labaume and the châtelaine had arrived in Hagetmau and sent word to Boisset that they had new instructions from the intendant. They agreed to meet next morning after mass in the church of Saint-Girons on the western side of the town. The captain did not see madame de Sèvres during the service, and found her waiting for him alone as he emerged. He was expecting her to convey the sternest of reproaches from Pellot, but she appeared to be in a gay and insouciant mood.

'I am delighted to see you, monsieur,' she said with a smile. 'I yearn to get to know you better, for I can see you are a gallant man who would indulge my foolish whims. Let us walk together to the strongpoint you defended so well. I have heard that you and your men escaped by a secret tunnel, and I wish to see the place.'

'It is only a few steps from here,' Boisset replied with some embarrassment. 'But I thought you had come to tell me of the intendant's displeasure at the fiasco of the public execution.'

'Come, we have more pleasant things to discuss,' she said, taking his arm seductively.

'Is not lieutenant Labaume escorting you?'

'He is such a dull fellow. I much prefer your company. I left him to attend to the re-shoeing of one of the horses.'

As they strolled towards the embankment near the exit from the tunnel, Boisset's natural suspicion of his companion disappeared.

'What a splendid sword you have, captain,' said the châtelaine. 'I warrant few weapons have seen such service for His Majesty. May I see the blade?'

Boisset drew the sword from its scabbard and proffered the hilt, and the châtelaine stepped back, pretending to admire it. At the same moment the massive frame of Labaume emerged silently from a pile of masonry in the rear of his victim, a rope in his hands. Before Boisset could turn Labaume twisted it in a stranglehold round the captain's neck while the châtelaine held the point of the sword to his stomach.

'Such are the instructions Monsieur Pellot provides for a traitor,' she said savagely.

'Have done with it! Run him through,' said Labaume hoarsely.

'Not so fast! We keep to our plan. Did you bring the axe?'

'I – I cannot do this to a fellow officer,' Labaume stammered.

'Do it, or you lose my favours for ever,' came the merciless rejoinder.

Boisset was choking helplessly, and Labaume stunned him with a blow to the back of the neck. Then, retrieving an axe he had left in his former place of concealment, the lieutenant decapitated his prey.

'And now the notice,' cried the châtelaine.

Labaume produced a placard and pinned it to a tree beside the bloody corpse with Boisset's sword. 'Mort aux gabeleurs - Bernard d'Audijos,' it read.

The intendant had moved east to Agen on the river Garonne, but remained closely in touch with events in Chalosse. On 31 October he sent an account of the murder of Boisset to Colbert, asserting that the captain had been set upon by Audijos and his band:

'There were twenty or twenty-five of them, with Audijos at their head. As to the murdered man, he did not amount to much, and he twice failed to capture Audijos through his lack of enterprise and resolution. I had reproached him severely on several occasions, and had come to the conclusion that he would have to be cashiered.'

The Invisibles were warmly welcomed in Orthez, although some of the town notables began to have second thoughts when Audijos and his men began to conduct raids against Nogent's border outposts in the weeks that followed. They were more determined than ever to strike against their enemies when they received the news that Boisset had been cruelly put to death, and Audijos was held responsible.

'He was a gallant man and a worthy foe,' said Roger Dubourdieu. 'God rest his soul.'

'Yes,' added Bernard, 'and there are reports that that woman and her paramour, Labaume, were in Hagetmau at the time. It is another score we have to settle.'

Near the end of 1664, reports came in of more looting and rapine by the dragoons and gabeleurs in seigneurial manors in Chalosse, and early in the new year it was learnt that Pierre de Borrit, the royal provost at Saint-Sever, had been hanged for aiding and abetting the rebels. To Pellot's chagrin, his tribunal found the case against Borrit's colleague, Louis de Barry, less damning, and merely sentenced him to imprisonment. In face of Pellot's campaign against the local nobility Poudenx sent a secret message to Audijos telling him that he must cease to operate from Béarn.

Soon afterwards the vicomte's fears were realised. The king authorised Pellot to extend his operations into Béarn, and Colbert's colleague, the minister for war Louvois, sent word to the military commander in Guienne, lieutenant-général de Saint-Luc, that reinforcements were being sent in preparation for the march of a royal army into the southern provinces. Audijos heard of these measures from Duplantier in Bayonne, where the news had been received from the Bayonnais agent at court, David de Cheverry. The Invisibles left Béarn for Bigorre and the mountains of Lavedan.

28. The Revolt of the Mountain Men

At the royal court the maréchal-duc de Gramont had an unexpected visit from madame de Motteville.

'I have heard, monseigneur,' she said, 'that you have obtained an order from His Majesty for the withdrawal of the soldiers from your lands, but in exchange you have had to order the pursuit of Audijos. It happens that I know the young man and I wish to speak on his behalf.'

'Alas, madame,' Gramont replied, 'it is only my barony of Hagetmau that has been freed from the pillage of the dragoons and the gabeleurs. Saint-Sever and Coudures and the surrounding area are still occupied, and the king has now ordered his armies to invade Béarn and Bigorre. As to this fellow Audijos, I am told that all Chalosse and Béarn support him - gentry, townsfolk and the common people - but he has been proclaimed an outlaw and a rebel against the authority of His Majesty.'

'If only monsieur Colbert could be persuaded to withdraw the gabelle from the privileged lands and restore them to their former state. Then, perhaps, we might seek a pardon for monsieur d'Audijos, who is a gallant and resourceful man, as he showed when he escorted the duchesse de Navailles and myself on our journey in the Pyrenees.'

'I fear, madame, that Colbert is immovable on any issue that affects the finances of the kingdom. He coldly repulses those who seek favours from him. Not for nothing do they call him "the north wind." '

'Yes, but it seems the inflexibility of the minister and his agent, Claude Pellot, is converting the actions of Audijos and his band into a civil war where the nobility of the south defy the royal authority.'

'It will not come to that, madame. True, the marquis de Louvois seems willing to lend the royal troops to Colbert's campaign, but we who command the loyalty of the seigneurs and have the king's other ear can exert some counter-influence. I have some sympathy for this Audijos and I defend the privileges of the provinces in which my lands lie, but I have to play the courtier's role. So I have ordered the pursuit of your friend in exchange for regaining my rights in Hagetmau, but I have also made it clear to my agents that they are not expected to act. This is also the attitude of my brother Toulongeon and of monsieur de Poyanne, whom you also know, and it would be the view of Navailles if he were here to express it. I wish it were so with Saint-Luc, who will command the army the king sends into my province of Béarn and, I hear, into my brother's domains in Bigorre.'

Madame de Motteville was too used to the ways of the court to have expected much else from this interview. She knew that beneath Gramont's urbane and courteous exterior there burned a deep resentment at Pellot's attempt to challenge him. Pellot knew it too. At this very time he was writing a fawning letter to his patron:

> *I know very well, monsieur, that the maréchal de Gramont is extremely angry and exasperated with me, although I have not done or said anything that could displease him. On the contrary, I have been lenient with his officers, who are more to blame than anyone, and I have remitted almost half of the poll tax for the parishes of Hagetmau and Coudures, which belong to him. I am not to blame if by its obstinate rebellion Hagetmau has brought misfortune upon itself. I have done what I could to give the place relief. So, monsieur, I beg you to renew the protection you extend over me. I assure you that in all these conflicts I shall continue to do whatever I can to satisfy the maréchal and earn his good graces. Your most humble and obedient servant, Pellot.*

While composing this piece of hypocrisy the intendant was arranging with the marquis de Saint-Luc to concentrate a powerful force for the march into Bigorre, but he was soon to become aware that Audijos not only had powerful friends in high places but could also look to the ferocious, if volatile, support of the men of Lavedan.

Snow was falling in Argelès, the gateway to the mountain valleys. Arnaud Corade, his twisted lips curled in a smile of welcome, was awaiting Audijos, Dubourdieu and fifteen of their followers at the gates as they rode into the town.

'Come,' he said. 'I have a sight for you to see that will gladden your eyes.' The little troop dismounted, and led their horses over the ridge to the town square. A strange but impressive figure strode forward to meet them, the archpriest of Juncalas, with his polished cuirass gleaming on top of his soutane and a massive sword strapped to his side. Jean de Cauterets flung his arms wide to embrace Bernard, but his words of welcome were drowned by the roar of the crowd behind him. Hundreds of mountain men were assembled in the square, rank upon serried rank of bearded warriors, clad in rough leather jerkins covered with the fleeces of sheep or the skins of wild animals and dripping with melting snow. They shook their varied weapons above their heads – pitchforks and pikes, muskets and axes – and shouted their war cry: 'Biahore! Viva d'Audijos!'

'You see,' said the archpriest when the noise had abated, 'we have risen in your cause – and also in our own, for we shall not allow the valleys to be invaded. The enemy is already on the march. My scouts report that a company of dragoons is close behind you.'

An hour later a loose formation of some forty dragoons came within sight of the walls of Argelès. Their outriders reported that the fortifications appeared to be deserted, and the column closed up to ride through the gates. They were greeted with a volley of musketry from the Invisibles that killed three of them and wounded several others. Their captain, himself clutching his right arm, turned his frightened horse and ordered his men to retreat. As the cavaliers wheeled about and galloped headlong down the defile they had just ascended, a piercing whistle sounded and the bare hilltops on either side suddenly swarmed with armed men firing wildly at the rout below. None of the shots hit home, and the survivors disappeared in the gathering dusk.

'Not much improvement in the musketry of your reverence's men,' Audijos remarked with a smile to the archpriest, who stood beside him on one of the gate towers, watching the mountain men looting the bodies of the dead and cutting the throats of the wounded dragoons who had been left behind.

'They can do with a little more of your training,' replied Cauterets, 'but we can agree that this action provides a good basis for our future co-operation. Your men can provide the marksmanship, my ruffians the ferocity of their taste for close-quarter combat.'

It continued to snow on the following day, but this did not deter the archpriest from proposing a demonstration before the walls of Lourdes.

'I am told there are five companies of dragoons in the city in addition to the one that we defeated – about four hundred and fifty men' he said. 'The defences of the place were improved some years ago against the possibility of a Spanish incursion, and they have cannon mounted on the donjon that overlooks the plain. We cannot take Lourdes by assault, but we can manifest our presence with a token force in such a way that they will think twice before risking another raid into the valleys.'

Audijos did not want to dampen the ardour of his ally, but he inwardly questioned the wisdom of exposing the mountain men on open ground, where, despite their numbers, they could be ridden down by the dragoons. Roger Dubourdieu was of the opposite opinion.

'Morbleu!' he exclaimed, curling his mustachios, 'we have enough good men to storm the battlements of hell. Let us mine the gates and let me lead a charge to the very foot of their confounded donjon.'

The archpriest pulled at his beard and smiled.

'We would need artillery for such an assault. Besides, if we were to capture the town, we should ourselves soon be besieged by the regiments that even now are on the march for Lourdes. Don Joan has provided us with more muskets, but we have little enough powder and no cannon. I have trained five hundred men of the five thousand you see assembled here in Argelès. They are skilled in ambush and defence of the passes, and the rest are undisciplined but ready to fight. None of them have any experience of siege warfare, let alone a set-piece battle in the open plain. I would not have them slaughtered beneath those massive walls.'

'Then,' said Audijos, 'let us accept your plan and serve under your generalship, and if the dragoons attempt a foray my marksmen will be at your service.'

The swirling snow still persisted as three hundred mountain men marched down the road to Lourdes.

'In these conditions,' the archpriest remarked to Audijos, 'it will be difficult for our enemies to judge our strength.'

'This may be so,' said Bernard, who had accepted the offer of a foul smelling sheepskin to shield him from the weather, 'and it may also deter the dragoons from riding out to challenge us.'

'Let them come if they will,' Cauterets replied. 'We know how to disable horses if they come at us. I am more concerned about your friend Dubourdieu, and the detachment we let him lead to the western walls of Lourdes.'

Roger's insistence upon playing a more active part had resulted in agreement that he should take thirty men to cross the Gave de Pau, but he had had to promise Bernard that he would restrain his impetuosity, and merely test the outer defences of the town. He had forded the freezing waters with his contingent, and arrived at the Pont-Vieux below the walls even before the main body had assembled on the eastern side of Lourdes. There he was delighted to find a troop of dismounted dragoons guarding the bridge. In his view this did not qualify as the kind of action his chief had forbidden. With blood curdling yells the mountain men followed their leader in a charge upon the bridge. The dragoons fled back through the western gate, but not before the hindmost had been transfixed by Dubourdieu's sword, and another had been shot down by Corade, who had accompanied him on the reconnaissance. The gate had been shut with a resounding clang, and the mountain men contented themselves with taunting the guards on the walls above with cries of 'Viva d'Audijos!'

Inside the town the commander of the dragoons, captain de La Forest, was engaged in an altercation with the meagre garrison in the citadel. The commandant, Germain d'Antin, seigneur d'Ourout, was also Toulongeon's lieutenant as sénéchal of Bigorre with special responsibilities in Lavedan. Like his superior, he had some sympathy for the mountain men, whose customs he knew well, and he had no intention of handing over the donjon to La

Forest without Toulongeon's approval. In the outcome he agreed to fire the cannon at the throng upon the eastern approaches, but the conditions made it impossible to aim accurately, and in any case the gunners ensured that the shots fell short. The men of Lavedan stood their ground, and set up a strange cry that sounded for all the world like the howling of an enormous wolf pack. Even those citizens within the walls who supported the cause of Audijos and his allies shivered at the sound.

The archpriest waited until Dubourdieu and his men had completed the circuit of the walls and rejoined the main body from the north.

'Our work here is done,' he said. The mountain men marched back to Argelès.

29. Negotiations at Lourdes

At the beginning of March, Saint-Luc joined Pellot in Mont-de-Marsan with four companies of infantry and one of cavalry. Before setting off for Bigorre, the intendant reported to Colbert that a regiment of dragoons had occupied Lourdes and that one of its companies had found the valleys of Lavedan blocked by the mountain men, whom Audijos had incited to revolt. He did not describe the rout at Argelès, nor did he mention the descent of the men of Lavedan upon Lourdes. He added a postscript regretting that most of the troops who had been occupying and punishing parts of Béarn would have to be temporarily reassigned to Bigorre. With a covert sneer against Gramont, he blamed the Béarnais people for encouraging Audijos to undertake his audacious enterprises.

'They call him,' he wrote, 'the liberator, and this after his brutal murder of Boisset, commandant of the guards.' By this time the officers of the royal army had developed a healthier respect for Audijos than that evinced by the intendant. Nor did they welcome being deprived of comfortable quarters and the opportunity for profit in exchange for a winter campaign in the Pyrenees. Colonel Podewiltz, for instance, had arranged with the notables of Orthez to be paid a sizeable sum in return for mitigating the conditions of the occupation by his dragoons.

François d'Epinay, marquis de Saint-Luc and lieutenant-général for the king in Lower Guienne, had his own hesitations about co-operating with the intendant. Saint-Luc was the grandson of one of the favourites of the last Valois king, Henri III, and as a member of the high sword nobility he had a distaste for commissioners of the robe in general and a particular dislike for the ruthless single-mindedness of Pellot. But, as Gramont had remarked to madame de Motteville, he was a soldier who knew his duty, and if Pellot was responsible for the political aspects of their joint mission, he made it clear that in matters of war military considerations were paramount. He had expected to report to Louvois, but since the royal council had given Colbert control over the repression of the revolt, he was obliged to account for operations to the minister for finance. Thus on his arrival in Tarbes he wrote to Colbert:

Monsieur,

Having arrived with monsieur Pellot in the county of Chalosse to chastise the rebellion of Audijos and his accomplices there, I found that he had thrown himself and his troop into the valleys of Lavedan, which are the most populous and the most difficult to penetrate of any in the Pyrenees. I had him followed diligently, and at the approach of a regiment of dragoons he persuaded fully six thousand men to take up arms and block all entry points to the mountains. My presence has had some effect in preventing the sedition from spreading further. I am awaiting two hundred more infantry before attacking these rebels, who have engaged in this criminal activity because Audijos assured them that the gabelle was going to be introduced in their land.

In fact, by the time Saint-Luc and Pellot arrived in Lourdes on 7 March, they had at least fifteen hundred soldiers at their disposal, and the stage seemed set for a major campaign.

Behind the scenes negotiations for a settlement were already in train. The pacifically minded bishop of Tarbes, Claude Malier du Houssay, well knew that his clergy in the valleys were at the centre of the revolt and were likely to ignore any episcopal mandate he might send them, but he, like the comte de Toulongeon, had a sympathy for the mountain men. He first contacted the commandant of the donjon and had him suggest to captain de La Forest that the curé of Lourdes should bear an offer to the archpriest of Juncalas. If Audijos were delivered, dead or alive, a pardon might be granted to the rebels of Lavedan. The archpriest had no intention of betraying Bernard, but he felt obliged to convoke the syndics of the valley communities to consider the proposal. Such was their enthusiasm for the cause that they rejected it out of hand. In any case it was a dubious offer, since a pardon would need authority far greater than that which La

Forest possessed. This abortive negotiation took place a few days before Saint-Luc and Pellot entered Lourdes. They had hardly done so when Toulongeon himself demanded that he should personally treat with the valleys.

The sénéchal of Bigorre was much respected in Lavedan. As the younger brother of the maréchal-duc de Gramont, he had at first been trained as a priest with a view to inheriting the family's high ecclesiastical preferments. Although he had eventually pursued a distinguished military career, he retained something of his early religious vocation, and the clergy of the valleys trusted him more than they did their bishop. In fact, Toulongeon chose as his emissary a monk from the Benedictine abbey of Saint-Savin near Argelès who was on good terms with the archpriest of Juncalas. Saint-Luc, who had little taste for campaigning against the mountain men on their own terrain, welcomed this intervention, but Pellot was determined to destroy Audijos and to teach the rebels a lesson. These differences were apparent in the discussions that took place in the château of Lourdes, where La Forest had now replaced the garrison commanded by Germain d'Antin with his own men.

'By what right have you evicted my lieutenant from this place?' Toulongeon demanded of Saint-Luc.

'His lordship bears the king's commission as supreme military commander in these parts,' Pellot interposed.

'I can dispense with your impertinence, monsieur,' said the sénéchal, his anger rising. 'His Majesty is aware of your designs against our family, and has ordered your ruffians to leave my brother's estate at Hagetmau. This is Bigorre, and not Chalosse. My people of the valleys are defending their just rights, and the king should be told of the true state of affairs. Your commission does not run in these lands.'

The intendant was not to be cowed.

'That is not what monsieur Colbert has ordered. We have the forces to march into Lavedan, and bring the traitor Audijos to justice.'

It was time for Saint-Luc to intervene.

'Monsieur Pellot has the king's warrant to oversee the civil side of this matter,' he said to Toulongeon. 'But it is I who command His Majesty's army here, and in my view our troops have little hope of defeating thousands of armed men who know every hidden trail and pass in this waste of mountains. I welcome your mediation, although it must be firm.'

Pellot contained his rage, as he saw the tide turning against him.

'They are more like animals than men,' he muttered through his teeth. 'Remember how they cut the throats of the wounded at Argelès.'

'Well,' said Toulongeon, addressing Saint-Luc and ignoring the intendant, 'it is clear from the first contact that they will never surrender Audijos. The best we can do is to ask them to lay down their arms and let the troops march through the villages to show His Majesty's authority. In return we can promise to intercede with the king to grant them pardon for their revolt - but not, of course, for Audijos and his troop.'

These terms were agreed upon despite the continuing objections of Pellot, who came near to accusing Saint-Luc of cowardice. They were passed to Dom Roland of Saint-Savin, who delivered them to his friend the archpriest. On this occasion the deputies of the communities discussed the issue at length. Jean de Lanusse, the curé of Arrens, pointed out that Toulongeon had given his personal backing to the proposal, and that it contained no mention of Audijos, whose battle with the wolf pack at Arrens had made him a local hero. Thomas Voisin, curé of neighbouring Marsous, was suspicious of the motives of the intendant, and doubted that a pardon could be relied on.

'Besides,' he added,' if we are to surrender our arms, and allow the soldiery to march in triumph through our lands, they will burn our homes and ravish our women.'

Jean de Cauterets conferred with Dom Roland, and then entered the debate.

'Do you not see,' he said, 'that the sénéchal is offering us a peace that will cost us nothing? We are to lay down our arms, but we do not have to pass them to the soldiers. We simply hide them away for a while, and if we are betrayed we can bring them forth at need. All this is merely face-saving. We declare our loyalty to the king, and his army makes a token visit to the valleys. The good comte de Toulongeon has told this worthy monk that these are empty gestures that neither threaten our liberties nor undermine our power to defend them.'

Even this assurance did not persuade some of the deputies, who had little respect for royal officers and noble titles.

'We are free men who govern ourselves,' declared Jacques Tourdes of Argelès. 'We have fought and won against the lowlanders before now. What need have we for promises from counts and bishops and kings?'

Audijos, Dubourdieu and Corade were listening to the debate at the back of the room. They had pulled their cloaks round their faces to avoid recognition, for their presence might invalidate the proceedings in the eyes of the lowland authorities.

'S'blood! These wild men of the woods are democrats who would destroy the natural ranking of society,' whispered Roger.

'They have strange customs,' Bernard responded, 'but most of them have some loyalty to the king and the sénéchal. My friend the curé of Arrens told me how hard it is to persuade his parishioners to take the path of peace once their blood is up. Yet I wager they will follow the advice of our warrior archpriest, who now, it seems, acts as peacemaker.'

And so it proved to be. Four deputies were empowered to go to Lourdes to join Toulongeon, who promised to protect them and superintend their formal submission on behalf of the Lavedan communities. The sénéchal led them to the town square where, in the presence of Saint-Luc, Pellot, and local dignitaries, they knelt and solemnly swore that the roads to the mountains would be opened and the mountain men would lay down their weapons. The deputies returned to Argelès and reported that Toulongeon had informed them the royal army would march into the valleys on the morrow.

Meanwhile Pellot expressed his resentment in a despatch to Colbert. He pretended that 'these seditious rebels' had only agreed to stand aside because they had seen the forces Saint-Luc had assembled and knew he was about to attack them. He had no doubt that the troops could crush the opposition if faint-hearted counsels were set aside. As it was, 'this patched-up peace is likely to prejudice royal authority and make these people even more fractious. They may give the appearance of complete obedience, but they cannot be trusted and have broken their word on several occasions. We shall march in battle order, as if we are going to attack them. It is only this that has brought them to terms, and we hope fully to establish the king's authority in this region.' The intendant still hoped to punish Audijos's new allies at the point of the sword, and to put them under such pressure that they would break the agreement.

The weather had again deteriorated as the troops began to ascend the road to Argelès on 18 March. They were indeed in full battle array, but it proved difficult to keep contact between the companies in the blinding snow. They halted to bivouac for the night, and sent scouts forward into the town, which they found almost deserted. The rumour spread that the mountain men were assembled at arms in the villages along the high ridge to the west, and Saint-Luc decided to go no further. To Pellot's chagrin the army marched back to Lourdes. Toulongeon, assuming that the demonstration had accomplished its purpose and the peace would hold, returned to Tarbes. The intendant, however, had new plans to impose his will. If the attempt to provoke the mountain men to resume military action had been frustrated by the weather, he now hoped to exact a new retribution by summoning the deputies of the valleys to Lourdes under pretence of a more comprehensive submission, and to arrest and try them as rebels.

Audijos and his men had taken refuge in Arrens when Saint-Luc had marched on Argelès. There he conferred with the leaders of the mountain revolt. Jean de Lanusse, though he had never favoured the mass rising, was among the delegates.

'What has happened to the ancient charter of Chalosse, in which maître Legrange had reposed such trust?' he asked of Bernard.'

'It is a sorry story,' Audijos replied. 'I have it still in my saddle bags. Président de Gassion refused to proclaim it through the *parlement* of Pau, and returned it to me. We still have forces in Chalosse and Béarn, but they remain in hiding and I did not think it wise to leave it in any place of refuge while the gabeleurs and the dragoons were searching high and low for my supporters.'

'Do not renounce hope of finding some honest judge,' said the curé of Arrens. 'I have friends in the *parlement* of Bordeaux who may be prepared to challenge the intendant.'

'That is for the future,' Jean de Cauterets broke in. 'In the present, since we have come to terms with Saint-Luc, you must decide on your own plans. We can continue secretly to shelter you here, of course. You may also wish to cross the border and regroup in Sallent de Gallego with Miguel Joan. A third course is to return to Béarn and Chalosse, which is relatively unguarded while the dragoons have been sent to Lourdes.'

'We have given thought to the matter,' said Audijos, 'and we think it best to return to our homeland, and rally our scattered bands for a fresh campaign against the gabeleurs.' He was not unmindful, in making this decision, of Jeanne-Marie and the hiding place near Coudures.

In the days that followed the mountain men returned to their villages, while the archpriest, suspecting some treachery from the intendant, went back to Argelès with most of the deputies. Soon after their arrival a summons came from Pellot requiring four representatives from each of the communities to proceed to Lourdes to formalise the submission of the valleys. The demand sounded suspicious, but the deputies relied upon Toulongeon to keep them safe from reprisals. Even so, there were some who refused, and only fourteen delegates, including Jean de Lanusse and Voisin of Marsous, obeyed the summons. No sooner had they passed through the gates of the town when they were arrested on Pellot's orders. Saint-Luc expostulated with the intendant on this breach of the agreement, but he felt obliged to accept the intendant's insistence that some at least of the representatives should be interrogated as to the actions of Audijos in the revolt. Saint-Luc wrote to Colbert exaggerating the success of his forces, and explaining that he had agreed to the arrest of six of those who had come to throw themselves on the king's mercy. It might now be politic, he suggested, to expedite a general royal pardon in the valleys, Audijos and his men excepted.

When Toulongeon heard of the arrests, his indignation knew no bounds. He rode forthwith to Lourdes and confronted the intendant, saying that if all the deputies were not immediately released he would go to Argelès and offer himself to the mountain men as a hostage for their safety. Once again Pellot reluctantly gave way. The prisoners were released, and the pardon granted. By this time Audijos and his followers had returned to Béarn.

30. The Double Agent

Exasperated by Toulongeon's intervention in Lavedan, and resentful of Saint-Luc's unwillingness to press further into the mountains, Claude Pellot spent the last week of March 1665 in Pau, where his spies brought reports of the earlier passage of Audijos and his band through Nay and Lescar. Nor did events in the Béarnais capital assuage the intendant's sense of frustration. Bernard de Lavie, the presiding judge in the *parlement*, made it clear that he resented the extension of Pellot's judicial powers to Béarn, while Poudenx, the syndic of the local representative estates, and Jean du Haut de Salies, bishop of Lescar and president of the estates, saw his authority as an invasion of their traditional rights. Pellot knew, of course, of Audijos's attempt to enlist the *parlement* in his cause through the président-marquis de Gassion, and he had received reports of Poudenx's contact with the rebels. He was also aware, through the châtelaine de Sèvres, that Poyanne, the head of the military in Béarn, had received Audijos on the journey of the duchesse de Navailles to Bigorre. Experience had taught the intendant to pretend respect for high nobles and provincial authorities while turning them against each other in the interest of his royal commission. Thus he appeared impervious to the slights he encountered in Pau, and promised himself to vent his rage against Audijos's supporters in Chalosse. He sent messengers to Saint-Sever with instructions to reactivate his tribunal, and asked the châtelaine to report whatever seditious activities she had discovered in the area.

Meanwhile Bernard and his troop were joyfully received in the hidden cave near Coudures. The deep-throated growls of Patou at the approach of the cavalcade changed into ecstatic barks that his master hastened to repress.

'I knew it was you who had come back to us,' said Jeanne-Marie. 'He has been so well trained that no one but you would excite such a welcome from our sentinel.'

'There is need for greater caution than ever,' said Baillet, stepping forward in some embarrassment to interrupt the lovers' embrace.

'We have news that an informer has seen one of our men carrying supplies into the forest. Fortunately, our man followed the instructions and twice doubled back on his trail, so that the spy lost the scent, but we know he reported the matter to Labaume.'

'How could you be sure of that?' asked Bernard.

Baillet's slight figure swelled visibly with pride.

'Because, I have found a spy of our own who shares the confidence of the châtelaine and her paramour.'

'What,' responded Audijos, 'a double spy! How can we trust such a person?'

'He is here,' said Baillet, 'and you can judge for yourself. If he were not a man of his word, all of us would have been arrested or murdered long before this.'

A figure lingering behind madame de Talazuc at the mouth of the cave came forward. It was the bailiff, Christophe de Labat.

'Morbleu!' expostulated Roger Dubourdieu. 'You trust the cousin of the worst traitor in Coudures, whom we put to death!'

'My cousin met his just deserts,' said Labat. 'It is because of our relationship that the châtelaine has made me privy to her secrets. She knows not that I detest everything he stood for. I serve the cause of the people of Chalosse, and offer my allegiance to the sieur d'Audijos.' With these words he knelt at Bernard's feet.

'Stand up, man,' said Audijos, seizing his hand and pulling him to his feet. 'We accept you as one of our own, but beware the wiles of madame de Sèvres. She is clever enough to trick you into betraying yourself. What have you found out about her plans?'

'I know the identity of the informer who suspected that you were hiding in these woods,' replied Labat. 'He is none other than the syndic Bernard Dumartin, and the châtelaine instructed me to follow the trail he had taken and make a thorough search for your hiding place. It was in this way that I chanced upon your refuge and offered my services to monsieur Baillet. I told madame de

Sèvres that Dumartin was surely mistaken, and since she knows I am familiar with the forest she accepted my opinion.

'That gives us breathing space,' said Dubourdieu, 'but what new devilry does she have in mind?'

'Well, I am not told things she thinks I do not need to know, but I did hear her and Labaume give orders to watch for the return of Duplantier from Bayonne. They are aware he goes there to work for our cause, and it seems that the people of the town are ready to rise when the word is given."

'Yes,' Audijos interposed, 'we have received a message to that effect, but the time is not yet ripe. I shall visit Bayonne shortly to see the situation for myself. In the meantime we must prepare to resume our campaign against the guards of the bureau, and punish those informers who have betrayed us. Your task, Labat, is to discover the identity of such traitors. We shall undertake retribution in such a way that the châtelaine does not suspect you of playing a double game.'

'I know the dangers, monsieur,' replied the spy. 'I also overheard that woman telling Labaume that she had been summoned to Saint-Sever by the intendant. It would be well for you to make your dispositions in her absence. Moreover, there is only a skeleton force of dragoons left in Coudures. Most of their company has not yet returned from Lourdes.'

'It is well,' said Bernard, his ice-blue eyes fixed penetratingly on Labat, whose sharp features reminded him of the notary and caused him a twinge of anxiety that a man involved in so complex a web of betrayal held the safety of those he held dearest in his hands. But Audijos had become accustomed to taking desperate chances, and the responsibilities of command had become part of his nature. He looked for countermeasures for every contingency. While he knew the gentry and people of the region supported his cause, experience had taught him that there were always some who, when faced with personal sacrifice, would forget their loyalty.

In the days that followed Audijos sent messengers instructing the leaders of local bands to regroup and prepare for the new campaign against the gabeleurs. He arranged for his mother to travel with an escort of local gentlemen led by the seigneur de

Montaut to Foix, where she might live in safety. He tried to make similar plans for Jeanne-Marie, but she refused to endure any more separation than was necessary.

'I shall not go. It seems it is my destiny to watch and wait for you, my love,' she said to Bernard, 'and I would not forego an hour of your company to avoid dangers that in any case will follow me wherever I go.'

'So be it,' said Audijos. 'It is a perilous road that we travel, with death awaiting us round every corner.'

The next morning a scout was posted to watch the house of Bernard Dumartin. The man who volunteered for the task was the messenger Duplantier had sent from Bayonne, a young apprentice tailor named Thomas Aramitz. Audijos was at first unwilling to send someone possessing little familiarity with the byways of Coudures, but he yielded to the boy's enthusiasm. Aramitz returned with the news that two of the guards of the bureau were visiting the syndic.

'Now is our opportunity to attack,' said Dubourdieu. 'Labaume will think we have followed the guards, and the bailiff's hand in the matter will not be suspect.'

Roger and four of the Invisibles put on their masks and rode to the northern end of the township. Dubourdieu signalled his men to dismount and cover Dumartin's house with their muskets. He himself strode boldly forward and set alight to some kindling wood stacked against the wall. While he bent to his task the two guards emerged from the door. He had scarcely drawn his sword when the crackle of musketry sounded. The wounded men staggered back inside, where within a few minutes they were consumed in the blaze. The syndic himself took refuge in his wine cellar and survived the flames, although this was not known until later.

Audijos welcomed the party on their return. He had thrown down the gauntlet on his home territory in defiance of the intendant, but he planned to shift his campaign to districts where he was least expected. In the meantime he prepared to see for himself what was happening in Bayonne, where he sent young Aramitz with a return message for Duplantier.

Reports of the killings in Coudures reached Pellot soon after the châtelaine had arrived in Saint-Sever.

'It seems your intelligence network is not infallible, madame,' he remarked.

'I blame Labaume,' she said. 'He ought not to have sent the guards to Dumartin's house in broad daylight and compromised our source, the worthy syndic, who has survived but who will now be of little use to us. However, I have acquired a new agent in the bailiff, Labat, who promises to continue the work of his late cousin.'

'I doubt if he can do much,' Pellot replied. 'As someone close to the notary, he is surely a marked man in Coudures. Set him to work to extend our list of those who have given the slightest indication of support for the rebel Audijos, and then we shall see if the noose and the rack will bring this canaille to heel. I have had to admit to monsieur Colbert that the disaffection is spreading. No sooner did the marquis de Saint-Luc and I put out the flames in Lavedan and Béarn, than new troubles have flared up in Bayonne. The marquis has passed through Bayonne on his way to report on the frontier defences, and he says the town is bubbling with sedition.'

'I have some information in that respect,' said the châtelaine. 'One of our spies there has reported that the rebel Duplantier recently sent a messenger to Chalosse. While we cannot find where Duplantier is hiding, we know who the messenger is.'

'That will serve us well. I shall send Nogent and a sergeant to Bayonne to arrest this man, and we can test the loyalty of the city council by ordering them to co-operate in the matter.'

On her return to Coudures madame de Sèvres summoned Labat by night.

'Here,' she said,' is a list of all the suspects we know in the area. They include many seigneurs whose estates you manage, and you may well find evidence to incriminate them. There must be others who have spoken favourably of Audijos and his band or given them shelter and supplies. Monsieur Pellot is about to order new arrests and interrogations, and he wants as many names as you can find.'

Labat tried to conceal his nervousness as he scanned the list carefully.

'I note,' he said, 'that it is not quite up to date. I see the provost Pierre de Borrit here, and he received what he deserved for aiding the rebel Audijos. His corpse still hangs from the gibbet. And here is his friend the lieutenant Louis de Barry, whom I thought you had arrested.'

The châtelaine gestured impatiently.

'The Bordeaux judges ordered his release for lack of evidence, and you should try to find something tangible against him. Now get you gone.'

Labat checked carefully to see he was not being followed, and made his way to the cave in the woods. He gave the password to the sentinel on duty beside Patou, and reported his conversation with the châtelaine to Audijos, who summoned Dubourdieu, Corade and Baillet to join them.

'By all the devils in hell,' exclaimed Roger, 'this is an opportunity to pay back that woman in her own coin. Let our ingenious spy add the names of some of our enemies to the list.'

'Not so,' Corade interjected. 'The accusations would be seen to be false, and the bailiff would pay with his life.'

'You are right,' said Bernard. 'The best we can do is to have Labat add one or two names of our true supporters who have powerful friends to protect them or who are willing to go into hiding. By so doing the châtelaine will repose more trust in our new recruit, and he may discover more of her secrets.'

'Perhaps,' added Baillet,' but if each new addition to the list is spirited away as soon as his name is mentioned, suspicion will be attached to our double spy.'

'It is tangled affair,' Audijos concluded. 'We must consider each case on its merits, and, above all, protect our ability to find out the secret plans of our foes.'

'I am at your disposal, gentlemen,' said Christophe de Labat. 'All our lives are at stake in this game, and I am prepared to wager mine in our cause.'

31. Riot in Bayonne

It was 8 April 1665, and in the gallery of the town hall in Bayonne the members of the civic council were discussing a letter received from the marquis de Saint-Luc. Four held the rank of échevin and three of jurat, while the town syndic and the registrar completed the company. Though few in numbers, it was their practice to be long in deliberation. Monsieur Duvergier, sieur de Belay, presided in his capacity as mayor or premier échevin. He was a large man, ponderous in gait and manner, who took his duties to defend the town's privileges and to maintain order through the militia and the watch with the utmost seriousness. Unfortunately these two areas of responsibility seemed about to clash. Saint-Luc had ordered him to issue a proclamation requiring citizens to report the presence of Audijos and his accomplices and to ensure their arrest. If he failed to do so it was clear that his authority would be superseded not only by monsieur d'Artagnan, the commander of the garrison in the Château Vieux, but also by outside military force.

'The artisans have already paraded through the streets in support of Audijos in defiance of the guild masters, and the people sing some doggerel in the cabarets declaring him their hero,' said Duvergier. 'We must tread carefully or we shall provoke a rising. At the same time we must keep control of the town's government in our own hands, or our rights under our charter will be lost.'

'To speak the truth,' volunteered one of the junior échevins, 'this man Audijos has some right on his side. We have had trouble enough with the intendant's attempt to take half our dues from the shipping tax, and there is talk, as we have heard from our representative at court, monsieur de Cheverry, of introducing the gabelle here in the peremptory style adopted in Tursan and Chalosse.'

'Yes, yes, but he is a rebel and an assassin with a price on his head, sought by regiments of the king's dragoons from Lourdes to

Mont-de-Marsan,' said Duvergier. 'We must conform, but let us do so in such a way that we do not inflame the populace.'

'And we must also take care not to offend the king's lieutenant-général,' said one of the jurats. 'Why do we not do what we have done to win the favour of past governors? Let us present him with the finest Spanish horse that money can buy.'

This suggestion was greeted with acclamation, and the council adjourned to their midday meal, agreeing to consider the draft of the proclamation on another occasion.

When the council's proclamation was posted in the town square to the sound of trumpets from the watch, and read in stentorian tones by the town crier, it was greeted with instant derision. Copies were also distributed to inns and cabarets, where they provoked indignant remarks directed against the city fathers. Duplantier and Jatxou participated in one such conversation.

'Did you hear how the words 'Vive d'Audijos' were scrawled all over the proclamation?' asked Duplantier.

'Yes, my friend,' replied Jatxou, 'and the urchins are singing his song outside the Château Vieux. Your efforts have created a movement that will sweep away all opposition. My people in Labourd are also with us.'

'It is not so much what I have done but the merits of the man and the cause. Yesterday the boatmen promised their support. Even the notables are wavering, as you may judge from the way Duvergier has worded the proclamation. But what will happen if Saint-Luc and the intendant send in the soldiers? I would that Audijos himself were here to guide us.'

'He is coming,' said Jatxou. 'Carla Baroja has told me so.'

'How could she know that? Young Aramitz returned from Chalosse an hour ago with a message that he will soon be with us, and you are the first person to whom I have mentioned this.'

'Our witch has ways of knowing that surpass our understanding. But let us take care that the news does not get abroad. Captain Bonnicart, who commands the watch, has the habit of following his orders whatever the situation. There are many who would betray us in the hope of reward. Someone came to the Aramitz household several days ago, asking the whereabouts of the boy Thomas.'

An hour after this exchange a loud knocking was heard at the back door of the house where Duplantier had taken refuge.

'Who is there?' called the innkeeper, a loaded musket in his hand. 'Give the password, whoever you are.'

'It is I, madame Aramitz,' came the tremulous reply. 'I know no password. Help me, for the love of Christ. They have taken Thomas.'

It took several minutes for Duplantier to calm the distressed woman, and by this time two other witnesses to the arrest of Aramitz had arrived on the scene. They were both members of Duplantier's network, and with their aid he was able to piece together the sequence of events incoherently blurted out by the mother of Thomas Aramitz. It appeared that a certain officer bearing a warrant signed by the intendant himself had forced his way into the house accompanied by a sergeant, and discovered young Thomas hiding under a bed. They had placed chains on his wrists and taken him outside where several members of the town militia were guarding two other prisoners, also in chains, who were known to the witnesses as fellow supporters of their movement. Closing ranks round their victims, the escort had set off in the direction of the house of the premier échevin.

'Did you catch the officer's name?' asked Duplantier of madame Aramitz.

'Yes, I tried to delay him by reading his warrant. He pushed me aside, but I had time to see it was a lieutenant Nogent.'

'Ah, I thought it might be one of our worst foes if Pellot himself had provided the warrant,' said Duplantier. 'Clearly, some informant has betrayed us.'

'Let us not stand here talking. There is still time to save our friends,' said one of the two witnesses. 'We sent madame Aramitz to you while we followed the party for a short distance. It looks as though our worthy mayor has declined to receive the prisoners, and they are on the way to the municipal jail. The alarm has spread from house to house, and a crowd is gathering to block the street. The militia men are hanging back as if they do not like the task they have been given.'

'Yes, it is time to act,' said Duplantier, wrapping his musket in a cloak and slipping a long dagger into a sheath hidden in his hose.

Riot in Bayonne

As the three men stepped outside the tocsin began to sound from the bells of a nearby church. Hurrying through the streets, they saw men, women and children erupting from houses on all sides and converging on the town hall.

There, in the central square, they came upon Nogent's escort surrounded by a threatening crowd who set up the cry of 'Vive d'Audijos!' until it reverberated from the rooftops. Stones began to fly. Nogent was waving his sword and turning from side to side to see if he could force a passage. The sergeant had raised his musket to his shoulder, but the rest of the escort stood by passively. There were many women in the front ranks of the crowd who taunted the militia men and shouted insults at Nogent and the sergeant.

Suddenly the two older prisoners pushed the guards aside and disappeared into the mob. Young Aramitz tried to do the same but Nogent stabbed him in the stomach. He cried out in pain and fell forward on his knees. At this the militia men threw down their arms and the crowd surged forward, engulfing Nogent and the sergeant in a flurry of limbs and giving them no chance to use their weapons. The two would have been beaten to death were it not for a new intervention. A trumpet sounded and the crowd fell back as captain Bonnicart and a contingent of mounted militia forced their way forward. He dismounted and raised the bruised and dishevelled Nogent to his feet. Thomas Aramitz had disappeared.

Bonnicart was a grizzled old soldier who had little time for political subtleties and even less regard for the fickle passions of the populace he was called on to control. He glanced cynically at the battered officer and his sergeant.

'Well, monsieur,' he remarked, 'clearly you have had little experience in dealing with riffraff. A few well placed shots would have dispersed them.'

'I thank you both for your aid and your comment, monsieur,' Nogent replied, spitting a broken tooth from his bloodied mouth. 'The fault was not mine. These guards you provided on the orders of monsieur Pellot refused to fire on the canaille.'

'That's as may be. I have orders from the premier échevin to place you in protective custody. You and your sergeant are to accompany me to the Château Vieux, where you will be safe from further assaults.'

'What!' said Nogent. 'I have a mission from the intendant, and I call on you and your men to clear the square and search for my prisoners - or do you side with these rebels?'

'I follow my orders, sir. Hand me your sword.'

Nogent had no choice but to obey. One of the militia men dismounted and helped him climb painfully into the saddle. With a muttered curse, the humiliated Nogent rode behind Bonnicart in the midst of the town guards, while the sergeant stumbled along beside him and the crowd fell back, still shouting insults.

At dusk on the day following the riot Audijos and an escort of fifteen Invisibles arrived at their appointed rendezvous near Bayonne. The place chosen by Duplantier was a fortified house on the Nive about two miles south of the town. The portly innkeeper was awaiting them there, together with his brother-in-law, Cambo Jatxou, and five local leaders of the organisation Duplantier had established. One was a barrel maker named Georges Chanda; another a hatter called David Massé; a third a Basque sailor named Iñaki Yndurrain who led the boatmen and the wharf labourers; while the fourth and fifth were two oar makers, Pierre Lajus and Jean Boucheron. The eighth person waiting to welcome Audijos rendered most of the others uneasy by her presence. It was Carla Baroja, whom Duplantier had had Jatxou summon to Bayonne in the hope that the powers she had exercised in arranging his escape at Saint-Jean-de-Luz would prove useful in his conspiratorial network. As soon as Audijos and his men entered the room she caught his eye.

The group greeted their leader warmly, but also with a kind of reverential awe, for Audijos had become a kind of living legend among them. Duplantier described the events provoked by Nogent's mission and the escape of the prisoners.

'That was a splendid victory, mine host,' said Bernard. 'It is not the first time we have crossed swords with lieutenant Nogent. But what will be the response of the town council? They will have to act firmly if they want to avoid an order from Pellot to have troops occupy the town, and if they do act they will face mass opposition in Bayonne.'

'Yes,' said Duplantier eagerly, 'this is the moment for which we have prepared. The good people of Bayonne will rise up at your call. All the Basques of Labourd and the gentry of Gascony will unite with them against our oppressors.'

'Not so fast.' said Audijos, smiling at his lieutenant's enthusiasm. 'I know there is support for our cause among all ranks and peoples in the south-west, but remember that these provinces are crammed full of the king's soldiers. There would be sieges and bloody massacres, and we could only survive if we called the Spaniards or the English to help us. That would be treason instead of the just defence of our rights.'

'I know your plan,' interposed Jatxou. 'You fight a war of attrition by forest ambushes and raids by night, hoping to wear down the patience of the king's ministers to the point where His Majesty agrees to keep his promises to respect our charters and abolish the gabelle.'

'That is indeed my strategy,' said Audijos, 'and I know the price those who give us food and shelter will pay as the intendant extends terror and repression. But what else can we do? Should we raise town and province, as Duplantier suggests, and recreate the peasant armies of the Croquants, or launch a new Fronde? The king's armies are stronger now than they were in the time of cardinals Richelieu and Mazarin.'

'You are our leader, and we follow your wishes,' said Duplantier resignedly. 'All I can say is that we have here an army of artisans and apprentices ready to fight and die. My only fear is betrayal, and we know there is a spy among us responsible for the arrest of young Aramitz and his friends. It was I who snatched the lad from under Nogent's nose, and had madame Baroja tend his wound. No one can be sure how much this traitor has divulged to the authorities. For all I know, this place may be watched and our enemies about to arrest us.'

'Not, I think, likely at the moment,' said Jatxou. 'Nogent is locked up in the Château Vieux, and the town council is dithering about its next move. But the spy among us must be found, and for that reason my cousin and I have asked the widow Baroja to attend this meeting.'

All eyes turned to Carla Baroja, who had been sitting quietly at the back of the room.

'I welcome you, my lord Audijos,' said the witch in her lilting, low-pitched voice. 'I have come to do you another service. I have spoken with the widow Aramitz about the man who came asking about her son while he was bringing you the message in Chalosse, and I know that he is here among us.'

The room became deathly still. Audijos studied the reactions of the four leaders of the artisan groups. The barrel maker pressed his lips together and seemed agitated. The two oar makers shifted their chairs as if to distance themselves from their companions. The hatter's hands fluttered nervously, and he gripped the table to steady them. Only the Basque sailor remained unmoved.

Carla Baroja rose to her feet and moved sinuously across the room to confront Iñaki Yndurrain.

'You are the bearer of a cawl,' she said. 'Perhaps you did not know that madame Aramitz shares some of the powers I possess. She sensed the presence of the charm concealed in the amulet that even now hangs from the necklace you wear."

Yndurrain's demeanour changed in an instant. He snarled like a cornered beast, and drew a long Basque knife from his belt.

'Witch,' he hissed, 'you will die for your meddling.'

As he stepped forward to stab his accuser, the sword of Audijos flashed from its scabbard.

'Die, traitor!' said Bernard as he impaled the sailor through the heart. The man crashed to the floor, and Duplantier tore open his shirt to reveal the amulet.

'What is this thing?' he asked, opening the lid and regarding the shrunken object within.

'It is a cawl we Basques sometimes carry to ward off evil spirits, ' explained Carla Baroja. 'We of the sisterhood know at once when we are close to it.'

Sanchez, Dupin and Lemercier gave voluble expression to their relief and thanked the witch effusively.

'Enough!' said Duplantier, holding up his hand. 'Let us throw this carrion into the river, and return to our deliberations. We must hear what our leader has in mind for us.'

As Audijos was holding his council of war in the house by the Nive, the premier échevin had reassembled the city fathers in the town hall. Fearing the wrath of Pellot when he learnt of the escape of the prisoners and the incarceration of Nogent, they sent Bonnicart post haste to the intendant at Mont-de-Marsan with a report defending their actions. Duvergier also authorised the jurat Peyrelongue, who happened to be a nephew of De Cheverry and a man of wide influence, to conduct a judicial investigation of the riot, so that a formal procès-verbal could be prepared for Pellot. The council ordered the guilds to be assembled to hear a new proclamation to be issued against Audijos and his followers. Gatherings of more than ten persons were forbidden without special permission; the singing of Audijos's song became an indictable offence; cabarets were to be closed at 8 p.m.; and anyone with knowledge of the Invisibles was to report immediately and in person to the premier échevin.

The town council also concerned itself with finding a way to have Nogent and his sergeant released from the Château Vieux and escorted safely beyond city limits. Nogent himself scornfully rejected these overtures. He made his way surreptitiously to the wharves and tried unsuccessfully to hire a boat to take him up the Adour to Mont-de-Marsan. The boatmen responded by raising a hue and cry, and Nogent was lucky to regain the château without injury. Before dawn on the following morning he and the sergeant managed to ride out of Bayonne without being intercepted.

Reverberations from the riot continued to be heard for several weeks. Pellot reacted first to Bonnicart and his report, and then to the sieur de Peyrelongue and his interminable procès-verbal, with calculated coldness. He did not hide his contempt for the city fathers, and told the jurat that he had asked the king to send several regiments to punish the city.

32. Lake Trasimene

Audijos and his band stayed on at the house on the Nive for a further day after the conference with Duplantier and his friends. The unmasking and death of Yndurrain was all the more disturbing because the Basque had been a trusted member of the inner circle. While they kept good watch, there was reassurance in the presence of someone who could sense danger better than any sentinel. Bernard welcomed the role Carla Baroja had assumed, but he kept his emotions carefully in check.

'Will young Aramitz survive that vicious wound?' he asked her.

'Yes, my lord. He is resting comfortably in a safe place, and his mother is nursing him. But you are about to receive unexpected news from another quarter. Someone close to you is about to join us.'

'Another of your riddles,' Bernard commented. 'I know better than to doubt you.'

Within the hour a sentinel reported a strange figure approaching the house. It was Roger Dubourdieu enveloped in a tattered cloak and shouting 'Alms, alms, for the love of Our Lady!' in a futile attempt to impersonate a beggar. The two Invisibles guarding the front of the house rose from their places of concealment and mockingly dropped some leaden bullets into his begging bowl.

'Morbleu! You rogues and vagabonds,' said the beggar. 'Can't you see I am a poor destitute soul on the brink of starvation?'

'About as famished as a horse that has eaten a regimental supply of oats,' said Audijos, stepping through the doorway and embracing his friend. 'What brings you here, and how did you find us?'

'I rode hard for two days from Hagetmau and left my mount in Jatxou's stables, where I found this accursed sackcloth and asked his servant the way to your meeting place. God's blood!

How could you penetrate my disguise? I have walked for miles in this craven habit and worked up an appetite that would shame the hungriest beggar.'

'I fancy we can feed you,' said Bernard laughingly. 'It is not every beggar that comes in cavalry boots with a sword beneath his rags. But what news do you bring?'

'That accursed Pellot has condemned some forty poor devils to the galleys. Their only crime was to have spoken in our favour, or, in a few cases, to have given our men food and shelter. In a few days they are to be taken from Mont-de-Marsan to Agen and thence to Toulouse and Narbonne under heavy guard. I thought you would wish to attempt a rescue, but we shall need to concentrate all our bands to do so.'

'That is a worthy mission, my friend,' replied Audijos. 'For once you have shown prudence, and not galloped headlong into the cannon's mouth. I shall send messengers to have our scattered forces assemble, and we shall ride tomorrow to join them.'

That evening Audijos, Dubourdien and their men, less four who had been despatched with messages for separate groups of Invisibles, wined and dined on the sumptuous fare Duplantier had provided. Roger had gone back to Jatxou's house with two men to recover his horse. They did not assume any disguise, but they saw no sign of the watch or any other threat. When they returned, shortly before Duplantier called the company to table, Roger was surprised to find that it was the widow Baroja who opened the door for them.

'So, my gallant cavalier is no longer a starving beggar,' she said with a smile.

Roger had previously been more than a little afraid of the witch, but now his suspicions had disappeared, and he looked admiringly at her comely figure.

'Boots and saddles!' he said, attempting a bow. 'It is a pleasure to be welcomed by so charming a hostess.'

She took his hand and led him to the table where Audijos and Jatxou were sitting. Before the night was out, Roger and Carla were exchanging intimate confidences, to the amusement of their friends. They embraced warmly before retiring.

'Alas!' said the swaggering cavalier. 'Tomorrow we must ride on our next adventure. By all the muskets in Gascony, I wish I could spend more time in your company.'

'I wish it too,' said Carla. 'I begin to understand your strange oaths. Perhaps they resemble my harmless spells. But I can tell you that destiny has linked our futures. I like you because you are no subtle lady's man, but a man of strength and courage who will accept a woman for what she is. My heart will go with you.'

Before leaving on the following morning Audijos instructed Duplantier to have his network in Bayonne maintain the utmost vigilance and to avoid any acts of provocation.

'You can be sure,' he said, 'that there will be reprisals after the riot. We must hope that Duvergier and the other échevins and jurats retain their authority, for they will defend the town's privileges against the intendant, even if they follow his orders to make an example of some of the citizens who support you. Let us hope there are no more spies in your organisation who may incriminate members of the inner circle.'

'We shall keep out of sight,' replied the innkeeper. 'We can look to the widow Baroja to preserve our security. I shall send reports of events to Coudures. May you succeed in your mission to rescue the unfortunates whom Pellot has consigned to the galleys.'

When farewells had been completed (and Roger's parting kiss with Carla was more public and more fervent than Audijos would have wished), the little troop of Invisibles rode east to Peyrehorade, and thence by hidden ways to Doazit, where they were welcomed by the old baron of Foix-Candale. They were joined there by another group from Hagetmau. At Coudures, where Bernard was briefly reunited with Jeanne-Marie, a third contingent met them, and a fourth swelled their ranks just south of Aire. Audijos now had nearly sixty men at his command.

Christophe de Labat had discovered that the prisoners were to ascend the Douze by boat past Roquefort to the village of Eauze, where they would disembark and march across the hills to Nérac and Agen. They were to be guarded by a company of some forty dragoons. This information gave Audijos a number of choices for an ambush, but his secret agent had not known when the quarry was to set out. He made camp in the woods south of Eauze and posted men along the banks of the river to give early warning of the enemy's approach. They waited for two days, during which the road to Nérac was carefully reconnoitred. One of the scouts found a narrow defile that opened beside a small lake into a plain beyond, and Audijos decided that this was the place to bring the dragoons to bay.

'Do you recall how maître Legrange used to read to us Livy's account of the battle of Lake Trasimene?' he asked Roger.

'Yes, I recall something of it,' Dubourdieu answered. 'It was where Hannibal trapped the legions of the consul Flaminius by drawing them towards the plain and then having his men descend from the hills when they were still within the gorge by the lake.'

'Such will be our plan,' said Audijos.

The Invisibles shadowed the barges on which the prisoners were conveyed past Saint-Justin and Cazaubon, and watched them disembark at Eauze, The dragoons had ridden beside the boats on either side of the river. Those on the southern bank forded the Douze at the point where the prisoners were brought ashore by their guards, and formed a column with one troop of horse in the van and another in the rear. After marching for an hour or so the column entered the defile. The remnants of the morning mist still hung about the hills, and the place seemed eerily silent, save for the snorting of the horses and the clanking of the prisoners' chains as they shuffled along the track.

Suddenly a scout rode back to the lieutenant commanding the company and reported that a body of horsemen was present at the mouth of the gorge.

'There are no more than fifteen of them,' he said. 'We should easily brush them aside.'

The lieutenant took no chances. He halted the column and ordered most of the rearguard to join him. Leaving the prisoners behind, he advanced at the trot, twelve men abreast. As they emerged into the plain, they were met by a volley of musketry from Audijos and his troop, who had dismounted and left their horses under cover. Down from the hills on one side came Corade and another contingent. Across the valley Baillet descended through the mist with another group in open order, while Dubourdieu and ten men, who had been following the rearguard at a safe distance, cantered forward and engaged the five or six soldiers left at the tail of the column. These rapidly threw down their arms, and had to be saved from the galley slaves, who shook their manacled fists partly in rapture at their deliverance and partly to threaten their former guards. Four hundred yards ahead, the lieutenant, seeing several of his men fall to the accurate fire of Audijos and his marksmen, ordered a retreat, only to find the Invisibles from the hills were now between him and the mouth of the defile. Audijos emerged from his cover and hailed the lieutenant.

'You are outnumbered and surrounded on all sides,' he said. Order your men to dismount and stack their arms, and you will have safe passage on foot to Nérac.'

The lieutenant ground his teeth.

'I might have known it was you, monsieur d'Audijos. I accept your terms.' He proffered the hilt of his sword as Bernard and his men came forward.

'You may retain your sword, monsieur, but I must take your men's horses and firearms to replenish my resources, and I need the keys to the manacles borne by these unfortunates you were escorting. We can provide you with litters to carry your wounded.'

'I have no choice, but perhaps our roles will be reversed if we meet again. My name is Bernardin de Marassé, at your service.

The dragoons handed over their mounts and weapons, and set off on foot northwards in dejected fashion. The Invisibles and the ex-prisoners silently watched them depart. When they had disappeared behind a grove of trees, all those at the mouth of the defile broke into cheers. Some of the peasants who had so providentially escaped the galleys knelt and held up their chains to Audijos in token of their gratitude. The grim mood that always held Bernard at times of action did not soften. He held up his hand to demand silence.

'There is work to be done,' he said. 'Corade, take four men and watch the dragoons at a distance to see they keep to their route. Baillet, look to the freeing of the prisoners, and have them bury the three dead soldiers who still lie on the grass.' He raised his voice to address the men he had rescued: 'Those of you who were condemned by the tribunal will now be marked men. Take the horses and the weapons and ride with us to a place of safety. We shall see that your wives and children are told of your escape.'

The Invisibles had not lost a single man in the encounter. After resting for an hour, they and their new recruits set off down the defile in the direction of Eauze. Dubourdieu rode forward beside his leader.

'Morbleu!' he exclaimed, 'you have out-generalled Hannibal himself. We Carthaginians have won a famous victory – and with less opposition than that offered by those Romans of the old times.'

'Perhaps,' replied Audijos,' but in that young lieutenant we have left a man as bitter as the consul Flaminius.'

33. The Bishop and The Charter

Pellot's fury at the news of Audijos's rescue of the galley slaves knew no bounds. He pored over maps with colonel Podewiltz, and designed an interlocking system of disposing the troops and guards that enabled small detachments to concentrate from all directions upon any place where Audijos or one of his bands might be reported. At the same time he hit upon a plan to impose heavy communal fines upon villages that aided the Invisibles, hoping by this means, as well as by administering summary justice to individuals through his tribunal, to cut off support for the rebels.

Pellot's new strategy was soon to be tested. Audijos had returned to the tactic of dividing his forces into small bands, which kept on the move and struck at the guards of the bureau without warning. He himself appeared with fifteen men at Montaner, a small town north west of Tarbes. When one of the châtelaine's informers reported his presence, the intendant immediately despatched a strong force of dragoons. Their approach was observed by peasants working in the outlying fields, and one of them ran swiftly to the curé, who ordered the tocsin to be sounded on the church bells. Audijos had no desire to fight a pitched battle in the streets, and he and his band melted into the woods on the far side of the town. Acting on their new instructions, the dragoons arrested twenty-three of the inhabitants, including the curé, who happened to be the archpriest of the district, and took them to Saint-Sever for interrogation.

This was the most blatant of a number of arbitrary actions by agents of the intendant, who carried writs of *pareatis* overriding the Béarnais system of justice and transferring jurisdiction to the intendant's commission. These violations of local and clerical rights stirred Poudenx to convene the standing committee of the estates of Béarn. Jean de Salies du Haut, bishop of Lescar and president of the estates, sought the aid of Poyanne in demanding that Pellot respect the Béarnais *fors* and either liberate the prisoners or allow them to be tried by local judges. Poyanne, however, proved evasive. The estates also sent a deputation to the *parlement* at Pau, and Thibaud de Lavie, the premier president, then remonstrated to Pellot that he was usurping the judicial powers of the court.

Audijos heard of these endeavours to restrict the powers of the intendant in Béarn through the curé of Saint-Sever, who had a clerical friend close to the bishop of Lescar. He thought for a moment of asking Lavie to invoke the charter of Chalosse, which he had left in the custody of Jeanne-Marie because of the dangers of his new campaign. It was as well he did not pursue the idea, for the premier président turned out to be almost as remorseless an enemy of his movement as Pellot himself. While Lavie firmly opposed the extension of the intendant's authority to Béarn, he regarded the Invisibles as rebels who should be exterminated by the rigorous application of the law. He was also jealous of the role of the Béarnais estates as a rival to the *parlement* at Pau, and he saw Poudenx as a covert supporter of Audijos.

For his part, the intendant sought to profit from the division between the two bodies that sought to curtail his jurisdiction. Like Lavie, he suspected Poudenx, whose secret earlier contact with Audijos he had discovered, and he considered Poyanne also to be sympathetic to the rebels. While insisting on his jurisdiction under his royal warrant, he decided to let Lavie have his way and released some of his suspects to the tender mercies of the Béarnais magistrates. At the same time he asked Colbert to persuade the king to send letters to Poyanne and Poudenx ordering the vigorous pursuit of Audijos. The copies he obtained of these letters would, he believed, enable him to bring to heel those members of the local nobility who sheltered under the patronage of the maréchal-duc de Gramont. However, he had also to deal with the high clergy, who exercised considerable political influence and protected the village curés in their participation in the struggle against the gabelle.

Bertrand de Sariac, bishop of Aire, had another mission in life besides his episcopal duties – the abolition of bull fighting in Chalosse. He had for long instructed his clergy that the practice was contrary to God's will, and they in turn had preached to their parishioners that present troubles resulted from divine wrath at their failure to stop the blood sport. An assembly of notables at Saint-Sever had finally agreed to ban the killing. A few weeks later an even larger meeting of deputies from a number of towns in the region was called to deal with the disturbances and financial obligations caused by the activities of the gabeleurs. It suggested to the bishop that the ban might be extended throughout Chalosse if he were to intercede with the intendant to have the troops withdrawn. Should Pellot prove obdurate, as the assembly expected, the bishop would lead a deputation to the royal court. In fulfilment of this bizarre bargain monseigneur de Sariac first obtained an interview with the intendant.

Pellot knew the bishop's reputation for supporting the causes of the unprivileged and his campaign to stop the ritual slaughter of the bulls. He decided to set his august visitor on the wrong foot.

'We are honoured by your presence, monseigneur,' he said. 'Rumour has it that you have persuaded the notables of Chalosse to deprive the poor of their most cherished spectacle in the bull ring.'

Sariac manoeuvred as adroitly as any matador.

'My good intendant,' he replied, 'the people of Chalosse know well that the miseries that have descended upon them come from God's anger at the continuance of this bloody pastime.'

'If by miseries you mean the gabelle and the rebellion against the king's servants,' said Pellot, 'you seem to imply that His Majesty is abetting a wrong cause.'

'Do not mince words with me,' said the bishop, his ruddy cheeks swelling with annoyance. 'I have come on behalf of the people of Chalosse to request you to withdraw the soldiers and the guards of the bureau who infringe their rights and persecute the innocent. In return, the notables offer their complete obedience.'

'I think you misunderstand the situation, monseigneur. What His Majesty requires is the full installation of the gabelle, and the acceptance of its burdens for the general good of the kingdom. When the smuggling of salt is terminated, and the rebellion led by that scoundrel Audijos is put down then, and then only, will the troops be withdrawn.'

'Many years ago,' said Sariac, trying another tack, ' I held in my possession an original copy of the ancient *for* of Chalosse. When it was presented to an officer of the bureau of the gabelle in protest against the illegal actions of his guards in the very seat of my diocese, he seized the document. It was subsequently recovered and passed to a learned schoolmaster in Saint-Sever, who claimed that it made the imposition of the gabelle illegal in Chalosse. I know not what became of it, but I truly believe that if the king were to see it he would support the liberties it guarantees.'

'Your grace is grasping at straws,' said the intendant. 'The law is what His Majesty wills, and he has made clear his intention to sustain the gabelle. If it is any consolation to you, I can tell you that this worthless piece of vellum is now in the possession of the rebel Audijos. Have a care that you do not associate yourself with this sedition.'

'How dare you threaten me in my sacred office!' Sariac expostulated.' I should warn you, monsieur, that your refusal to listen to reason will result in my going to His Majesty to inform him of the suffering that your intransigence has entailed.'

'I fancy your lordship will have more success in your mission to save the bulls,' retorted Pellot, smiling sarcastically.

'May God forgive you,' said the affronted bishop, turning on his heel.

The intendant sat down to write a report to Colbert, warning him that yet another meddlesome cleric was likely to seek an audience at court. The bishop, for his part, reported the failure of his interview with Pellot to the notables, and began to prepare for his journey to the north. He wrote indignantly about Pellot to his friend, the bishop of Lescar, who was using the Béarnais estates in a similar conflict with the intendant about the liberties of the province. Salies du Haut mentioned the passage in Sariac's letter concerning the *for* of Chalosse to the canon of the cathedral chapter, who was the correspondent of the curé of Saint-Sever. In due course Audijos learnt from the curé that the charter was again at issue. He began to wonder if he should entrust the *for* to the bishop of Aire in case Sariac actually succeeded in seeing the king. The notables had deputised Louis de Barry, the judicial officer arrested by Pellot and subsequently freed, to accompany the bishop. Remembering Barry's presence among the guests of the baron de Foix-Candale and Pellot's accusations against him, Audijos felt sure that Barry could be trusted as a man of the law to make good use of the charter.

It was no easy matter making contact with Louis de Barry, who, as Bernard knew, had been carefully watched by Pellot's spies since his release from house arrest. He discussed the problem with Jeanne-Marie during a visit to the refuge near Coudures.

'You must not go yourself, my love,' she said. 'Even in disguise you are likely to be recognised in a place where you are so well known. Perhaps I should seek out the lieutenant-civil in Saint-Sever under the pretence that I have a law suit to put before him.'

'On no account.' Bernard replied. 'You can be sure that that diabolic woman, madame de Sèvres, will have accused you of the death of Prugues, and you are just as likely to be recognised as I. But the idea of sending someone under pretence of legal business is a good one.'

They decided to send Olivier Sirgos, a member of the band from another district who had shown his worth in taking care of the security arrangements for the hidden refuge. Sirgos rode into Saint-Sever on the following day and requested the registrar of the prévôté to admit him to the presence of the lieutenant.

'You say you have a family law suit to place before monsieur de Barry, baron de Batz,' said the registrar, a surly man who liked to control the business in hand. 'You can leave the details with me.'

'This is an extremely delicate matter,' replied Sirgos. 'What I have to say is for the ears of the lieutenant-civil alone.'

The registrar looked at him suspiciously, and grudgingly ushered him into an inner office. Half an hour later Barry entered the room.

'I am told you wish to see me personally on a confidential legal matter,' he said.

The Bishop and The Charter

'Yes, monsieur. Are you sure we cannot be overheard? I bring a message from Bernard d'Audijos.'

'Lower your voice, man,' said the lieutenant in some alarm. 'Do you not know that any association with that proclaimed rebel brings death?'

'He believes you can be trusted secretly to support his cause, and what he has to tell you is of the utmost importance.'

Although the duties of his office had obliged Barry to sign several declarations against the Invisibles, he was prepared to take risks in support of their cause provided secrecy was preserved. He agreed to meet Audijos at dusk at the confluence of the Gabas and the Bas.

Audijos stepped out of a grove of trees as the lieutenant approached the rendezvous.

'I much appreciate your coming, monsieur,' he said. 'It does not seem you have been followed. I posted one of my men to watch the road, and he saw how you doubled back and hid for a time – a wise precaution.'

'That was only the last of my evasions,' Barry replied. 'I do not want to suffer the fate of my colleague, monsieur Pierre de Borrit, our late prévôté. I was indeed followed, but I shook off the spy by starting on a different route. What is this message you have for me?'

Bernard explained the background to the *for* of Chalosse, and the hopes maître Legrange had had for its efficacy in preventing the extension of the gabelle.

'I have it here,' he said, 'and I understand you are to accompany the good bishop of Aire on his mission to the king on behalf of the oppressed people of Chalosse.'

'I do not share your expectations, monsieur,' said Barry, 'but I am prepared to venture my life in the cause. The times have changed, and I do not think His Majesty shares the attitudes of his grandfather, the good king Henri. Nevertheless, I shall try. I shall need to keep the charter well hidden, for the intendant's spies are everywhere.'

'That I have foreseen,' said Audijos, producing a bible from his saddlebag. 'It is sewn into the binding of this holy book. Bonne chance, and may God go with you. My men will shadow you for part of the way on your journey in case you are intercepted.'

On the day after this scene Pellot summoned the châtelaine.

'I have a mission for you, madame. I have set a trap for our friend Audijos. When that windbag bishop came to me with his impossible petition I let slip the fact that the charter of Chalosse, which he thinks the king may respect, has found its way into the possession of that rebel. My lord bishop may well implicate himself in the sedition by trying to retrieve it and take it to court. If he does so, we can be sure that Audijos will follow. At the least we shall get our hands on that so-called *for* and have it destroyed.'

Madame de Sèvres smiled at the intendant.

'That fits well with what I was about to report to you, monsieur,' she replied. 'As you well know, the lieutenant-civil escaped us once and is high on our list of suspects. Yesterday, according to his registrar, who is one of our informants, a suspicious character was granted an interview with monsieur de Barry. They spoke in low voices, so he did not overhear their conversation. Knowing that the lieutenant is to accompany the bishop of Aire on his much publicised mission to court, I had him more closely watched than ever. He rode off in the late afternoon to what must have been some secret assignation. He took various measures to elude the man who followed him, and, unfortunately, succeeded in giving him the slip.'

'No matter,' said Pellot. 'It certainly seems that he has been given the supposed charter. Tell Labaume to take a troop of horse, and intercept the bishop's entourage. Here is a warrant justifying a thorough search of their persons and belongings. More importantly, have Labaume keep a sharp watch for any of Audijos's band that may be escorting them at a distance. We may even catch the leader himself, since he esteems the document so much that he will want to safeguard it.'

'The plan appeals to me,' said the châtelaine. 'With your permission, I shall myself accompany Labaume. Nothing would give me greater pleasure than to see Audijos shot down.'

The intendant looked at her intently.

'I believe you have more motives in this than you care to disclose,' he said. 'Take care to keep in the background. Audijos will not surrender without a struggle, and you are too valuable to His Majesty's service to be killed in some dark encounter.'

It was a week before the bishop was ready to depart. He might have travelled by river to Bayonne and thence by ship to the Seine, but he wished to visit his friend, the bishop of Bazas, some thirty miles north of Aire, and then to Bordeaux for the sea passage. He took with him an entourage of twelve persons, including his chaplain, Godefroy Forbin. Louis de Barry brought with him Henri de Foix-Candale, the grandson of the old baron. Henri had completed his studies at the University of Bordeaux, and was anxious to go to Paris. Unlike his invalid father, the youth was a secret adherent of his cousin, Audijos. Barry knew him well and revealed to him his own feelings about the gabelle. On the second day on the road he told him of the mission with which Bernard had entrusted him. They found the chaplain to have similar opinions and shared their secret with him.

'My lord bishop would be delighted to know the charter was travelling with us,' said Forbin. 'He has related to me the story of how it came into his possession, and was then lost.'

'It would be unwise to inform him at this point,' said Barry. 'It could be embarrassing for his grace. The intendant has had me watched, and he might well interfere with our journey.'

'And you said Bernard d'Audijos may also be following us.' put in Henri de Foix-Candale, his eyes glistening. 'There could even be a fight. I have my grandfather's sword.'

'Monseigneur would not want violence,' said the chaplain. 'Perhaps it would be wise for me to carry the holy book in which the charter is concealed. It may be safer with a man of the cloth.'

The lieutenant-civil thought this a prudent suggestion and passed the bible to Forbin. For a time he rode on ahead of the bishop's slow-moving carriage, and perceived a group of horsemen on the crest of a hill in the far distance. Young Foix-Candale dropped back, and noticed the dust raised by another troop half a mile in the rear.

Labaume and the châtelaine, together with twenty dragoons, had taken the road ahead of the bishop's party. Scouts kept level with them several hundred yards on either side of the road, watching carefully for any sign of the Invisibles. They worked in pairs and reported to Labaume every hour, but the difficulties of the terrain, and the need to conceal themselves from the bishop's entourage, made their contact with their commander irregular.

A few miles north of Roquefort, Labaume decided to halt round a bend in the road, and prepare to challenge the bishop's caravan when it caught up with them. While they waited the châtelaine reminded him that there had been no report from the scouts on the flanks ever since they had crossed the river Douze two hours earlier. Low hills covered with forest lay on either side of the road, but a number of tracks could be seen winding between the trees.

'Perhaps I should send someone into the hills to check if there is anything amiss,' said Labaume in some uncertainty.

'I think I shall go myself to the western side,' said madame de Sèvres. 'It would not look well if I were to be seen in your party when you confront the worthy bishop. A ride through the woods appeals to me after this dust-filled route.'

Labaume was clearly disturbed at this suggestion, but he was so accustomed to taking orders from the châtelaine that he did not demur.

'Go if you must,' he said, 'but return at once if you encounter danger.'

The châtelaine looked at him scornfully, and cantered off into the hills. Twenty minutes later the bishop's carriage and its outriders rounded the bend and saw the dragoons blocking their passage. Labaume rode forward, waving his warrant.

'I have orders from monsieur Pellot to search your party for an illicit document you are carrying,' he said to Louis de Barry at the head of the convoy.

'You have no right to interfere with his grace's mission to see the king by the resolution of the notables of Chalosse,' replied the lieutenant-civil.

'My right is in my warrant,' said Labaume, motioning to his troops to surround the group. Henri de Foix-Candale put his hand on the hilt of his sword, but Barry restrained him. The bishop descended from his carriage, bursting with indignation. His chaplain followed him, clutching the bible.

'This is sacrilege,' said monseigneur de Sariac. 'I know nothing of any document. Stand back or I shall pronounce anathema against you.'

Labaume ignored the bishop's fulminations, and his men began systematically to search his entourage. They had begun to tear the linings from the interior of the carriage when three horsemen emerged from the trees beside the road, Two wore the blue cloaks of the dragoons. The third, on a leading rein, was the châtelaine, her hands tied behind her back and a gag across her mouth. Assuming the dragoons were his errant scouts, Labaume did not at first notice her predicament.

'Stop!' thundered Audijos, casting off the cloak and levelling a pistol at the head of the châtelaine. 'Call off your men, Labaume, and let the good bishop proceed upon his way, or this lady dies.' Meanwhile the second supposed dragoon aimed his musket at the lieutenant. Labaume looked around wildly, but could see no way out of the trap.

'In case you are thinking of sacrificing yourself and madame de Sèvres,' Bernard added, 'look to the further side of the road.' Clearly visible among the trees were the levelled muskets of the Invisibles. 'We have followed you all the way from Aire. You should have guarded your rear as well as your flanks. Your scouts on either side resisted and have been eliminated. Now tell your men to throw down their arms and sit down. They will be tied and kept under guard for several hours. You and the lady will be held as hostages until the bishop reaches Bazas.'

The humiliated Labaume followed his instructions, and Bernard released the bonds and gag of the châtelaine.

'You will pay dearly for this,' she hissed.

Despite their gratitude neither the bishop nor Barry dared to address Audijos in public, but Henri de Foix-Candale stepped forward and laid his sword at Bernard's feet.

'Let me serve you and your cause,' he said.

34. The Net Tightens

Audijos had intercepted the châtelaine within a few hundred yards of the place where Labaume had blocked the road with his men. He had been sorely tempted to treat her in the way in which he had dealt with the two scouts a mile further back, but something had restrained him. While he fully realised what a malevolent threat she was to his movement, the memory of their early sexual encounters still lingered in the back of his mind. For her part madame de Sèvres was well aware that she faced death, and exerted all her charms in begging her captor for mercy. It was for this reason, as much as any fear that the châtelaine might give the alarm, that he had bound and gagged her. He now faced the question of how to hold her and her paramour in safe custody. Remembering the death of Boisset, Dubourdieu and other leaders of the Invisibles were in favour of immediate execution, but Audijos had given his word that they would be hostages for the bishop's safe journey. In the end it was decided to imprison them both in a deserted manoir near Serres-Gaston, well to the south of Coudures.

On the day after Labaume and the châtelaine had been locked up separately in the fortified farm house, a report came in that a strong party of the guards of the bureau were in the woods near the village of Sainte-Colombe, a few miles away. Audijos decided to take the fifteen men who were with him and launch an attack, but someone had to guard the prisoners. He turned to Henri de Foix-Candale.

'I want you to stay here,' he said, 'and keep close watch upon these two. This is your first important service, and you will need to keep constant vigilance.' The new recruit was bitterly disappointed to be left behind, but he knew that his inexperience in forest warfare might be costly to his leader, and obeyed without question. An hour after Audijos had departed, madame de Sèvres called plaintively to him: 'Help me, for the love of God. I have caught my attire in the lock of the armoire and I cannot reach the key.'

Carrying the loaded pistol that Audijos had left with him, Henri cautiously unbolted the door and looked inside. The châtelaine had locked the fringe of her dress in the heavy wardrobe and had partially disrobed in her effort to free herself – or so it appeared to young Foix-Candale. He put down the pistol and picked up the key to the armoire doors, which had fallen just beyond the châtelaine's reach. As he freed his half-naked prisoner she fell into his arms.

'My saviour,' she murmured, kissing him passionately. Foix-Candale forgot all his chief's warnings, and groped for her breasts. She responded to his lovemaking, and then, as he disengaged himself, she seized the pistol and struck him savagely on the head. Pushing his unconscious body aside, she adjusted her clothing, descended to the cellar below, and freed the distraught Labaume.

'He assaulted me,' she gasped. 'He had no mercy and took me by force.'

'May he burn in hell,' said Labaume. 'I could hear the struggle, and surely he deserves to die.' He grasped the sword that his jailer had left in the anteroom, but the châtelaine had other ideas.

'Let him be,' she said.

An hour later Audijos and ten of his men returned to the manor. The encounter in the woods had been a desperate affair in which, for once, the Invisibles had been caught in a crossfire. They had killed several of the guards in hand-to-hand combat, but had lost as many of their own band. Carrying their wounded, they entered the farmhouse to find the prisoners escaped and the body of their new recruit lying unconscious on the floor.

After their arrival in Paris the bishop of Aire made contact with the duc de Gramont to see if he would be received by the king at the palace of Saint-Germain.

'His Majesty can hardly refuse to see you, monseigneur,' said Gramont, 'but these things take time. You must remember that he has good cause to be suspicious of churchmen who come with political agenda to fulfil, and you bear a petition that favours the cause of armed rebels. He may see you as another cardinal de

Retz, who played so great a part in the Fronde, but he can be forgiving, as in Retz's case. You may have heard that the cardinal has been allowed to live in Commercy in Lorraine, and there is even some talk that he will return to Paris.'

'Your grace pays me no compliment by such a comparison,' replied Sariac. 'I have never countenanced rebellion, but they do say Audijos has many good qualities, and he has done less harm in Gascony than that unscrupulous intendant, Claude Pellot, as you well know.'

'Yes, he has despoiled my lands and made my people suffer. It is unwise, however, to praise Audijos in these parts. It is true that he does have his admirers, even at court. Madame de Motteville has sung his praises ever since he escorted her into the wilds of Lavedan. But she has little influence at court now. The queen mother is sinking fast and may not live out the year.'

While the bishop was concealing his own fortuitous contact with Audijos and pulling all the strings he could to secure a royal audience, Louis de Barry was consulting David de Cheverry, the agent for the town council of Bayonne, who still remained in the good graces of the government. De Cheverry was sceptical about the king's likely reaction to the *for* of Chalosse, and sent him to a celebrated historian, François Eudes de Mézeray, to test the validity of the document. He also recommended that Barry have a fair copy of the charter made and notarised, in case the original met with some misadventure. The lieutenant-civil improved on this suggestion, and obtained several certified copies. He also managed to see Mézeray, and found to his surprise that the historian was a freethinking man of letters who was prepared to criticise the government's policies in front of a stranger. In fact, the sight of the charter set him off on a diatribe about mismanagement of taxation in general and the evils of the gabelle in particular. But at least he seemed convinced that the *for* was genuine, and he suggested that it should be registered with the *parlement* of Bordeaux.

When the day for the royal audience finally arrived, the bishop of Aire and the lieutenant-civil of Saint-Sever, who had informed his grace about the *for* of Chalosse, were first ushered into

Colbert's bureau, where the minister briefed them on what to expect.

'We have been fully informed by monsieur Pellot,' he said, 'of the state of the rebellion against the gabelle, and we have been assured that the new measures we have instituted will destroy these bandits. Then, perhaps, the pressures caused by the presence of the troops will be alleviated. The disaffection of the people of Chalosse, Tursan and Béarn has deeply grieved His Majesty, and he expects support for the regime of the gabelle from the notables who commissioned you and their participation in the suppression of sedition.'

'If you will permit, monsieur,' said Sariac, 'we have in our possession an ancient charter that defends the liberties of Chalosse, and His Majesty has sworn to uphold those liberties.'

'Monseigneur,' said Colbert coldly, 'we have been told about your document. You may leave it with me.'

When Barry presented one of his copies, the minister seemed surprised.

'But this is not the original,' he said.

'No, monsieur,' replied Barry. 'That is to be placed before the *parlement* of Bordeaux.'

Colbert raised his eyebrows but said nothing further except to instruct the deputation to proceed to the royal anteroom. There they waited for an hour while a throng of petitioners chattered about everything from securing an office to the king's dalliance with his mistress, mademoiselle de la Vallière. When at last they were ushered into the royal presence, they passed between long lines of perruqued and beribboned courtiers before approaching the throne. The master of ceremonies announced their names and business, and the bishop launched forth into an impassioned address about the loyalty of the people of Chalosse and the wrongs that had been done to them. His Majesty appeared to listen patiently for about five minutes, and then raised his hand.

'We are pleased to hear that our good subjects of Chalosse are now ready to manifest their obedience. The matter will be taken into consideration.'

This formulaic utterance terminated the audience.

'And for this we have travelled countless leagues by land and sea!' the bishop whispered to the lieutenant-civil as they withdrew, walking backwards and bowing low at every third step.

'Yes,' whispered Barry in return. 'I am glad now that we had no chance to speak of the charter and to remind His Majesty of his oath. Perhaps it is as well that we did not surrender the original document.'

During the absence of the bishop's deputation, Pellot tightened his repressive measures, imposing more fines on villages that had harboured the Invisibles and condemning the suspects he had arrested on trivial grounds. His military dispositions restricted Audijos's plans and caused him several losses. The most grievous was the surprising of Corade and his band by Nogent's troops in the woods near Hagetmau, where the Invisibles suffered several casualties, some of them being the result of summary execution after capture. Audijos felt the loss of his men deeply, and with each new death he became more merciless towards his enemies and regretful of his leniency after his successes near Eauze and Roquefort. The adherence of young Foix-Candale to the movement had one unexpected consequence. His ailing father, once the friend of Prugues and the châtelaine's informant, repented of his treachery and confessed his spying to his own father, the old baron. Audijos, of course, had long suspected him as the source of Pellot's information about the local gentry, but now he learnt the details of what had been divulged.

The raids of the Invisibles became less frequent as the net drawn by the intendant began to tighten. They seldom stayed in the same refuge for more than a day, travelling through the woods and hidden byways between Tursan, Chalosse and Béarn. It was fortunate for them that the local populace still provided early warnings of the movements of the troops. At times such information came from unexpected quarters. Pellot sought to test the loyalty of the marquis de Poyanne by having one of the châtelaine's spies inform him of the presence of Audijos's band near Orthez. Poyanne sensed the trap and passed on the information to Nogent, but at the same time he saw to it that Audijos was warned first. By the time Nogent had arrived the birds had flown.

Audijos decided to dissolve the subsidiary bands of the Invisibles. He recalled Corade and Baillet, and yielded to Dubourdieu's request that he join Duplantier in Bayonne. Roger's real motive, to renew his pursuit of Carla Baroja, was transparent, but Bernard foresaw a need to provide new bases near the city. As it turned out, Duvergier and the other city fathers stepped up their campaign against the dissidents in the town when they received news of the approach of the two regiments Colbert had had sent from Dauphiné. Duplantier followed the path of prudence, and evacuated his ring of some two hundred citizens, much to the distress of Roger Dubourdieu, who wanted to resist the soldiers in the streets. It was Carla who persuaded him of the futility of such a course, and who arranged for a safe refuge in Labourd.

Meanwhile the security of the hideaway near Coudures was cast in doubt. Labat reported that the châtelaine's spies had followed some of Sirgos's men to within a few hundred yards of the cave. Fearful of the fate that madame de Sèvres would mete out to Jeanne-Marie if she were to be captured, Audijos gave orders for the evacuation of the place. He instructed Sirgos to move the party southwards to La Bastide-Villefranche near the border between Navarre and Béarn. They were to adopt the guise of shepherds moving a flock of sheep with their dogs. This involved slow progress, but it would account for the presence of Patou, upon whose preservation Jeanne-Marie was adamant.

Audijos and the remaining body of the Invisibles, comprising twenty-four men divided into two groups, set out for the same destination a week later. They were skirting the bourg of Salies-de-Béarn, the centre of the salt trade, when a scout reported a troop of dragoons following their trail a mile behind. Bernard ordered one group of his men to ride down a streambed to hide their tracks and then to conceal themselves in a wood. He and the remaining Invisibles increased their speed, and crossed the Gave d'Oloron near the village of Abitain. A scout, sent back to report the whereabouts of the dragoons, whom Audijos had hoped to catch between his two detachments, returned with the news that the soldiers had crossed the river lower down, at Escot. From the tracks left by their horses they appeared to be riding hard. Audijos frowned and ordered the first party of the Invisibles to spread out and proceed with the utmost caution. The scout was sent back again, this time to make contact with the second group and instruct them to keep well to the rear. Near midday Audijos and his men were approaching a low ridge when a volley of musketry rang out. The dragoons had placed themselves across his path and prepared an ambush.

Audijos wheeled his men to the right and galloped for cover. One had already fallen. Another had had his horse shot from under him and rode pillion behind a comrade. They entered a sparsely wooded area, beyond which lay a large low building. As they made for the house across an open space, more shots came from their flank, and yet another Invisible fell from his horse with a scream. They entered a narrow gateway and found themselves in a courtyard. Dismounting, Audijos hastily surveyed the defences, and placed his surviving men on the roof and at the windows of what had once been a fortified manor. As he was making these arrangements, a bedraggled, longhaired figure emerged from an inner door, carrying a musket.

'I am Jean d'Hauteville, sieur de Boueren,' he said. 'You must be Bernard d'Audijos, and I bid you welcome to my abode. This place is half ruined but still defensible, and I am ready to serve by your side. Would that I could provide you with more men, but I live here alone.'

'My thanks to you, monsieur,' Audijos replied. 'I know not how many of my enemies have trapped me in this place, but their commander must be a skilful officer to have devised such a stratagem.'

The identity of the officer was soon to be revealed. Lieutenant Marassé emerged into the open and approached the hermit's dwelling with a man beside him carrying a white flag.

'We have met before, monsieur d'Audijos,' he shouted. 'You let me keep my sword at our last encounter, and now I demand yours. You are surrounded and cannot escape. There are reinforcements close behind, and I think you would prefer to surrender to me than to their commandant.'

'We do not surrender to you or anyone else,' Bernard shouted in return. 'Withdraw before we open fire.'

As if to substantiate Marassé's words, a trumpet sounded, and a full company of dragoons and a body of guards of the bureau could be seen riding up between the trees. They were led by none other than lieutenant Labaume, who had ridden hard from Orthez when word had been received of Audijos's route. His men joined their fellows, and set up guard posts at intervals, entirely surrounding the house of Boueren and just out of musket range. Hours passed, and when darkness came the campfires lit by the dragoons illuminated their positions.

Towards midnight Audijos tried to break out. Sword in hand, he led his men at the run towards two posts on the western side. The dragoons had placed several men lying prostrate on the ground half way between the house and their guard posts to give warning of just such a sortie. As the Invisibles emerged they opened fire. A half moon had risen in a cloudless sky, but it was still too dark to shoot accurately at a rapidly moving target. The shots went wide but the soldiers in the guard posts stood to at the sound of musketry, and when he reached the tree line Audijos found himself vastly outnumbered. He pistolled one man and passed his sword through another. On his left one of his own men was clubbed to the ground, and on his right Corade and a dragoon grappled each other and rolled over and over, trying to use their daggers. Bernard realised he could not penetrate the lines without heavy casualties, and gave the signal to retreat to the house. As he did so he saw that Corade had been wounded by his opponent and dragged away. There was no time to attempt to rescue his lieutenant, and he shepherded his remaining men back to safety.

Back in the hermit's house, the Invisibles nursed their wounds and counted their losses. Strangely, although another man besides Corade had fallen, their company was only one short.

'It is I, Sirgos,' said an unexpected voice.

'By what miracle—?' Bernard began, but the new arrival cut him short.

'I have left our group of shepherds at the rendezvous ten miles from here,' he went on. 'Then I walked eastwards, hoping to come upon you. I found your second detachment about a mile away. We heard the sound of musketry at noon. When we came nearer to this place we found it surrounded by soldiers. I have placed the detachment well back in the woods on the southern side, and we planned to create a diversion two hours before dawn to enable your escape. For this to succeed someone had to tell you of our plan, so I crawled through the enemy lines and came to the outside southern wall just as you attempted your sortie to the west. I was about to join the mêlée when you ordered the retreat.'

'You have done well,' said Audijos, seeing a new gleam of hope. 'We knew we had to abandon our horses, but I thought to break the lines on foot in a sudden rush. I did not count on finding sentinels on the ground waiting for our coming.'

'No,' said Sirgos, 'but I can tell you there is at least one sentinel the less. I crawled up behind him in the dark, put my hand over his mouth and stabbed him as he lay there.'

Audijos made preparations for the second sortie, this time to the south. The hermit, who had not taken part in the first attempt, told him that in that direction a shallow ditch ran outwards from the wall. Two and a half-hours before dawn, Bernard crawled along it with all the stealth of an American Indian, his knife between his teeth. He disposed of the sentinel in that direction the more easily because the man had fallen asleep and was snoring gently. Having reconnoitred the ditch as far as the tree line, he returned to the house of Boueren.

It was nearly the appointed hour, and Audijos and his men crawled noiselessly in line ahead along the ditch. They had almost reached the end when loud shouts and random musket fire sounded through the woods. The dragoons in the two adjacent posts took up arms and sent some of their number to investigate. Audijos and his men rose to their feet and set off after them. It was another scene of complete confusion in the darkness. Many of the dragoons and guards turned when they realised what was afoot, and the Invisibles fought desperately to break through. Audijos was himself brought down by three men who hung on to him like terriers. Sirgos cut his leader free, but was himself shot at point blank range by a musketeer. Bernard and six others, together with the hermit, succeeded in escaping. They turned sharply westward to avoid contact with the soldiers who had been lured to the south by the second detachment of the Invisibles. The two groups met a mile away at a rallying point, mounted the horses that had been left there, and set off, sometimes two riders on one animal, towards the place where the late Sirgos had left his pretended shepherds.

35. Across the Pyrenees

The first sound Audijos heard, as he and the survivors of the battle of Boueren stumbled wearily into the village of Arancou, a little to the west of La Bastide-Villefranche, was the deep-throated bark of Patou, who bounded forward in unrestrained joy at the approach of his master. Behind him came Jeanne-Marie, still clad in the rough sheepskins that had served as her disguise on the long slow march from Coudures. As the lovers embraced, five men who had accompanied her emerged from a hut, clutching weapons in the expectation of an attack. They set up a cheer when they saw Audijos, but their mood turned rapidly to sadness at the news of the death or capture of their comrades, especially their leaders, Corade and Sirgos.

'They fought bravely and well,' said Bernard. 'I fear the worst for Corade, for if he survives his wounds those devils will put him to the torture.'

'No man, however brave, can withstand such pain,' said Baillet, who had led the detachment that created the diversion at Boueren. 'They will force our secrets from him, and our hidden ways and refuges will become known to the intendant.'

Grim-faced, Audijos knew his campaign was over.

'We have sustained many losses,' he said to the group. 'The dragoons are now intercepting us at every point, and the people who shelter us suffer under a merciless régime that rides roughshod over our liberties. The high and mighty in our land can no longer protect us. Our laws are flouted at every turn. The time has come for us to disband, and I must ride tomorrow for Aragon with no more than four companions. The rest of you should return to your homes, hide your weapons, and wait until I give you the call. My way will be perilous, and I cannot tell what the future holds. May God be with you.'

That night the Invisibles feasted on two of the sheep brought from Chalosse. The rest were given to the local villagers in exchange for spare horses. Despite the relaxed air of the festivities, Audijos took the precaution of posting sentinels in the woods, for he knew his antagonists would be searching for his trail. The next morning he said farewell to his followers, and rode off with Jeanne-Marie and Baillet, accompanied by Thomas Lejay, an expert marksman and former soldier, and Elias Navarro, a shepherd from Aragon who had migrated to Lavedan, where he had joined the Invisibles at the time of the revolt of the mountain men. He knew the mountains like the back of his hand. It was he who had controlled the flock of sheep on the journey from Chalosse, and who now brought with him his two dogs, much to the approval of Patou, who was, of course, included in the party. At the last moment the hermit of Boueren stepped forward.

'Take me with you, monsieur,' he begged Audijos. 'I have had my fill of loneliness, and I can serve you well, for if I die I have no one to mourn my passing.'

'Mount up, my friend,' said Audijos, 'and bring your sword and fusil with you. We may have need of them.'

Both monsieur Pellot and the marquis de Saint-Luc were in Bordeaux when news of the battle near La Bastide-Villefranche came through. They wrote separately to Colbert, blaming Labaume for not mounting a frontal attack in the house of Boueren while light remained. The intendant stated that the dragoons and guards had outnumbered Audijos and his men twenty to one, whereas the king's lieutenant-général in Guienne reported, more accurately, half that number. In any case it was clear that a golden opportunity had been missed. In another letter, Pellot said that the vicomte de Poudenx had informed him that Audijos might be escaping to Spain, and would be vigorously pursued in accordance with the orders sent personally to the syndic by the king. Pellot commented on the continuing rivalry between Poudenx and président de Lavie, and praised the latter for being the more effective in repressing the sedition.

In yet another of his missives to the minister the intendant told of arrests in Bayonne, where one suspect had described under torture the role of Duplantier in organising the artisans. It was now clear, he said, that the disaffected were planning a massacre of the notables, the seizure of the city, and the calling in of either Spanish or English forces. Pellot did not say that these were details his agents had put in the mouth of their victim during interrogation. Duplantier and many other suspects, he reported, had fled from Bayonne.

Labaume, who had sustained a serious wound in the hand during the breakout from Boueren, returned to Orthez, where the châtelaine had now installed herself. She gave him little solace, and reproached him for failing to capitalise on the information her spies had secured about the movements of Audijos.

'What is the good of providing you and the guards with such valuable intelligence,' she railed, 'when our quarry slips through your fingers time and time again? Perhaps it was not your fault on this occasion but we almost caught the Dubourdieu woman who murdered Prugues. Labat found their nest, which was right under our noses in the woods beside the Gabas. The guards moved in at daybreak one morning during your absence in Orthez, but the cave in which she and other rebels had been sheltering for so long was deserted. I am beginning to think we have a traitor in our midst.'

Labaume grunted in noncommittal fashion, wincing from the pain in his bandaged hand. In his obtuse way even he had come to realise that liaison with the châtelaine caused pain of a different kind.

Bernard and Jeanne-Marie felt their spirits lift as they followed the western bank of the Gave d'Oloron past Sauveterre and the old walled city of Navarrenx. She had exchanged her peasant garb for that of a cavalier, carrying a sword and pistol provided by the indefatigable Baillet. They had faced dangers separately in the past, and now that they were reunited the perils of the route seemed slight in comparison with their happiness. Despite his mood, Bernard took precautions. Patou trotted behind them, followed by Baillet and the hermit, who sat dejectedly in the saddle, his bedraggled locks obscuring his face. Navarro and his dogs formed a kind of advance guard, the shepherd sending his animals into the woods in wide sweeping movements as if they were searching for stray sheep. This, Navarro had insisted to Audijos, would flush out anyone watching their progress or lying in ambush. Lejay rode a hundred yards in the rear, his keen eyes watching the road behind and his musket slung to hand. The main road ran along the further bank, and the travellers met few passers-by on the paths they were following. There was one false alarm when Navarro's dogs barked at a hunter tracking a deer a hundred yards away. A shrill whistle from the shepherd brought them to heel, and the man made off into the trees.

It was growing dark as the party approached the outskirts of Oloron, which commanded the two routes that climbed vertiginously beside the mountain streams of the Aspe and the Ossau to the passes across the Pyrenees. Audijos knew that they could not count upon hospitality in the town because Lavie had sent a warrant to the jurats ordering them to apprehend any troop of Invisibles that came that way. One of the jurats had protested to Poudenx that the premier président was exceeding his jurisdiction, and the dispute had come to the ears of one of Audijos's supporters. It was also possible that there might be a patrol of dragoons in the place. The party camped in a secluded gully a little to the south, near the rocky banks of the Gave d'Aspe.

That night the hermit decided to tell the story of his life to his new friends.

'I have lived as a solitary for seven years,' he said. 'I was once a happy man, descended from a noble family near Saint-Cloud, and married to a wife I respected, who bore me four children. My lands brought me a plentiful revenue, and I had powerful friends at court. My own folly caused my downfall. I fell in with the libertines of Paris, who followed the tradition of Cyrano de Bergerac. Perhaps you know his fantastic romances that mocked the ways of society. We used to assemble at his ancestral home, close to my own estates, and there the wits and writers of Paris would gather in his memory, for he had died soon after the Fronde. Among the guests was a high born and beautiful widow, who turned out to be the devil incarnate. My father had followed the teaching of the convent of Port-Royal, which condemned the loose morality that despises the marriage vows. One day, when my wife and children were absent, he visited my home and found me in the arms of that woman. Such was his shock and anger that he incurred an apoplexy and died shortly afterwards.'

'I can understand your grief,' said Audijos, 'but surely you repented and turned back to your own family.'

'I wish it had been so,' the hermit continued,' but I was so ensnared by the pleasures of the flesh that I continued my liaison, and saw my wife and children less and less. True, my conduct was not so unusual in the circles I frequented, for marriage within our order, as you will know, is often arranged as a conveyance of property, and husbands and wives tolerate each other's infidelities.'

'So it may be among the old nobility,' put in Jeanne-Marie, 'but for me true love involves commitment, and surely there are many marriages where loyalty and affection go hand in hand. But you must tell us the outcome in your own case.'

'Well, something of my father's conscience suddenly caught my heart. I told the widow that I could see her no more. She turned on me in fury, and swore to be revenged. Two days later, when I was visiting Paris, fire broke out in my château and my family was consumed in the flames. The prévôté had his men investigate, and found that the fire had been set and the doors blocked from the outside. They could find no suspects, and for a time I was myself accused of murder. My liaison was widely known, and some said that that woman was in search of a rich husband and I a beautiful new wife. Her own consort had died some years before - it was said by poison. Evidence was lacking, and I was eventually released. I cared not whether I lived or died, and gave all my lands to the church. It was then that my patron, the noble duc de Gramont, took pity on me and granted me the deserted seigneurie of Boueren, which was part of his estates. There I have lived alone ever since, while this canker eats my soul.'

'Could you find no priest to give you consolation?' asked Baillet, who found this tragic story beyond his comprehension.

'It is useless,' said Jean d'Hauteville. 'I shall burn in hell, as I deserve – and so, too, will that infernal woman, the châtelaine de Sèvres.'

At this revelation, a shocked silence fell upon the group. Lejay, who had paid little attention to the hermit's story, went with Patou to relieve Navarro from his watch above the gully. Bernard rose and placed his hand upon the hermit's shoulder.

'I understand better than you might imagine,' he said.

When Navarro and his dogs returned, the rest of the party tried to compose themselves for sleep, except for the hermit, who sat, wild-eyed, staring at the dark and tumbling waters below.

Next morning they decided to follow the Aspe southwards to the village of Escot. The foothills of the Pyrenees were steeper in this region, and a variety of mountain streams descended through gorges to meet the main river. They might have climbed eastwards to meet the parallel course of the Gave d'Ossau earlier, but Navarro insisted that the trail from Escot would be the only practicable one. As their horses picked their way up the rocky path, Bernard and Jeanne-Marie discussed the tale the hermit had told.

'He is like the ghost of a man,' she said. 'His tragedy haunts him at every moment. And what a strange twist of fate it is that his nemesis is also ours.'

'Or would want to be,' replied Bernard. 'Let us hope that fortune will continue to favour us. There were many things he said that reminded me of the conversation of madame de Motteville and the duchesse de Navailles. They spoke of this Cyrano, who besides his fantasies was an accomplished duellist. They say he killed more men for insulting his grotesque nose than he did as a soldier in battle.'

'Well, the company our hermit kept in that circle seems preferable to his father's connection with Port-Royal. My convent in Saint-Sever also had Cistercian links, and the nuns used to repeat stories about the austerities practised by their sisters of the family of Arnauld in that place.'

'My fine ladies on the journey to Lavedan also spoke of them. Their cult, if I remember aright, was called Jansenism, and if their strictness was contrary to human nature, they did much to counterbalance the laxity of the Jesuits in the theological disputes about the nature of God's grace that were apparently the talk of

Paris. Our hermit's problems may owe something to his Jansenist upbringing.'

'You seem to have learnt much from your ladies, and I do not mean the châtelaine,' said Jeanne-Marie, blushing. 'Let us hope our love for each other may find a way between extremes.'

'We need not fence with words in the manner of those society games,' Audijos responded. 'What we have is precious and inexpressible. God grant us a happy outcome to our troubles!'

'You are a better lover than a philosopher,' added Jeanne-Marie, reaching across her saddle to place her hand in his.

As they passed through Escot, a man ran out of a farmhouse.

'You must be the lord d'Audijos' he said breathlessly. 'I am the syndic of this place. A troop of horsemen stopped here two hours ago. I overheard them saying they were searching for you. They passed on southwards but they promised to come back on their tracks if they found no trace of you. God be with you and damnation to the gabeleurs!'

'My thanks, monsieur,' replied Bernard. 'We ride east to Bielle on the Ossau. Should they return, send them on a false trail.'

Evidently the hunters were not to be deceived by the village syndic. Audijos and his group had been riding for nearly an hour along a ridge when Lejay reported they were being followed. Taking advantage of the cover provided by some trees, the party dismounted and led their horses, slipping and sliding, down a steep slope to a circle of high rocks, where they were well concealed. As he looked back to the trail they had left, Bernard was surprised to see the vicomte de Poudenx himself leading a group of gentry along the path. Although the ground was stony, the horses' hooves must have left some imprint, for Poudenx halted at the spot where his quarry had quit the path, and conferred with the other cavaliers. Then one of them dismounted and began to clamber down towards the hiding place. At a signal from Audijos the party took up firing positions, covering the horsemen on the ridge some fifty yards away. Bernard waited until the man who had been sent to reconnoitre rounded the rocks where the fugitives and their horses lay hid. Before the scout could cry out he levelled his pistol at him and said quietly:

'Not a sound, monsieur, or you and your friends above are dead men.'

'Well met, Bernard d'Audijos,' said the man. 'I believe we are acquainted.' It was the baron de Navailles-Banos, who had been among the guests to welcome Audijos at the château of Foix-Candale near Doazit.

'Well or ill met,' Bernard replied. 'I had thought that you and your leader were my friends.'

'You have our sympathy,' said Navailles-Banos, 'but the vicomte is now under direct orders from the king to arrest you. It is no longer possible for any of us to remain neutral, for we face retribution from the intendant if we do not act. Our hearts are still with you, but our hands must be against you.'

'A sorry affair when loyalties clash,' said Bernard bitterly. 'The way is clear to me. I may be a rebel but I fight for a just cause, and you and your party, monsieur, seem at this moment to be at a considerable disadvantage.'

Apart from his own danger, the baron could see three muskets and a pistol aimed at his companions on the ridge, and he knew the reputation of the man with whom he had to deal.

'So be it,' he said. 'If you will trust me I shall reclimb that slope and tell the vicomte that I could find no trace of your party. Should you decide to press on, let me tell you that the fort on the Spanish border is manned, and there are patrols lurking in the defiles of the Ossau.'

'Agreed,' said Audijos. 'I thank you for your warning. Adieu.'

Navailles-Banos could be seen returning to the ridge and talking animatedly with Poudenx. Whatever was said, the apprehensions of the watchers were relieved when the cavaliers turned their horses and rode back towards Escot. Audijos waited for half an hour before he and his party forced their protesting mounts back up the slippery slope and resumed their journey. They reached Bielle without incident, and camped to the south of the village under a cliff overhanging the Ossau. Next day they picked their way upstream on the western bank, and came finally to the town of Laruns.

Laruns was nestled among the hills at the confluence of three mountain streams with the Ossau. Behind the four valleys that debouched into the town rose snow covered peaks obscured by mists. It was raining as the party approached the outskirts, and even the dogs seemed wet and dejected. Audijos decided to seek an inn for the night, although he was aware of the risks involved. They found a humble establishment and settled the horses and the two sheepdogs in the stables. Patou, as a Pyrenean, received special privileges, and crouched beside the table in the taproom where the rest of the group was eating.

'A fine dog, monsieur,' said the landlord, 'but will his presence not betray you?'

'I do not follow your meaning, mine host,' replied Audijos. 'We are simple wayfarers who need shelter for the night.'

'Come, come! You are monsieur d'Audijos, the friend of the unprivileged and the defender of our rights. There is a troop of soldiers in the town who have told us to be on watch for a small group such as yours, accompanied by this splendid animal. I shall not betray you, but I must warn you that patrols have been checking on all the hostelries in the vicinity.'

Bernard had not counted on the description of his party being circulated so quickly, and he began to wonder if Navailles-Banos, who had had time to view their composition in their place of ambush between Escot and Bielle, had said more to Poudenx than he had promised. The vicomte must have honoured their compact in part, but this might not have prevented him from sending word of their coming to Laruns. In any case there was no opportunity to speculate. Sensing a hostile presence, Patou growled savagely, and the next instant the door was thrown open, and there stood Sébastien de Nogent with two dragoons at his heels.

'A pretty scene,' sneered Bernard's old enemy, 'especially in such charming company.' He bowed mockingly to Jeanne-Marie. 'We have secured your horses in the stables, and this time there is no escape.'

Incensed at the unwanted compliment, Jeanne-Marie was the first to react.

'Ça ho!' she shouted, giving the hunting call to Patou. The gigantic dog launched himself at Nogent, his jaws agape as if they were breathing fire like some beast from the apocalypse. Nogent had no time to draw his sword, and his men were still in the room behind him. Nogent sprang back and slammed the door, which shuddered as the weight of the dog crashed into it. In a flash Audijos crossed the room and wedged his dagger in the rustic lock.

'Quick!' said the landlord. 'There is a way out to the stables at the back.'

The party stumbled out into the courtyard, Patou unwillingly obeying his master's signal to follow. Two dragoons were standing there, one holding the horses of his companions, the other wiping a bloodied sword at the stable door. D'Hauteville stepped in front of Audijos and engaged the first soldier with his sword. There was a clash of steel and the man fell. Heedless of danger, Navarro pushed past the second dragoon into the stables. Two tangled heaps of fur lay upon the straw. Bernard disarmed the man with a flick of his wrist as the soldier half turned to check the shepherd's passage. The next moment the dragoon was seized from behind by Navarro, who cut his throat with his long knife as if he were killing a sheep.

'Vida por vida,' he muttered in his Aragonese dialect, as his victim subsided with a hideous bubbling noise.

The party entered the stables, where Patou whined softly at the sight of the corpses of the sheepdogs. They mounted swiftly, seized the leading reins of the horses of the dragoons, and cantered into the streets behind. Nogent, who had been delayed by an attempt to force the door of the taproom, rounded the inn into the yard too late. One of his men got off a shot as Audijos and the others disappeared into the darkness, but it hit no one. The officer stood there in the pouring rain, cursing eloquently.

They took the treacherous road beside the Ossau, breathing hard and riding slowly, for the wet, black night restricted vision to a few yards. After half an hour they stopped to rest beneath some trees in an adjoining ravine.

'We shall be pursued,' said Audijos, 'but we have gained some time by taking the horses of the patrol.' He looked round at his shivering followers. 'You have more skills than you told us of,' he said to the hermit, remembering the latter's sword play. 'We shall change our order of march. You shall form the rearguard. Lejay, Navarro and the dog will lead us, with the demoiselle Dubourdieu, Baillet and myself behind you. I fear the landlord will pay for his part in this night's work. I owe you my apologies for not setting one of us on watch by the inn, but luck and your courage have seen us through. Now we must press on, tired as we are. At daybreak, when we reach some mountain village, we shall change mounts, for the horses we lead are better than ours and we can leave our own with the village folk.'

Jeanne-Marie smiled at him.

'But not, of course, your mare, which I have brought all the way from Chalosse,' she said.

As day dawned they reached the hamlet of Miégebat, and rested for an hour. The rain had stopped but the mist clouded the peaks of the mountains of Goupey and Sesques to east and west. Knowing the likelihood of reprisals against those who offered them aid, they sought out none of the few mountain people who inhabited the place. Indeed, no one emerged from the five or six dwellings that composed the village, but the travellers sensed that they were being watched. They left the horses they had acquired at Arancou in a field nearby, and rode on, past the Pic de la Sagette, to the town of Gabas, where the gorges of the Ossau opened into more open country. Then they followed a swollen tributary of the Ossau upwards to rolling barren hills dotted with enormous boulders. They were now above the tree line, but since it was midsummer only a few patches of snow lay beside the smooth rocks as they approached the pass of Pourtalet.

The hermit kept a sharp lookout to the rear, but there was no sign of Nogent and his men. Ahead, Lejay saw a patrol on its way back to the fort on the border, and Audijos had the party take cover and wait for an hour. Then Navarro led them on a by-path that circled the fort and hid them from observation. On the 22 July 1665 they crossed into Spain, just twelve miles from their destination, Sallent de Gallego.

36. Sallent de Gallego

The sun was shining as Audijos and his friends approached the Spanish frontier post of El Formigal. They were no longer in defensive formation, although d'Hauteville continued to glance over his shoulder in case they were still being pursued. They were too fatigued to be apprehensive about their reception. Whatever lay ahead, they thought, must be better than the dangers and travails they had endured.

A troop of cavaliers rode out from the fort and cantered towards them. Their captain reined in his horse with a flourish before Audijos and doffed his hat.

'You and your party are welcome in Aragon, señor,' he said. 'We were told to expect you and to assure you that you will be fully protected here. Don Miguel Joan awaits you in Sallent, and I have orders to escort you.'

The officer sent one of his men ahead to give notice of their arrival. As they descended an ancient road they came upon the town nestled among clumps of trees in a valley and dominated by a lone mountain peak to the north. Fed by melting snow from a higher range on the French side of the border, a stream ran between substantial stone houses. Joan's dwelling was the largest of them all, and lay between a Gothic-styled fifteenth-century church and the market square. Its owner, who had been standing on a portico above the courtyard, climbed hurriedly down the stairs to meet them, his face beaming.

'So you have come at last,' he said. 'I have had reports of your progress from Miégebat, where you left your spare horses.'

Bernard wondered how Joan's messenger had managed to arrive before them, and vowed to ask Navarro if he had led them by a longer route.

'We thank you for your hospitality,' he said. 'Much has happened since we were together in Lavedan five months ago, and my enemies have driven me into exile.'

'I have heard of your exploits,' Joan replied, 'and now you and your companions must stay here some time to recuperate. I see you have brought one friend who will never desert you.' He whistled, and Patou's mother came gambolling into the courtyard to greet her offspring. While the dogs disported themselves and the travellers dismounted, Miguel Joan realised he had committed a faux pas.

'I meant no disrespect to the demoiselle Dubourdieu,' he said. 'Fidelity is not the attribute of beasts alone.'

'At least I am not divided in my allegiance, señor,' Jeanne-Marie laughed. 'Patou is torn between me and monsieur d'Audijos, so that he prefers us to be together.'

'May it be so henceforth,' said Bernard, 'but I may have to recross the frontier, and I would not needlessly expose you or the dog to danger.'

'Let us talk later about past, present and future,' said Joan. 'Now my servants will show you to your quarters so that you may rest and regain your strength.'

With the exception of Elias Navarro, the party slept for several hours. The shepherd was too exhilarated at being back in his native land to rest, and spent some time conversing with the servants. Lejay, who was ill at ease in such surroundings and unable to understand the language of his hosts, kept his musket by his side and slept fitfully. That evening Navarro escorted him to the kitchens and acted as his interpreter while he ate with the servants. Bernard, Jeanne-Marie, Baillet and d'Hauteville dined more sumptuously with Miguel Joan and two or three of the town notables and their wives. After the meal Jeanne-Marie resented having to sit apart with the ladies, whose language she found it difficult to understand. Meanwhile Bernard provided some details of the last stages of the campaign against the gabelle, and found to his surprise that his host seemed better informed of events than he.

'I marvel at your knowledge of affairs in Gascony and Béarn,' said Audijos. 'The network that my mentor, maître Legrange, bequeathed to me has long since broken down, and yet my supporters throughout the lands that monsieur Pellot represses with an iron hand send me what news they can. Perhaps it is because I have been so much on the move that I lack the information of which you speak.'

'It is my business to acquire what intelligence I can,' replied Miguel Joan. 'This is not simply because of my own interests in the border lands but also because the viceroys of Navarre and Aragon seek to learn from me the movements of French forces that threaten the frontiers. As you may know, the understanding between Madrid and Paris at the time of the peace has been replaced by renewed hostility.' He glanced meaningfully at the notables of Sallent, who dwelt upon every word he uttered.

'That is something beyond my knowledge,' Audijos replied. 'I should like to think I am still a loyal subject of my king, even though he has branded me a rebel and placed a price on my head.'

'These are conflicting loyalties, but remember you are now under the protection of the crowns of Castile and Aragon. Remember, too, that the people of the mountains on both sides of the border have many interests in common. I should not be surprised if this lieutenant Nogent who pursued you is ordered to cross the frontier to arrest you and your followers. If he tries we shall be ready for him, and you can be sure that any movement he makes will be observed and reported to me by my agents in France.

The conversation continued in this vein for an hour or more. Audijos noted the deference with which the notables treated Don Miguel, and concluded that he enjoyed the confidence of the highest Spanish authorities. He learnt something of high politics in Aragon and Castile, and the parlous state of the government in Madrid, where the authority of the infant king, Carlos II, was exercised by his mother, queen Mariana, whose regency was closely supervised by a junta of grandees appointed under the will of the late king, Felipe IV. At the other extreme he heard news of his friends in Lavedan. The archpriest of Juncalas and the curé of Arrens, Joan told him, had promised to visit Sallent in the immediate future.

Joan's surmise about Nogent proved prophetic. Three weeks after the arrival of Audijos the lieutenant and a troop of dragoons crossed the border on the way to Sallent. Warned of their coming, the garrison of El Formigal took up positions on either side of the road, and the militia of Sallent de Gallego marched out to support them. Confronted with superior force, Nogent hastily withdrew and reported that it was impossible to fulfil his mission. A month later he tried again, this time with twenty veteran cavaliers. On this occasion he managed to bypass the fort and enter a wood on the outskirts of the town. His presence was soon detected, and once again the militia stood to arms. Audijos was anxious to bring Nogent to bay, but Joan insisted that an armed clash would involve awkward diplomatic repercussions. To make matters doubly safe Bernard and his party were temporarily obliged to leave Sallent in case the French attempted a sudden foray. As chief magistrate of the town, Joan sent an officer to parley with the dragoons and inform them that their prey had departed. The frustrated Nogent recrossed the frontier and again reported failure.

During Nogent's incursions, Baillet and Lejay, equipped with papers in false names, made their way through Spanish Navarre to the pass of Roncesvalles, whence they proceeded to Saint-Jean-Pied-de-Port, the principal town in Labourd. There they made contact with Roger Dubourdieu, Duplantier and the leaders of the refugees from Bayonne. Most of their followers had made their way back to the city or found relatives with whom to stay in other parts of the Basque lands. Although there were royal troops in Saint-Jean, Cambo Jatxou and Carla Baroja had secured the loyalty of the local Basque community, and the group felt reasonably safe from pursuit. They had taken care to breath no word of Carla's occult powers lest Basque fears of witchcraft be aroused.

Roger was relieved to hear that his sister and Bernard had escaped to Sallent.

'Does he plan a new campaign in Béarn and Chalosse?' he asked Baillet. 'Morbleu! We need to teach Nogent a lesson, and Labaume and that woman who calls herself the châtelaine must be brought to book. We should never have let that pair escape from Serres-Gaston.'

'I fancy our leader is conferring with Miguel Joan as to future action, but he does not intend to renew our attacks on the gabeleurs until most of the dragoons are withdrawn. As to the escape of our two most dangerous enemies, we have heard from Don Joan that young Henri de Foix-Candale is still in poor condition from his head wound and is back in his grandfather's château. The old baron, by the way, is reported to be sinking fast, and may not live out the year.'

'This does not bode well for the house of Foix-Candale,' Duplantier interjected. 'The next baron is an invalid in failing health and, if the grandson does not recover, the direct line will be extinguished.'

'Yes,' said Dubourdieu, 'they have rallied many of the gentry to our cause, but now too many seigneurs have been forced to act against us. It must have been a sad blow to our leader to find himself hunted by the vicomte de Poudenx and his friends.'

'Now that I have made contact with your group here,' said Baillet, 'I think I should return to Chalosse to discover the fate of my poor friend, Corade. Lejay can return to Sallent and report to the sieur d'Audijos on the state of Labourd.'

'Then I shall accompany you,' said Duplantier. 'I need to see what has become of Coudures.'

'And I too,' added Roger. 'I cannot sit here and let my sword rust in its scabbard.'

There was a sigh from Carla Baroja, but she said nothing.

Pellot at this time was in Dax, establishing a new bureau for the gabelle and reporting confidently to Colbert that the inhabitants were too cowed to protest. In a different vein he complained of Nogent's failure to seize Audijos in Sallent, blaming the lieutenant's lack of enterprise in much the same manner in which he had earlier criticised Labaume's failure at La Bastide-Villefranche. From Dax the intendant went to Saint-Sever, where he was joined by colonel Podewiltz and président de Lavie, and extended his persecution of the supporters of Audijos. Lavie was as enthusiastic as Pellot in this bloody work, and the intendant no longer attempted to transfer all cases in Béarn to his own jurisdiction. New executions occurred at Hagetmau, where the rotting corpse of Corade, who had died under torture some weeks before, was exposed beside the bodies of more recent victims. As in the past, the châtelaine's network of informers kept the tribunals well supplied with suspects. From time to time members of the Invisibles who had gone to earth in their own villages took revenge upon those who betrayed their comrades and supporters, but they took no new initiatives against the guards of the convoy or the dragoons. Inevitably, the murders and house-burnings in the countryside gave rise to rumours that Audijos had returned.

From Bordeaux in mid-October, Pellot reported to Colbert that he was now concentrating on the arrest of the Invisibles themselves. He was offering indemnity for their own involvement to those who could identify them, and found this method 'a good means to exterminate this canaille.' Affairs, he said, had reached the point where he could reduce the number of troops. He wrote also that the village communities in Béarn on which he had imposed fines for sheltering Audijos were now disposed to meet their obligations. This was by no means true, for the villages were protesting vigorously to the estates. However, the emergency did seem to be subsiding since Audijos's retreat to Aragon, and in November Pellot drafted for the king's approval a general pardon, excluding Audijos and a few of his close associates. This received the royal assent in the following month, although some weeks passed before the *parlements* in Bordeaux and Pau registered it, and in the meantime the estates of Béarn and the city council of Bayonne complained that the terms in which the pardon was expressed implied a general culpability.

Winter snows closed the passes on the frontier, but in the spring Jean de Lanusse and Jean de Cauterets arrived in Sallent with news from the north. They were made welcome by Don Miguel, and even more warmly received by Bernard and Jeanne-Marie.

'So all is quiet in Lavedan?' asked Audijos.

'Let us say things have returned to normal,' replied the archpriest. 'Before the freeze set in, there were the customary disputes between the villages. It takes an outside threat or a cause such as yours to unite the mountain folk.'

'And in the lowlands there have been but few incidents of violence concerning the gabelle,' added the curé of Arrens. 'The main news consists of the efforts of his eminence the bishop of Lescar and the vicomte de Poudenx to have the estates of Béarn protest against the intendant's levies. They succeeded in persuading the *parlement* to join them in a new deputation to the king, and this despite président de Lavie's continuing feud with the vicomte. Before the royal pardon there were various arrests by monsieur Pellot's agents. I myself was taken on suspicion of being one of your accomplices, and held for a time in the donjon at Lourdes.'

'You may well imagine the fuss we made about it in the valleys,' said Cauterets. 'The comte de Toulongeon intervened, and so did the bishop of Tarbes. I suppose bishops sometimes have their uses.'

'It was just as well that Pellot was not in Lourdes,' said Joan, amused at the archpriest's irreverence. 'You will recall how at the time of the negotiations he arrested some of the deputies who had safe conduct, and would have arrested more if it had not been for Toulongeon and Saint-Luc.'

The conversation ranged widely over past events and plans for the future. The revolt had ended and the liberties of Béarn were still intact, but in Chalosse the gabelle was still in force, while in Bayonne the intendant was trying to change the city's form of government and tap its fiscal resources. Jean de Lanusse reminded Audijos of the charter of Chalosse, which was still in the possession of Louis de Barry in Saint-Sever.

'I still believe it can be invoked,' he said, 'if only we could arrange for its registration in a *parlement*. You may remember that I told you I know an influential judge in Bordeaux, who is an antiquarian and might be of help to us. His name is Jacques de Leydet.'

'We shall see,' said Bernard. 'My effort to persuade président de Gassion at Pau proved fruitless.'

Later during the visit of the two clergymen Bernard and Jeanne-Marie raised a matter very dear to their hearts.

'As you have probably assumed,' said Audijos, 'we have been living together as man and wife since arriving in Sallent, but we should like to have the blessing of the church. There are two obstacles: we do not have the permission of Arnaud Dubourdieu, and we are cousins in the fourth degree. My grandfather married the sister of Jeanne-Marie's grandfather.'

'In the circumstances I could marry you without the leave of your father,' said the archpriest to Jeanne-Marie, 'but only a bishop can issue a dispensation from this degree of proximity. I told you bishops have their uses, but I do not see any French bishop issuing such a document while your intended husband remains an outlaw.'

Jeanne-Marie glanced sadly at Bernard.

'We have our love and we can wait,' she said.

'And despite your sin I give my blessing on that love,' said Cauterets, 'even if I cannot unite you in holy matrimony.'

The curé of Arrens later had a private talk with Jean d'Hauteville. The hermit had tried to improve his unkempt appearance for the benefit of Don Miguel, in whose political opinions he had begun to take a lively interest. Yet his mind was still obsessed by his personal tragedy, and he hoped that the curé might somehow assuage his guilt. At the same time his memories of the salon conversations in which he had participated in Paris left lingering traces of scepticism.

'The Lord is merciful if you truly repent,' said Lanusse when he had heard Hauteville's story.

'I have tried to believe, father, but how can there be a beneficent and omnipotent God when the world is full of evil. Reason suggests otherwise.'

'Look into your own heart, my son,' replied the curé. 'Realisation of sin is a step towards belief. Your friends in Paris must have spoken of Blaise Pascal, a man of faith as well as a philosopher.'

'Of course,' said Hauteville. 'He was one of the Jansenists of Port-Royal.'

'Well, think upon his saying, my friend: the heart has its reasons that reason can never know.'

The hermit looked into the eyes of the priest, buried his face in his hands, and began to sob bitterly.

37. Conspiracy and Betrayal

Hauteville remained in a state of depression for several days after the departure of the archpriest and the curé. Jeanne-Marie tried to draw him out by asking about his experiences in the salons of Paris, a world utterly unknown to her. Her infectious gaiety enabled the hermit to recover memories of happier days and in the course of their conversation he managed to throw off his brooding gloom. Bernard looked askance at their talk of the parlour games and amorous pursuits with which the wits and fops of the capital passed their time, but he was too busy gathering news about events in Gascony to pay much attention to Jeanne-Marie's efforts to restore Hauteville's spirits.

Audijos was surprised to hear of the softening in Pellot's policies, which he assumed was the result of a change in direction on the part of the royal council. At the same time he noted that, despite the general pardon, the intendant was continuing to demand payment of the fines he had levied on selected villages. Travellers from the north also brought news that a few of the former Invisibles and their supporters were still being arrested and punished on the grounds that they had acted against the gabelle since the promulgation of the pardon. No reports arrived from Baillet, Dubourdieu and Duplantier, and Bernard became increasingly worried about his friends and lieutenants, who, like himself, were specifically excluded from the pardon. By June 1666 he had decided to recross the frontier and track them down in person, but first he had to fulfil a promise he had made to Miguel Joan to accompany him on a journey southwards to Zaragoza, the capital of the kingdom of Aragon.

Don Cristobal Crespi de Valldaura, vice-chancellor of Aragon and a member of the junta supervising the regency of queen Mariana, had ordered Joan to bring his notorious guest to Zaragoza so that he might explore the willingness of Audijos to co-operate with a possible Spanish invasion across the Pyrenees. It was also his intention to put the exiled rebel leader in contact with a group of French conspirators who were secretly planning to set up an independent republic in the south of France. The vice-chancellor was accustomed to the deceits and tensions of high politics in Madrid, where the grandees of the junta were engaged in checking the political activities of the regent's confessor, an Austrian Jesuit known as 'el padre Everado', and at the same time resisting claims to share in the government advanced on behalf of the popular military leader and natural son of the late Felipe IV, Don Juan José. Intrigue had become second nature to Don Cristobal.

It took three days for Audijos and Joan to reach Zaragoza, and within an hour of their arrival they were ushered into a room high up in the palace of the kings of Aragon, where the vice-chancellor was dictating a letter to his secretary.

'Convey my usual respects to the viceroy,' he said, 'and now you may leave us.' He turned towards his guests with an air of contemptuous hauteur that Bernard instinctively resented.

'Don Miguel has probably told you,' he said to Audijos without bothering to use the customary form of welcome, 'that the understanding between Paris and Madrid has broken down. Your king has laid claim to our domains in the Netherlands in the name of his queen, the sister of our infant sovereign. He is preparing to invade our territory, and when he does so we shall strike across the Pyrenees. What I demand of you is to support us with the forces you raised to oppose the gabelle in your lands.'

Bernard drew himself up to his full height and glared at Don Cristobal with his pale blue eyes, but he answered softly.

'It is one thing, my lord, to fight against the wrongs my king's misguided servants have inflicted on the people, and quite another to lead a rebellion against my sovereign in co-operation with a foreign power. I am grateful for the protection you have afforded me but I cannot commit so flagrant an act of treason.'

The vice-chancellor raised his eyebrows.

'There are others of your countrymen who think otherwise,' he said, motioning to a lackey standing beside another entrance to the room. 'Abre la puerta, mozo. Entre, señor.' As the door opened, a strange, bent figure shambled forward, his white hair descending to his shoulders and a long-handled lorgnette held before his myopic eyes.

'Tengo el honor de presentar el señor Van den Enden de Holanda – el señor d'Audijos,' said Don Cristobal with more formality in his introduction than he had used previously.

'A great pleasure to meet someone so famed for his defence of the common people against tyranny,' said the Dutchman in perfect Gascon. 'I have travelled much in your country in the course of my researches into the languages spoken on either side of the mountains.'

'Well met, my friend!' said Miguel Joan. 'Monsieur d'Audijos, who is something of a linguist himself, is my guest at Sallent de Gallego, as you were last year at the time of the revolt in Lavedan. I should tell you,' he went on, turning to Bernard, 'that monsieur Van den Enden is a celebrated professor from Amsterdam, now established in Paris, where students from all over Europe come to learn from him. He can manage more tongues, living and dead, than most men can imagine.'

'We have not brought monsieur d'Audijos here to discuss the professor's arcane studies,' interrupted Don Cristobal. 'It is his other role that is relevant to our purpose. This is something of which you, Don Miguel, have some slight knowledge. It is a secret of state that must be carefully guarded. You, monsieur,' he said, looking at Audijos, 'must swear never to divulge what you are about to hear.'

'I am accustomed to secrets,' replied Audijos. 'You must be aware, my lord, that secrecy is governed by interest, and you would not have brought me here if you thought it would be to my advantage to betray you.'

'Spoken like a politician,' said the Dutchman. 'You should know that my mission began when I was in Flanders. The count of Monterey, the viceroy and son of the former minister, Luis de Haro, suggested I should go to Paris and secretly work for the interest of the crown of Aragon and Castile under the cover of my studies. As his lordship the vice-chancellor knows, I have long been persuaded that republics are a better form of government than monarchies, and I have found like-minded persons who have studied with me the fate of Rome after the death of Caesar. Now that Flanders and Holland have a common need to check the aggressions of the king of France, the movement I have founded will serve the needs of my own republic and dismember the realm of the most powerful monarch in Europe.'

Audijos found it difficult to conceal his astonishment at this speech. It reminded him of maître Legrange, who had tried to explain to his pupils how Livy could idealise the ancient virtues of republican Rome while serving the emperor Augustus. Here was Van den Enden preaching the virtues of republicanism while creating an international conspiracy in terms of reason of state. Idealism and pragmatism seemed to be hand in hand. Such thoughts made Audijos reflect that his impulsive response to Don Cristobal's invitation had been more than a little hasty. He might have much to gain by discovering the secret designs of his country's enemies.

'I can see,' he said, 'how it could be in the real interests of France to put the public welfare before the glories of foreign conquest. Perhaps I spoke unwisely when I said that it would be treasonous to support his excellency's plans.'

Don Cristobal smiled ironically at this change of front. He sensed that his guest had divided loyalties, and could not be trusted with too many secrets until he had been tested further.

'That is well,' he said. 'In due course you will be informed of our intentions. The interview is terminated.'

Audijos and Joan were conducted to the lodgings that had been arranged for them, and on the following day they were informed that they should return to Sallent de Gallego.

'You should not be offended by Don Cristobal's peremptory manner,' said Don Miguel. 'This is the way in which such matters are conducted in Madrid. His Excellency is accustomed to looking over his shoulder, and I should not be surprised if one day he and the rest of the junta are sent packing by the regent and her confessor or, indeed by the worthy Don Juan José. As for me, I keep my options open, and I make it my business to keep my own knowledge of these affairs concealed from those who could do me harm.'

'I appreciate your confidence,' replied Bernard. 'That Dutch scholar intrigues me, and I wonder how far his conspiracy extends, and what his republican ideas portend for Gascony. I wish we had had the opportunity to talk more with him.'

'Don Cristobal prevented that. I should not take Van den Enden too seriously. He is the conduit for several wild plots, but he does not control them. If there is a genuine plan to erect a republic in the south of France, it comes not from the Dutchman's antiquarian studies but from two Huguenots who have designs of their own. How far Van den Enden is privy to their scheming I know not. One of them, who visited me in Sallent, is Sardan de Paul, who uses the alias of the comte de Foncenade. The other is a certain Claude Roux from Nîmes who has adopted the title of Roux de Marcilly. I learnt of him from Sardan. If you are to become embroiled in these devious schemes it may help you to know these names.'

'By some extraordinary chance I believe I have met the latter,' said Audijos. 'A man called Claude Roux served in the Cavalerie Etrangère during the Catalan campaign – an undisciplined fellow who was wounded several times in battle. His captain was Louis de Marcilly, and doubtless Roux stole his sobriquet from him. But all this seems like some fantasy to me.'

'That is the nature of such things. There are times when too much knowledge of this kind can be dangerous, and what I know I tell you from friendship.'

This conversation occurred as the two men set out on their return journey to Sallent. Audijos did not inquire as to the sources from which Don Miguel derived his knowledge of high politics in Madrid and Zaragoza, dark conspiracies in Paris and Brussels, and local feuds in the Pyrenean region, but he realised that Joan kept an open mind and followed his own best interest. It was for this reason, perhaps, that powers high and low valued their contact with him. In any event Bernard felt himself fortunate to have the wily Spaniard as his friend, and confident that Jeanne-Marie would have a safe refuge when he undertook his dangerous mission to find out the fate of his friends in Chalosse.

Audijos remained in Sallent for several days before recrossing the frontier. Jeanne-Marie begged him to remain longer, but she shared his anxiety about her brother, and made Bernard promise to send back word as soon as he had found Roger. He enlisted

Navarro as a guide for the first part of his journey, and refused the request of Hauteville and Lejay to accompany him, claiming that he could more easily avoid interception if he travelled alone. With the aid of Joan he disguised himself as a merchant, hiding his sword and musket in bales of fabric loaded on a mule. Taking two of the strongest of the horses they had commandeered from the dragoons, he and Navarro threaded their way westwards between the mountains and reached the boundary near the Col du Somport. There Audijos ordered the shepherd to return to Aragon, and began the descent of the ravines of the Aspe.

Dubourdieu, Ballet and Duplantier had reached Chalosse several weeks before Bernard set out to find them. They skirted Coudures and made their way to Ancos, resolving to return to the town under cover of darkness on the following night. Baillet's farmlet lay just outside Ancos, and he and his companions were joyfully received by a family of peasants who had worked for him as day labourers. The peasants could not provide much information about events since the granting of the general pardon, but they knew that there were still soldiers in Coudures and Saint-Sever, and that the property of the three visitors had been confiscated by the bureau and sold to new owners.

'We no longer visit your cabaret, monsieur,' said their host to Duplantier. 'It was bought by the syndic, monsieur Dumartin, and leased by him to some fellow who caters to the needs of the dragoons.'

'And what has happened to my small estate just west of here?' asked Dubourdieu.

'Your father, the judge, was able to repossess it,' came the reply. 'We saw him visiting the place the other day, and he seemed in good health. Take care, my lord, if you plan to visit your home in Coudures. There are still paid informants in the town, and everyone has been warned to report the presence of those exempted from the pardon.'

On the following morning Duplantier decided to leave his companions and ride south to inspect a parcel of land he owned near Serres-Gaston. Dubourdieu and Baillet waited until the late afternoon and set off for Coudures. It was growing dark as they approached the place, and they passed several peasants returning from the fields. As they led their horses into the courtyard of the Dubourdieu house, Bernard Dumartin emerged and walked past them without giving any sign of recognition.

'We cannot trust the syndic,' whispered Baillet. 'Remember that Christophe de Labat identified him as an informer and we burned his house. Perhaps he did not know us in the gloom.'

'Devil take him!' replied Roger. 'Even if he recognised us he may have chosen not to make trouble. A thousand curses on the treacherous rogue, may he burn in hell. Let us greet my parents.'

Arnaud Dubourdieu and his wife welcomed Roger as if he were the prodigal son, and expressed their relief at the news that Jeanne-Marie was safe with Audijos in Sallent de Gallego. Baillet was received as an honoured guest, and it was clear that the judge, although still standing on his dignity and unwilling to admit his past uncertainty about the Invisibles, now took pride in the reputation of Audijos and his bands.

'The king's pardon,' he said, 'implies that His Majesty knows of the wrongs the gabeleurs have inflicted upon us all. If only he had included Bernard d'Audijos and yourselves, but it seems that the malign influence of the intendant still prevents the full extension of the royal grace.'

'Yes,' said Roger, 'we have heard that monsieur Pellot is still insisting on the payment of the fines he levied on the communities, and his troops are still arresting individuals unwise enough to take revenge against those who informed against them.

'If only we had deputies to defend us as the estates in Béarn protect their people,' said the elder Dubourdieu. 'As to the dragoons, the latest outrage has been their occupation of the château of Foix-Candale, where the old baron and his son have both died, and the new baron is suspected of supporting your leader. By the way, madame de Talazuc had come back from Foix and was living in the château. She was arrested, but, thanks to the influence of Louis de Barry of Saint-Sever, she has been allowed to return to her home in Coudures.'

Roger and Baillet thought immediately that Audijos would welcome news of his mother. The other details mentioned by the judge reminded them that young Henri de Foix-Candale had been one of their most enthusiastic recruits and might still be suffering from the wound he received at Serres-Gaston, while the allusion to Barry called to mind the fact that he was probably still in possession of the ancient charter of Chalosse. But the conversation was interrupted at this point by Christophe de Labat, who brushed past the servants and burst unceremoniously into the room.

'You have been betrayed by the syndic,' the bailiff blurted out. 'The dragoons are already on their way here. You must leave at once.'

'Are you sure of that?' demanded Baillet.

'I know because I have continued to play the double game for which you recruited me. The châtelaine still thinks I am her spy. The gabeleurs trust me with their secrets, but they will do so no longer if they find me here and know that I have warned you. Come, we must waste no more time with words.'

At that moment the neighing of a horse and the clatter of hooves could be heard in the courtyard. Arnaud Dubourdieu moved to the vestibule in an attempt to delay the intruders, while his son, together with Labat and Baillet, fled into the garden through a rear exit. The front door was flung open in the judge's face, and he was pushed aside as an officer and several soldiers entered the house.

'How dare you invade these precincts! I am an officer of the duc de Gramont,' expostulated Dubourdieu. 'You will find no one here save my family.'

A pistol shot and the clash of steel in the garden belied these words. The officer, who had replaced the wounded Labaume, had sent some of his detachment to the back of the house before riding into the courtyard. Labat fell, mortally wounded. Baillet rolled sideways, stunned a soldier with the butt of his pistol, and fled into the darkness. Roger was less fortunate. For a moment he broke free from four or five men who assailed him, but then he tripped and fell, and his attackers swarmed over him.

The officer stepped into the garden, summed up the situation, and directed some of his men to pursue Baillet.

'So,' he said to his sergeant, 'we have captured one principal rebel, and disposed of the traitor long suspected by madame de Sèvres.'

Roger's parents, silent and aghast at what had happened, stood aside as their son was led back to the courtyard, his face bleeding from wounds and his hands tied behind his back. The soldiers remounted and, leading their prisoner with a rope round his waist, passed through the gateway into the street.

38. Bordeaux

Géronce Baillet knew the byways of Coudures far better than his pursuers. He doubled back on his tracks and hid in a hayloft where he could see Roger Dubourdieu being dragged along the main street by the dragoons. He waited there for several long hours and shortly before dawn set out in the direction of Doazit in the hope of making contact with the new baron de Foix-Candale. He anticipated a house-to-house search in Coudures and mounted patrols in the vicinity, and made as much speed as he could to distance himself from the town. At the village of Sainte-Colombe he cautiously approached the home of a former member of the Invisibles. To his good fortune the man was saddling his horse in the stable, and when he heard of Baillet's plight he did not hesitate to lend him the beast.

By noon Ballet had reached the outskirts of Doazit, where he enquired at an inn about the situation in the château of Candale a mile to the south. He was told that the dragoons were still occupying the place, and that the young baron had moved to a manor house on the fringe of his estates. Tired and hungry as he was, Baillet was soon at the baron's door. A servant asked him to wait while he reported his presence to his master. Henri de Foix-Candale came out to meet him with a smile on his emaciated face.

'You are more then welcome here,' he said, 'but where are Audijos and Dubourdieu?'

Baillet told him that, as far as he knew, his leader was still in Aragon and Roger had been captured at Coudures through the perfidy of the syndic, Dumartin.

'My sympathies, my lord, on the passing of your father and grandfather,' he went on. 'The old baron was a powerful support for us. And you yourself, have you recovered from your wound at the hands of that terrible woman?'

'It has been a slow recovery,' replied Henri de Foix-Candale. 'It has not just been the head wound. I fear I have inherited something of my father's ailment. He died before my grandfather passed away, deeply regretting the path of betrayal on which his evil friend, Prugues, had set him. But there, at least, there is some good news. Madame de Sèvres has withdrawn the information about Prugues's death that she registered with the lieutenant civil-et-criminel, Louis de Barry.'

'Why by all the saints would she do that?' asked Baillet in astonishment.

'Some say it is part of the intendant's new policy of moderation and appeasement, but I suspect that it is part of a plot to lure demoiselle Dubourdieu back to Coudures as bait for monsieur d' Audijos. Monsieur Pellot has returned to Bordeaux, and I plan to ride there soon to use what influence I can in this new climate of affairs to have the dragoons withdrawn from my lands. Perhaps, since Audijos is my cousin, I could even negotiate the terms of an agreement to extend the pardon to those who are exempted from it.'

'It would be a bold venture, my lord, since you are yourself regarded as an enemy of the gabelle. If you go to Bordeaux, I should dearly love to accompany you in some suitable disguise. However, there are two other matters that need attention. Roger Dubourdieu will face the executioner unless something can be done, and Bernard d'Audijos still hopes that the charter of Chalosse may be proclaimed by the *parlement* of Bordeaux. It is now, I believe, in the hands of monsieur de Barry.'

'Then I shall ride first to Saint-Sever. Barry may also be able to intervene on Dubourdieu's behalf. I am not inclined to try my sword to effect his rescue. Judicial mercy has long been a scarce commodity in these parts, but I shall see what can be done. It would not be wise for you to enter Saint-Sever in present circumstances. Wait here until I return, and then you can come with me to Bordeaux.'

Despite his physical frailty, the young baron had acquired a commanding air since his adventures with the Invisibles at Roquefort and Serres-Gaston, and Baillet readily fell in with his plans. When he arrived in Saint-Sever he found Louis de Barry deep in conversation with père Anselme, whom he knew well, and another cleric unknown to him.

'We know your sympathies and welcome you to our conversation,' said Barry to Foix-Candale. 'This is père Jean de Lanusse, curé of Arrens, who is a close friend of our own curé, and who once had the celebrated *for* of Chalosse in his possession. He has come to suggest that it is time we took it to the *parlement* of Bordeaux. You will remember that I accompanied monseigneur Sariac all the way to court in the vain hope that the king would acknowledge it.' He looked archly at the young baron, who had deserted that mission to give his loyalty to Audijos.

'I am not likely to forget,' smiled Foix-Candale, 'and while we are perhaps unwilling to mention names, a certain gentleman who has just escaped from an affray in Coudures has sought my protection and, by strange coincidence, has suggested that his nameless leader would be well pleased if I took the said charter to Bordeaux.

'The saints be praised!' returned Lanusse. 'Perhaps I might give you a letter to my friend, conseiller Jacques de Leydet, who may be willing to promote the charter with his fellow judges.'

'That would indeed be welcome,' said Foix-Candale. 'I too have some contacts, though of lesser weight. I studied law at the university of Bordeaux, and some of my friends are now practising at the bar of the *parlement*.'

And so it was decided. Louis de Barry handed over the precious charter, and père Lanusse wrote his letter. Barry also agreed to do what he could for Roger Dubourdieu. He pointed out that several circumstances favoured the case. Pellot's personal tribunal was not at the time acting in the district, so that another court, the sénéchaussée, would have jurisdiction, and Roger would not be tortured. The accused's father, in whose presence the arrest had been made, was a man of substance and good repute. Moreover, the châtelaine, whose sinister role was becoming widely known, had just left Saint-Sever to join Pellot in Bordeaux. But since Dubourdieu was a named exemption from the king's pardon, he would almost certainly be found guilty. If he confessed his alleged crimes, Barry believed, his sentence might be commuted to some years in the galleys.

'I suppose this likely outcome is the best we can hope for,' said Jean de Lanusse. 'As to the charter, its acceptance by the *parlement* at Bordeaux would have pleased my late friend and Audijos's mentor, maître Legrange, had he survived the assassins of the gabelle. It is important that Audijos be informed of these matters. I shall set off at once for Sallent de Gallego.'

When Henri de Foix-Candale returned to Doazit he found Baillet dressed as a gentlewoman, and ready for the journey to Bordeaux. 'Your disguise becomes you well,' said the young baron, 'but are you supposed to be my wife or my doxy?'

'Perhaps I could be your sister, my lord. I know I can pass well enough for a woman. Once when we were attempting to rescue two of our band at Hagetmau, I adopted the habit of a nun.'

This recollection reminded Baillet of Arnaud Corade, and he smiled sadly at the thought of his dead friend's impersonation of a friar. There was much time to reflect about the past on the long journey, for Foix-Candale's weakness obliged them to travel slowly. When they arrived at last, they lodged with one of the baron's friends from his student days, who was newly registered at the bar of the *parlement*. Raymond de Sallegourde belonged to a noble dynasty of the robe. His father, Odet, whose office he would in due course inherit, was a colleague of Leydet in the main chamber of the court.

Henri de Foix-Candale trusted his friend so well that he decided to inform him of their mission. Sallegourde looked curiously at Baillet.

'You play your part well, madame – uh – monsieur,' he said. 'I would not have suspected your disguise had I not noticed the way you dismounted from your horse in the courtyard. You need not continue the charade here, but I think you must conceal your real name. He turned to Foix-Candale. 'My father is a man of extreme caution. He would have a fit if he knew that someone with a price on his head was sheltering under his roof. We must hide from him your association with the notorious Audijos, but there is no harm in telling him about the charter of Chalosse. In fact he is something of an antiquary himself.'

Shortly after this conversation, Odet de Sallegourde returned from the *parlement*. The conseiller was a rather pompous little man, some fifty years of age. He made Foix-Candale welcome, but did not meet Baillet, who, having shed his disguise and assumed the role of the baron's valet, had taken himself off to the servants' quarters. The elder Sallegourde was indeed intrigued with the charter, perusing it through a magnifying glass and handling it as though it were about to dissolve into fragments.

'Extraordinary!' he muttered, rubbing his hands. 'This is a document of the greatest importance. To read it is to see how all the ancient liberties of Gascony have been set aside in recent times, despite all the fine promises of our kings. You say you hope to persuade my friend, conseiller de Leydet, to have the charter registered by the *parlement*. It is the kind of thing he might well do. A rash cause indeed, but one for which I might cast my vote if others had a mind to support it.'

On the following day Foix-Candale accompanied Raymond de Sallegourde and his father to the *parlement*, where they found Leydet sitting at his desk in a room close to the great chamber. He was an intense, cadaverous man, whose dark eyes glittered as if he were consumed by some inner fire. He read the letter provided by père Lanusse, examined the charter carefully and then insisted that Foix-Candale tell him every detail he knew of its provenance and recent history. It was as well that the curé of Arrens had briefed the baron about the research on the *for* conducted by maître Legrange.

'I have heard of the Legrange you mention,' said Leydet. 'He left the law faculty at Toulouse with a reputation for backing lost causes, but some of them were causes with which I am in sympathy. Perhaps it is unfortunate that the document he so treasured has become associated with the rebel Audijos, but a general pardon has now been issued for his followers, and one cannot suppress the truth just because it was invoked imprudently. Yes, I shall sponsor the charter's registration.'

'Eventually I may support you,' said Odet de Sallegourde, 'but first I must think more on the matter. It will not sit well with the intendant.'

In contrast with this tepid opinion, Foix-Candale was so overjoyed by Leydet's statement that all discretion vanished.

'Monsieur Pellot has stamped on the rights of Gascony for long enough,' he blurted out. 'Now that his superiors are reining him in it is time for the restoration of the old laws. He has yielded on much and he may yield more. I must tell you that it was not just the charter of Chalosse that brought me to Bordeaux. I seek an audience with the intendant to have the troops withdrawn from my lands. If all goes well I may even request a pardon for my cousin, Bernard d'Audijos.'

These words visibly shocked conseiller de Sallegourde, for whom this was the first intimation that his son's friend was linked with Audijos. Leydet, on the other hand, was amused at his colleague's consternation.

'I shall ask monsieur Pellot to grant you an interview,' he said. 'I do not trust the man, but you may be right in thinking that this is the time to ask his indulgence.'

Foix-Candale thanked the judge, and handed him the charter of Chalosse. Two days later he was admitted to Pellot's bureau.

'With all respect, monsieur,' he said, 'I have come to beg the removal of the dragoons from my château and my estates.'

The intendant twitched his heavy eyebrows.

'We are reliably informed, monsieur, of your close association with the rebel Audijos. However, it is now our policy to heal wounds and lead the people of Gascony back to their loyalty to His Majesty. Give me your assurance that you will no longer engage in treasonable activities, and I shall withdraw the soldiers.'

'I am most grateful and do so promise, but there is one more matter I wish to present to you. A true peace may never be attained unless you seek His Majesty's pardon for my cousin Audijos and his lieutenants. He has so won the hearts of the people that resentment and disobedience will only cease when my cousin receives the royal grace.'

'There was a time when such advocacy would smell of treason. However, I can tell you that some consideration has already been given this question in the king's council. Exemptions from the general pardon may be cancelled if your cousin agrees to depart permanently from this land and reside in New France on the other side of the ocean. Our problem is to establish contact with the rebel so that he may know of our offer.' Pellot looked quizzically at Henri de Foix-Candale.

'It is my understanding that Bernard d'Audijos now resides in Aragon,' said the latter, who immediately perceived that this gesture stemmed not from mercy but rather from the desire to forestall Audijos's co-operation with Spain in the impending hostilities. 'I shall explore ways of making contact,' he added cautiously.

After the baron's departure Pellot sent for the châtelaine. She swept into the room as if she resented the summons, and ignored the intendant's clumsy bow.

'I hear we have wasted an opportunity,' she said. 'Young Dubourdieu has been taken at his parents' house in Coudures, but his case has been handled by the lieutenant civil-et-criminel, and he has merely been condemned to the galleys without proper interrogation.'

'All is not lost,' replied Pellot. 'He is still being held at Saint-Sever, and I have a mind to put him to the question to see if we can learn more of the designs of the rebel Audijos.'

'I doubt if you will discover anything of value. My agents have reported that the two have now been apart for some months. Dubourdieu arrived in Chalosse in company with Baillet and Duplantier. The latter is said to be in Serres-Gaston, but Baillet was in Coudures and managed to escape. No one knows what has become of him.'

The intendant's eyes gleamed in triumph.

'We shall send the guards of the convoy to Serres-Gaston. As to Baillet, I have news for you. An informant in the house of Sallegourde has told me that a man disguised as a woman arrived there with young Candale. I have just seen the new baron, and he has fallen for our plan to offer pardon to Audijos if he consents to go to America. If we track Candale's contact with our enemy, we may well lay our hands on him. As to the transvestite, I have every reason to believe it is Baillet. His effeminate ways hide the traits of a dangerous assassin. I have already sent guards to arrest him.'

'Good news indeed,' said the châtelaine. 'But will not Candale react so strongly to the arrest of Baillet that he renounces his promise to make contact with Audijos?'

'No, I believe he will convey the offer, come what may. At last we are bringing the scum that led this revolt to heel. It compensates a little for the humiliation I have felt by being obliged to pursue this feigned policy of reconciliation. Monsieur Colbert has even conceded the demands of the city of Bayonne. I have had to abandon my planned revision of its charter of government, to allow some of the prominent exiles to return, and to cancel new fortifications that would have given the royal garrison greater control of the place. I have pretended, of course, that it was my intercession with the minister that secured these bumbling bourgeois their demands.'

When Henri de Foix-Candale returned to the home of his friend Raymond de Sallegourde, he found the place in uproar. In his absence a sergeant and a file of militia had burst into the mansion with a warrant from the intendant, and taken Baillet away in chains. The conseiller sat in the library with a wet towel over his head, bemoaning his aching brow and bleating about invoking the privileges of the *parlement*. His son stood enraged before the stables, calling for the servants to saddle a horse so that he might ride to the house of Jacques de Leydet. In an instant Foix-Candale's high hopes were replaced by something close to despair. He no longer had any hope for a pardon for Audijos, although he felt bound to inform Bernard of its terms. Perhaps the dragoons would leave Candale – perhaps not. Above all, he feared for the terrible suffering he knew Baillet would endure.

Géronce Baillet showed incredible fortitude in keeping silent through two sessions of torture. On the third he broke, but his string of incoherent words about the Invisibles provided no information of value to the intendant. He clung to life for some days after his torment, and died alone from his injuries. Not long afterwards Duplantier was ambushed in Serres-Gaston, and killed two of his assailants before he expired. His corpse was taken on a farm cart to Saint-Sever, where it was suspended from a gibbet. In the jail nearby, Roger Dubourdieu lay chained to the wall, swearing monstrous oaths. At night he dreamed that Carla Baroja was standing before him, saying, 'Fear not – your rescuer is coming.' Meanwhile a merchant in fabrics encountered the curé of Arrens on the banks of the Gave d'Oloron.

39. A Perilous Rescue

It had been raining, and Audijos had been having trouble with Joan's recalcitrant mule on the downward slope of the track beside the river near Oloron. There had been few passers by, and he had been too intent on observing the rough terrain beneath his horse's hooves, and too busy tugging on the lead rein of the mule, to pay attention to other travellers. As he crouched forward in the saddle with his hat pulled down over his ears and his sodden cloak concealing his accoutrements, he was unlikely to be recognised as the notorious leader who had defied the king's regiments. Certainly Jean de Lanusse, riding in the opposite direction, would not have guessed the identity of the figure in his path. Yet some unknown impulse caused Audijos to glance forward at the curé of Arrens.

'Hold, monsieur le curé!' called Bernard. 'What do you here, so far from your parishioners in Lavedan?'

That commanding voice and those steely blue eyes provided instant recognition.

'The Lord be praised,' replied Lanusse. 'It is Bernard d'Audijos, for whom I have travelled all these leagues in the hope of finding him in Sallent.'

'No, no,' said Bernard, 'it is Gaston Pérrier, dealer in fine cloths. Well met, my friend. Come, let us find some safe inn in Oloron. I am starved for food and yet more for news.'

An hour later, seated before a fire, the two men exchanged accounts of all that had befallen them since their last meeting. Bernard was deeply distressed at the news of Roger's capture, but delighted to hear that Foix-Candale and Baillet had gone to Bordeaux with the charter of Chalosse and an introduction to a sympathetic senior judge in the *parlement*. He was relieved to know, too, that Louis de Barry would mitigate Dubourdieu's punishment, and that Jeanne-Marie was no longer threatened should she return to Coudures.

'I shall find Duplantier in Serres-Gaston,' he said, 'and we shall see if we can rescue Roger. Will you ride on to Sallent and inform his sister of my plans?'

'I should prefer that to accompanying you,' said Lanusse. 'Violence is not my way, and I trust you will take what precautions you can when you reach Chalosse.'

'I shall not court unnecessary danger, but such a rescue involves perils that must be faced. There is one more favour you may do me. I tire of this foolish disguise, and have no mind to drag this accursed mule all the way to Saint-Sever. Señor Joan generously provided me with the animal and its cargo. Perhaps you may take them back to Sallent? Besides, if someone were to ask me the cost of a yard of worsted, I should be utterly lost.'

Somewhat ruefully the curé accepted this charge. Audijos recovered his sword and musket from the bales of fabric, and the next day the two friends parted. Looking back, Bernard smiled as he saw Lanusse wrestling with the unwilling mule.

The horse that Audijos had taken from the dragoons at Laruns was a vigorous animal, and he made good progress to Navarrenx. Thence he struck northwards through the wooded hills he knew so well, and crossed the Gave de Pau near Lescar, where he spent the night in a farmhouse. The owner had recognised him immediately, despite the full beard he had grown in his persona of the merchant, Gaston Pérrier. To his host, Audijos was the hero of many exploits against oppression, and particularly of the adventure in which he had freed the district of the bandit Mazerolles seven years earlier.

'Why, that was even before you took up the cause against the gabeleurs, my lord,' said the man.

'Not quite,' replied Audijos, remembering the affray at the ford across the Adour that had incurred the reproaches of the duchesse de Navailles.

'But now the king has issued a general pardon, and the times have changed,' he went on. 'You know, of course, that there is a price on my head, and that you risk death by sheltering me.'

'It is an honour, my lord,' said his host. 'There are many hereabouts who would gladly die for you. But the times have not changed that much. We still have the gabelle.'

Audijos knew the risk he ran, despite the support of the rural populace. He recalled Lanusse's parting words, but he had grown accustomed to constant danger, and luck had been with him so far. He rode on to Hagetmau, where he learnt that the dragoons had been withdrawn from Doazit and the lands of Foix-Candale. He visited the young baron on the following night, taking elaborate precautions to ensure he had not been followed. He climbed in unseen through a side entrance and surprised the baron in his cabinet. After the initial shock of this unexpected appearance, Henri de Foix-Candale greeted Audijos warmly and told him of the support conseiller Leydet had promised to give the *for* of Chalosse in the *parlement* of Bordeaux. The news of Baillet's terrible death was a cruel blow, and made Audijos reflect on the urgent need to rescue Roger Dubourdieu before the intendant turned his attention to the prisoner in Saint-Sever. Bernard bade farewell to the baron, and before daybreak was on the outskirts of Saint-Sever. He resolved to reconnoitre the place before making contact with Duplantier.

As he passed his old school, Audijos thought to himself that with the publication of the charter he would have fulfilled some part of the mission entrusted to him by maître Legrange. He had intended to consult the curé of Saint-Sever, whom he knew he could trust, but a servant told him his master was absent so he rode on to the town square. There a scene of horror confronted him. Hanging from a gibbet was the rotting corpse of his old friend Duplantier – the generous host of the tavern, the indefatigable organiser of the resistance in Bayonne, the man of infinite resource and courage – there he hung twisting lifeless in the stiff morning breeze.

For once Bernard's *sang froid* deserted him. He gasped and nearly fell from his horse. Then, dismounting, he sat listlessly beside the well, while the horse, insensible to the emotion of the moment, sank its head in the drinking trough. It was still early in the morning. There was some movement on the other side of the square, and Bernard noticed a number of soldiers leading their mounts from the courtyard of the hôtel de ville. They climbed into the saddle and rode off on patrol. A cold fury possessed Bernard, driving caution to the winds. He primed his fusil, inspected his pistol, and loosened his sword in the scabbard. With his musket under his arm, he strode across the square, tethered his horse in the yard, and entered the building.

Inside the doorway a young soldier was sitting listlessly, chewing on a crust of bread that served as his breakfast. Bernard levelled his weapon at the sentry's chest.

'I have come to take delivery of monsieur Dubourdieu,' he said. 'Lead me to the jailer and thence to the cells, or you are a dead man.'

The soldier blanched and rose unsteadily to his feet.

'You have papers, monsieur?' he gasped, half realising with whom he had to deal.

'I am Bernard d'Audijos, and this is my warrant.' The musket was thrust beneath the boy's chin. 'Now lead on, and make no sound if you want to live.'

They proceeded down a corridor, passing various rooms where other members of the garrison were rising from their beds and preparing for the day. Some of the doors were open but no one happened to look up and see Audijos and the sentry. They climbed down a twisting stairway, inhaling the stench of the dank and noisome air from below. The sentry stopped at a heavy doorway that led to the jailer's room and the cells beyond. Audijos knocked lightly and the door opened to reveal a squat, burly man, his eyes rheumy with sleep and a ring of keys in his hand.

'What—?' he growled. Audijos struck him down with the butt of his musket before he could utter another word. Pushing the terrified soldier before him, Audijos picked up the keys and opened the cell in which Roger was confined.

Roger could scarcely believe his eyes when he saw his friend. He began to utter some stentorian oath of welcome, but Bernard had crossed the cell in a second and placed his hand over the mouth of the prisoner.

'Make no noise,' he whispered. 'We have yet to escape from this place and there is a hornets' nest above through which we must pass.' He freed Roger from his chains and began rubbing his limbs to restore some circulation.

'I have been lying here in this filth for longer than I can remember,' said Dubourdieu as he tried to rise to his feet. 'I think there are four or five poor fellows in the other cells who, like me, are awaiting convoy to the galleys. If we have to fight our way out of this hell hole, they may be useful.'

The young soldier, who might have tried to escape while this conversation was occurring, chose instead to assist in helping Roger regain his strength.

'You may think it strange that I aid you, monsieur,' he said,' but if you don't shoot me my lieutenant, monsieur Labaume, probably will for failing to give the alarm.'

'Once again Labaume crosses our path,' Audijos remarked grimly. 'How many men does he command above us?'

'Some fifteen or so. The rest have set out on the dawn patrol.'

Bernard released the other convicts, who had not been considered as dangerous as Roger, and consequently were not manacled and in better condition for action. He entered the jailer's room in search of weapons, and found to his consternation that the man had disappeared. At the same time the muffled sounds that had come from the floor above were replaced by shouts and the tramp of feet.

'He has given the alarm,' said Roger. 'We are caught like rats in a trap.'

A familiar voice was heard at the top of the stairs.

'There is no escape,' shouted Labaume. 'Throw down your weapons and come up one at a time.'

'Wait, messieurs,' said the soldier quietly. 'Some days ago I heard my officer disputing with the town officials about our occupation of the hôtel de ville and the prison. They particularly objected to the storage of munitions in the place, but the lieutenant defied them. If I am not mistaken, casks of powder are hidden in a recess along the passage before us.'

Audijos looked curiously at the boy.

'You have done us a signal service. What is your name?'

'Gilbert Defaux, my lord. Fate has cast my lot with yours. I seek only to survive.'

'You remind me of my youth,' replied Bernard. 'We shall see what fate provides.'

Audijos directed the freed prisoners to place the barrels below the topmost turn of the stairway, and ran a trail of gunpowder down the remaining stairs and along the passageway. He lit the fuse and retired with Roger and the others to the furthest cell, closing the jail's heavy door on the way.

'Part of the blast will shoot towards us,' he said. 'We must hope that the main jet will blow upwards in the line of least resistance.

The force of the explosion blew the prison door off its hinges but harmed none of those lying on the floor of the most distant cell. Above stairs was a scene of devastation. The stairway was blocked and the men stationed by Labaume in the corridor near it were killed instantly. Others, further back, were screaming from the pain of their injuries or lying unconscious. Labaume and two of his men were the only ones unscathed. Audijos and his party threw aside pieces of broken wood and stone and emerged into the vestibule of the ruined building. Half blinded, Labaume stood sword in hand among the smoking ruins to bar their passage. Killer though he might be, he did not lack courage.

'You shall not pass,' he cried.

'By the blood of Christ, this is my honour,' said Roger, taking Bernard's sword from his hand. Steel clashed against steel. The conflict was not uneven, for, though Roger was the more skilful of the two, his muscles were weak from his confinement. Labaume had recovered from his wound at the battle of Boueren, and he seemed to be gaining the upper hand when one of the freed convicts, unused to the conventions honoured by Audijos, threw an axe he had taken from the jailer's room. Its blade caught Labaume full in the face and his massive frame crashed to the ground.

'So be it,' said Bernard. 'It was in like fashion that he is said to have slaughtered Captain Boisset.'

There was no time to be lost. Audijos knew that the explosion must have been heard by the patrol, who were probably riding with all speed back to their headquarters. His own horse had broken its tie-rein and bolted in terror at the time of the blast, but there were fresh horses in the stables. Roger's fellow convicts chose to go their separate ways, while he and Bernard mounted and galloped towards the river. The noise of the explosion had brought the people of Saint-Sever into the square, and a cheer went up as Audijos and the former prisoners disappeared into the side streets. Young Gilbert Defaux stood in the smoking ruins awaiting the return of the patrol and wondering, somewhat remorsefully, whether his part in the escape would be discovered.

Bernard and Roger dismounted by the river and slapped their horses on the rump in the hope they would return to the town hall. They commandeered a skiff, and pushed off into the Adour, trusting that their pursuers would not expect them to travel by water. The journey proved to be slow and uneventful. They passed the town of Dax and the junction with the Gave de Pau, and arrived at last in Bayonne. There they made contact with Cambo Jatxou and imparted the sad news of the death of his brother-in-law. Roger asked the whereabouts of Carla Baroja, and was told she had gone to the Basque city of Bilbao.

'Perhaps,' he said, 'we too should cross the frontier and avoid retribution against those who shelter us in France.' Audijos, anxious to find some way to return to Aragon, readily agreed, and Jatxou arranged for them to take passage to Bilbao on a Basque vessel owned by one of his friends.

The harbour of Bilbao was crammed with ships of all kinds. Audijos asked the captain of the fishing boat on which he and Roger were the only passengers whether so much of a bustle was normal for the port.

'Oh no, monsieur,' the man replied. 'This is the royal fleet of Spain fitting out to transport reinforcements to the Low Countries, which have been invaded by the king of France. We Basques on either side of the border do not pick sides in such hostilities.'

When Audijos looked more carefully, he saw that many of the vessels were equipped with cannon, and Dubourdieu, standing beside him, drew his attention to several formations of troops drawn up on the quays. Suddenly his eyes picked out a figure on the nearest wharf, and he forgot all about military matters.

'Look, look!' he shouted, pulling Audijos by the sleeve. 'By all the angels in heaven, it is Carla who has come to greet us.'

40. Deception and Disaster

As their vessel approached the wharf, Roger waved energetically to Carla Baroja, but instead of responding she pointed to a group of armed men on the quay, and the thought came into his mind that they would cause trouble. The men came aboard the moment the ship docked, and Audijos looked inquiringly at the Basque captain.

'There are new formalities,' the latter said. 'The presence of the king's fleet in Bilbao requires these officials to check all persons going ashore in case there are spies or saboteurs.'

'We have no deed to disguise our identity,' Bernard declared. 'I have already been granted sanctuary in Aragon, and my friend, monsieur Dubourdieu, will, I am sure, be given the same status.'

So it proved to be, but the officials had clearly been warned to be on the lookout for Audijos, for when they heard his name they insisted that the two arrivals accompany them immediately to the fortress where the corregidor resided. Carla smiled at them as they passed by her under escort, and once again Roger had the impression that she was telling them to be on guard.

The corregidor, or governor of Vizcaya, the almost independent province of which Bilbao was the capital, was himself a Basque, although he spoke both Castilian and French. He received them with considerable ceremony.

'You have a reputation, monsieur,' he said to Audijos, 'as a valiant friend of Spain, and here, as in the other ports and frontier posts, we have been told to bid you welcome. It so happens that the noble admiral Don Juan is in this town to inspect the fleet before its departure, and he most certainly will wish to see you. In the meantime you will be my guests.'

Roger Dubourdieu did not welcome this enforced hospitality when his principal desire was to see Carla Baroja, but Bernard convinced him that it would be prudent to restrain his impulse to leave the fortress and he knew, in any case, that Carla would make contact when opportunity offered. The next morning the two men were ushered into the imposing presence of Don Juan José, Knight of Saint John and Grand Prior of Castile and Leon. Don Juan had lived up to his honorary title of Prince of the Sea through his exploits against the French in Barcelona and his repression of a revolt in Naples when he was viceroy in Sicily. His last command, when he had led the Spanish forces opposing the Portuguese attempt to reassert their independence, had been less successful. It had suited the junta in Madrid to offer him the governorship of the Spanish Netherlands, now under threat of French invasion, but Don Juan, after inspecting the fleet in Bilbao, had decided that this was a ploy designed to remove him from the centre of power at a time when the conflict between the regent and the junta was in flux. On the very morning that he saw Audijos and Dubourdieu he had sent a messenger to Madrid declining the post in Brussels.

'I bid you welcome, messieurs,' he said as the corregidor presented the two and then withdrew. 'We are familiar with your campaign north of the Pyrenees, and we have been informed, monsieur d'Audijos, of your presence in Aragon and your visit to Zaragoza.'

'Yes, your excellency,' replied Bernard. 'Don Cristobal told me something of a plot against my king, and asked me to co-operate with a possible invasion of my country.'

'I have been told of your hesitation, and I can understand it, but these are troubled times and loyalties are not always clear cut.' As he said these words Don Juan smiled wryly, thinking of the devious intrigues in which he himself was involved. In Aragon he knew that the vicar-general, Don Cristobal, was at odds with the viceroy, the count of Aranda, and he fancied that the former had given him information for reasons connected with his ambitions. Aranda was known as a critic of the boy king's elder half-brother, and Don Juan's rehabilitation meant Don Cristobal's advancement.

'You see,' Don Juan continued, 'I too have been made privy to some part of this conspiracy to dismember France, and I believe that factions in Spain are uncertain of its efficacy. I am frank with you because there is a man here called Roux de Marcilly whose real intentions I find hard to fathom. I want you to talk with him and draw him out. I was told you knew him in the Catalan campaign fifteen years ago.'

'We can try,' replied Bernard, anxious to associate Roger with this bizarre turn of events.

'Yes, my lord,' interposed Roger, who had found the conversation difficult to follow. 'We can certainly try, and in the meantime, perhaps, you may grant us leave to explore Bilbao.'

But Don Juan kept the two men for a further half hour, talking of affairs in Gascony, and asking their opinion of Miguel Joan.

'He has been a good friend to us and knows far more of politics and events on both sides of the Pyrenees than any man,' replied Audijos. 'He told us of another plotter, the so-called comte de Foncenade, who had visited him in Sallent.'

'Yes, he is another mysterious figure. But it is the loyalty of Don Miguel that interests me. I have many supporters among the caballeros of these kingdoms, but I also have enemies in high places, so I need to evaluate the intelligence he provides.'

'It is hardly for me to say, your Excellency,' replied Audijos. 'I can only report that he has spoken of you with admiration.'

Bernard and Roger had evidently made a good impression on the prince, who offered them places in his entourage should they wish to stay in Spain. He gave them the address of the hostelry where Roux was to be found, and asked them to return when they had discovered more about the conspirator's plans. They departed with the conviction that they had found a valuable patron, who, like themselves, was more at home on the battlefield than in the corridors of power.

Soon after leaving the fortress they were met by a man who claimed to have been sent to conduct them to Carla Baroja. They followed him with some caution, for Bilbao seemed to them a strange and hostile place. They were led to a house on the waterfront, where Carla was waiting. She embraced Roger warmly, and curtseyed low to Bernard.

'You are my saviour, my lord,' she said to the latter, 'and now you have brought back to me the man whose love I have been fortunate to win.'

Audijos smiled.

'I need not ask how you knew of monsieur Dubourdieu's capture and imprisonment in Saint-Sever. Your powers are beyond my understanding.'

'I did not know anything precisely,' she answered, 'but I sensed he was in great danger and somehow I felt that you were coming to rescue him.'

'So that is how you sent me a message in my dreams,' said Roger.

'It may have been so,' Carla went on. 'I sensed, too, that you were both following me to Bilbao. Here there are many things that will affect our future. My cousin, who led you here, has told me of a man who is staying at an inn nearby who seems surrounded by mysteries.'

'And, since coincidence is part of the occult world you seem to control,' said Audijos, 'he is doubtless this Claude Roux we have been asked to interrogate.'

'Hobgoblins and imps from hell!' exclaimed Dubourdieu. 'Is it any wonder I am bewitched?'

'I forgive you the quip,' returned Carla. 'My cousin says he is a tall, long-faced man with dark hair who never stops talking and makes no secret of his identity.'

'Strange for a secret agent,' mused Bernard. 'I doubt we should recognise him now after all these years, but let us go find him.'

The two friends proceeded to the adjoining tavern and sat down near a man who answered Carla's description, and who was holding forth in a mixture of French and broken Castilian on international diplomacy.

'The interests of Spain are bound up with the Protestant countries of the north,' he said to the two or three bystanders who seemed more amused than convinced by the speaker's discourse. 'France under its tyrant king is the common enemy. The great fleet in this harbour will soon sail, not just to defend Flanders and Brabant, but also to aid the Dutch Low Countries against the French threat. England has ended its war with the United Provinces and should join in alliance to stop the tyrant's aggression. He is withdrawing the liberties of French Protestants like myself, and soon he will abrogate the fundamental edict by which his grandfather guaranteed us toleration.'

Audijos and Dubourdieu waited until the man had lost his audience, and then approached him.

'We overheard your words, monsieur,' said Bernard. 'Are you not Claude Roux of the Cavalerie Etrangère of the Catalan campaign?'

'I am Roux de Marcilly,' said the man, looking intently at the two. 'Yes, I had the honour to serve there, and now I have a greater mission to perform. Do I know you?'

'Do you recall the action in the hills of Manresa, where your company fought alongside the Créquy Cavalerie? We are Bernard d'Audijos and Roger Dubourdieu, who aided you when you were wounded in that engagement.'

'The good Lord has designed this meeting,' replied the surprised conspirator. 'The years have changed us all, but now I do remember you. There are great things afoot, and you two, who have led the resistance of Gascony against the tyrant, may have a role to play. I sail with the fleet to the Low Countries, but I have a powerful protector here in the prince, Don Juan José, and I can present you to him before I leave.'

'There is no need for that,' replied Audijos. 'We are more interested in the plan to establish a republic in the south of France, and we have been informed by monsieur Van den Enden that you are associated with a group that has that aim.'

'You have met Van den Enden?' said Roux. 'Then you have heard of the Committee of Ten and of Sardan de Paul?'

'In part,' said Dubourdieu, catching the drift of Bernard's questions. 'What exactly is this secret association?'

'Only the initiates may know, but I can tell you it is spread through Switzerland, Franche-Comté, Lorraine and France.'

Roux would not be drawn further on this issue. He did, however, elaborate on the idea of a separate republic: 'It is not simply the ideals of ancient Roman republicanism of which you have doubtless heard Van den Enden speak. There are many seigneurs in Gascony and Languedoc who know that after the massacre of Saint Bartholomew's Night, nearly a century ago, those of the reformed religion set up virtual republics in the south, where nobles, towns and pastors enjoyed the rights of self rule through their representative bodies. What is more, I came to know one of Cromwell's agents in Savoy at the time of the English protectorate, and he convinced me of the evils inherent in monarchy. But this is a distant project. What I plan at present is to facilitate an alliance between the English, the Swedes, the Dutch, and perhaps the Protestant Swiss cantons, to check the French armies in the Netherlands, and that is why the Spanish support me.'

At this point a messenger arrived to tell Roux that he was required to embark immediately, as the fleet would soon get under way. Feeling that they had done their best to acquire the information Don Juan had requested, Audijos and Dubourdieu assured the unlikely conspirator that they would further consider his plans, and made their farewells.

They remained in Bilbao for a further week, during which Bernard described the grandiose ideas of Claude Roux to Don Juan, but saw little of Roger, who spent most of his time with Carla. Knowing that Roger felt bound to accompany Audijos to Aragon, Carla decided to return to her relatives in Saint-Jean-de-Luz, where she hoped her gallant suitor would eventually rejoin her. Meanwhile Don Juan sent a messenger to Sallent de Gallego carrying a letter from Bernard to Jeanne-Marie, and an instruction to Miguel Joan to procure what further information he could about the Gascon part of the supposed conspiracy. The corregidor made supplies available to the two cavaliers for their journey, provided them with a guide, and equipped them with passports.

The guide was a surly fellow, who seemed to resent having to accompany two Frenchmen, and was more interested in stopping to eat at every wayside inn than in making good progress. They passed through Vitoria, and thence to Pamplona, the capital of Spanish Navarre. There they debated whether to ride eastwards through less mountainous country before turning north to Sallent, or to ascend the pass of Roncesvalles and take the mountain tracks on the Spanish side of the border. The guide assured them that the latter route was the shorter.

'Besides,' he added, 'you can see the place where the army of your emperor Charlemagne was routed by the Basques.' In the old story where Roland and Olivier had died awaiting the return of Charlemagne it was Saracens, not Basques, who had ambushed the heroes, but Bernard and Roger let the remark pass without comment. They had travelled but a few hours on the road to the mountains when a horseman caught up with them from the direction of Pamplona. It was Jean d'Hauteville.

Hauteville had ridden hard. His horse was lathered, and he seemed out of breath.

'So glad I found you,' he gasped. 'I could not locate you in Pamplona, but I met some travellers who said they had seen two men answering your description take the mountain road. The demoiselle Dubourdieu asked me to ride to meet you as soon as she had received your letter. She is concerned about a new guest of Don Miguel, a fellow calling himself the comte de Foncenade.'

'Calm yourself, my friend,' said Audijos in reply to this torrent of words. 'I have heard this man is a conspirator in some wild scheme, and he has visited señor Joan before. But why does he alarm Jeanne-Marie?'

'He presses his attentions on her, and I fancy he is no gentleman. I offered to intervene, but she asked me not to disturb Don Miguel by provoking a quarrel.'

'Then we must hurry forward,' said Audijos. 'When do we reach the next village? It is growing dark,' he called to the guide.

'There are few villages in these hills,' replied the guide. 'This is the land of the Agotes of Navarre, mountain people who do not welcome travellers.

It became increasingly difficult to follow the treacherous path, and the party decided to camp for the night beneath some trees near the mouth of a ravine. Although they all felt fatigued by their journey, they lit a fire and prepared some food before settling down to sleep. There were animal noises further off in the woods, and the horses stirred uneasily in their pickets. Once Audijos thought he saw eyes reflecting the firelight among some bushes. He took the first watch himself, and sat by the fire with his musket primed. Shortly before midnight he awoke the guide, and told him to keep alert and to waken Roger, who was snoring stentoriously, after two hours. When Bernard and Hauteville awoke shortly before dawn, Dubourdieu was still snoring, but the guide and the horses had disappeared.

They followed a trail of blood into the woods, and found the body of the guide lying on his face with his head battered to pulp.

'This must be the work of a bear,' said Roger, still wiping the sleep from his eyes.

Audijos turned the corpse over.

'We are intended to think so,' he said, 'but bears do not cut a man's throat. Moreover, the traces of the horses have been severed cleanly. Let us follow their hoof marks, which are clear enough in this damp soil.'

There were strangely smudged footprints also, as if the men who made them wore rough moccasins of animal hide. Beyond the woods the ground was dry and the trail more difficult to discern. After an hour's trek over rugged terrain they saw smoke rising behind a steep hill. Climbing cautiously to the crest, they looked down over a cliff on a village where the habitations were made of dried mud and animal skins. Many of the people they could see walking between the huts were clad in the skins of wolves and bears.

'These must be the Agotes of whom our guide spoke,' said Audijos. 'Compared with them, the folk in the remotest valleys of Lavedan have attained the heights of civilisation. But if they are primitive, they are also great hunters. To have murdered our guide and stolen our horses without waking us was a singular feat.'

As he spoke a noise behind them made all three men turn suddenly. Some twenty figures stood there, hirsute and cloaked in skins, with axes and long knives in their hands. It was obvious from their menacing mien that they did not intend to parley, and in any case none of the three cavaliers knew what language they spoke. The hunting party moved forward, uttering low growling sounds.

'I see a path running down the side of the cliff towards the village,' said Jean d'Hauteville. 'It is our only means of escape.'

'Go while you can,' said Bernard. 'I shall hold them off for a while.'

'No,' roared Roger. 'We stand and fight side by side against this rabble of savages.'

'Two cannot stand abreast on this path,' said Bernard, pushing his friend behind him. He raised his musket and shot the foremost of their assailants. The rest were on him in an instant. Roger stepped forward, pistolled one and stabbed another. Picking up yet a third of the wild men, he threw him bodily over the cliff. Then his foot slipped on a stone and he went tumbling down the path towards Hauteville, who had turned and was climbing back to join in the struggle. But it was too late. Audijos was submerged by a crowd of attackers, striking and stabbing. Roger regained his feet and thought for a moment of re-entering the fray. He could see that there was no hope, so he began to descend the path with Hauteville, cursing and lamenting as he went. The hunters seemed to have had enough bloodshed and excitement for one day, and none of them followed.

The two survivors reached the bottom of the cliff, and skirted the village without interference. Then they returned to their campsite and gathered what provisions they could carry for their long hike to Pamplona. In the city they reported the assault by the Agotes and the death of Audijos and the guide, but the authorities merely shrugged their shoulders.

'If you were crazy enough to travel by such a route,' said one of them, 'you must expect such an outcome.'

Hauteville and Dubourdieu, who gained some respect by telling of his meeting with Don Juan, eventually were provided with fresh horses, and made their way by the easier road to Sallent de Gallego. There they described the disaster to Don Miguel.

'It was not far from Roncesvalles,' said Hauteville, 'and truly Audijos died like Roland in the old legend of Charlemagne and the Saracens at the pass.'

'But Olivier, his friend, survived,' said Dubourdieu, 'and will carry the shame of it to his dying day. And what am I to say to my sister, who loved him as no woman has loved man?'

'Let me break the news to her,' said Don Miguel. 'She has locked herself in her room, because she says my conspiratorial guest, Sardan de Paul, has been pursuing her. I cannot afford to see the man off because he is the source of much valuable information, and he has lingered here in the hope of telling Audijos of his plans.'

'Ah!' interrupted Roger. 'I suffer from no such hesitation, and my sword tingles in its scabbard to teach a lesson to a scoundrel who makes advances to my sister while waiting to unfold his plots to her absent lover.'

'I doubt if anything serious has occurred,' returned Joan. 'She is an attractive woman, and this fellow fancies himself as a ladies' man. I am sure she knew how to deny him her favours, even if she finds it impossible to be rid of him.'

'What is more,' Hauteville remarked, 'we still, I take it, want to continue the mission of Bernard d'Audijos. This plotter may have something to contribute to our cause.'

'Yes,' said Don Miguel, 'he has told me much, but there is more to discover. See if you can gain his confidence. If it does not help your cause, it might be used to secure your pardon.'

'Devil take it!' grunted the exasperated Dubourdieu. 'Must all honour be sacrificed to these deceptions?'

So it turned out that Jean d'Hauteville entered into the secret ways of Sardan de Paul, alias the comte de Foncenade, while the heartbroken Jeanne-Marie decided to return to Coudures with Patou, under Hauteville's escort. At first it was Roger who had insisted upon accompanying her, but it was pointed out to him with some firmness by his sister that it would be madness for a condemned galley slave to return to the district whence he had escaped. Instead, he resolved to make his way to Saint-Jean-de-Luz. In preparing for her journey, Jeanne-Marie was distressed by losing the letter Audijos had sent her from Bilbao. She searched high and low without success, and finally asked Don Miguel to forward it should it be found. For his part, Foncenade, thinking he had made a convert of Hauteville, set off for Bordeaux without even bothering to say farewell to the woman he had professed to admire. Meanwhile, in a vile smelling hut south of the pass of Roncesvalles, a gravely wounded man was gradually recovering his strength.

41. The Châtelaine's Date with Destiny

The spring of 1668 came slowly, and the great port of Bordeaux was once more crowded with vessels. In the *parlement* conseiller de Leydet succeeded in persuading his colleagues to register the charter of Chalosse as 'a document setting forth the principles on which these provinces were formerly governed.' As his friend, conseiller de Sallegourde, remarked, this was not likely to provoke the intendant since to say what used to be was very different from saying what ought to be. In fact the intendant chose to ignore the *parlement's* declaration. He had more important things to consider, notably the threads of a new conspiracy that had just come to his notice.

Pellot was discussing affairs with the châtelaine. 'We are entering a new phase,' he said. 'A plot has been spawned in the course of our war with Spain. As you know, we have taken Franche-Comté, but His Majesty has chosen to make peace rather than confront the alliance of England, Sweden and the Dutch republic. I have been informed that that alliance was promoted by a Huguenot exile called Roux de Marcilly, although his was but a minor part. A despatch has reached me from monsieur Hugues de Lionne, our minister for foreign affairs, reporting that monsieur de Ruvigny, our ambassador in London, has uncovered a conspiracy in which this fellow Roux is one of the confederates planning to detach certain provinces from the kingdom. In particular, one of his associates is said to be present in Gascony, and that is where you may have a role to play.'

'Well, monsieur,' the châtelaine responded, ' I am certainly tired of this petty spying against Audijos and his followers. We have disposed of most of the leaders, and, while there are many who are still disaffected, your gabelle remains solidly in place and the king's pardon is generally welcomed.'

'Yes, but Audijos is still in Aragon, and his friend Dubourdieu has not been recaptured.'

'I should dearly love to catch those two,' said the châtelaine, curling her lips vindictively. 'They killed my henchman Labaume – though, truth to tell, I had become weary of his bumbling ways. But what is this new task you offer me?'

'I want you to make contact with the conspirator in Bordeaux whom I mentioned. He goes by the name of the comte de Foncenade, and he has been reported as lodging in a house behind the cathedral of Saint-André. I know you have your own methods to win the confidence of such a man.' The intendant paused and glanced significantly at madame de Sèvres, who tossed her head and looked back at him through a cascade of auburn hair. 'We need to know his contacts and the nature of his plot. One of his associates is this Roux de Marcilly whom I mentioned, and it would be useful to discover his present whereabouts.'

'You could simply arrest this Foncenade and force him to talk'

'Yes, but it may be better to let things develop a little, so that others will incriminate themselves. There is said to be a circle in Paris run by some Dutch mountebank, and another in Rouen. I am most interested, of course, in Gascon and Béarnais noblemen, many of them heretics, who are thought to be trying to recreate the old Huguenot republics.'

'These schemes smell of fantasy to me,' said the châtelaine. 'This is a very different task from my pursuit of Audijos and his friends, who were men of daring and fought for a practical cause.'

'Yet it is more of a threat to His Majesty's authority. Rebels and hypocrites as they were, those who opposed the gabelle always professed loyalty to the king, whereas these conspirators seem to be convinced republicans. Moreover, they are desperadoes who take life cheaply. There is real danger in the role you are asked to play. Perhaps I should assign some swordsman to protect you in case of need. Lieutenant Nogent might serve the purpose.'

'As you will, but he seems to have been as inadequate as the late Labaume in dealing with Audijos.'

'It may be so,' said the intendant, his sunken eyes gleaming with malice, 'but he is resourceful and has some stake in redeeming his reputation.'

Two days later Sébastien de Nogent reported to the châtelaine.

'You have orders for me, madame?' he asked in a tone of resignation, as if being assigned to the service of so notorious a woman was a poor substitute for military command.

'Yes, monsieur. We are required to penetrate a ring of conspirators, and our first task is to make the acquaintance of a certain comte de Foncenade.'

Nogent recruited a group of urchins who soon located the false count and reported his daily comings and goings. He observed a pattern of walking to the wharves at a set time in the morning to visit a particular vessel. Madame de Sèvres arranged to have her coach lose a wheel as Sardan de Paul was emerging from his quarters. She pretended to fall from the vehicle and injure her arm.

'Monsieur,' she called plaintively, 'aid me, I beg you. I am in pain.'

The ruse was completely successful. Sardan was at once enthralled by this attractive and highborn lady, who seemed to have fallen into his arms. He curled his moustache, assumed his most charming manner, and assisted her to his rooms. There he offered to call a surgeon, but the lady assured him that the pain had departed, and she needed only to bathe her arm in warm water. Within an hour the châtelaine had accomplished the first part of her mission, and was exchanging intimate confidences in his bed.

'So this great mission on which you are engaged will alter the governance of this part of the kingdom,' she said. 'I have long been critical of the tyranny that has abased my own and many other noble families. We need to go back a century to the times when we controlled our own destinies.'

'Exactly so, my lady. The spirit of revolt is still alive in these provinces. Look at the success of that rural squireen Bernard d'Audijos, whose vision was limited to fighting the gabelle.'

'So you know of the exploits of the noble Audijos. He is something of a hero in these parts.'

'Yes indeed. I had hoped to enlist him in my venture, and was awaiting him in Sallent de Gallego when the news came through that he had been murdered by some wild mountain men.'

'Is he really dead?' asked the surprised châtelaine. 'I know something of the man, and I wonder how you would have persuaded him to join you.'

'Well, he was reliably reported as overcome by his assailants while fighting like a lion. Two of his companions escaped, thanks to his prowess, and gave me the details. One of them has already enlisted in my cause. As to persuading the man we now think has perished, I found out much about him from the woman he professed to love. I even managed to steal from her his last letter, which I thought might prove useful.'

'I should not write off Audijos yet,' said madame de Sèvres. 'He has an extraordinary capacity for survival. Tell me, you must know something of this Miguel Joan in Sallent.'

'He is man who seems to trade in commodities of all kinds, including valuable information about everything that goes on north and south of the border, but he would tell me little about Audijos, whom he seems to regard as his friend.'

'Perhaps he would trade more intelligence if you could supply him with fresh news of value. I happen to have contacts in high society who might give me such items of gossip. I know you will think it is mere idle curiosity on my part, but I have long been interested in Audijos and the movement he led. Who is this associate of his that you enlisted in your cause?'

'He is a man called Jean d'Hauteville who used to have estates near Paris and belongs to an illustrious family. He is due to visit me here today.'

The châtelaine sat up with a start.

'I think I met him in the salons of Paris long ago. It may be wise not to tell him of our association.'

'Ah!' said Sardan. 'I suspect he was your lover, and I shall respect your wish. We are both people of experience in such matters.'

'Yes, count,' replied the châtelaine, 'and I hope we shall continue to take pleasure in each other. You may be able to satisfy a whim of mine. I believe this Hauteville may have an interest in the woman you mentioned, a certain demoiselle Dubourdieu of Coudures. I should dearly love to have some piece of evidence of Hauteville's association with her.'

'I am inclined to think you have a grudge to pay,' said Sardan, smiling. 'It will be a pleasure. Clearly we have much in common in intrigues of love and politics.'

The châtelaine began to think she had gone too far. The false count had revealed himself not only as an ardent lover but also as a clever and perceptive conspirator. She was also afraid of meeting Hauteville, and took her leave after arranging their next assignation. Her carriage had been repaired, and Nogent was waiting for her.

The intendant was pleased by the châtelaine's progress. She took care not to reveal to him her conversation with Sardan about her personal interest in Audijos and her early affair with Hauteville, but she did report the story that Audijos had been killed in the mountains. Here Pellot had news for her.

'We have heard from an agent in Pamplona,' he said, 'that our main quarry has survived, though severely wounded. He is said to have been brought to Pamplona by some mountain men, and is recovering under the care of expert physicians.'

'I had a feeling it might be so,' replied madame de Sèvres. 'He will doubtless make for Sallent when he is well enough to travel. It might be a good idea for me to journey to Sallent myself. According to Foncenade, this Joan is a venal fellow who might give us more information if we give him something in return, and we might at the same time finally rid ourselves of Audijos. Nogent could accompany me in disguise, but we shall need some papers authorising our presence in Aragon.'

'I shall make arrangements,' said Pellot. 'After all, we are no longer at war.'

The false count had begun to communicate more and more of his schemes to Jean d'Hauteville, and in return he learned some of the personal secrets that Hauteville disclosed as a means of gaining the conspirator's confidence. He found out the details of Hauteville's liaison with madame de Sèvres, and the tragedy that had driven his new recruit to despair. He did not, of course, tell Hauteville of the lady's presence in Bordeaux, nor did he hint at his own involvement with her. This particular conversation led him to suspect that the châtelaine was a dangerous woman, whose interest in his own schemes might not be as innocent as she pretended. He also discovered that Hauteville had indeed been an admirer of Jeanne-Marie, that he credited her with saving him from his black mood, and that Hauteville had actually written a poem to his saviour. While hesitant about so intimate a matter, the former hermit was unconscionably proud of the skill as a versifier he had once practised in the salons. Professing a lively interest in verse, Sardan persuaded the poet to lend him a copy, and thought to himself that this would be exactly what the châtelaine had been seeking. For his part, Hauteville acquired details of the conspiratorial network in Paris and Rouen. Sardan told him that he was soon to travel to Normandy, and gave him the names of several Protestant seigneurs privy to the plot, to whom he could introduce himself, armed with the secret code words that would establish his credentials.

On the next occasion when he met the châtelaine, Sardan was no less enthusiastic in his lovemaking, but far more reticent about his conspiracy. In order to lull her suspicions he did provide some information, but most of it was entirely imagined. He promised to tell her more at their next meeting, and delighted her by handing over Hauteville's poem to Jeanne-Marie. But when madame de Sèvres returned for the next assignation, the comte de Foncenade had vanished, and no one could tell her what had become of him. Nogent's inquiries were equally unsuccessful, and the intendant fumed at the disappearance of his suspect.

When Audijos had regained consciousness in the woodsmen's hut, his body ached all over from his contusions, and he was aware of being weak from the loss of blood he had sustained from a number of stab-wounds. A bearded face was leaning over him, and spoke to him in Béarnais. 'You are very fortunate, monsieur d'Audijos. I am from Lavedan, and I recognised you in the mêlée and called off your attackers. We have carried you here and tended your wounds as best we could. When you are stronger we shall take you to Pamplona.'

Audijos remained in the hut for several weeks. He found that his rescuer was a man from Arrens, who had fled from his community and crossed the mountains after committing a murder. It had been a crime of passion not unusual in Lavedan, and Bernard promised he would intercede for him with his friend, the curé. He learned that Dubourdieu and Hauteville had been allowed to escape, but no one would undertake to deliver a message to his friends. He feared that Jeanne-Marie would think him dead. It was not until he reached Pamplona, some weeks later, that he could send a message to Sallent, and by this time only Miguel Joan was there to receive it. Another month passed before he was strong enough to travel to Sallent. He was still unable to ride, but the corregidor in Pamplona, discovering that his guest was high in the favour of Don Juan, provided a vehicle and escort for the journey.

Roger Dubourdieu grieved for his friend and cousin for at least half the long journey to Saint-Jean-de Luz, but, as he approached the town and thought more of being reunited with Carla, his heart began to lift. His father would never approve of such an association, he thought, but then he no longer had any status as an escaped convict and he decided he should try to find what happiness he could.

He was greeted with great joy by Carla Baroja, and warmly welcomed by her cousins. As time passed he started to take more and more to Basque ways, and even began haltingly to try a few words of the language. One of his principal interests was to learn how to swear in Basque, and he found greater help in this endeavour in the local tavern than he did among Carla's relatives. He came closer to Carla as time wore on, and accepted her strange insights without question. One day she told him she had had a vision.

'I dreamed that my lord Audijos was still alive,' she said. 'You must go to him at Sallent.'

'How can that be?' stammered Roger. 'I saw him overwhelmed by those savages. He had no chance of survival.'

'Be that as it may, I saw him clearly, and he seemed in extreme distress.'

'Then I shall go to find him, and perhaps I should get some kind of message to my sister. I have not tried to communicate with my family in Coudures for fear it might lead to my apprehension and my father's shame.'

'Do not tell your sister yet,' replied Carla, 'Verify my dream first.'

So it was that Roger Dubourdieu set out on his quest for the friend he thought he had lost.

In Sallent Don Miguel received information that madame de Sèvres had obtained permission to cross the frontier. He could only speculate about the purpose of her visit, and he guessed it had something to do with Audijos or perhaps with the conspiracy that Hauteville had infiltrated. The role that the châtelaine had fulfilled in the revolt against the gabelle was familiar to him, and he looked forward to a battle of wits with a dangerous antagonist. At the same time he needed to be forearmed about Sardan's plot, so he sent a message to Hauteville in Bordeaux to join him as urgently as possible.

Joan's first visitor was the last person he could have expected to see.

'Are you a ghost or flesh and blood?' he asked, his face beaming with pleasure.'

'A little of each,' said Bernard, 'and not as much of the latter two as I could wish. Where is Jeanne-Marie, and what has happened to Dubourdieu and Hauteville? I know they escaped from the affray in which I so nearly died. And what became of that scoundrel of a plotter, who, I was told, was bothering Jeanne-Marie with his attentions?'

Don Miguel explained how the so-called comte de Foncenade had left Sallent for Bordeaux soon after the return of Roger and Hauteville with the news of Bernard's death, how Jeanne-Marie and Hauteville had gone to Coudures, whence Hauteville had set off for Bordeaux to find out what he could of Sardan's conspiracy, and how Roger had gone to Saint-Jean-de-Luz. Joan also told Audijos about the impending visit of madame de Sèvres, and his supposition that she might now be seeking information about Sardan's plot.

'I cannot escape that infernal woman,' said Audijos. 'If I had known of her crime against poor Hauteville, I would have exacted justice against her when we held her at Serres-Gaston. But I must think first of Jeanne-Marie and my friends who believe me dead.'

'I beg you not to intervene against the châtelaine until we know the reason for her visit. I hope to gain more information from her than she will get out of me. As to the demoiselle Dubourdieu, you will risk your life if you go to Chalosse at this time. Even her impetuous brother thought twice about escorting her to Coudures, and that is why Hauteville went with her.'

Two days after this conversation a messenger arrived from Zaragoza with a request from Don Cristobal. He had heard from Pamplona that Audijos had been received by Don Juan in Bilbao, had been severely wounded in the mountains, and was going to Sallent. He wanted Audijos to return with the messenger and report what Don Juan had said about the plot of which Van den Enden had informed him.

'The vicar-general's real motive,' said Don Miguel, 'is probably to use you in his rivalry with the count of Aranda. In any case he is a supporter of Don Juan, and it will be to your advantage to obey. Moreover, it will avoid confrontation with the châtelaine.'

'I go unwillingly,' replied Bernard, 'and I shall return as soon as I can. One day that woman will meet her deserts. It is true that I am still not strong enough to dispose of whatever escort she brings with her, but I think I am now able to ride.'

Madame de Sèvres turned up the day after Audijos's departure, accompanied by Nogent disguised as one of her servants. Don Miguel received her with courtesy, and after she had rested asked her to join him in his cabinet.

'You have something to impart to me, madame?' he asked.

'I know that you think me an enemy of monsieur d'Audijos,' she said, 'but whatever he may have told you to the contrary, we once had an affection for each other that is not entirely extinguished.'

'Ah! So you know he still lives, madame. There was a rumour that he was killed in the mountains of Navarre.'

'Yes, señor. He is reported to be recuperating from his wounds in Pamplona, and sooner or later he will come to Sallent. In fact I have a letter for him which I shall entrust you with. Where, by the way, are your other guests?'

'They have departed,' Joan replied, refusing to be drawn. 'If monsieur d'Audijos returns, I shall ensure he receives your missive. I imagine, however, that it is not solely to deliver this letter that you have come here.'

'No, there is a conspiracy afoot of which you are doubtless aware. These are men, linked with Spain and Protestant countries abroad, who wish to separate the provinces of the south from the kingdom of France. We know that a certain Roux de Marcilly has been in Bilbao, and that some Dutchman and a man masquerading as the comte de Foncenade have visited Aragon.'

'You seem well informed, madame. When you say 'we' I take it you mean the highest authorities in France?'

'I would not presume to say as much, but it is true that I am in the confidence of the intendant in Bordeaux, monsieur Pellot, He knows something of the conspiracy and he is prepared to offer you privileges or money if you can add to his knowledge.'

'But, madame, if this plot is receiving support from my own country, I should be acting against its interests by meeting your request.'

'Come, come, señor, we need not pretend patriotism when we deal in matters such as this.'

'Well, I shall consider further madame. I do not think that at present I can add much to what you already know, but there may be means of discovering more. Would the privileges you mention include, for instance, a pardon for my friend Bernard d'Audijos?'

'Even that may be possible,' said the châtelaine, her lips tightening involuntarily.

They met again for discussion on the following day but made no substantial progress. Finding cold reason to be insufficient to persuade Don Miguel, madame de Sèvres assumed her most seductive pose and, running her hands over her breasts, hinted at personal favours she might grant. Joan, however, maintained his reserve. Their negotiations were interrupted by the captain of the frontier post of El Formigal, who took Don Miguel aside.

'There are two matters I must report,' he said. 'I have detained a man calling himself baron d'Hauteville as he crossed the pass. Second, I glimpsed some of the attendants of your present visitor as I entered your house, and I could swear that one of them is the commander of the French dragoons who crossed the border in their attempts to seize señor d'Audijos three years ago.'

'You have done well, señor,' said Don Miguel. 'You may return to your post. You may release monsieur d'Hauteville, but do not tell him of the presence of madame de Sèvres.'

'Madame,' he said on rejoining the châtelaine, 'an unfortunate obstacle to our talks has arisen. The officer who illegally invaded this territory in search of monsieur d'Audijos has been identified as a member of your entourage. We may perhaps resume our negotiations at some future date, but now I must ask you to return at once to France. Otherwise your attendant will be arrested.'

The châtelaine went white with fury and swept out of the room. Within an hour she and her retinue were on the road to the frontier. Soon after her departure Roger Dubourdieu rode into Sallent by the southern route from Pamplona.

'Señor,' bellowed Roger as he burst into Don Miguel's house. 'Where is Audijos? Does he still live?'

'Of course he still lives,' said Joan, descending the stairs. 'He is now in Zaragoza. There is no time now to tell you his story, for you must ride at once for the frontier. The châtelaine and her crew, including lieutenant Nogent, have been here. They left half an hour ago, and your friend Jean d'Hauteville is at El Formigal and may try to intercept them.

'Devil take me!' exclaimed Roger. 'Here is mystery piled on mystery.'

'Do not delay or another tragedy may occur. I should never have ordered Hauteville's release.'

The bewildered Dubourdieu asked no further questions, but sprang on his horse and galloped for El Formigal. He slackened his pace after a mile or two lest the animal founder under his weight. The sky was growing dark as a storm was crossing the mountains from the north. Soon heavy rain began to fall. Ahead he could just make out a carriage on the summit of a hill and several horsemen beside it. The vehicle was halted, and as Roger came closer he saw two figures apart from the others who were apparently engaged in an altercation. He dismounted, tethered his horse, and approached carefully.

Hauteville had left the fort with no inkling that the châtelaine was on the road before him. He was about to pass her carriage when some impulse made him glance at the woman within it.

'Stop!' he called. 'It is I, Jean d'Hauteville. I wish to speak with you, madame.'

Madame de Sèvres had no premonition of danger. Astonished as she was by Hauteville's sudden appearance, she was curious to hear what he might have to say.

'He is a deranged fellow I once knew,' she said to Nogent. 'Halt the carriage and I shall descend and talk with him a moment. Stay near and watch him closely.'

'But the rain, madame...' objected Nogent.

The châtelaine would not be dissuaded. She walked with Hauteville to the edge of a cliff a few yards from the road. Lightning flashed and thunder sounded, and the two had to shout to make themselves heard.

'What is it that you want, baron?' asked the châtelaine. 'I heard that you had become a Jansenist, and then a hermit. Was it from love of me? Would you like to share my bed again?'

'Murderess!' shouted Hauteville. 'God has delivered you to my vengeance.'

He advanced towards her, shaking with fury. The châtelaine suddenly realised her peril. She raised her hands with fingers curled like claws and raked his face as he drew a dagger from his belt. Then, forgetting the precipice behind her, she stepped backwards and went over with a scream. Down, down, she fell, and smashed in a twisted mess of blood and tangled flesh on the jagged rocks below.

This happened so quickly that Nogent, leaping forward with drawn sword, was unable to save her.

'You will die for this,' he snarled at Hauteville, and lunged forward, stabbing him in the chest.

'Turn, you dog,' said a voice, and there was Roger, his own blade beating down his opponent's weapon. Nogent jumped back.

'Rebel and galley slave,' he cried. 'Now I shall finish what we once began at Saint-Jean-d'Angély.'

It was a savage duel with no quarter given. Once Roger slipped and fell to the ground. Then he caught Nogent's sword in his left hand as his opponent thrust at his throat. Stabbing upwards he wounded Nogent in the groin. Nogent cried out in pain, and Roger, regaining his feet in a flash, struck him with the hilt of his sword and sent him tumbling to his death beside the corpse of the châtelaine.

The rest of her party did not attempt opposition, and mounted and fled as soon as Nogent disappeared over the cliff. Dubourdieu knelt beside Hauteville, who was failing fast.

'In my doublet there is a paper,' he gasped. 'Give it to Don Miguel – it contains the details of the plot I ascertained from Foncenade. Now justice is done, and I follow Audijos to the grave. May God forgive my sins.'

The storm had passed and a ray of sunlight descended through the clouds.

'He is not dead. He lives and is in Aragon,' whispered Roger. Hauteville lifted his bloodied face, smiled weakly, and expired.

42. The Pardon

Three days after these events Bernard d'Audijos dismounted in Don Miguel's courtyard. In Zaragoza he had informed Don Cristobal of his conversation with Don Juan and of the bizarre behaviour of Roux de Marcilly in Bilbao. Of course, he knew nothing of the more valuable details of the conspiracy that Hauteville had acquired from Sardan de Paul. Don Cristobal had treated Bernard with far more courtesy than he had on their first encounter, and assured him that Don Juan would become the paramount voice in the government. If Audijos were to accept the prince's offer to join his entourage, Don Cristobal observed, he could be certain of a prosperous future. Although his main objective was to secure a pardon and return to Jeanne-Marie, Bernard felt elated by the success of his mission. All this was to change when he heard what had happened in Sallent in his absence, and when he experienced the venom of the document, which the late châtelaine had left as her memento.

Bernard was told the news by Don Miguel and Roger, the latter still wincing from the pain in his left hand.

'What,' he said, 'the châtelaine and Nogent both dead, and poor Hauteville too? Does not the Lord discriminate between the wicked and the good?'

'Well,' replied Joan, 'that woman did not dismiss the possibility of your pardon in return for intelligence of this hare-brained conspiracy, and we now know more of the plot through the paper that Hauteville left us at his death. Further, a message has been received from your cousin, the baron de Foix-Candale, saying that Pellot would obtain your pardon if you consented to go to America.'

'I have no intention of crossing the ocean,' said Audijos, 'but I am now ready to use the information we have about the plot as a bargaining counter.'

'And there is something I had forgotten in the trauma of all these events,' Don Miguel continued. 'That infamous woman left you a package.'

Audijos opened the package in private. It contained his last letter to Jeanne-Marie, torn in fragments. There was also a poem addressed to her by Jean d'Hauteville which ended:

> You saved me from the valley of despair,
> You gave me hope and taught me how to care,
> And now I know my heart is born anew,
> My life henceforth I dedicate to you.

The châtelaine had also added a line from Virgil, although Bernard would not have recognised the tag: *'Varium et mutabile semper femina,'* to which a translation was appended: 'Woman is ever changeable and capricious'.

A blackness enveloped Bernard. The world had turned upside down. He recalled how he had seen Jeanne-Marie and Hauteville engrossed in conversation and remembered the pang of jealousy he had told himself was quite unjustified. And it was Hauteville who had taken her back to Coudures! He had felt so confident of their love that he had trusted her completely. Could she have betrayed him? Could her sympathy for that depressed and guilty soul have turned to affection and then to love? Now the man was dead, but could he forgive such a breach of their mutual understanding? Wounded pride struggled with the deep sentiment that had possessed him for so many years.

The abrupt entry of Roger Dubourdieu broke in upon this dark reverie.

'What in heaven's name possesses you, man?' he demanded, as he saw his friend white-faced and disconsolate. 'Have you seen a ghost?'

'The ghost of that evil woman,' Bernard replied. 'She has left me proof that your sister has betrayed me.' He threw the contents of the package on a table.

Roger scanned the torn letter, the poem, and the note.

'This is some plot. How could that sinister trollop have obtained these papers? I cannot believe my sister would do what you suggest, and in any case Hauteville is dead. By the horns of

Beelzebub, the sun is shining on you. Don Miguel has told you how to win your pardon. Forget this evil shadow.'

Roger's half acceptance of the possibility of Jean-Marie's infidelity was more than Audijos could bear.

'I want no more of this,' he shouted. 'That part of my life is over and finished. I go back to Don Juan and will accept his offer.'

'Wait, wait,' called Roger.

But Audijos, reckless in his despair, was a man transformed. He strode out of the room, collected his weapons and his few belongings, and rode out of Sallent. Dubourdieu, distressed beyond measure, tried to explain his sudden departure to Don Miguel.

'We can only hope that time will restore him to his senses,' said the Spaniard.

As Audijos rode deeper into Aragon he tried to come to terms with his emotions. He convinced himself that Jeanne-Marie was probably well rid of him. Here he was, a rebel with a price on his head seeking service with the enemies of France. Jeanne-Marie would find a happier life without him. If she repented of her dalliance with Hauteville now that he was dead, she would have no future in resuming her association with a permanent exile. In this way he allowed his pride and his lack of magnanimity to hide the love still embedded in his heart. Had he recalled those maxims of La Rochefoucauld that he had once heard madame de Motteville quote, he might have realised that he was deceiving himself, but it was not to be.

Roger Dubourdieu was in a quandary of his own. He did not believe that his sister had lost her love for Bernard. Sooner or later she would learn that he was still alive, but he could not bring himself to tell her so. How could he say that his friend had believed she had betrayed him, and had turned his back upon the past? So he did nothing except to wish that he had Carla beside him to solve these problems. He resolved to rejoin her, perhaps to marry her if she would have him, and to live in hiding in the Basque lands far from his family in Chalosse.

Jeanne-Marie did indeed hear eventually of Bernard's survival and of the death of the man she had innocently befriended, Jean d'Hauteville. It was Jean de Lanusse who wrote of the events at

Sallent to his friend the curé of Saint-Sever, and père Anselme, who passed the details to the grieving woman. She seemed to have lost all joy in life. That Bernard was still alive inspired a spark of hope, but she heard nothing from him or her brother, and as time went by she lapsed into a numbness of spirit from which neither priest nor parent could awake her. But always there was Patou, now growing old and stiff, to whom she confided her sadness.

Except for some aches from his wounds Audijos found his strength returned. He had heard that Don Juan was in Huesca with a small entourage, and when he arrived there the prince appointed him to his personal guard. He was treated as a confidant and soon became so proficient in Castilian that he no longer needed to converse with Don Juan in French. Don Cristobal could no longer perform his duties as vicar-general because of illness, and the count of Aranda's antagonism to the prince obliged the latter to leave Aragon and find a refuge in Catalonia. There the viceroy, the duke of Osuna, supported Don Juan, who established himself in the monastery of Santa Eulalia on the hill of Tibidabo overlooking Barcelona.

The Catalan government at this time was supporting the continued revolt of the Angelets in the mountains of south Roussillon. The rebellion was similar to that which Audijos had led in the western Pyrenees, as the Catalan-speaking peasants of the region were protesting against the gabelle and the infringement of their own charters of liberties, the *usatges,* which resembled the *fors* of Béarn and Bigorre familiar to Audijos. For some weeks Audijos acted as an adviser to the rebels, who were gradually driven further into the mountains by the army sent by the French government.

When he returned to Barcelona, he found Don Juan engaged in a propaganda campaign against queen Mariana's Jesuit favourite. The junta in Madrid eventually succeeded in having el padre Everado sent to Rome, but they remained suspicious of the prince. Osuna acted as intermediary between the regent Mariana and Don Juan, and in January 1669 the prince set out for Aragon with a force of four hundred caballeros. Audijos played a part in organising the march. Don Juan's following grew as he moved westwards, until he finally entered Zaragoza and arrested Aranda. Don Cristobal had died, and the prince was appointed vicar-general of Aragon.

In Zaragoza Audijos was able to establish contact with Don Miguel and to obtain news of events in Gascony. Pellot had been sent to Rouen as first president of the *parlement* there, and Bernard wondered if among the former intendant's new assignments was an investigation of the Norman branch of the conspiracy of Van den Enden and Sardan. Joan had evidently continued to take an interest in the plot, for among the messages he sent to Audijos was a report that Claude Roux had been captured in the Swiss canton of Berne by a French detachment that had shown no more respect for boundaries than had Nogent at the Col du Pourtalet. Don Miguel wrote that the talkative conspirator had been taken to Paris, interrogated, and executed. Audijos had not forgotten Jeanne-Marie, and was tempted to ask his friend in Sallent if there was any news from Chalosse, but, once again, he convinced himself that it was better not to stir up the past.

Within Chalosse and Béarn a movement developed among the nobility to petition the king for Audijos's pardon. Foix-Candale, Navailles-Banos, and madame de Talazuc-Bahus were at the centre of the scheme, and the bishop of Aire gave it his support. The new intendant in Gascony, monsieur d'Aguesseau, was not unsympathetic, but he was soon replaced by a certain monsieur de Scève, who assumed that Audijos was responsible for attacks on villages in Lavedan by wandering groups of bandits. There was no evidence to support this supposition, but the fact that Louis XIV had now declared war against the United Provinces, and that other powers, including Spain, had allied themselves with the Dutch, did not incline the king to look favourably on an outlaw who was sheltered by the government of Aragon. It was at this point that the reappearance of the conspiracy to dismember France afforded Audijos a fresh opportunity.

The plot was now centered on Normandy, and its leading figure was a disciple of Van den Enden known as Latréaumont. Sardan de Paul, still using his false identity as the comte de Foncenade, was acting as its emissary in Madrid, and in due course he arrived in Zaragoza to renew his invitation to Audijos to lead an invasion across the Pyrenees. Don Juan was unsympathetic to this venture, and when Bernard consulted his protector the prince offered some surprising advice.

'I have long known that your loyalties remain on the other side of the mountains,' he said. 'You have served me well, but perhaps it is time for you to serve your own king. I do not believe this strange intrigue is really in the interest of Spain, although the junta may think otherwise. Don Miguel shares my opinion, doubtless because his personal interests lie in keeping hostilities away from the Pyrenees. You have told me how your friend Hauteville acquired many of the conspirators' secrets. If you now gain more information by pretending to enter into their schemes, you may be able to strike a bargain with His Majesty in Paris. Why do you not consult señor Joan, who can facilitate your return to France?'

'I do not care for such intrigues and deceits,' replied Audijos, 'but it is true I yearn to return to Chalosse and receive pardon from my king. I believe the cause I defended was just, but I also know that the dust of years has covered the path I took, and it may be time to follow a different road.'

After considerable reflection Bernard resolved to play a double game with the comte de Foncenade. Don Miguel made secret contact with conseiller Leydet in Bordeaux, who passed on to the intendant Audijos's offer to reveal the details of the conspiracy in return for the king's grace. To make it seem that rebel leader was still regarded as a traitor, and thus to lull any suspicion Foncenade might have of the sincerity of Audijos, a royal decree was enacted in council confirming his outlawry. Despite his misgivings, Bernard played his part well in his contact with the false count, and succeeded in obtaining more details of the plot from the conspirator. This information, together with the names and codes discovered by Hauteville some years earlier, was transmitted to an agent of the intendant, and in due course reached Louvois, the minister for war. The latter had some difficulty in the inner council in overcoming the prejudice against Audijos that Colbert had inherited from his client, the former intendant Pellot. In Rouen, however, Pellot welcomed new proof of the dangerous intentions of the plotters. Latréaumont was wounded while resisting arrest, and committed suicide. The figurehead of the movement, the high born chevalier de Rohan, together with the befuddled ideologue, Van den Enden, were taken to the Bastille and executed. In the south, Sardan's contacts went into hiding. Audijos had earned his pardon.

The so-called letters of abolition enacted by the royal council constituted a lengthy document which began:

Louis, by the Grace of God King of France and Navarre, gives greeting to all present. The sieur d'Audijos of our land of Chalosse, having not only forgotten the fidelity that he owes us as our subject, but also having allowed himself to persuade various persons disaffected towards the good of the state and our service, made several journeys to Spain and engaged himself in the party of our enemies, to such effect that, having committed many crimes and excited a number of rebellions and uprisings in our province of Guienne, notably near our frontier at Bayonne and in the lands of Béarn, Bigorre and the valley of Lavedan...

The pardon went on to revoke decrees requiring the arrest and trial of Audijos and his adherents on account of 'his having recently acknowledged his fault and found the means to render us considerable service, thereby deserving pardon for his crimes.'

The document engaged Audijos and his followers to abandon their links with Spain and thenceforth to remain steadfast in their loyalty to the French crown. The *parlement* of Bordeaux was to register and proclaim the pardon in a ceremony where Audijos confessed his crimes, named his accomplices, and promised his perpetual allegiance. On this solemn occasion, where he knelt before the judges in their red robes in the grand'chambre, Audijos appeared, in the words recorded by the registrar of the court, 'with head bare and his feet in chains, and, having been interrogated, took an oath with hand raised that the said letters contained the truth and that he would truly subscribe to them.'

Bernard was not without friends during these humiliating formalities. The official to whom he gave a list of accomplices was none other than Lespès de Hureaux, whom he had last seen at the rescue of Carla Baroja in Bidart. Conseillers Leydet and

Sallegourde, the latter accompanied by his son the advocate, congratulated him after the chains had been removed from his legs, and reminded him that the charter of Chalosse was now inscribed in the records of the *parlement*.

'It may not have the effect that your maître Legrange would have wished,' said the younger Sallegourde, 'but, as Henri de Foix-Candale told me at the time of its registration, it will serve as a tribute to his memory.'

During much of the ceremony Bernard's thoughts had been elsewhere. He recalled the generosity of Don Juan, and wondered how someone who had spent his life commanding Spanish armies against the French could have seen fit to advise his reconciliation with the national enemy. Then he remembered how the prince had once told him that he had visited the court of Louis XIV on returning to Spain from the Netherlands, and that he and the young king had immediately liked each other. Mazarin had then ruled France under the regency of the queen mother, Anne of Austria – a situation, Don Juan had said, not unlike that of the boy king Carlos under his mother Mariana and her advisers. Perhaps, thought Audijos, dynastic ties worked at a different level from national interests and governmental intrigues.

The motives of Don Miguel, the real instrument of Bernard's pardon, were more easy to discern. It had been he who had set Hauteville the task of penetrating Sardan's conspiracy when both of them had thought him dead. If Joan's personal interests outweighed conventional loyalties, it was none the less true that he had been a genuine friend. Thinking of Hauteville's role turned Bernard's mind to Jeanne-Marie. He had to find out what had become of her. Would she forgive him for his silence through these long years of separation? Now that he was pardoned, they would be able to obtain a dispensation and to marry. But perhaps, after all this time, she had married someone else? He resolved to visit Chalosse and find out for himself. He would adopt a disguise so that she would not know of his presence, and if she were happily settled he would steal away unnoticed.

In Coudures Arnaud Dubourdieu was discussing his son and daughter with his wife.

'Could there be more ungrateful offspring?' he said. 'Roger has dishonoured our house by marrying a Basque woman, and now, according to the letter he wrote us, he has been pardoned and asks whether he may visit us.'

'He is our son, and surely he deserves your forgiveness,' replied madame Dubourdieu. 'He has been for long an outlaw and a convict, but you yourself have admitted that he and Bernard d'Audijos fought and suffered in a just cause.'

'Tush, woman! Then what do you make of our daughter who sits and pines with that useless animal when she might marry the most eligible man in Chalosse, and restore wealth and prestige to our family?'

'It is true that, since he became a widower, the baron de Navailles-Banos has tried to pay court to her, but she will hardly give him the time of day. I fear she is inconsolable, having heard nothing from Bernard d'Audijos.'

'This is ridiculous,' said Arnaud Dubourdieu. 'That fellow Audijos may be a fine soldier, and now that he is pardoned the king may appoint him to some regiment. Yet clearly he cares nothing for our daughter. Think how my master, the noble duc de Gramont, would congratulate us if she married Banos. Why, she might even be presented at court.'

At the time when these words were spoken Audijos had reached the château of Foix-Candale, where he was welcomed rapturously not only by the baron but also by madame de Talazuc-Bahus, who was once again staying with her cousin. The next morning they were surprised by the arrival of old Podewiltz, who still held his post of colonel commandant of the dragoons.

'You must forgive my intrusion,' said the colonel to Bernard's mother, 'but I have been following your son from Bordeaux with a special despatch from the war ministry.'

Audijos entered the room at this moment, and Podewiltz turned to him. 'My congratulations,' he said. 'You have been commissioned by the king with the brevet of colonel to raise a special regiment of light horse to fight the Spaniards in Catalonia. It is hoped you will recruit some of the men who caused us so much trouble in the irregulars you led against us.'

'I am deeply honoured, colonel,' replied Bernard. 'I hope to redeem myself in His Majesty's service. But first, if you will permit, I have a personal mission to fulfil, and would appreciate it if you gave me some time before I report for duty.'

'Agreed,' said Podewiltz. 'Your commission will be gazetted a month from today.'

Audijos had confided to his mother and Foix-Candale that he intended to go secretly to Coudures to find out what had happened to Jeanne-Marie. He put on the habit of a monk and, somewhat incongruously, rode off next day to the town of his birth. Leaving his horse at the tavern that had once belonged to Duplantier, he cautiously approached the Dubourdieu residence from the rear.

In the garden where the châtelaine had once interrupted the lovers' embrace an aged dog, his senses almost gone, raised his head as an intruder stopped at the garden gate. He moved forward stiffly and sniffed at the monk's garments. Then with a deep baying bark, he launched himself at his master, his tail wagging in ecstasy. Jeanne-Marie, busy with some embroidery, lifted her head, and knew immediately who it was. She discarded her sewing, and ran to meet Bernard. With no questions asked they threw themselves into each other's arms.

Bertrand de Sariac had died, but the new bishop of Aire shared his predecessor's sentiments, and granted the dispensation within a week. Arnaud Dubourdieu was reconciled to his daughter's marriage to Audijos by the fact that his prospective son-in-law was a colonel commanding a regiment. Much to his wife's delight, he even received his son Roger and his wife Carla Baroja when they came to attend the wedding. The ceremony was performed at the church of Saint-Martin in Coudures by père Anselme from Saint-Sever, with the assistance of Jean de Lanusse, who came all the way from Arrens, and brought with him the blessing of the archpriest of Juncalas.

Two weeks later, Audijos set up his standard at the town of Salies in Béarn, close to the border with Chalosse, and the centre of the illicit salt trade that had so antagonised Pellot and the gabeleurs.

The duc de Gramont and the duc de Navailles, who had recently been promoted to Gramont's rank as a marshal of France, passed the word to their clients among the lesser nobility that service in the Audijos dragoons would bring them much honour. The news spread even faster among the surviving Invisibles, who had no such claim to status. Audijos found a considerable crowd awaiting him in the town square close to the salt fountain. Roger was there as the newly appointed captain of one of the companies, and Navailles-Banos was by his side as the commandant of another. There were some unexpected faces. Lejay, carrying his long-barrelled musket, had answered the call, and even Gilbert Defaux, who had aided the escape from the prison of Saint-Sever, had obtained permission to transfer from his regiment. As Audijos strode forward to welcome old friends and new recruits a cry went up from two hundred throats: 'Vive le roi! Vive d'Audijos!